A Parcel for Anna Browne

Miranda Dickinson has always had a head full of stories. From an early age she dreamed of writing a book that would make the heady heights of Kingswinford Library and today she is a bestselling author. She began to write in earnest when a friend gave her The World's Slowest PC, and has subsequently written six bestselling novels: *Fairytale of New York, Welcome to My World, It Started With a Kiss, When I Fall in Love, Take A Look At Me Now* and *I'll Take New York*. Miranda lives with her husband Bob and daughter Flo in Dudley.

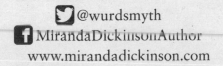

@wurdsmyth
MirandaDickinsonAuthor
www.mirandadickinson.com

A Parcel for Anna Browne

Miranda Dickinson

PAN BOOKS

First published 2015 by Pan Books
an imprint of Pan Macmillan
20 New Wharf Road, London N1 9RR
Associated companies throughout the world
www.panmacmillan.com

ISBN 978-1-4472-7605-0

3 5 7 9 8 6 4 2

A CIP catalogue record for this book is available from the British Library.

Typeset by Palimpsest Book Production Ltd, Falkirk, Stirlingshire
Printed and bound by CPI Group (UK) Ltd, Croydon, CR0 4YY

Visit www.panmacmillan.com to read more about all our books
and to buy them. You will also find features, author interviews and
news of any author events, and you can sign up for e-newsletters
so that you're always first to hear about our new releases.

For Claire Smith
Giver of gifts too precious to wrap
in brown-paper packages.
Thank you for being a true friend.

Dear Reader

Imagine the most amazing, beautiful gift, chosen especially for you and wrapped with great care, so that the unwrapping is as delicious as the gift itself. That's what I hope this book is for you. It's a story I've wanted to tell for a long time and I'm over the moon to be able to share it now.

I'm still pinching myself that I get to write stories for a living. Huge thanks to the team at my new book home, Pan Macmillan: to my editors, Caroline Hogg and Victoria Hughes-Williams, for their insight and huge faith in me; Wayne Brookes (bostin' in every sense!); Mandy Greenfield, Kathryn Wolfendale and Claire Gatzen. Enormous love to my brilliant agent, Hannah Ferguson, for her phenomenal support and excitement about everything I do.

I have the gift of awesome fellow writers, whose encouragement means the world to me – heartfelt thanks to Julie Cohen, Rowan Coleman, Cally Taylor, Kate Harrison, Tamsyn Murray, Kim Curran, Hannah Beckerman and A.G. Smith.

Much love, as always, to my amazing Twitter and Facebook lovelies, who once again have inspired elements of the book:

* Babs the cleaner named by Denise @samsonite11111
* Spill the Beans coffee shop named by Mell Greenfield @thislittlemell
* Bennett the collie named by Meriel Flint @mezzabel
* Daisy-chain necklace chosen by Cheryl Saunders @cherylsaunders3

* Rea and Megan inspired by @bookreviewbyrea and @ MeganInTheSun
* Florence, the ice-cream VW camper-van at the Charity Fair, kindly loaned by Polly's Parlour and is a real-life star! www.pollys-parlour.co.uk
* Freya & Georgie's coffee shop named in honour of my nieces, Freya Smith and Georgie Davis.
* Much love to Anna Perkins for being my inspiration for Anna Browne.
* Happy 30th Wedding Anniversary to Mandy and Alan Cooke, who won a mention here!
* Lucy the blogger is inspired by all the lovely bloggers I've met over the years. You rock!

Thank you to my fantastic family, the legendary Peppermint massive and my brilliant Dreamers writing group, for keeping me sane! This book is written in loving memory of Doris Ellis, my Gran and biggest fan.

And lastly, all my love to my lovely husband Bob and gorgeous daughter Flo, for being the most precious surprises in my life. I love you to the moon and back.

This book is about life's ability to surprise us. I hope it inspires you to seek out extraordinary gifts of possibility hidden in everyday life.

Brightest wishes
Miranda xx

'Surprise is the greatest gift which life can grant us.'

Boris Pasternak, novelist (1890–1960)

One

The UPS deliveryman waited in line, checking his watch. It had been a long day already and he still had two hours of his shift remaining. Traffic was backed up two miles out of the city on the main arteries and it was only going to get worse as the weekend rush began. He would be late – as he was nearly every Friday evening. His wife would not be happy. Neither would his kid, waiting for Daddy to come home and try out his new football in the back garden. Like he'd *promised* . . .

Ahead of him a line of three people waited not so patiently to receive security passes. They were red-faced and rude, loudly voicing their annoyance as a young receptionist did her best to remain affable. Too many people in this city were willing to engage their mouths before their brains, the deliveryman concluded. God forbid he should ever have to work in a city building. Trapped inside steel walls, breathing everyone else's recycled air, office politics as unforgiving as the air con – that wasn't the life for him. Visiting them on his round was bad enough. The sense of relief he felt climbing back into his delivery van confirmed the rightness of his career choice. At least he could drive away from places like these, even if it was to visit identical buildings somewhere else in the city.

He glanced up at the large atrium, rising six storeys to a domed glass ceiling, the imposing architecture befitting a national newspaper. Marble floors and mahogany fixtures, subtle uplighting and large brushed-steel planters filled with greenery at the feet of a glass lift, which reminded him of a Roald Dahl story he'd read as a boy. It was the kind of building his brother Warren would kill to enter, with his cheap suit and greedy ambition. Not that the dodgy knock-offs his brother peddled were ever likely to get him into this place. Warren could take the mickey out of him all he liked for being a 'jumped-up postie', but it meant he could enter fancy city buildings where his brother would never be admitted. That was something. Smiling to himself a little unkindly, the deliveryman stepped forward as the party ahead of him moved on.

The young woman behind the reception desk apologised for his wait. She had a pretty smile, he thought, the kind that transforms a face when it appears.

'How can I help you today?'

The deliveryman lifted up a package. 'I have a parcel . . .' he checked the label, 'for Anna Browne?'

The woman's pale-blue eyes widened. 'Oh. That's me.'

Her apparent shock made him grin. In a round made up exclusively of business deliveries to corporate offices,

2

it wasn't often that somebody was surprised to receive a package.

'You weren't expecting anything?'

'No, not at all.' She leaned forward a little, lowering her voice. 'I never get parcels – not here or at home,' she confided, peering at the package.

'Must be your lucky day, sweetheart,' the deliveryman smiled, giving her his handheld device and leaning against the desk while she signed. 'You have a good day.' He paused while he debated whether or not to say more, and then went ahead. 'Hope it's something nice.'

Two

It had just been an ordinary Friday for Anna Browne. She arrived for work exactly twenty minutes early, as she always did, stowed her belongings in the small staff kitchen behind the huge slate wall of the reception area and took her place behind the desk. First task of the day was checking for notes in the diary for any important meetings due to take place at the *Daily Messenger*. There had been three marked for today: a visit from a trio of Board members to see the newspaper's editor, Juliet Evans – the purpose of which was no doubt likely to set tongues wagging among the *Messenger*'s employees; a team of accountants due to meet the Finance Department at midday; and a raft of hopefuls expected from two o'clock for the next intake of the paper's highly prized internship scheme.

There had been nothing to suggest today would be remarkable, save perhaps for an official-looking brown envelope waiting for Anna in her pigeonhole. A glance across the wall of uniform wooden boxes when she'd arrived confirmed that every employee had received an identical letter – the contents of which were soon the hot topic of conversation amongst her colleagues.

'I won't do it,' snapped Sheniece Wilson, junior receptionist, her carefully straightened blonde hair bobbing with indignity. 'I don't care if it is official.'

Newly arrived receptionist Ashraf Guram looked worried. 'But they can fire you if you don't take part, can't they? I mean, it says here . . .'

Ted Blaskiewicz, chief security officer, chuckled and slapped a comradely hand on the young man's back. 'You don't want to pay too much attention to that, son. Trust me. They only fire you if they're *really* angry. Mind you, you know what they say: last in, first out . . .'

As Ashraf's brow furrowed further, Anna passed around the mugs of tea she had made for everyone – another Friday tradition. 'What's up?'

'So, you haven't heard the latest, then?' Sheniece was waving a sheet of paper like it was covered in something unmentionable.

Anna surveyed the identically disgusted expressions of her three work colleagues. 'I take it that it's not good news?'

'Read your memo,' Ted said. 'Turns out we're all pointlessly job-swapping for a fortnight.'

'Doing the work of someone else for less money, more like.' Journalist Rea Sinfield had appeared at reception – her favourite place to be whenever she could get away from the newsroom, and *especially* when there was gossip to be had.

'Work-shadowing,' Sheniece spat the words like a fly from her mouth. 'Another of the Dragon's stonking ideas. It's *pathetic*. What am I going to learn from . . .' she squinted at the name handwritten on her letter, 'Alan Drake in Logistics?'

'I would've thought it was more about what *you* could teach *him*,' Rea chuckled. 'Sam from Accounts reckons he's fit.'

'Does she?' Sheniece brightened a little as she considered this.

'I'll tell you what it is,' Ted said, gravely. 'It's rearranging the chairs on the *Titanic*. Making us think everything is tickety-boo when it isn't.'

Anna sighed. Rumours had been circulating like leaves in the wind for a month now, following a report in the *Daily Post* – the *Messenger*'s biggest rival – that unreliable accounting and questionable Board decisions had led to a dangerous shortfall at the newspaper. While Juliet Evans, inimitable *Daily Messenger* editor, insisted that all was well, the majority of her staff were yet to be convinced. Anna, however, was more inclined to believe her employer than the notoriously unreliable *Messenger* building's grapevine. She had worked here long enough to see countless supposed threats to the paper come to nothing. 'Things aren't that bad, Ted. Ms Evans said as much in last week's staff briefing. If anyone can get the *Messenger* through a tough time, it's her.'

'You mark my words, girl, the more she tells us it's under control, the more in trouble this place is.'

'Who'd you get, Anna?' Rea asked, blanking Ted's portent of doom.

Anna opened her letter – and her heart jumped. The name on the page caused her voice to squeak a little when she spoke it aloud. 'Ben McAra.' The air around her seemed to heat inexplicably.

Ben McAra had a reputation as the wunderkind of Fleet Street – a young, ambitious reporter who had quickly risen through the ranks of journalism-school hopefuls to become one of the major voices in British print media. The *Messenger* had headhunted him from a junior news-desk job at *The Times* and promoted him to chief correspondent, thus making him a star. All of this was impressive, but what Anna liked most about him was that he wore his success as casually as a weekend jacket, seemingly unaltered by his professional position. It was what she had first noticed about him when he came to work at the *Messenger* three years ago. And her respect for the easygoing reporter had gradually become something more.

Rea and Sheniece gawped at her. 'You only bagged the best-looking bloke in the building! Way to go, Anna!'

Flushing, Anna fixed her gaze on the handwritten name on the memo. She knew it well – although admitting it to her colleagues was more than her sanity was worth. Ben McAra, dark-haired, cheeky-smiled star reporter of the *Daily Messenger*, who had never so much as cast a glance in her direction, but whom Anna had secretly admired since he arrived at the newspaper. 'I don't know why I've been paired with someone from the newsroom,' she mumbled, hoping to draw attention away from the burning beacons of her cheeks.

Sheniece stared at Anna as if she'd just turned green. 'He isn't just "someone from the newsroom" – he's the chief reporter. The fittest bloke on Fleet Street; the fella half the women in the city would walk over hot coals to get close to!'

'He's annoying, but you wouldn't kick him out of bed,' Rea agreed, with all the indelicacy of a tabloid journalist.

'There must be some mistake,' Anna said, her racing thoughts made audible. 'I can't work in the newsroom.'

Sheniece's false eyelashes fluttered with excitement. 'It's *perfect*, though! Think about it: you have two whole weeks to cosy up with a sexy journo, chasing headline stories. All that danger and passion and deadlines – it'll get the blood pumping, bringing the two of you together . . . He'll be jumping your bones in no time!'

Anna felt sick. 'It won't be like that . . .'

'You obviously haven't heard the rumours about Ben McAra,' Rea smirked. 'He's *very* single right now, and more than willing to come to the aid of a pretty damsel in distress.'

'You watch that McAra, Anna,' Ted warned, as Sheniece and Rea drifted away to loudly concoct increasingly filthy scenarios about Ben and her. 'He's a snake. Murray Henderson-Vitt in the newsroom says he has no scruples when it comes to getting what he wants.'

Anna rolled her eyes. 'Murray would know. Honestly, Ted, I'll be fetching Ben coffee and typing up his notes, that'll be all.' But, secretly, the thought of spending a fortnight with the man she had been fascinated by for months both thrilled and terrified her. What would she say to him? And what could she possibly offer him in return? She liked her job in reception and was good at it. But she had never even considered she could do anything else at the paper. Comfortable with what she knew, the thought of a new work situation – even a temporary one – scared her. What if she made a fool of herself? What if everyone saw her mistakes?

A memory of a village-hall stage and the cruel laughter of a packed audience forced its way to the forefront of her mind, the affront twisting her stomach. Feigning a coughing fit, she hurried to the small kitchen behind the reception wall to steady herself against the stainless-steel sink while she pushed the recollection away.

I won't go back there, she vowed. *I'll never do that again . . .*

Scrambling to control her thoughts, she tried to think rationally. Of course she would be fine. Work-shadowing would probably be like work experience had been at school: no matter where you were placed, the tasks were the same – filing, making coffee, doing the boring stuff nobody else wanted to do. Anna could *do* boring and mundane, happy to be out of the spotlight. And this would be no different. So she would just follow Ben McAra around, willingly taking the unimaginative jobs he offered her, and keep her head down. Two weeks would pass soon enough. And then she could return to what she knew best – safe behind the reception desk of the *Daily Messenger*.

The sound of a barking voice summoned her back to

her post, where Sheniece was now struggling to be polite to a newly arrived group of visitors who were voicing their frustration at the security procedures Ted had recently introduced.

'I shouldn't have to give you all this information,' a portly man bellowed. 'Do you *know* who I *am*?'

'Perhaps I can be of assistance?' Gently nudging her colleague out of the firing line, Anna proffered a bright smile, instantly diffusing a little of the visitor's anger. Sheniece didn't argue: it was well known that irate members of the public were her least favourite thing to deal with. Of all the reception team, Anna's coolness in the face of fury placed her firmly ahead of her colleagues for crisis management. It was a skill honed over many years, in a season of her life that nobody here knew about.

After much blustering and threats of dire consequences when the Board heard of their ordeal, Anna furnished all the visitors with passes, collected the details required by the new security protocol and sent them, grumbling but defeated, on their way to the top-floor boardroom. As they left, a smiling UPS deliveryman stepped forward.

'I have a parcel . . . for Anna Browne?'

Three

Anna Browne stared at the package in her hands. It was bigger than a shoebox, wrapped in brown paper with a neatly written address label. She didn't recognise the handwriting. Turning it over, she found no return address. Which was odd. Packages from delivery couriers almost always had a sender label stuck on the top, useful for the deliveries the newspaper often received in error, meant for the large international banking corporation up the street. Two digits wrongly arranged in the street number meant a lunchtime excursion for Anna, dropping off the misplaced parcels in Hanson Holdings' glass-and-steel reception. Couriers had made so many mistaken deliveries lately that she was now on first-name terms with the two receptionists there.

This package was different. It was addressed correctly to *her*. But who would be sending her parcels? Hardly anybody she knew could even say where she worked. In fact, of those Anna Browne called her friends, only one person would even bother to ask for that information. For a moment she wondered if her expat American neighbour Tish might have sent it. But while they exchanged cards and gifts for Christmas and birthdays, Tish and Anna were not yet at the stage of friendship for unexpected gift-giving. Their friendship had begun when they'd recognised one another when queuing for coffee in the small coffee shop below their apartment building on the edge of the city. They had met once before, in the temperamental lift making its unsteady way up from the lobby of Walton Tower, and had shared their frustrations with the unreliability of the building's amenities. In the coffee queue, Tish had turned to Anna to complain about the slackness of service and had recognised her. They had shared a table and the bond began. The friendship that grew from that initial meeting was strong, but remained largely in the here and now – in the tradition of many of her London acquaintances, Anna actually knew very little of Tish's life before she'd emigrated to England.

Anna dismissed Tish as a possible sender. If she had decided to send Anna gifts, she would have sent them to Anna's home address anyway, and as Tish Gornick was fond of attention, she was most unlikely to want her generosity to go unaccredited.

Her younger brother Ruari could have sent the parcel, Anna supposed. But why wouldn't he send it to her home? Anyway, he was wrapped up in his own life, finally on an even keel back in Cornwall, after many years chasing surf around the world – and as the birthday cards he sent her were always three weeks late, this level of spontaneity was out of character for him.

Two other unlikely candidates remained: Isadora Smedley, Anna's elderly neighbour; and Jonah Rawdon, who was the closest person Anna had to a best friend in the city. Mrs Smedley was known for her generosity, but didn't know where Anna worked, so Anna decided she could be ruled out immediately.

Could it be Jonah? Unlike Tish or Isadora, he knew what Anna did for a living and had occasionally met her after work near the *Daily Messenger*'s building. He was naturally a little shy and was definitely capable of concealing secrets, but why would he have chosen to send Anna a gift now, several years into their friendship? While there was undoubtedly a connection between them, and Anna had even on occasion found them flirting together, she couldn't quite picture Jonah choosing this method to declare a long-held regard for her. The no-nonsense Yorkshireman was far more likely to come right out with a confession in the middle of a field somewhere, during one of their weekend trips out to the countryside, than go to all the trouble of sending her secret gifts.

But if not him, who else could it be? Certainly not Anna's mother, stuck like a stubborn stick in Tamar Estuary mud, who still hadn't forgiven her for 'abandoning your family and running away to *that* city . . .' Cornish people should remain Cornish, she maintained; Anna's decision to move out of blessed Kernow was tantamount to treason. Consequently Ms Senara Browne hadn't sent Anna a birthday card in six years; a parcel with no specified reason

13

for sending it was therefore out of the question. And as her father was long gone, before Anna was old enough to notice, it was highly unlikely to be from him, either.

'Hey, Anna, what you got there?'

Anna looked up to see the smiling face of Ted Blaskie-wicz. Most days the chief security officer appeared around this time to help himself to coffee from the percolator behind reception and to chew the cud. There was nothing in the *Daily Messenger*'s building that Ted didn't know: he took security to a new heights of conscientiousness.

'Sanjay from Obits has split from his wife,' he grinned, this gem of gossip a prized possession. 'I told you that was going to happen.'

'I think it's sad,' Anna replied, never one to revel in another's misfortune. 'Poor Sanjay.'

'Poor Sanjay's *ex*,' Ted retorted. 'He's been doing over-time with Claire Connors from Features, if you know what I mean. Growing his personal *column inches*, in more ways than one.'

'Ted!'

He shrugged like a Mafia don after a massacre. 'It's just an observation. So,' he eyed the unopened parcel in Anna's hands, 'what's in the box, Anna Browne?'

'I have no idea.'

'Ain't you going to look?'

'No.'

Ted was wounded. 'Whyever not? It could be a bomb.'

Anna shot him a look. 'Well, in that case tell the BBC I was a hero, for opening it at home to save the *Messenger* staff.'

14

'You are no fun, woman.'

Anna grinned. 'I just want to enjoy having a parcel. I don't get parcels. Ever.'

Even for a hardened gossipmonger, Ted accepted this, being rather fond of the occasional parcel that arrived at reception addressed to him, quickly snaffled away to his office. It was common knowledge amongst his colleagues that these deliveries were box sets of prized American crime series, purchased months before they were due to be screened in the UK. 'Okay. But I'll be here tomorrow demanding to know what it was.'

'Of course you will.'

Anna watched Ted's hulking frame slope off and smiled to herself. No doubt he would blab the news to the first person he met. Ted always did. But how unusual for Anna to be the topic of gossip – little, quiet Anna Browne on reception, who nobody ever noticed! The thought of it made her smile all afternoon.

Four

Friday early evening in Spill the Beans coffee shop was bustling: tired city workers hunched over lattes and macchiatos as if their lives depended upon them. The beaten-up sofas and armchairs were all occupied when Anna arrived, but she spotted a red-faced Tish Gornick waving from a table by the counter.

'It's bat-crazy in here,' she said, when Anna sat down. 'I had to fight three people for this table. I'll bruise tomorrow, you'll see.'

'You got a great one,' Anna said, amused by the drama her friend could inject into the most mundane of events. 'Those bruises are well earned.'

Tish nodded, her mind elsewhere. 'You know, my therapist tells me confrontation is good for my soul. I'm not so sure. Feel my heart – I mean it, Anna, *feel* my heart . . .' She grabbed Anna's hand and held it against her chest, all consideration for personal space dismissed in one movement.

16

'You see? I had to sit down for five minutes just to get it to this rate, and it's still way too fast.'

She relinquished her grip and Anna pulled her hand back, resting it safely on her lap underneath the table.

'I'm sure you'll survive,' Anna smiled. 'Shall I get coffees for us?'

'Would you? I'm gonna need a while to compose myself.'

Leaving Tish recovering from her ordeal, Anna joined the back of the long queue that stretched from the counter almost to the door. Normally this wait was frustrating, her feet aching from the long day, and the customers ahead of her maddeningly indecisive about their orders. But this evening Anna didn't mind.

She thought of the parcel, waiting still unopened in her apartment – a parcel sent especially for her. The thought of it lifted her, as if she was stepping on pockets of air beneath her feet. Was it possible that something as small as an unexpected parcel with her name on it could so dramatically alter how she felt? Maybe it was.

An unkind onlooker might have suggested that the impact of this singular small happening in Anna Browne's life was a sad indictment on the rest of it. A tiny part of Anna suspected it, too. But for now all that mattered was that somebody had sent her a gift – and it was waiting for her upstairs.

'What's with you?' Tish frowned when Anna returned to their table. 'I watched you in the line: you were smiling.'

'There's nothing wrong with smiling,' Anna replied, surprised that her friend had even noticed in the midst of her heart palpitations. 'Maybe I'm happy.'

17

'Happy? When you're as single as I am? Damn, girl, whatever you're on, I need some. What happened to you today? Have you got a date tonight?'

Anna stirred clouds of pristine milk-froth into her coffee. 'No, I don't have a date.'

'What happened to that guy with the cheap roses?'

'Which guy?'

Tish folded her arms. 'Last Thursday. I'd just arrived on your floor to accompany Mrs Smedley to the supermarket and I saw him. He knocked on your door with a bunch of roses he'd clearly picked up at a gas station.'

Anna giggled. 'Gary? He wasn't my date. He's my dentist. And the roses were from Waitrose, actually. They were lovely.'

Tish stared. 'Since when did dentists start making house-calls with cheap roses? He had his best suit on.'

'He came straight from a meeting at the bank. I helped him to work out a business plan a while ago; when the bank approved his loan, he brought me flowers.' What had started as a chance remark by Gary about his expansion plans for the dental surgery had led Anna to offer her help. She had studied Business Management at university and had recently helped her brother Ruari make a plan for his surf school in Perranporth, so the method was fresh in her mind. To her surprise, she had enjoyed the experience – and her dentist had been over the moon. It amused her that Tish had been spying on her. She shook her head. 'I can't believe you thought I was going out with Gary.'

'When I see a man in his best suit with cheap flowers

knocking on your door, what else am I going to think?'
Tish sipped her coffee. 'And you still haven't answered my
question. What's made you happy?'

'I had a good day today, that's all.'

'In *your* job?'

'Yes. Sometimes people surprise you. Today, that
happened.'

'Make the most of it,' Tish snorted. 'You don't get too
much of that in this city.'

By the time Anna closed her door she was buzzing with
caffeine and anticipation. Tish, who'd had a bad Friday,
insisted that she buy a second round of coffee, in order
to explain the offences of her day in full. Anna did her
best to listen, but the promise of the package upstairs was
too strong to ignore.

And now here she was: alone with the parcel at last.

She almost didn't want to open it, the sight of mail
addressed to her more precious than the contents could
ever be. It was like the time when, as a child, she once
received a Christmas present from the Santa at Trago Mills
– the closest thing to a shopping centre that her mother
would take her to. The gaudy paper and irresistible rustle
it made in her hands was as close to perfection as it was
possible to be; the slightly spicy fragrance of the printed
design and metallic tang of the elastic string wrapped
around it too lovely to rip into. Unlike Ruari, who had
torn open his parcel and immediately thrown a tantrum
when an inexpensive bag of sweets fell out, Anna had
cradled her gift all the way home, hiding it under her bed

until Christmas Day. The thought of it waiting beneath her, unopened and sparkly, as she slept each night brought her the sweetest of dreams for a week. Of course, on opening it, the contents were revealed to be identical to those so hated by her brother, but that didn't matter. Little Anna Browne had been given a gift, just for her.

The parcel sat now in the middle of the small dining table in her living room. Anna drew up a chair and sat, staring at it. All day she had eliminated possible senders and had drawn a blank. There was only one way to discover the identity of the kind gift-giver. Taking a breath, she reached out and slid the parcel towards her.

It was neatly wrapped, the folds at each end of the box forming two identically sized triangles. Anna appreciated the care and concentration required to achieve this. As a sixteen-year-old she had worked on Saturdays in the gift-wrapping department of Purefoy's, the faded department store in Liskeard, long since demolished. Miss Miller, the pinch-faced spinster who ran gift-wrap like an army barracks, insisted on nothing less than symmetry for the piles of boxes awaiting adornment. More out of fear than anything else, Anna had learned the art of accurate folding, measuring the overhang of each end of wrapping paper before daring to crease it. Symmetry was what mattered, Miss Miller said. People always appreciated a well-wrapped parcel.

Looking at the package in her hands, Anna now knew what Miss Miller meant. Somebody had not only taken the time to think of her and select a gift, but had also ensured it was beautifully wrapped – albeit in brown paper.

But if this much care and attention had been lavished on the unremarkable outer garment of the parcel, what did that bode for whatever lay inside?

The moment Anna had waited for all day had arrived. Determined to enjoy every minute of its unveiling, she took a deep breath and began to peel away the sticky tape holding down the perfect parcel corners. The paper shivered away across the table, revealing a pale, duck-egg-blue box embossed in the centre with the words *Et voilà!* in midnight-blue foil. Anna lifted the lid – and lost her breath.

There, nestled between gossamer sheets of the palest green tissue, was the most wonderful silk scarf Anna had ever laid eyes on. Almost afraid to disturb its exquisite folds, she reached into the box and carefully lifted the garment out. Its sheen caught the light from the pendant lamp above her table and, as she raised the scarf further, a delicious scent filled the air. It was like sugared almonds and royal icing – sweet and inviting. Gently she found the corners and shook out the folds, revealing a beautiful design of tiny yellow roses laid across a background the colour of the sky before the snow: a glowing cream with the smallest hint of pale gold. The scarf moved with a mercurial elegance through her hands, and when Anna lifted it to her neck it felt like the caress of a summer breeze across her skin.

Trembling, she rose and stood by the mirror that hung on the wall between her bathroom and bedroom. How had somebody chosen this perfect gift for her? The colours in the scarf seemed to make her skin glow, each shade a perfect complement for her colouring. In all her life she had never received a gift like this. Her reflection smiled back and she was surprised at how different she appeared. Could a scarf make such a change?

It was beautiful; what was more, she *felt* beautiful wearing it.

But who had sent this to her? And why?

Five

At the *Daily Messenger* nobody knew the building as intimately as Barbara 'Babs' Braithwaite. She had been cleaning its nooks and crannies for nearly forty years and in that time had witnessed many changes. Even her own job had undergone several transformations: from Cleaner to Cleaning Operative to Assistant Sanitation Officer to Head of 'Clean Team'. She was now in charge of ten cleaners, who worked shifts to prepare the newspaper offices hours before staff arrived and late after they had left. Consequently not much passed her attention.

So she was the first to notice when the friendly receptionist arrived almost an hour early that Monday morning. Babs had always liked the girl, and on the occasional times she'd been able to share a conversation had noticed how easily she maintained eye contact. Not like those stuck-up journalists, who mostly ignored the Clean Team as if they were designed to be invisible. Eye contact was an underrated skill, Babs believed. Her mother – Heaven bless her – had always laid great store by developing the ability. 'If you can look someone in the eye, they'll know you're honest,' she'd often say. The poor woman might have died practically penniless, but she'd left a legacy of lifelong friends who appreciated her honesty. Eye contact was her unique talent that drew them to her. Not many seemed to value it these days. That nice Anna on reception was one of the few young people Babs had met who could do it.

Today, there was something different about the girl, although Babs couldn't quite put her finger on what it was. She was always pleasant and friendly, quiet of course – but that was a nice change, in a place that attracted people with more mouth than sense. Today, she seemed happier, glowing even. Maybe she was in love. If that was the case, she was likely to keep her beau a secret from the loudmouths she worked with. That Sheniece girl broadcast her shenanigans with all and sundry, to anyone within earshot. No class, that one. Whatever happened to maintaining a little bit of mystery?

Or maybe she was pregnant. That would be lovely, Babs thought. People in this building tended to leave when they had babies, the tick of their biological clocks providing the excuse they needed to quit the newspaper business. Anna didn't strike her as the sort to do that. She seemed to love her job. A baby on the way would be just what reception needed. Bring a bit of joy into the place. But if that was true, Babs was certain she would have already heard about it from Ted Blaskiewicz. That sort of gossip was his favourite kind . . .

While the reason was unclear, Anna certainly seemed

keen to come into work this morning – and that alone was remarkable. Babs hoped it might become a regular thing. She met very few people at this hour, and the chance of a bit of chat before the end of her shift would be very welcome indeed.

'You're in early,' Babs noted as she ran a duster over the reception counter. 'It's nice to see a friendly face before the rush starts.'

'I thought I'd catch an earlier bus,' Anna replied. She had a lovely smile, Babs thought. Pretty girl, pretty soul – that's what her old ma would have said.

'Good idea. I bet you found a seat, too.'

'As a matter of fact, I did.'

'But why come straight here, though? You could be having one of those posh coffees somewhere. My grand-daughter tells me they're all the rage nowadays.'

'I suppose I could have. I just fancied getting here before everyone else.'

More power to you, flower, Babs thought to herself as she pushed her cleaning trolley back to the Clean Team storeroom. *Wish there were more like you in this place . . .*

Anna was enjoying the space that being so early at work afforded her. More by luck than design, she had woken before her alarm and felt a sudden urge to do something different. Babs was right: she had considered stopping to buy a leisurely breakfast in one of the expensive coffee shops that lined the street on which the *Daily Messenger* building stood, but decided to go straight into work instead. She had never arrived before her colleagues, but today she found the prospect appealing. It was a little thing, barely enough to count as a small detail of her day, but the opportunity to do something different just to see what it was like was a new thing for Anna. It wasn't that she was particularly fond of her routine, more that she had settled into a way of living that rarely changed. Today, she felt a new urge to challenge that.

This morning everything felt new. Even the bus journey into work had revealed details Anna had never seen before. She noticed beautiful alabaster spirals above the window of a shop she had passed, without seeing them, countless times before; the corner florist's where her street met the main route into the city bore a sign announcing: *It's a GIRL!*; an elderly lady sitting behind her began reminiscing to her guide dog about the London of her childhood; and a harmonica-playing busker by her stop was playing *Nevermind* as she alighted. She had never particularly dreaded this journey, but neither had she smiled so much as she did today.

The *Daily Messenger*'s building was strangely quiet and smelled of newly applied floor polish when Anna arrived, her footsteps echoing around the brightly lit atrium. Instead of attempting to quieten her heels, as she might have done, Anna revelled in the sharp clack-clack announcement of her arrival. *That* was new, too.

Standing behind the reception desk, she gazed out across the empty atrium. Usually she felt part of the furniture – she knew her place and was happy to be invisible. Today, looking out from her position, she felt like a ruler surveying

26

her kingdom. Completely at one with her surroundings, she dared the day to notice her.

I feel at home here, she thought, with a fizz of excitement.

She was keen to get started, while the building belonged only to her. Without the pressure of waiting couriers, Ted hovering around wanting to talk and her colleagues moaning about the traffic, she was able to prepare the day's diary, sort outstanding parcels and post and clear the reception desk of the weekend staff's detritus. Every one was a small action, but today each felt like an achievement.

I wonder why I feel so different today?

As she took the last of the weekend staff's dirty mugs to the small kitchen area hidden behind the slate wall bearing the large *Daily Messenger* sign at the back of reception, she caught sight of herself in the shaving mirror that one of her colleagues had suspended above the sink. Her new scarf was tied around her neck, secured with a brooch she'd found on a second-hand jewellery stand in a local market at the weekend. As soon as she had put it on this morning she felt the same sensation she'd felt on Friday evening. All weekend she had been looking forward to wearing it: now, with her navy-blue skirt suit, it was working its magic again.

I feel a change in me: like I'm taller, somehow.

She liked the Anna Browne who smiled back at her from the dust-speckled glass. She looked happy.

'Bloody hell, Anna, you chasing a promotion or something?' Ted Blaskiewicz's ruddy-cheeked face appeared over her shoulder.

Anna turned. 'Morning, Ted.' She rinsed the mugs and laid them out on the stainless-steel drainer.

'*Early* morning,' Ted reiterated, following her through to reception, where the coffee percolator was already at work. 'Emphasis on the early. What happened? You hoping for a pay rise? Because you can whistle for it in this place, girl, if you are.'

Anna smiled and handed him a mug of coffee. 'No. I just thought I'd come in early for a change. I don't see why it's headline news. Babs acted like I'd done something shocking.'

'It *is* shocking. I know this place, girl: no one is ever in a hurry to get here in the morning, not even the great Juliet Evans herself.' He gave a mock-bow to the photo of the *Daily Messenger*'s infamous editor that hung by the side of the reception desk.

'I wasn't in a hurry. I just caught an early bus – which, by the way, was a revelation because I actually found a seat. I've sorted everything before the rush starts and now I have time to relax a little, which never normally happens. It's been a successful experiment all round.' She lifted her mug of coffee and took a celebratory sip. It had been a long time since her first coffee of the morning had been anywhere above tepid, interrupted often as it was by the first hour's busyness.

Ted Blaskiewicz was watching her like she was a suspicious package. 'What's up with you?'

'Sorry?'

'There's something about you this morning. Something – different.'

28

'Is there?' Anna hid her smile as best she could. 'I hadn't noticed.'

'There *has* to be a reason,' Ted muttered, oblivious to Anna's answer. 'New boyfriend?'

'No.'

'New medication?'

'Hardly.' Her smile broadened.

'I don't know, these days, do I? Everyone seems to be popping a pill for something.'

'Thanks for the insinuation! Can't a girl just be happy?'

'Stop teasing me, Anna Browne! I know you're enjoying this . . . Ah!' He snapped his fingers. 'What did you get up to at the weekend?'

'Nothing special. I went to the market in Sheep Street on Saturday, met some friends for lunch at the pub, but other than that I had a quiet one. How about you?'

But Ted was not one to be diverted so easily. 'Something's happened. Don't try to deny it, girl, I can tell. One-night stand?'

Anna laughed. 'No, Ted.'

'Win some money on the lottery?'

'I don't play it.'

'Then what is it? Did you hear something about this place? Something you needed to be in early for? There's talk of the paper being in trouble – do you know more about that than we do? What do you know?' He was getting flustered now, the tips of his ears turning flame red against the dark-grey felt of his security guard's cap.

Anna patted his arm. 'You're the font of all gossip, Ted:

I wouldn't dream of challenging your position. There really is no mystery. I'm just having a good day.'

'So what was in your mystery parcel on Friday?' he asked, pointing a nicotine-shaded finger at her as the memory returned.

Anna beamed back at him and touched the cool silk of her scarf. 'This, actually.'

Ted peered closer to inspect it, giving Anna a sudden waft of his too-sweet cheap aftershave as he did so. 'Ni-i-ice. Expensive, that.'

'You think?'

'Without a doubt. What did the card say?'

'What card?'

Ted frowned. 'The card with the parcel.'

'There wasn't one.'

The furrows in Ted's brow deepened, but his eyes sparked into life. *This* was the kind of juicy gossip he could do something with. 'You're telling me somebody spent a small fortune on a scarf like that and sent it to you anonymously?'

'Yes. Wonderful, isn't it?'

'Wonderful. Or *weird* . . .'

Anna knew where this was heading. When Ted Blaskiewicz retired (in ten years' time, as he was so fond of frequently informing anyone within earshot), he should get a job concocting preposterous conspiracy thrillers for Hollywood. Ted's work-related scandals were almost legendary in the *Messenger* building. Last month he had heroically foiled what he thought was a covert spying ring in the post room, only to discover a group of workers

30

who were attending slimming classes and sharing their experience away from the other staff. He had wrongly accused a senior journalist of fiddling her expense account, after spotting a printed list of expensive gifts on her desk, only to eat humble pie when it was revealed to be a gift list she was circulating for her husband's fiftieth birthday. And he still turned a pinker shade of mauve over his attempt to forcibly eject the 'shady-looking man hovering suspiciously around the top-floor offices', who was subsequently revealed as the newest member of the DayBreak Corp Board who had arrived early for a meeting.

'It isn't weird,' Anna replied. 'It's lovely.'

'You say that now, girl, but what do you know? I saw this kind of thing on *Taggart* once,' he lowered his voice. 'It starts with attractive gifts to woo the victim and then, when the killer has them in his grasp, the parcels start to get nasty . . .'

'You watch too much television,' Anna replied, refilling her mug from the coffee percolator.

'Mock all you want,' Ted answered, finishing his drink and walking away, 'but when you're lying on a mortuary slab, don't say I didn't warn you.'

All day Anna was aware of how different everything was. As if the very air around her had changed, eliciting curious glances from people who ordinarily wouldn't have noticed the quiet receptionist. The new chief sports reporter – whose name nobody could remember – made a point of saying how nice she looked when he arrived for the afternoon news-desk shift.

'Thank you.'

'No, I mean it. Have you had your hair done different?'

Anna laughed. It was a typically bloke-like comment, but she appreciated the thought behind it. 'No. New scarf, actually.'

'Ah, right. That was going to be my second guess.' With a broad smile, he checked his watch. 'Well, I'd better – you know.'

'Of course. Nice to talk to you, Mr . . . ?'

The journalist shouted something unintelligible over his shoulder as he hurried to the lift. Anna turned back to Ted and shrugged. 'Nope. Still didn't catch his name.'

The surprises kept arriving. Three visitors remained by the reception desk to chat with her, instead of waiting on the wide black leather armchairs for their appointments. Anna learned about the brand-new baby of one of the male visitors and was then treated to an impromptu slide-show of gurgling, sleeping and grinning images on his phone. Ted proudly informed Anna that one of the single male journalists in the newsroom had been enquiring after her – although he refused to tell her which reporter it was. And when even Juliet Evans remembered Anna's name, Ted was so shocked he required a ten-minute sit-down with a restorative cup of tea.

Anna received the new attention with cautious optimism. It was not altogether unpleasant, but so alien to anything she had encountered before. All her life Anna Browne had assumed the role of the invisible woman. Growing up in the shadow of her flamboyant mother, she had quickly learned that being quietly amiable was the best course of action. As Senara Browne dominated the social hub of Polperro with her lurid wardrobe, questionable lifestyle and unbridled opinion, Anna hurried along in her wake, repairing the damage with apologetic smiles. Moving to the city had afforded her more freedom to carve out her own life but, by her own admission, it was a quieter existence than her former life in Cornwall. She liked it that way. Far better to have a circle of close friends you could rely on than the ability to command a room.

Anna had always had friends, but never thought it necessary to try to attract more. The people who mattered were naturally drawn to her. At work she made an effort to speak to anyone who seemed interested, but few of her colleagues bothered to do the same in return. Until today.

'Get you, Miss Popular,' Sheniece jibed. 'I've been trying to get Joe from the news-desk to speak to me for *months* – and there you are, chatting with him as if you've been chums for life!'

Anna ignored the hot flush of her cheeks and stared at the visitor logbook. 'He was just being nice.'

'Nice, my *ass*. He either wants to get into your knickers or into your bank account.' She inspected a chip on her gel nails. 'Joe Adams doesn't do nice.'

'So why do you want him to speak to you?'

Sheniece shrugged. 'I'm broke. There's only one other thing I could offer him.'

Anna hid her smile. She was still getting used to her colleague's candidness, a year after Sheniece had arrived at the *Messenger*. 'Well, I'm not offering him anything apart from conversation.'

'Seems like everyone wants to talk to you today. Like you're our very own celebrity. What happened?'

'Nothing.'

'Ted reckons you've got an admirer. Maybe it's Joe.'

Anna considered the possibility. As the good-looking journalist had never so much as glanced in her direction before, it really wasn't likely. 'I don't think so.'

'Point is, though, you don't know, do you? It could be anyone in this building. Sending you anonymous presents, for reasons yet to be revealed. It's like a movie or something.' She shuddered. 'Freaky, if you ask me.'

Anna was quickly learning this was the conclusion reached by most people who had heard about her mystery parcel, courtesy of Ted. Must be someone who wants something, they suggested, their tone heavy with concern. Must have ulterior motives. *Nobody* sends anonymous gifts without an agenda. You should be careful, Anna: you don't know what you're dealing with . . .

But Anna wasn't concerned. She'd encountered enough doomsayers in her life not to be affected by their pessimism. Her neighbours back in Cornwall had been only too happy to prophesy untold misery for the 'poor girl with a car-crash of a mother' – and on the rare occasions when fortune had smiled on Senara Browne and her two children, it was quickly deemed dodgy by the village commentators. Why was it gospel that someone doing something selfless, like sending a lovely gift, automatically implied questionable motives? Life could surprise you – both for good and for bad. This was obviously one of the good surprises. Knowing the unbridled delight with which

34

Ted was spreading news of her secret admirer, Anna could practically feel the whispers of the building around her. Glances were cast in her direction as people buzzed in and out of the atrium, muffled giggles echoing across its marble floor as they moved away again. Secretly she liked that for once she was the hot topic of conversation at work. What would the village gossips back in Cornwall make of that, she wondered? Quiet little Anna Browne being the centre of attention, and not because of her shameful mother's exploits! Ms Senara Browne would *not* be happy at having her thunder so comprehensively stolen . . .

It would quickly pass, of that Anna was certain. In a newspaper building more stories passed through its walls than through its columns. Soon Anna Browne's mystery gift would be old news. But today she liked the attention.

At the end of her extraordinary workday Anna said goodbye to her colleagues and walked out of the building. As it had been a day of firsts, she decided to take Babs' advice and treat herself, before joining the bus queue. Ordering a takeaway tea and a sticky almond flapjack for the journey home was almost negligible in its ability to change the world, but – added to her experiences of this remarkable Monday – it shone. Anna couldn't stop smiling as she waited for her bus, her happiness a sharp contrast to the line of world-weary expressions queuing up in front.

'Had some good news, have you?'

So rare was it for anybody to speak to her in the bus queue that Anna jumped. Looking to her left, she saw an older man huddled on the too-small orange plastic seat attached to the Perspex bus shelter. He looked cold, despite the mild air temperature.

'Just a good day,' she replied.

'Don't see smiles at this stop normally,' the man continued. 'Nice to see one.'

'Thank you.'

'Probably won't last, mind.' He dug in the pocket of his padded plaid bomber jacket and handed Anna a crumpled leaflet, which proclaimed: *END-TIMES ARE NEAR!* 'Armageddon's coming, you know. The End and that. Soon be here.'

'Nutter,' someone muttered behind Anna in the queue.

'Right. Well, thanks for letting me know.' Not knowing what else to do, she pocketed the tract.

'You're still smiling, though,' the bus-shelter prophet noted, a little piqued.

The queue shuffled along as the bus arrived.

'The way I see it,' Anna said, before the push of people behind her moved her away, 'if The End is coming, we might as well be as happy as we can before it arrives.'

'Fair point.' The man didn't smile, but seemed to be considering her words as Anna left.

'So I said to him, "I don't care if you got down on bended knee and begged me to reconsider. I wouldn't date you again if the President ordered me to!" . . .' Tish gave a tut as she sipped her macchiato. 'Guy's a *loser*.'

'I take it your fascination with the sales reps at work is over, then?' Anna asked.

Spill the Beans coffee shop was as packed as ever,

36

customers eager to celebrate surviving another city Monday. Anna rested against the leather upholstery of the bench seat as her friend regaled her with the details of her latest failed foray into dating. If Tish was to be believed, the financial services company she worked for seemed to attract an unusually high proportion of decent-looking, single salesmen, the ranks of whom she had been steadily dating her way through.

'Oh, I am *more than* done,' Tish scoffed. 'Gary was the last straw. Do you know he tried to say it was my fault for not knowing he had a wife and kids? Sales reps are masters of spinning tales. I should have guessed they were all liars. So. You look happy. *Again.*'

The emphasis wasn't lost on Anna. Sometimes she wondered if Tish was ever really pleased about things happening in her friend's life. It was best not to consider this too much, as she strongly suspected the answer wouldn't be positive.

'I had a good day.'

'Okay, now I know you must be on drugs. *Nobody* has a good Monday in this city, unless they're crooks, deluded or high.'

'I'm none of those. Maybe good Mondays happen occasionally. Maybe I was lucky.' She straightened her scarf, enjoying its soft caress against her neck. 'Don't worry, though, I'm sure tomorrow will be doubly depressing, to compensate.'

'It'd better be,' Tish muttered. 'Or else I'll start to worry about you.'

The American expat's pessimism came as no surprise

to Anna, after encountering it almost daily for four years. Bad news made Tish Gornick tick – but her saving grace was that it also brought out her rapier wit, which was entertaining, if not entirely comfortable all the time. Anna was amused by her friend's wry take on life, in particular her willingness to give voice to the thoughts everyone else concealed out of politeness. In a city where rudeness was perfectly acceptable as long as it wasn't vocalised, Tish stood out. But she was unrepentant, believing it was far worse to 'resort to British passive-aggressive silent rage, which isn't good for your colon'.

Secretly, Anna was impressed by Tish's forthrightness. Today, she found herself wondering if one day she would ever muster the courage to be like that.

The magic of the silk scarf was still working when she arrived home, her smile as broad as it had been all day. She remembered Laurel, a friend from her college days who believed new shoes were magical. Whenever she bought new shoes, she said, people noticed her. She would excitedly share tales of encounters and conversations brought about by the effect of her latest purchase, as if stardust was sewn into the seams of the leather. Until her scarf arrived, Anna hadn't really understood what this meant. But now she knew exactly what Laurel was talking about. It had been an unusual day, as if she had been allowed to live someone else's life for twenty-four hours. She had been given a glimpse of what life *could be* – of how differently she could live. It reminded her of a *Mr Men* story that her grand-mother Morwenna had read to her, in which the character who lived in a permanently snow-covered land and sneezed all the time was granted one day of summer.

What a difference one length of printed silk had made to her day! Anna was certain that when the garment was back in her wardrobe, things would return to normal. But today had been a rare gift: a chance to be different in her everyday ordinariness.

That night Anna slept deeper and more contentedly than she could remember. Her dreams were filled with smiling faces and the sensation of being as light as a feather.

When I wake up, this will be over, she told herself in the dreamlike half-awake moments before her alarm, as daylight began to filter through her closed eyelids.

But Anna was wrong.

Six

In her thirty years at the coalface of the British media, Juliet Evans had rarely been wrong-footed. She prided herself on her ability to weather any storm – from the two failed marriages that had rocked her life in her early twenties and late thirties, to attempted coups, professional scandals and the best attempts of her rivals to sully her name.

But then something had happened, unexpectedly tearing the ground from beneath her feet. And her own heart was responsible for the earthquake. Her mother died – and it was only then that Juliet realised how deeply she'd loved her.

Her mother's death wasn't a surprise. The human body didn't encounter such an all-consuming blow as Alzheimer's without eventually succumbing to it. But when the end came, it ripped a hole in Juliet's steel defences.

She wasn't expecting to grieve.

She'd lost plenty of other people over the years, all of

them dearer to her heart than her rigid, unemotional mother had ever been, yet the weight of loss didn't come close to the hollowing, empty ache she now felt. Was she grieving for a relationship she had never known, or for the definite end to any possibility of future reconciliation? She didn't know. But the pain was the keenest, most unforgiving sensation – and it refused to go away.

Had she had children, she would have turned to them now, seeking comfort there, where with her mother she'd had none. Had she still a constant partner in her life, she could have shared her pain. But the overwhelming feeling Juliet had was one of true loneliness. People had been polite, of course, even overstepping the usual boundaries of their acquaintance to offer condolences. But something was missing – something their kind words couldn't give her.

That was, until a chance remark in a lift journey three weeks ago had brought unexpected comfort.

Juliet had returned from a week's leave, aware that her staff had been given sketchy details of her recent bereavement. Piers, her faithful PA, had tentatively offered a hug in addition to his usual air-kiss greeting, and she could see sympathy in her colleagues' eyes as they attended that morning's editorial meeting. But by mid-morning she was feeling decidedly shaky, heading out of the building for a walk to calm her nerves. That was most unlike her, she knew, but she needed space to think. When she returned, she sprinted for the lift as the doors were closing, meeting the startled expression of Anna Browne, the pretty woman from reception.

41

'Thank you,' she'd managed as the lift began to rise. 'Anna, isn't it?'

The woman had nodded and immediately offered her hand. 'Yes. Anna Browne. I work on the reception team.'

What a sweet accent she had – Juliet recognised it immediately. Cornish. After her second divorce she had rented a house on the cliffs overlooking the sea near Padstow for a four-month sabbatical to lick her wounds, and had pottered down to the local village every day to buy a newspaper and essentials. She remembered the soothing nature of her new neighbours' conversation, its soft, lilting tones like the gentle undulation of the sea.

'I know who you are,' Juliet had replied, her smile beginning to fade as the conversation died between them.

And then Anna Browne spoke.

'Forgive me, but I was really sorry to hear about your mum.'

In the week since Juliet's return from compassionate leave, the young woman was the first person to actually refer to her loss. Taken aback, Juliet had shaken her head. 'Thank you. But we weren't close.'

For anyone else, her curtness would have been a warning sign. But not for Anna. 'I understand. I'm not close to mine, either. But still, your mum's your mum.'

It was a casual observation, but in that lift, that day, a young woman spoke to Juliet Evans' life in a way that few others had. And she realised that the ache weighing within her was guilt – for wanting to grieve for someone who had done nothing in her life to deserve it. The receptionist's words had finally given her the permission she needed to grieve, regardless of whether her mother merited it or not.

So, when her company-wide work-shadowing scheme was finally given the go-ahead by the senior management team, Juliet remembered the kindness and took a particular interest in Anna Browne's placement. Now, looking at the completed list of work-shadowing placements on her desk as last-minute preparations were signed off, her finger momentarily rested against two names: Ben McAra and Anna Browne. Smiling, she leaned back into her expensive white leather executive chair. If she said so herself, the resulting pairing was *perfect*.

In all the excitement surrounding the arrival of Anna's mysterious gift, she had temporarily forgotten her fear of the work-shadowing placement. But, as the week continued, the looming spectre of it returned, growing darker and more ominous. All weekend her nerves increased, until the waiting ended and the day she had been dreading arrived.

On the pavement outside the *Daily Messenger* building, Anna looked up involuntarily, her eyes fixing on the windows of the third floor, which housed the newsroom – the beating heart of the newspaper, and the place she was destined to be for the next two weeks. She had tried her best not to be apprehensive about this, but today nerves were getting the better of her. Last night her dreams had been filled with blunders and mishaps, always returning to an image of her facing a crowd of mocking faces. If she made a mistake here, not knowing what she was meant to do, *everyone* would see it. What happened if she became a laughing stock on her first day shadowing Ben?

And that was another problem entirely. Despite admiring the handsome journalist for months, from the safety and anonymity of the reception desk, she hadn't exchanged more than five words with him – and even when, on occasion, he'd wished her a good morning, she had been so befuddled with embarrassment that she'd hardly managed to reply before he'd walked away. She couldn't explain her reaction. She was usually confident around men, if a little self-conscious (which was her initial reaction to everyone new she met). Nearly two years ago she had been in what she'd assumed to be a long-term relationship with a young architect, Tom, until he'd left her to take a job in New York. With other men at work – Ted, Ashraf and the assorted male journalists she occasionally met from the newsroom – she could hold her own in conversation. But Ben McAra was a different prospect entirely. And now she was stuck with him for two weeks. What if she couldn't find the courage to string a sentence together?

Tish had dismissed her concern immediately, of course. They had walked from Walton Tower the day before to a small, antiquarian bookshop a few streets away, where Tish had an ongoing flirtation with the silver-haired bookseller. In a brief moment when the object of Tish's affection was otherwise engaged with a genuine customer, Anna had confided her fears.

'I just don't know what I'll say to him,' she admitted, selecting a dusty volume of First World War poetry from the shelves and inhaling the vintage scent of paper and ink.

'You'll say whatever comes up at the time, honey.'

'But what if nothing comes?'

Tish discarded a cloth-bound copy of Rossetti poems on the top of a row of books and tutted when Anna replaced it in line with the others. 'You have a problem with *neatness*, you know? Relax. This is just because you're in unfamiliar territory. After tomorrow, you won't be.'

'I really don't want to do it.'

'I know you don't. But life is full of things we don't want to do. I don't like monthly sales meetings with my creepy boss, but it's in my job description. At least you get to do something exciting. You *do* want to do exciting things, don't you?'

'I'm here with you, chasing good-looking bookshop owners, aren't I?' Her joke had been a deflection: the truth was, Anna didn't relish the prospect of excitement – not the kind that might shine an unwanted spotlight on her, anyway. She had grown up with the uncertainty that a life of drama brought, and had fought hard to leave it behind. Her job, her trusted circle of friends and her careful life in the city suited her. She knew where she was with it all, with no room for nasty surprises or uncertainty to ambush her.

But today, all that could change . . .

Steeling herself, she walked through the entrance doors and across the polished floor of the atrium, her shoulders back and her head as high as she could manage. It was only when the lift doors parted and the flood of newsroom noise hit her that she felt herself sagging. Panicking, she reached for the Door Close button, but a friendly face appeared in the doorway before she got there, grabbing her sleeve and pulling her into the hubbub of the unfamiliar floor.

'Hey, Anna! It's *so cool* that you're going to be here for a while.' Rea Sinfield clamped a friendly arm about Anna's shoulders, propelling them both through the frenzied mass of journalists. 'It's a little crazy in here this morning – big news just broke about a well-respected BBC news anchor having illicit meetings with a rent-boy.' She grinned. 'We have his exclusive story, and the other rags are murderous about it! Don't look so worried; it's not always like this. Let me get you a coffee and then I'll introduce you to Mr Wonderful.'

Paling, Anna let herself be manoeuvred between desks and dodging bodies, the shouts and activity of the newsroom dizzying to her unaccustomed senses. She was used to dealing with busy periods in reception, but this was a different kind of busyness. Tension hung almost visibly above the heads of the journalists, its presence squeezing the corners of the space and raising the volume of conversations. Even people collecting paper cups of water from the large coolers at one end of the newsroom appeared to be doing so as if their livelihoods depended upon it. Anna knew she was staring, but couldn't stop. It was claustrophobic and thrilling, a contradictive experience that awed her.

'How does anyone work here without having a heart attack?' she asked.

'You get used to it.' Rea smiled as she handed Anna a mug of dark, smoky coffee. When Anna tasted it, the caffeine nearly knocked her off her feet. 'This stuff helps. Come on.'

Trailing like a bewildered child behind her colleague, Anna followed her through the newsroom to a row of desks that appeared to be made of better-quality wood-effect laminate than the rest.

'Senior editorial team,' Rea explained. 'They get better chairs than us minions, too. Ah, here's the man of the hour! McAra, you have a visitor.'

The dark-haired man swung his office chair around and suddenly Anna was face-to-face with the object of her anonymous affection. She forced a smile, and prayed to all that was good that her cheeks weren't matching the scarlet upholstery of Ben's chair. 'Hey. You must be Anna Browne.' He held out his hand as he stood. 'I'm Ben.'

'Our *star* reporter,' Rea mocked.

'Hardly. Thanks, Sinfield. I'll take it from here.'

With a final encouraging smile, Rea returned to her desk in the middle of the newsroom scrum, leaving Anna feeling self-consciously on show by Ben's desk.

He was smiling at her and she couldn't work out whether this was friendliness or fascination for an unfamiliar face. Remembering his manners, he grabbed a grey office chair and wheeled it beside his. 'Please, have a seat. I'm just firming up my appointments for this morning, so give me five minutes and then we'll get cracking.'

Without waiting for her answer, he turned back to his computer screen and began to make a phone call. Anna

47

sat on the slightly uneven seat of the chair, which seemed to possess the loudest squeak known to man, feeling completely conspicuous. It was as she'd feared: her confidence had evaporated and she was stuck here for what already felt like hours, unable to do anything until Ben returned his attention to her.

Two weeks of *this* was going to be hell . . .

The TV anchorman's exclusive reverberated around the newsroom for most of the day, but as it was the property of Eric Mullins, Ben's fast-talking, self-assured colleague, the story made little impact on the work Anna and Ben had to do. As she'd expected, Anna quickly learned where the coffee machine, photocopier and stationery cupboard were situated, Ben sending her on mundane errands more to occupy her while he arranged his week's schedule than because any of it was crucial to his work. As she printed off copies of Ben's recent research, she took the opportunity to watch the newsroom. She remembered her friend Jonah – a freelance TV cameraman who worked on nature documentaries – telling her that much of his job entailed watching 'the everyday activity of unfamiliar environments'. Today, she understood what he meant. The flora and fauna of the *Daily Messenger*'s news hub were most definitely alien: the pallid skin and uniform dark circles beneath eyes hollowed out by lack of sleep at odds with the frenetic activity of all of its inhabitants. Spikes of laughter punctuated the constant din of voices, phones and tapping keyboard keys, but Anna saw few genuine smiles. What she felt, though, was an unseen force driving everything: an urgency that seemed to sweep every person along.

She watched Ben from this safe distance, too. It was impossible not to – he seemed to be the centre of the action, whether participating or not. Her eyes were drawn to him, noting the way he was aware of everything happening around him, yet able to appear completely absorbed in his own tasks at the same time. It didn't hurt that he was undeniably pleasant to look at, of course – a fact not lost on several of his female colleagues, who flitted close to him whenever an opportunity presented itself. If Ben knew the effect he had on them, he was careful not to show it, but his satisfied expression made Anna think that he was more than happy with the situation.

Anna was quickly learning that Ben McAra was a series of contradictions. He moved faster than anyone she'd met before, yet seemed to take his time over every task. He was driven but laconic, a natural comedian but prone to moments of dark seriousness. All of which made him fascinating and frustrating all at once. As the day progressed she found herself more able to talk to him, becoming less concerned with the stark newness of her temporary work surroundings. Procedures and protocols gradually formed coherent lists in her mind and she settled into the strange rhythm of the journalist's day. There appeared to be much sitting around waiting for interviews, interspersed with frenetic sessions of Internet research and information-gathering. And coffee. A *lot* of coffee. Fearing she might not sleep again during her entire work-shadowing placement, Anna made a note to herself to bring in peppermint tea tomorrow. One day of newsroom rocket-fuel sludge was enough to bear.

What did Ben make of her? Anna couldn't tell yet, but he certainly seemed to be interested in his temporary work colleague. In the gaps between actual work he bombarded her with questions, from banal to personal, on every topic under the sun:

'*That accent isn't local. Where are you from?*'

'*Did you go to university?*'

'*What was the first record you bought?*'

'*Bourbons or custard creams? Personally, I can never choose. Do you have a favourite biscuit?*'

'*What's your five-year plan? What do you mean, you "haven't got one"?*'

By half-past three that afternoon, Anna felt thoroughly grilled.

'You ask a lot of questions.'

Ben stared at her, mid-coffee-sip. 'Occupational hazard. Sorry, I've been annoying you, haven't I?'

'Not annoying as such . . .'

He shook his head. 'My apologies. I do this. My friends regularly tell me to shut up. Feel free to do the same.'

Anna smiled. 'Shut up, Ben.'

'There. Makes you feel better, doesn't it?'

'Much.'

'So, why don't you like answering questions?'

'Shut up, Ben.'

'Oh, come on, just this one question? It's my best one.'

'Shut up.'

Groaning, he raised his hands in defeat. 'Fine. Wish I

hadn't told you that. Let's mix it up, then. Why don't you ask me something?'

Anna thought for a moment. There were many things she wanted to know about Ben McAra, but where to begin? 'Why all the questions?'

'Because I'm interested. Don't roll your eyes, Anna – I am. I'm a natural inquisitor. Plus, my own life is never as interesting as other people's.'

'Why say that? You're a star reporter, you have the news-room at your feet . . .'

'And you do the same job, day in, day out, yet you seem more content in your career than I have ever been.'

It was an observation Anna hadn't anticipated and it took her by surprise. Could Ben really have concluded that, from the little she had actually told him of her own life? Of course, she loved her job – it was comforting in its everyday usualness, and her colleagues made her work-days enjoyable. But that her happiness was so obvious to a relative stranger surprised her. *Am I happy?* She supposed she was, even if happiness for Anna Browne was a quiet, safe kind of happiness.

'Aren't you content? I thought you loved your job?'

'Oh, I do. I mean, I can't see myself ever doing anything else. But I'm always chasing the next story, the next big headline – and while the pressure is what drives me in this job, it also creates a permanent sense of dissatisfaction. I need to feel like I'm missing something to keep going, I guess.' A wry smile appeared and Ben reached for his notebook. 'Heck, that was *deep*. I'd better write it down before I forget what a shallow newspaper hack I really am.'

His humour was disarming and certainly put Anna at her ease, but she noticed that he also used it as a shield when he felt challenged.

'It's endearing,' she explained to Tish later that afternoon, as they sat in the coffee shop, Anna enjoying the caffeine-free soothing of a peach tea while her friend fuelled her neuroses with a triple-shot of espresso. 'He's a confident man, but he hides very quickly from anything too revealing of himself.'

'And that makes you like the guy even more, huh?' Tish nodded knowingly. 'Classic unattainable-male syndrome.'

'I don't want to *attain* him,' Anna corrected her, feeling her cheeks reddening despite her best efforts. 'But, I'll admit, the prospect of working with him for a fortnight is much more appealing.'

'Because you're intrigued?'

'Yes.'

Tish's expression was hard to decipher. 'Good.'

Seven

'Nice scarf, Anna.'

Murray Henderson-Vitt, staff reporter, leaned back in his chair from his desk behind Anna. He appeared to have half the contents of his breakfast sandwich displayed across the front of his greying work shirt, the other half clearly visible rolling about in his mouth as he spoke.

'Thanks. It was a gift.' Anna did her best to focus on Murray's eyes instead of the food flopping around beneath them.

'So I heard. From Ted.'

'Ah.' *Of course you did.* Ted Blaskiewicz was obviously not slipping in his gossip-spreading duties.

'So, any idea who sent it?'

'Nope.'

'Bet you're intrigued, though? I know my wife would be, if she received a gift like that. She'd have good reason to wonder, mind you, seeing as she'd know it wasn't from me. Last year I bought her a new steam-iron for her birthday, so you can imagine the stick I got for that.' He picked up a paper napkin and wiped his mouth. 'So, how's it going with McAra?'

'Good, thanks.' Anna had heard from Rea that there was little love lost between Murray and Ben, so she was careful to keep her answer neutral. 'We're going out to interview a theatre producer today.'

Ben had informed her of their appointment when Anna arrived for work first thing, and she was both excited by the prospect of watching Ben in action and a little nervous about being alone with him. Still, it would be good to leave the noisy newsroom for a few hours, not least because of the beautiful sunshine bathing the city this morning.

'Your first field trip. Bless. Still remember mine: visiting a local mayor in Norfolk in his shoddy little office that smelled of fish. Years ago, of course, but the memory of that smell never quite left me. Can't walk past the fish counter in Morrisons without gagging. Oh, look lively, here comes your boss . . .' He raised a hand in salute to Ben, who was heading back to his desk. 'Ah, McAra. I hear you and this delightful young lady are off gallivanting this morning.'

Ben flopped into his chair. 'We will be, yes. Jealous, are you?'

Murray's eyes betrayed contempt as he smiled. 'Sitting in a cab in lunchtime traffic in the West End? No chance. Better make sure you rehearse your big song, though. You know what these theatre impresarios are like – always on the lookout for new talent. Could be the big break you've been waiting for.'

54

'Not me, H-V. I'll be in this job until the day I retire. I'll send you a note when that day comes. Which care-home will you be in by then, do you reckon?'

'So funny. Well, if you'll excuse me, *some* of us have *real* news stories to write. Anna, have fun.'

Anna watched the two journalists return to their work like stalking stags after a rut. It was her fourth day in the newsroom, but already she had deciphered the unspoken tensions between various reporters, editors and interns. Ben's colleagues fell into two distinct camps when it came to their opinion of him: those who liked him and those who were irritated by him. The former group was, it had to be said, overwhelmingly female, ranging from junior reporters to older picture editors and columnists who found everything he said unfeasibly amusing. The latter were a more diverse and, consequently, far more interesting group. Within their ranks Anna saw jealousy, annoyance, bitterness and disgust, mostly aimed at the actions of Ben's fan club. She couldn't work out whether the relationship between Ben and Murray was good-natured banter or something deeper, but she was enjoying unravelling the puzzle from her vantage point at Ben's desk.

'Do you go to the theatre much?' Ben asked when they were in a taxi heading to the Dominion Theatre, half an hour later.

'More than I used to,' Anna replied. 'My friends Jonah, Tish and I take our neighbour Isadora to local theatre productions when we can. We don't tend to go to the big West End theatres often, but every now and again we'll treat ourselves. How about you?

'Only when my mum visits,' he admitted. 'But if you tell anyone at work, I'll put you on filing duty for the rest of your time with me.' He flicked through his notes. '*So*, the theatre bod we're chatting to today has recently returned to the UK after twenty years living in New York. Which means his first West End production after a raft of Tony Awards on Broadway is a big deal. Plus, he's secured serious funding for the production. We're talking *big* bucks.'

The taxi swerved to the kerb beside the impressive theatre.

'Here we are. Ready?'

Anna nodded, surprised by an attack of stomach butterflies. 'What's the production?'

Ben opened the door and hopped out. '*The Sound of Music*.'

Anna froze. Why hadn't she checked that fact before they left the newsroom this morning? At least then she would have been forewarned . . .

'Anna?' Ben was peering back into the taxi. 'You coming?'

Dismissing her reaction, she hurried out, following him into the opulent lobby of the theatre. She had to keep her mind on the job.

I can do this.

Rufus Sigmund was as charming as Anna had expected him to be. Known as much for his very public, very flamboyant lifestyle, he was larger-than-life in both character and physique. With almost shoulder-length flowing blue-grey hair and powder-blue eyes, he was striking to look

56

at. He towered over Ben as they walked into the Dominion's auditorium, his jovial laugh booming around the empty theatre space.

'I might look in control, but let me tell you, darlings, it's been *hell* on *earth*. Press viewings begin this evening, and you would not *believe* the problems we've had securing work visas for half the cast. My Elsa Schraeder only became official an hour ago!'

'Why didn't you choose a British cast?' Ben asked, making covert notes as he maintained eye contact with his subject. Anna noticed that his smile remained steady as a thousand questions raced across his face. 'Surely that would have been easier?'

'No time, love. We moved the production from Broadway two weeks ago. The slot we got at the Dominion was too good to miss. Should it be a success, of course we will recast local actors for the onward run.' He smiled at Anna. 'Do you sing?'

Anna felt herself redden. 'Not in public.' *Not any more.*

Rufus shrugged. 'Forgive me, I'm a terror for talent-scouting. My partner reprimands me for it constantly.'

Ben asked the questions he had gone over with Anna that morning, and Anna watched the interaction between the two men. She noted the subtle changes in conversation as the subject moved from Rufus' latest production to a recent scandal involving one of his leading actors in his most recent Broadway production. It was well known that the actor – a personal friend for many years – had turned tail on Rufus when he was accused of arriving stoned for performances, and had sold a raft of increasingly lurid stories about the producer. Ben broached the subject carefully, but Anna still saw Rufus Sigmund wince when the actor's name was mentioned.

'Danny Raphael is a very angry man,' Rufus answered – and Anna saw pain wash over his eyes. 'We are no longer on speaking terms.'

'Did that prompt your move back to London?'

'Not at all, love. Despite what your colleagues in the US tabloids would care to believe, my return is purely coincidental. But that's really old news, Mr McAra, so I trust you'll be more creative in your report.'

Ben nodded his understanding. 'Of course.'

'Excellent. Now, I think it's time our company showed you why this production of Rodgers and Hammerstein's masterpiece will become known as *definitive*.' He brightened as he motioned to a stagehand and the house lights dimmed.

The cast walked onto the stage in full costume, performing a medley of the musical's famous songs. In the darkness Anna sank further into her seat, waiting. Sure enough, it came – a young actor and actress stepping forward as their cast-mates retreated from the spotlight.

'*You are sixteen going on seventeen . . .*'

Anna tensed as the song began. At one time this had been the only song she had sung for almost an entire summer. Thrilled at winning the role of Liesl in the Polperro Drama Players' production of *The Sound of Music*, she had proudly rehearsed the song on the clifftops above the harbour bay, treating the gulls and skylarks cruising the coastal air currents to her best vocal performances. Like the character

58

she was preparing to portray, she was approaching her seventeenth birthday, the promise of college and, further still, the much longed-for escape from Cornwall beckoning as brightly as the sunlight dancing on the waves beneath her. This would be her final summer restricted to the village, with its too-harsh spotlight on every aspect of her life. But as Anna began to sing there had been an unscripted crash from the back of the village hall . . .

'Not a fan of musicals?' Ben's whispered question nudged Anna from her memories.

'Just this one,' she replied, before she could think of a better answer.

'What's *The Sound of Music* ever done to you?'

'Nothing. Just not my favourite.' Anna forced a smile. Ben didn't need to know the reason her insides were knotting so tightly as Liesl's song played.

'Nazis and nuns – not a sequin in sight,' he joked, blind to Anna's discomfort. 'As a teenager it was the only one I found acceptable, trying to be an alpha-male . . . That was a *joke*, Anna.'

'I know. Sorry. I'm not on the ball today.'

'Late night?'

'Couldn't sleep.'

If Ben thought she was lying, he didn't show it. 'That'll be the excitement of working with me.'

'Could be.' She felt herself relax as the song ended and the cast returned to finish with a rousing rendition of 'Edelweiss'. But the feeling of injustice remained as they sang: the memory of her stolen moment in the spotlight – her mother's alcohol-fuelled rant at what she saw as a 'room full of hypocrites' silencing Anna's song. Frozen to the spot, she'd been forced to see the pity in her neighbours' eyes and hear their muttered opinions reverberating with the sound of a drunken woman's wails around the walls of the hall . . .

Safely back on Tottenham Court Road after walking from the theatre, Anna was aware that Ben was observing her carefully.

'That was fun,' she said brightly, keen to deflect his concern. 'I liked Rufus.'

'He's a character, for sure. But I promise we'll steer clear of West End theatre stories for the remainder of your work-shadowing, okay?'

'Deal. So, where next?'

Ben grinned. 'Illicit work lunch, I think. *Essential* perk of my job.'

The experience in the Dominion Theatre had shocked Anna with its intensity, but as Friday passed into the weekend, the smarting of it began to fade. Ben hadn't pressed her for an explanation or sought to find out more – and for that she was grateful. Now, with the weekend stretching ahead of her, she decided to have fun.

Tish gave her a wry look as they walked from Walton Tower, heading for the Tube.

'Good week, huh?'

'Different,' Anna conceded. 'The newsroom is like another planet, though. Two weeks there will be plenty for me.'

'And handsome Ben?'

'Still handsome. And still interesting.' Anna smiled. 'He manages to be utterly relaxed and totally on the job at the same time. It's fascinating to watch.'

'A man multitasking: who knew? So, where are we headed?'

'I thought you could show me that shop in Marylebone you're always going on about.'

Tish brightened immediately. 'Mia Casa, Mio Cuore? Oh my, Anna, you're going to *love* it!'

The idea had come about quite by chance that morning as Anna was eating breakfast, gazing out at the overcast cityscape beyond her apartment window. Perhaps it had been the memory of her past that prompted it. Whatever it was, she had been struck by the urge to buy something new for her home. Her apartment was comfortably furnished, but she hadn't changed it much since she had arrived at Walton Tower. Every item of furniture, every picture and every object had a memory attached to it – something that gave Anna a sense of peace. But now, with the extraordinary events of the past couple of weeks, she wanted something to mark the present.

The small shop on Marylebone High Street had been the object of Tish's affections for nearly a year now, and Anna had lost count of the number of prized purchases from the shop that her friend had proudly shown her. It was a part of London she hadn't ventured into much before, but as soon as they entered the High Street she liked it. Unlike other areas of the city, it had a more relaxed feel. People walked more slowly, pausing to look at shop-window displays or browse menus in gilt-edged glass frames outside restaurants and cafés. One couple, walking arm-in-arm, actually wished Anna and Tish good morning as they passed – an occurrence so unusual in the city that Tish turned to stare at their backs to check they weren't a mirage.

Mia Casa, Mio Cuore had a bright-turquoise painted facade and a brass-handled door that creaked satisfyingly when it opened. Inside, the shop was bright and minimally decorated, the whitewashed floorboards and reclaimed-oak display tables a perfect canvas for the beautiful ornaments, kitchen accessories and textiles. The space smelled of orange, cinnamon and sandalwood, reminding Anna of the New Age shops in Newquay she'd visited as a teenager with Ruari.

Tish dashed from one display to the next, loudly proclaiming her love for every item she saw, while Anna wandered slowly between the tables and shelves, pausing to run her fingers over rich embroidered fabrics, carefully lift glass ornaments and inhale the fragrance of hand-dipped candles. She wondered if her scarf had been bought from a boutique like this: had the parcel-sender taken time to select the right gift for her, as she was doing for herself today?

Rea had taken her aside by the newsroom coffee machine yesterday to dig for more details of her gift.

'Don't you have any idea who sent it?'

'No. I've considered everyone I know and drawn a complete blank.'

'Do you want to know?'

Anna confessed she did. The more she had worn the

beautiful scarf, the more curious she had become about its sender. It felt as if it had been made just for her – and that made her wonder how well she was known by the sender. If it had been a random choice, it had been a lucky guess. But Anna couldn't help feeling there was more to the gift than just a kind thought.

'It's heaven, right?' Tish's eyes shone now, and Anna saw her wicker basket contained several items already. 'It's too long till my next pay-cheque, but I can't resist.' She waggled a credit card in front of Anna. 'Thank the Lord for plastic, that's what I say. What you gonna get?'

Anna had seen several possible purchases, but one drew her back to it. 'This, I think,' she said, leading Tish to a display of silvered glass birds. In the middle, one rose up above the rest, its stylised wings spreading out as if preparing to fly. It caused a flutter of excitement within Anna, reminding her of the strange mix of apprehension and anticipation she had experienced in the *Daily Messenger*'s newsroom that week – and, no doubt, would feel during the next few days. It seemed the perfect choice.

Later that day Anna unwrapped the bird and placed it on the top shelf of her bookcase, where a shaft of sunlight caused the silver flecks within its surface to sparkle and shine. Her second week in the newsroom lay ahead of her like an uncharted ocean – but, to her surprise, she no longer felt afraid.

Eight

First thing on Monday morning the entire editorial team was called into the newspaper's boardroom on the sixth floor, its full-height windows inviting the neighbouring buildings to peer in on proceedings with glassy eyes. Anna followed Ben into the room, feeling the anticipation of the people around her prickling along her skin. Nobody smiled, but by now she was used to the serious expressions the newsroom incumbents wore.

The available seats were snapped up quickly, the remainder of the staff leaning against the walls and perching on the edge of tables and planters around the perimeter of the room. Ben offered Anna his seat, much to the amusement of his colleagues. Reddening, she accepted, hunkering down as best she could to avoid their eyes.

The door opened and immediately the room fell silent. Juliet Evans, flanked by her ever-present PA, Piers Langley, breezed into the room, taking her seat at the head of the table.

'Good morning, all.'

Mumbled greetings sounded from around the board-room.

'*So*, what do you have for me?'

One by one, the senior journalists ran through their current projects, the bones of the week's papers taking shape as each column, section and department added their contributions. The editor listened dispassionately, nodding her approval and making notes. Occasionally she would interject with questions, quickly dismissing points she didn't agree with. Some of the reporters challenged her, and Anna saw the younger staff writers shrinking back when Juliet disagreed. She could feel tides of respect and resentment in the air, rising and falling as the meeting progressed. Ben had told her that morning that most of the senior writers enjoyed the verbal sparring with their editor, in their own way.

'It gives them ulcers, but it's addictive. You fight for your words and, occasionally, you win.'

'McAra,' Juliet barked. 'How about you?'

'A few leads I'm working on, but the oil story, the government report on the Stafford case and my interview with the Deputy PM are all ready to rock.'

'So, we're expecting standard politician answers?'

Ben chuckled. 'As ever. But I'll make it work.'

'*Boring!*'

The eyes of the boardroom lifted as one.

Ben stared back. 'Sorry?'

'We need an angle the other titles don't have.' Frowning, Juliet slapped her hand on the pale wood of the boardroom table. 'Come *on*, people! This is a crucial time for the *Messenger*, as you have no doubt all been speculating. We need to approach our stories from a different perspective – appeal to readers who are looking for a fresh approach. Standard interviews with politicians are *old*. They know exactly which questions we'll ask, and they've been media-trained into avoiding giving us anything. People are sick of reading it. *I'm* sick of reading it. So, how do we avoid it?'

Uniform silence met her question.

'Seriously? The greatest talent gathered on Fleet Street, and yet not *one* of you can offer anything different?' Her sharp green stare swivelled without warning to Anna. 'Anna Browne. What do you think?'

Juliet Evans was not a woman to notice anyone, being more inclined to expect the whole world to notice her. Wherever she walked in the *Messenger* building, people parted like the Red Sea under Moses' outstretched arm, clearing a path for the woman *Time* magazine listed as One of the Most Influential Women in Business Today. A posse of hangers-on scurried behind her – security, assistants, associate editors and anyone who dared request an audience with her in her busy day. Outside editorial gatherings such as this, Juliet rarely entertained *Messenger* staff in her office, preferring instead to have them stutter their requests at breakneck pace as she swept from one department to the next. 'Walk with me!' was her favourite order, barked at cowering employees as they hurried alongside her. She was, in short, *terrifying*.

And now she was fixing Anna with her stare, demanding a reply . . .

It was as if the air had suddenly been sucked from the room. Anna's mouth dried in an instant, her body shrinking into the uncomfortable chair. *Everyone* was looking at her now, expecting her to answer. She looked over at Ben for reassurance – or even a look of friendly solidarity – but he was staring a hole into his lap.

'I . . .' *Think, Anna, think!* Her heart beat so quickly she thought she might faint, all rational thought leaving her.

'Well?'

The bark of the *Messenger*'s powerful editor hooked the flailing words in her mouth, dragging them forth in panic, like a fish struggling from the water on the end of a fly line. Anna closed her eyes and heard her voice speaking words she hadn't formed.

'Ask them different questions . . . Things the politicians aren't expecting.'

When she dared to look, something approaching a smile had taken residence on Juliet's lips.

'Good. Such as?'

Anna's mind whirred into action. 'Personal things. I read political interviews and I never feel I'm getting an insight into real people, just rhetoric. If you met someone for the first time, you wouldn't only talk about their job. You'd ask questions about their lives, their likes and dislikes – all of which would inform your opinion of them.'

'Go on.'

Anna considered her own experience of meeting and

greeting strangers as they entered the building. 'I find, in my job, that establishing common ground is a good way to get the measure of someone in a short time. When people are waiting in reception, they usually like it when you put them at their ease with a little chat. I've often discovered surprising things about people during short conversations.'

Juliet clapped her hands, making her audience jump. 'And *that*, people, is why the work-shadowing project is going to be so valuable to this paper. People from different departments, offering a fresh perspective. *That* is what will give us the edge. McAra, make sure you give Miss Browne more to do than photocopying and fetching coffee, yes?'

Ben nodded dumbly as Anna stared at her lap, feeling relief flood her frame as she was released from the weight of the editorial team's stares.

'Well, weren't you the star of the show?' Murray Henderson-Vitt jibed as Anna and Ben returned to the newsroom.

'I don't know about that. Just common sense, I think,' Anna said quickly, noticing Ben's amusement at her reply.

'Yeah, you know, H-V – that thing we're supposed to have?'

'I've read about it. So, what challenging assignment are you going to set the Teacher's Pet today, McAra?'

Ben's smile faded a little. 'Riveting research for the oil-company story.' He mouthed *Sorry* to Anna.

'Welcome to the wonderful adventure of a national

newspaper,' Murray chuckled. 'One minute you're dining with stars, the next you're shovelling the—'

'Quite. Well, we must be getting on, H-V. I'm sure your headlines are screaming for you.'

Anna heard the older journalist mumble something unprintable as he turned back to his computer screen. She was becoming accustomed to the banter in the newsroom and was growing to like it, despite its ferocity.

'Sorry about the Internet-trawling,' Ben said, once Murray was hunched over his work. 'I need background on three of the biggest oil companies. Bit of a boring job, but it needs to be done.'

'I don't mind,' Anna replied, happy to have a quiet, steady task to focus on after her experience in the editorial meeting. Why had the editor singled her out like that? They had barely spoken in the past, apart from saying hello, and one brief conversation in the lift a while ago; aside from that, they were as good as strangers. Anna hadn't liked Juliet's condescending tone, either. If she wanted a poster-girl for her precious work-shadowing programme, Anna didn't want the job.

'You did well, though, in the meeting,' Ben said, as if reading her thoughts. 'Juliet can be terrifying when she jumps on you like that.'

'It was a bit of a shock. I don't know why she picked on me.'

'You're new. And she has a point to prove with this scheme. Don't worry, she'll have forgotten about you tomorrow.'

Anna hoped Ben was right.

*

Her feelings about the experience in the editorial meeting remained conflicted for the next few days as she accompanied Ben to several interviews and completed hours of background research for the assignment he was working on. She *had* spoken up in the middle of a packed room full of people she didn't know: that was new. And they listened to her suggestion and didn't shoot her down in flames (as she'd seen several of them do to one another on the newsroom floor), which was even more surprising. She'd hated all eyes turning to her when Juliet barked her name, but had emerged unscathed from a situation that, even a week ago, she couldn't have coped with.

Her work-shadowing task was turning out to be a place for unusual happenings and Anna was quietly satisfied by her reaction to it all. That said, she was glad her remaining days in the newsroom were fast dwindling now. It would be good to return to reception and her usual routine. She would miss working alongside Ben, though. Despite his unremitting questions and questionable sense of humour, she felt at ease in his company and was even beginning to sense a chemistry growing between them. She was certain she would never quite reach the banter levels of his closest colleagues, but she enjoyed the jovial conversations and good-natured jibes they had shared.

As the end of her time with Ben approached, Anna marvelled at how much had happened to her since the arrival of her surprise parcel. She had started to feel a little differently about herself recently, and the scarf's appearance in her life was the only thing she could pinpoint as being responsible for it. Intriguingly, her most challenging and surprising experiences in the newsroom seemed to happen on the days she wore her scarf. Deciding to test the theory one last time, she wrapped the scarf around her neck as she left her apartment for her final day in the newsroom.

For the first two hours nothing happened. The work they had done during the week was complete and Ben's calendar was empty until the following Tuesday morning. It seemed that a slow news day was in progress across the news floor, with journalists wandering between the desks and hanging around the coffee machine in an attempt to look busy. Even the phones were strangely silent. Anna could see Ben's frustration building, the tap-tap-tap of his pen against his notebook a telling sign.

'I'm sorry, Anna. I thought we'd have more to do for your last day.'

'Don't worry, it's fine,' she replied, smiling brightly to conceal her disappointment. *Next week I'll return to my everyday life*, she told herself sternly, feeling foolish for wanting more.

'This doesn't happen often, but when it does it's a killer.' He grimaced, absent-mindedly stirring the coffee in his insulated mug with his pen. 'Drives me *insane*, to be honest. What do you do downstairs when it goes quiet?'

'Ted usually entertains us with his latest conspiracy theories.'

Ben laughed, the sound warm and familiar to Anna now. 'Well, our Teddy B could keep you entertained with that for *years*. It's a wonder Channel 5 haven't done a series on his crazy theories. Maybe we should get him up here, just to kill a few hundred years.'

71

Anna could just picture Ted Blaskiewicz holding court in the newsroom, spinning tales of covert corruption, devious deeds and shameful secrets. He would be in his element. 'He should have been a spy. I think he always wanted to be one. He thinks he's one already, truth be told, but at least if MI5 had actually hired him, he'd have all the surveillance gadgets he lusts over.' A thought occurred to her. 'Did you always want to be a journalist?'

'Actually, no. I wanted to be an explorer when I was a kid. I had dreams of travelling the world and writing about my adventures.' He laughed and flicked a screwed-up sticky note off his desk, missing the waste-paper basket by millimetres. 'It's probably good that I reconsidered. Can't really picture myself in a pith-helmet, can you?'

'What made you change your mind?' Anna was astonished by how easily she could question Ben now, without a hint of nerves. It was another surprise from her time with him.

'I was offered work experience with the local paper when I was fifteen. And, let me tell you, it was nowhere near as exciting as the things you've done this week. But, I don't know . . . there was something about the buzz of the place that I liked. They printed one of my stories, too – a tiny piece about a sinkhole that had appeared in the High Street overnight. When I saw my words in print, that was it for me.' He shrugged. 'Maybe we should run one of the stories you've been working on for me, and enchant you into the business.'

'No, thank you. I mean, it's been fun, but I'm no writer.'

'So, did you always want to be a receptionist?' Mischief danced in his eyes.

'Oh yes,' Anna replied, playing along. 'I used to line my teddies up and sign them in as visitors.'

'Aw. Did you make little security badges for them, too?'

'The whole shebang.' It felt good to laugh at a joke she'd made. 'I don't know what I wanted to be, really. I just wanted a job where I could meet people. And I wanted to come to London. When this job came up, I took it and I really enjoy it.'

'Why did you want to come to London?'

His question took her by surprise: she hadn't realised she'd offered the information until Ben jumped on it. Why London? In truth it was because it was the one place her mother wouldn't follow her to.

But there had been another reason – one that even Jonah and Tish didn't know: she believed her father lived in the city. It had stemmed from a casual remark Senara had made during one of her drunken rants about how sorry her life was. *Your dad was the worst of 'em! Running back to his comfy life in London, forgetting all about me – like it was that easy! T'ain't fair, Anna! Why am I always the one that gets left?*

She knew nothing more about her father – not even his name, a detail Senara refused point-blank to share. But even knowing he was somewhere in the city gave Anna a tangible connection to him. London became the object of her ambitions from that moment on: a plan hatching in her early teens that would lead to her leaving everything behind to follow it. Maybe she had already met him;

perhaps he had visited the *Messenger* building and wished her a good morning as he collected his pass. She often thought about him as she travelled to work, visited galleries and bookshops and cafés with Tish and Jonah, or walked through London's beautiful parks. In her deepest dreams he would emerge from the crowds and take hold of her hand. She would see herself in his eyes and feel, at last, as if she belonged . . .

'I thought it would be great to live here. And it is.'

'But you don't miss – where is it you come from?'

'Cornwall – Polperro. No, not much.'

'Don't think I've ever been. My family always took us to the Norfolk Broads or Margate—' He was interrupted by the shrill ringing of his desk phone. 'Here we go – something to do at last!'

Anna turned away a little to look at the notes she'd made for Ben yesterday. As she did so, she could hear the journalist's voice rising beside her.

'You *will*? Definitely? Perfect! No, don't bring anyone else – and tell no one you're meeting me, okay? I'll text you the location.' Slamming down the phone, he shook his head. 'I *knew* today wasn't going to be slow. Anna, this is *huge*!'

With no further explanation offered, she watched as Ben flew into action, the change in him startling. She could almost see the adrenaline coursing through his body as he arranged an interview venue and time, fired off texts and scribbled lines in his notebook. After a full ten minutes of activity he finally turned back to her, his eyes alive.

'We got it!'

'Got what?'

'An exclusive I've been working on for *months*. I'll explain on the way there. But this is what I do this job for! Come on . . .'

His excitement fired Anna's own and she hurried after him down to a waiting taxi. She wasn't sure what to expect, or what lay ahead – the prospect both unnerving and thrilling.

'This story could bring down a major politician,' Ben explained, still adding questions to the list in his notebook as their taxi wove through midday traffic. 'Scratch that: it *will* bring him down. With an election looming and his party polishing him as the PM's spotless right-hand man, it's *explosive*! Juliet told me to lay off the story last week, but I knew it was coming, you know? I felt it, *there*.' He jabbed his thumb at his heart. 'This doesn't happen often, but when it does, the rush is incredible! Don't look so scared, I'll handle everything.'

'And what do I do?' Anna asked, suddenly feeling like a spare part.

'Just watch,' he grinned, 'and enjoy!'

Nine

Vanessa Milburn was not accustomed to nerves. But today she seemed beset by them. Of course, dishing the dirt on your soon-to-be-former boss was never going to happen completely without jitters, but she hadn't expected to feel quite as apprehensive as she did. The hotel room hired for the exclusive interview with the *Daily Messenger* didn't help, either; it was furnished to look sumptuously comfortable, but was anything but. Even as she wriggled on the painfully rock-hard upholstery of a chaise longue at the bottom of a palatial bed, Vanessa felt out of place.

She couldn't reconsider. Not now. Alistair had cooked his chips when he denied their long-standing affair and made her out to be a liar and a cheat. *She* wasn't the one with the media-friendly, doe-eyed wife and simpering kids. She'd maintained her deliciously single status: the only person she had cheated was herself. Alistair had used her, betrayed both her and his family, and now he expected her to fall on her sword for him? Not likely! Vanessa

Milburn was a survivor. Her entire career had been built on weathering storms. Now it was *her* turn to have her say.

Unfortunately the *Daily Messenger*'s star reporter was fast revealing himself to be a Class A idiot. Already this morning he had insulted her, wrongly guessed her age (who *did* that these days, anyway?) and now was trying to insinuate that he was her erstwhile saviour. *You're just a hack*, she thought, as he fired a set of increasingly patronising questions at her. Everything within her screamed back at him: *I'm not some dim-witted teenager selling a story on a celebrity! What I have to share will undermine the credibility of one of the country's most respected politicians, the heir-apparent to the Prime Minister himself!*

She should have talked to the *Post* instead. They were crass and devoid of conscience, but at least you got what you expected with them. She should leave, chuck this annoying young man out and rethink her strategy.

But . . . the young woman sitting next to him interested her. She seemed to have an air of calmness around her – and also appeared to be becoming increasingly embarrassed by the questions of her colleague. So far she had only spoken to give her name and say hello. According to the journalist, she was on some kind of work-experience programme, although she looked too old to be a college student. Vanessa found herself drawn to the woman's kind eyes. And that was when the idea occurred.

'I think we're done here,' she snapped, registering with no small satisfaction the shock that laid siege to Ben McAra's smugness.

'What? You – you can't!' he protested. 'You promised me an exclusive.'

'I promised the *Daily Messenger* the exclusive, not you.' A thrill of returning power fired through her backbone as she focused on his female companion. 'So I'll talk to *her*.'

It was the young woman's turn to be shocked. 'No! I'm just shadowing . . . I'm not a journalist . . .'

'All the better for me then. I might get some sense out of you.'

The journalist had abandoned his self-assured air and was glaring at her with barely concealed rage. '*No*,' he growled. 'Absolutely not.'

Oh, this was becoming more enjoyable by the second! Vanessa raised her chin to give the floundering reporter the full weight of her superior stare. 'That's the deal, McAra, take it or leave it. Either I talk to *her* or I find another paper that'll buy my story. Believe me, I've had *plenty* of offers.'

It was a lie, of course, but the journalist didn't know that. This way, Vanessa could say what she wanted, get her money and move on with her life – with the added bonus of getting one over on the annoying young man who had insulted her for the past half-hour.

Observing the aftermath of her verbal bombshell with delight, she leaned back against the unforgiving velvet of the chaise longue and waited . . .

This was the *worst* possible thing to happen.

Anna looked at Ben helplessly, not knowing what to do. It was exactly this sort of situation that she had dreaded, and she found herself wishing she had never agreed to the work-shadowing project. It was one thing to be challenged by Juliet Evans in a room of editorial staff, but this was another prospect entirely. This was Ben's story; from what he had told her, she knew how much it mattered to him. It was the *big one* – the rare kind of bombshell that he craved, the kind of exposé that could boost his career.

Anna could see that the interview wasn't going well. Part of her understood Vanessa Milburn's frustration – the woman's livelihood depended on her story being handled well, and she needed assurances. Whether it was a simple personality clash or Ben was too eager to get his story, Anna couldn't tell, but she'd been taken aback by some of the remarks he had made this morning. It seemed at odds with the charming, quick-witted person she had seen in other interviews she'd sat in on. But she never expected that his bumpy beginning to the interview could lead to this . . .

She knew Ben was affronted: his huge exclusive snatched away and offered to a receptionist, of all people! She wasn't even a newsroom intern, which in itself would have been enough of a snub to him. His eyes darted between her and the well-dressed woman on the chaise longue. What was he thinking?

She realised her fingers were gripping the silk scarf around her neck as she desperately tried to regain the sense of confidence that had surrounded her whenever she'd worn it previously. But the magic eluded her.

'No. You promised *me* the story, Ms Milburn. I'm a journalist; Anna isn't.'

79

The woman shook her head. 'Then we have no deal.'

Anna saw abject panic fill Ben's eyes as the woman stood.

'Wait!'

She paused, realising it was her voice that had summoned Ben's and Vanessa's stares. Her heartbeat crashed in her ears, making her dizzy as she gathered her words. 'I'll do it – but only if I can ask you the questions Mr McAra has already prepared.'

Though she was thinking on her feet, it seemed to make sense. Asking Ben's questions would mean the interview was still his – she would merely be a mouthpiece for him. At least she could help Ben get the story he'd worked so hard to win. But would Vanessa agree?

She could feel the weight of Ben's eyes on her: was he offended or impressed?

As Vanessa considered this suggestion for several dragging moments, Anna fought the urge to run from the room. Why had she ever thought she could do this? How had she come to be in this situation?

And then –

'Fine.' The woman resumed her seat and turned to Ben. 'You can go.'

Ben nodded slowly. 'I will. But I need a moment with my colleague.' He caught Anna's elbow gently and led her towards the hallway of the hotel suite.

'*I can't do this,*' Anna hissed, panic setting in.

'Yes, you can. You have to.' He pressed his black leather notebook into her palm as if conferring the Holy Grail. 'Just ask these questions and . . . and you'll be fine.' He was clearly improvising as much as Anna had been moments before – unsmiling, his eyes were insistent on her. 'And if something else occurs to you, ask it. She likes you: that's an advantage you can use.'

'I don't know what to say or how to do this.'

'Yes, you do. Think of it as a conversation with a new friend. And don't worry if you stumble – she won't be expecting you to be professional, which means she'll tell you more than she would me. Just do it. I'll be waiting outside.'

Ben didn't wait to hear her protest, slipping quickly out of the room, leaving Anna alone, frantically studying his unkempt scrawl across the notebook pages. She felt sick and reached out to steady herself on an ornate plaster pillar.

You can do this, she repeated, pushing away her concern about Ben's true feelings. There would be plenty of time to deal with that later. She understood how important this interview was to him: she couldn't let him down. Her fingers found comfort in the cool silk of the scarf, where minutes before there had been none. She knew this must be her imagination attributing such power to an inanimate object, but right now she was willing to take strength from anything, however unlikely.

Vanessa Milburn was a different woman when Anna returned. Gone were the hard lines across her brow, her firmly folded arms now unfurled and resting on the aubergine-velvet seat of the chaise longue on either side of her knees.

She smiled as Anna resumed her seat. 'So. Shall we start again?'

An hour later Anna was still shaking. But this time nerves were not to blame. She had taken a risk and succeeded. It had been a long time since she'd been so brave. The thrill that shook her now was the same as she'd last experienced as a teenager, when a friend persuaded her to dive from a cliff near her home on a balmy summer's day. So all-encompassing and invigorating had that risk been that she'd been rendered speechless for several hours afterwards as she and her friends gathered on the beach around a fire, with a blazing red sunset spreading across the sky.

She felt *alive*, as if awoken from a sepia-toned dream to find herself in a Technicolor world. Her solo interview with the politician's mistress was little more than a fog in her mind, the questions of her own that she had asked only coming back to her now as she and Ben leaned over the voice recorder at a table tucked back from the main hub of the hotel's restaurant. Hearing her own confident voice coming from the speakers was a surreal experience, as if listening to a version of herself she hadn't yet met.

Ben had said little when she'd emerged from the hotel suite and Anna still couldn't tell what his true reaction was. Instead he had fiddled with the notebook and voice recorder in the lift down to the lobby and had busied himself with talking to the stern-faced maître d' in the elegant restaurant, to secure a secluded table. He'd ordered coffee without asking Anna's preference, his face betraying none of his emotions. Anna waited: she would find out soon enough how he felt. For now, she wanted to capture this moment and hang it on her wall – this self-assured, other-Anna-Browne, improvising questions and even sharing jokes with the woman she was interviewing. It was proof of what she *could* be – and of what she could be again . . .

The recording came to an end and Ben clicked off the recorder. The sound of clinking cutlery and muted conversation rushed in between them like a wave, as Anna stared at Ben and he kept his eyes on the pressed white linen tablecloth beneath his hands. Finally she could bear it no longer.

'What do you think?'

Ben shook his head. 'You did it.' His voice was flat, neither angry nor triumphant.

'Did I ask the right questions? I mean, I asked all the ones you'd written, but then we carried on and I just went with what felt right at the time . . .' Realising she was jabbering, she took a breath. 'Ben?'

He gave her a half-smile when his eyes met hers. 'You did a great job. I mean it. Thank you.'

Anna felt the tension in her shoulders release. 'That's good. For a moment I thought you'd be angry with me.'

'Angry? Why? You saved the exclusive – surprisingly well, considering it was your first interview. Juliet Evans will be over the moon . . .' His eyes strayed to the curled edges of his notebook. 'Speaking of whom, we should be getting back.' He raised his hand for the bill, signalling the end of the conversation.

They spoke little in the taxi back to the *Messenger*

83

building, Ben checking emails on his phone as Anna gazed out at the greyness of the city passing by. His reaction irked her a little, but it couldn't take away the thrill of what she had achieved today. She was determined to enjoy it, just as she had all the unusual things that had happened to her since the scarf arrived. When today was over – and she returned to the warm familiarity of her real life – she would package up her extraordinary memories and store them safely where she could revisit them like keepsakes whenever she wished. It was another, even more precious gift than the sender of her scarf could ever have anticipated. It made her all the more determined to find out who the sender was. One day she would thank them in person.

Back at Ben's desk, Anna assisted quietly while he typed the story. Tomorrow morning, as her life resumed its usual rhythm, the story she had brought into being would rock the country from the news boards of the nation's newsagents. She could hardly believe today's turn of events.

'I should give you billing on this,' Ben said, so suddenly that Anna nearly spilled coffee over his desk.

'No, you shouldn't. It's your exclusive.'

He turned to her. 'By rights, it's become yours. The questions you asked brought about the biggest revelations – some of this stuff is so explosive Vanessa Milburn would never have offered it if she hadn't felt at ease. *You* made it happen.'

He had a point, but Anna couldn't let him lose the story that he had told her was so important for his career. However the interview had gone, it had been Ben's dogged pursuit of the subject that had brought about the meeting. He couldn't have foreseen the personality clash that threatened to scupper it. Besides, the uplift Anna had experienced was enough. Despite the thrill-ride of today, she didn't want to be a journalist. Her experience of Ben's working life had been enough to convince her of that: his strange working hours, his ability to shelve his conscience as the job required, not to mention his reliance on far too much caffeine than could ever be healthy. It was not for her.

'It's your exclusive, your story. I don't want to be credited for it.'

Ben sat back in his chair. 'You are a genuine surprise, Anna Browne. Anyone else I know would jump at the chance of a front-page byline.'

'I'm not like that. It doesn't matter to me.' She looked at the clock hung high on the newsroom wall. 'And, as of five minutes ago, I am no longer work-shadowing you.' She offered her hand to him. 'Thanks for an enlightening fortnight.'

Ben stood and shook her hand. 'So. I . . . guess I'll see you around?'

Gathering her bag and coat, Anna smiled. 'I hope so.'

She walked from the newsroom as if propelled by air, surprised by how different she felt from her hesitant arrival, two weeks ago. As she turned in the lift, she noticed that Ben had returned to his work, the scurrying bodies of the newsroom staff blurring him from view as the lift doors slowly closed on the strange chapter of Anna's life.

That night Anna slept soundly, the memory of her day

mingling with the sense of being surrounded by billowing lengths of rose-printed, sugar-scented silk, feeling completely at ease with herself and utterly at peace.

Ten

Saturday morning was warm and bright, flooding Anna's apartment with light as she emerged from her bedroom in search of breakfast. Her work-shadowing fortnight over, she was exhausted but happy, the kind of bone-tiredness she remembered feeling after childhood Christmases spent with her grandmother and brother while her mother worked at the local pub. It was past nine o'clock – far later than she would normally wake up on a Saturday – but this morning her lie-in had felt like a reward.

She opened her front door to retrieve the carefully folded weekend paper from the doormat outside. Seamus, the caretaker, let the local paperboy deliver to Walton Tower residents' doors, rather than stuff the thick newspapers into the bank of apartment post-boxes in the entrance hall.

'The last thing anybody needs is post-boxes gummed up with paper and newspapers they can't read for creases,' he would intone, his deep Belfast brogue making the statement sound like a matter of dire importance. 'Plus, the kid needs the exercise. Have you *seen* the gut on him?'

Hot buttered toast and tea in hand, Anna settled at her dining-room table to read the Travel section of the paper. She was admiring a photograph of an Indian Ocean archipelago when a knock sounded on her door.

The smiling man on her doorstep was a sight for sore eyes.

'Jonah! You're back!'

Her friend patted his faded blue T-shirt with suntanned hands as if checking his existence. 'So it would seem.'

'Come in! The kettle's just boiled. Have you had breakfast? I can make you some toast if you like.'

Jonah Rawdon watched Anna dashing around her kitchen with amusement. 'I don't think you've ever been this chuffed to see me before.'

Anna laughed, but Jonah was right. He had been away on a filming assignment for a month now and she had missed his company. They had been friends for several years, from the day Jonah had moved in when they'd met in the hall as the removal men were bringing in the last of his furniture. His no-nonsense Yorkshire outlook and laid-back attitude were a breath of fresh air to Anna: he, like her, was an 'outsider' in the city, unaffected by the conventions of London life. This had drawn them together, and Anna valued Jonah's friendship more than anyone else in her life.

In nature, he reminded her of her brother Ruari – Jonah's love of the outdoors and wry sense of humour were infectious and Anna felt better for spending time with him.

Furnishing him with a mug of tea and a stack of toast, she thought of how much had happened in her life while he had been away. There was a great deal to tell him, but where to begin?

'How was Spain?' she asked, revelling in the sight of her good-looking and delightfully unkempt friend reclining on the sofa. It was so good to have him back.

'Hot. *Spanish*. I've eaten enough paella and chorizo to do me for life.'

'Seriously, though, did you enjoy the assignment?'

'I did, aye. For what it was, it were good enough. The money was good, too, so at least I'm not panicking about the rent for the time being. Nice bunch of blokes, though. I met a fella who works for the BBC and he said he'd put in a word for me when we got back. So, you never know.' His grey eyes narrowed slightly. 'All good with you?'

'Yes. And for a change I've got quite a lot to tell you.' She noted Jonah's surprise with satisfaction. 'What are your plans for today? Fancy lunch out somewhere?'

'Funny you should mention that. I'm heading out to the sticks for a bit of location-scouting this morning and wondered if you fancied tagging along? It's been a while since we did any weekend field-yomping and I thought you might like it. There's a half-decent pub near the place, so I'll shout you lunch, too?'

Anna didn't need any further convincing. The prospect of being outside on a beautiful morning with her best friend was wonderful. An hour later they were driving out towards Hampshire in Jonah's ageing VW camper-van. The air grew sweeter through their open windows as urban sprawl gave way to fields and pretty little villages snuggled between rolling hills. It was a beautiful part of the world, and Anna relaxed against the warm vinyl of the front seat as sunlight bathed the road ahead.

They parked in an innocuous-looking lay-by beside a field of tall, wild grasses.

'What a lovely day,' Anna said, feeling the warmth of the sun on her back as she climbed out of the camper-van. Although it was spring, the weather had more of a feel of summer about it, unseasonably warm for the time of year. It seemed strange to be without layers of woollens today, with the damp chill of winter still only a recent memory. While she loved her job and the building in which she worked, a part of her would always long for the countryside. Senara had been right about one thing: the country was in Anna's blood, and no amount of living in London would change that.

'I don't know how you stay indoors all day. It would have me climbing the walls in minutes.' Jonah handed her a pair of mud-splattered wellington boots. 'Here, you'll probably need these. They might be a bit big, but I've spare socks in the van to pack them out a bit.'

Anna giggled as she pulled the boots on, their generous proportions dwarfing her feet. 'I never realised your job was so glamorous. There. Will I do?'

'Aye.' He gave her an appreciative smile. 'Very nice.'

Jonah's faithful Border collie, Bennett, jumped out of the back seat and bounced around their feet as they set off across the lush grass of the wildflower meadow, his barks and yelps mirroring Anna's mood today. She found

90

a stick and threw it high for the delighted dog, laughing out loud as he jumped to catch it mid-air. The lazy hum of bumblebees surrounded them and clouds of midges rose from the grass as they walked. It wasn't yet midday but the morning had a promise of heat about it, the expanse of cloudless sky above them suggesting a beautiful day ahead.

Jonah had a tripod bag slung over his shoulder and carried a camera bag, which brushed the tops of the grass and flowers as he walked. It fascinated Anna to see her friend in his native environment. He was completely at ease with his surroundings, as much a part of it as it was of him. She couldn't imagine him surviving long in a corporate environment. He was made to work outside.

At the edge of the wildflower meadow they reached a roughly hewn wooden stile that breached the dry-stone wall. Jonah bounded over it almost as if it wasn't there, holding out his hand for Anna to take as she tentatively negotiated the obstacle.

'It's not far now,' he promised, indicating a wooded area where the path became sandier and cloaked in a thickly matted carpet of brown pine needles. 'Just through that copse.'

Anna followed, the coolness of the pine plantation prickling across the bare skin of her forearms as they moved out of the morning sun. 'How did you find this place?' she asked, picking her way carefully around exposed tree roots and hummocks of spiky grass.

'One of the researchers on the Spain job mentioned it. She walks her dog here at weekends. I'd never have found it by myself. But I think it has potential for some great wildlife shots.'

'It's lovely here. Your office certainly beats mine.'

He laughed. 'I'd say that's pretty easy to do. I don't know how you relax in that glorified tin box.'

'It's not so bad. Besides, it's the people who make it for me. Being out here on my own wouldn't suit me.'

'Probably not. Now – look at *that* . . .'

They emerged, quite unexpectedly, on the shores of a gorgeously glassy lake, its mercurial waters lapping red sand-coves where bright-blue and green dragonflies dipped and hovered. Surrounded by the dark wash of pine forest and illuminated by morning sunbeams, the effect was sublime.

'Wow!'

Jonah's smile broadened as Anna drank in the view. 'Pretty good, eh?'

'I love it.' She unknotted the arms of her anorak from around her waist and laid it over the mossy bulk of a tree root to sit down on. The air above the water was cool against the warmth of the sun hitting her face – the contrast reminiscent of childhood days rowing out towards Looe Island with Ruari and their Uncle Jabez. The only thing missing was the smell of salt and the wheel of gulls.

Jonah set up his tripod and video camera, taking stills-shots with a digital camera hung around his neck as he worked. Anna watched the lake's insect residents skimming along the soft ripples of the water where it met the shore. The scene couldn't have been more at odds with where she had spent the last two weeks and she found herself wondering if Ben would enjoy the stillness of this place as much as she did. She smiled to herself: the lack of action would probably drive him to distraction.

'Penny for them?' Anna looked up to see Jonah standing beside her. 'You were miles away just then.' He flopped down onto a large, flat rock next to her and flicked through the photographs he had taken so that Anna could see them on the small screen of the digital camera.

'I was just thinking about my work-shadowing,' she replied.

Jonah frowned. 'Your what?'

'It's a scheme at the paper, where you go to a different department for a fortnight and get to see how someone else in the building works.'

'What, like *Wife Swap*, but for jobs?'

Anna giggled. 'You watch too much trashy telly when you're between jobs. No, not like that. More like an extended work experience. So my placement was in the newsroom shadowing the chief reporter.'

Impressed, Jonah sat back a little. 'Heck, that's a bit of a change, isn't it? How'd you get on?'

Beside the gently rippling waters of the quiet lake, Anna told Jonah about her extraordinary time shadowing Ben, concluding with her unexpected promotion to journalist on his exclusive story.

'Ouch! How did he take that?'

'I think he was okay about it, in the end.' Ben had seemed perfectly fine when she'd left yesterday, but whether or not he harboured any resentment she supposed she'd discover in time. 'Anyway, it doesn't matter. On Monday everything will go back to how it always was.'

'Are you happy about that? No drama, no exciting assignments across town?'

Anna considered the question. Ordinarily her answer would have been yes, a return to the safety of familiar surroundings being exactly what she wanted. Now, she wasn't sure.

Eleven

Ted Blaskiewicz was worried. This was not an unusual thing, considering his vital role as head of security for the *Daily Messenger*'s headquarters. You had to have eyes and ears everywhere, as he often told his junior officers in their weekly security briefing. Thinking the worst was practically in the job description. During his time as a security chief, Ted had seen many dodgy sights – most of which would shock the average city worker. Petty crime, drugs, attempted fraud and business espionage were just the tip of the iceberg. And the number of clandestine office affairs beggared belief.

But this was something new.

That it was happening right under his nose was bad enough. But that the potential victim was a colleague for whom he had great personal affection was deeply concerning. From the first day Anna Browne began working for the newspaper, Ted sensed she was special. His brother Ivan had the temerity to suggest once that Ted carried a candle for her, which was, of course, a completely crazy comment to make, given that he was in his early fifties and wouldn't date a woman so much younger. He didn't fancy her, but he did feel unusually protective towards the kind-hearted young woman.

And now some ne'er-do-well had taken an interest in her. An interest that Ted highly suspected of being unhealthy.

What made the whole thing worse was that he suspected the culprit was already in the building. Anna didn't mention family much, so it seemed safe to assume that none of her relatives knew where she worked. Anyone else would send gifts to the recipient's home address, not their place of work. Ted congratulated himself on his sly deductions. Sherlock himself would have approved, he was sure. Or Dr Gil Grissom on *CSI* (the best character, in his opinion). Ted would be happy to take the plaudits from either eminent investigator.

Following the arrival of the mystery parcel, he had spent evenings poring over his *True Crime* magazines and old episodes of his favourite crime shows. He was sure he'd seen a similar plot somewhere. Frustratingly, he hadn't found it, but his conviction remained strong. Columbo would never have let such a small detail as lack of evidence stop him, so neither should Ted Blaskiewicz. Whoever had their eye on lovely Anna Browne should know that he was on their tail already – and he wouldn't stint in his investigation until the guilty party was revealed.

And this morning, exactly four weeks from the arrival of Anna's mystery parcel, the need for his skills intensified –

because he had just signed for a second, smaller package, delivered before Ms Browne arrived. As with the first, no sender details were given, the label (this time printed) offering no clue as to the sender's identity. He cursed the Finance Department for refusing his third request for a fingerprint kit. If he had one now, things could be *very* different indeed.

But the sender should still be afraid. Ted Blaskiewicz was *not* a man to give up.

Anna couldn't believe her eyes. Neither, it seemed, could the *Daily Messenger*'s chief of security, although his reaction was the polar opposite of hers.

'Another one?' She had not expected this when she arrived for work this morning. She had enjoyed the afterglow of the first parcel's arrival for four weeks, but had assumed it was a one-off. 'That's amazing!'

'Is it?' He wasn't smiling, his dark, beady eyes narrowing.

'You don't think it is?'

'Depends what's in the box, girl.' He straightened his jacket, appearing to grow an inch taller. 'I think, in the interests of security, you should open it now. While I'm here to protect you.'

Ted Blaskiewicz was a constant source of amusement to Anna. His preposterous theories, and dogged commitment to them, endeared him to her in a way that few other *Messenger* employees appreciated. She was buzzing from the unexpected parcel, and Ted's concern only made it more entertaining.

'Protect me? What from? The last parcel had a pretty

scarf in it. Do you think someone's trying to charm me to death with lovely gifts?'

Ted harrumphed and refused to be swayed. 'And what if it's *not* lovely, eh? What if it's a severed body part or . . . or a *dead* thing?'

'That's one heck of a progression from a silk scarf, Ted.'

'The scarf could have been a hint at how they wanted to kill you.'

Anna chuckled. 'You have such a charming imagination. I think I'll take my chances and open it at home.' She took the parcel from the desk and put it in a drawer, turning the key to secure it from any further investigation.

'I could dust it for prints,' he suggested, clearly clutching at straws.

'What with, Ted?' Sheniece shook her head as she took off her coat.

'I was thinking icing sugar. Saw it on *Midsomer Murders* once.'

'Moron!'

Ted's face turned a fetching shade of puce. 'Oi, less of your cheek, Sheniece Wilson! Mocking an important security official is an offence, you know.'

'It might be. But I was mocking *you*.'

In utter frustration, Ted threw his hands up. 'Impossible, the lot of you! I only have your best interests at heart but, oh no, you know better. Well, I'll tell you this for nothing, Anna, whoever's sending you those parcels had better be on their guard, because Ted Blaskiewicz *always* gets his man!'

Anna and Sheniece shared a knowing grin as the security officer stormed back to his office.

'I think we upset him.'

Sheniece dismissed Anna's concern. 'He'll get over it. He's just miffed he didn't get to watch you open the parcel. But now he's gone, maybe you and I could have a little look inside?'

Anna was wise to her colleague's scheme, long before Sheniece finished speaking. 'I'm opening it at home,' she repeated firmly. It didn't matter what her colleagues thought: the thrill of a second parcel arriving was enough to make her stand her ground.

At midday, when Sheniece and new junior receptionist Ashraf disappeared for lunch, Anna allowed herself a small peek at the new parcel. Taking it from its safe place in the drawer beneath the reception desk, she gave it a little shake next to her ear and inspected its perfect wrapping, quickly transferring it to her handbag in the kitchen cloakroom when she heard Ted's booming voice echoing through the atrium towards her. She was thrilled that a second Friday had been blessed with more promise.

Just knowing another gift was waiting to be uncovered fuelled her smile and good mood for the rest of the day. While Ted, Sheniece and Ashraf taunted her with dark and dastardly theories, Anna couldn't think of anything other than the surprise concealed in her handbag, far from prying eyes. It couldn't have come at a better time. Almost a week back into her usual job, she had felt like something was missing. The excitement of her work-shadowing had been exhausting, but she found she missed it. To compound this, she had also noticed that Ben avoided her, choosing to sign in visitors when Sheniece or Ashraf manned reception and hurrying away when he caught Anna's eye. She was probably imagining it, she told herself, but the possibility had bothered her all week.

She thought of the parcel and wondered what might be inside it. *Someone, somewhere is thinking of me.* It was a beautiful thought.

What was most special was that Anna knew the parcel was uniquely hers. In a life that had many shared experiences, joys and frustrations, she realised she'd had very little she could lay sole ownership to. In her childhood, many of her possessions had been shared with Ruari, their mother blaming financial restrictions for this necessity. Her clothes were often hand-me-downs from her Uncle Jabez's children and from older girls in the village. Senara Browne loathed charity and viewed it as yet another damning verdict on her abilities as a mother, so young Anna quickly learned to hide any bags of clothes left on the family's doorstep by kind neighbours, before her mother saw them. Senara was too wrapped up in her own life to notice when Anna or Ruari wore something new, which meant the Browne siblings were able to enjoy the kindness of others without incurring their mother's wrath.

Since moving to London and achieving financial independence Anna had taken great pleasure in buying her own things, but the parcels represented a new experience: being given gifts by somebody else. That, coupled with the anonymity of the sender, imbued them with an almost magical quality.

Regardless of what the new parcel contained, to Anna Browne it meant more than she could ever find words to express.

As the hours until its unveiling dwindled to minutes, her excitement grew. All that lay between her and the opening of the parcel was a bus journey and a regular, end-of-the-week coffee date with a certain cantankerous American . . .

Twelve

Tish Gornick was not the kind of woman to be suspicious of her friends. Even given her deeply cynical, dyed-in-the-wool New York mind, she liked to think she was a good friend and therefore trusting of their motives. But lately one person she thought she knew was acting *very* strangely indeed. And Tish didn't like it.

She had known Anna since their chance meeting in the queue for coffee at Spill the Beans four years ago, and their subsequent friendship had developed over many after-work meetings and weekend trips into the city. It had become what Tish's mother back in the Bronx would call a '*thing*'. *You gotta* thing *with her, now? Is this a* thing? If you had a *thing* with someone, it was pretty much a friendship for life.

Tish liked Anna. Her sense of humour seemed to take her as much by surprise as it did anyone who witnessed it; while Anna's oh-so-British reticence kept her from acknowledging any of her considerable gifts (her loyalty, her sweet nature and her deep empathy, for starters). Tish also loved the way Anna listened to her. The latter was what had most endeared Anna to Tish, largely because working in a faceless office building for an equally anonymous financial services company meant very few people were willing to listen to her.

But on several occasions now Tish had noticed that Anna wasn't listening like she usually did. She was distracted again this evening, her gaze far beyond the coffee shop's faux-brick walls. At first, Tish had dismissed this as a symptom of a long day at work. But then it had really begun to bug her. And today it had become plain *weird* . . .

'What's *with* you, Anna?'

Anna was a little surprised by the venom in her friend's question. 'What do you mean?'

'You're not yourself. You haven't been the last two times we've met. What gives?'

Tish's expression threatened thunder, but Anna couldn't help smiling. If she was acting differently, the parcel nestled safely at the bottom of her handbag could well be the reason why. It was waiting for her, ready to be opened . . . The thought of what might be in the small package filled her with happiness she could barely contain. 'Actually, I feel fine,' she replied, resting her hand on the rose leather of her bag.

Tish put her coffee mug down with more force than usual. 'I don't buy it. And I'm not letting you leave this coffee shop until you tell me what's going on.'

Anna hesitated. Should she tell Tish about her parcels?

She's my friend, one side of her argued. *She should know about them* . . .

But this is mine – *truly mine – bought for me, intended for me to enjoy*, a new, unfamiliar voice insisted in her mind. *It's been a long time since anyone bought me a gift as a surprise.*

Could she hang onto her secret a while longer? There might not be any more parcels, in which case was it really worth making a song and dance about it, if it turned out to be nothing?

She was about to brush off her friend's comments when Tish spoke again.

'Just say it, Anna. I know I'm not the easiest friend in the world. My mother would confirm this. I –' she looked away and suddenly Anna was aware of a vulnerability she hadn't witnessed before, '– I'd rather you just told me to get lost. I don't do subtle hints, Anna, and lately I feel like I'm boring you. If that's true, then just tell me and I won't bother you again.'

Anna was shocked by Tish's assumption. How could she interpret Anna's lightened mood with wanting to be rid of their friendship? 'Don't be daft, Tish. You're my friend – why would I want that to stop?'

'But you've been so distracted lately. You don't seem interested in what I tell you . . .'

'Well, I am. And if I'm distracted, it isn't because I'm bored.' This turn of conversation made up Anna's mind. It was going to be far easier to tell Tish than to conceal it. She took a breath, inhaling the warm scent of coffee. 'Someone is sending me parcels. I've had two, both with

104

no sender details, both addressed to me. And I *never* get parcels. It's just made me smile, that's all.'

Tish was clearly not expecting this. 'Who would do that?'

'I don't know.'

'Don't you think you should find out?'

'How? They've given me no clues. Maybe they're just being nice. A random act of kindness.'

'Really?' Aghast, Tish faced her. 'So a *random stranger* sends you parcels, and you don't for a minute think there's an ulterior motive?'

'No. Why should there be?'

'Are you *kidding* me? Who sends gifts without expecting something in return?'

Anna sighed. Clearly Tish was at one with every other person who knew about her mystery deliveries. Perhaps she should have felt more cautious, but Anna couldn't see the parcels as anything other than a kind, beautiful gesture. 'If he or she wanted something in return, surely they would have included a note. Or a return address. Everyone at work thinks the sender is some kind of murderer-in-waiting.'

'They *could* be. They could, Anna! Trust me, honey, no one in this world does anything without an agenda.'

'I wish I hadn't told you now.' Anna stood. 'I'm sorry, I have to go.'

'So, what did they send this time?'

She let out a sigh, torn between wanting to leave and not wanting to offend a friend. 'I don't know yet. I'm going to open it when I get home.'

'You have it with you now? Open it! Let's see what you got.'

Anna thought of the parcel lying in her bag – the precious gift that it seemed only she saw the value of. And she considered what Tish would make of it. Would her friend's view of the actual object tarnish her own? So, Anna made a decision. The gift was intended for her, and her alone. To share it would almost remove some of the magic that in her eyes still surrounded it.

'No,' she lied. 'It's at home. I'm going back to open it now.' Remembering her friend's concern from earlier, she smiled. 'But I'll show you what it is next week, okay? And I would very much like us to remain friends. I'm sorry if I've been distracted.'

Tish shrugged. 'As long as we keep meeting up, it's good. Go. Open your parcel.'

As the lift shuddered and squeaked up to her floor, Anna considered her response to Tish. Why had sharing the moment with her friend been such a dreadful thing? She rarely told lies – a reaction to years spent enduring her mother's tall tales. Why had she lied to Tish today? Tish said Anna had been different recently, and this certainly seemed to be true. Anna wasn't sure whether she should like this version of herself, but she couldn't help thinking she had made the right decision today. People at work – and now Tish – had all taken it upon themselves to pass damning judgement on the parcels. So what right did they have to share the wonder and excitement that Anna felt at opening them?

106

The first parcel had made her happy for weeks. The second was just as unexpected, and meant just as much. She deserved to enjoy this moment, she decided. Because it might not last. While it did, she was determined to enjoy it – alone.

The parcel was considerably smaller than the first, a square box measuring no more than three inches across, but wrapped with identical care. The address label had been printed this time but, as before, gave no clue to the sender's address or identity. Anna turned the parcel over in her hands and heard a faint rattle from inside. She suppressed the urge to squeal – a childlike joy quivering up within her. Instantly, she was back in the small bedroom of her grandmother's house in St Agnes, long before the bitter battle ensued that would see young Anna and brother Ruari denied access to it. Until Anna's tenth birthday, she and Ruari spent every Christmas at Grandma Morwenna's fisherman's cottage perched high above the village looking out to the sea. Senara claimed that her bar work at the Blue Peter Inn in Polperro kept her away, but Anna was later to learn that she and Morwenna could not be in the same house for longer than a few hours. Morwenna got the grandchildren, while Senara had four child-free days over Christmas to do as she pleased: the perfect arrangement for both women.

Morwenna made Christmas the most exciting, magical time of the year for the Browne children – her home-made gifts and house filled with far too many fairy lights for the aged electrics in the cottage to cope with instilled a love of the festive season in Anna that time, trouble and experience couldn't shake. Her favourite time was early on Christmas morning – while the village outside still lay in darkness – when she would wriggle out from the too-tight sheets of her bed and reach down to pat the bulging pillowcase propped up beside it. The thrilling, muted rustle of wrapping paper was enough to make her Christmas even before it had properly begun, the promise of what lay within the folds of faded, candy-striped cotton far more important to her than the contents. When Senara called time on the children's St Agnes Christmases, without warning and with no explanation, Anna never experienced this again. She quickly learned – as she would with many other aspects of her childhood – that surprises and magic were not priorities for her mother. Where Grandma Morwenna delighted in awe and wonder, Senara mistrusted anything she was unprepared for. Instead of surprise Christmas presents, Anna and Ruari received money hastily crumpled into last year's leftover Christmas cards. Her mother's answer, whenever Anna asked for a surprise, was always the same: 'Trust me, girl, you don't want surprises. Life throws too many of 'em your way, and none of 'em good.'

Maybe that's why this means so much to me, Anna thought, as she carefully unstuck the tape holding down the corners of folded brown paper on the small parcel. *It proves not all surprises are bad . . .*

Within the folds of packaging paper and nestled within a plain white cardboard box lay a smaller, hinged box covered in dark-blue velvet, the colour of the night sky in Talland Bay, just around the headland from Polperro, where

Anna and Ruari would sneak after dark in their teens with bottles of local scrumpy smuggled out from their mother's not-so-secret stash. Gazing up at the star-strewn heavens from the dark beach, the two Browne siblings would dream of where their lives would take them. For Ruari, it was always going to be somewhere exciting: backpacking to the furthermost corners of the world – as far as possible from Cornwall. He achieved his dream at seventeen, travelling through Cambodia, Guam and Vietnam, until a beautiful girl called Jodie whom he met backpacking across Australia called him home to Cornwall, to embark upon a new adventure building his own surfing business, supported by a stable family life and kids. Anna was proud of her brother for his intrepid ambitions, but her wish on Talland Beach had been far simpler: to be somewhere she could be herself, instead of 'Senara Browne's daughter'. The city called her after university, and she never looked back as the train took her away from Cornwall. It was easy to be anonymous here: to have friends of her own choosing, or unlimited solitude if she so desired.

Anna gently lifted the lid of the velvet box, which opened with a satisfying creak, to reveal a beautiful costume-jewellery brooch in the shape of an owl. It looked old – perhaps fifty or sixty years of age. Made of shiny brass with green rhinestone eyes, it sat on a branch set with two coral stones and glinted in the light as she turned it. Something about the owl's expression made her smile.

'Now, where did you come from?' she asked, searching beneath its velvet-covered cushion in the box for any clue. But there was neither a maker's mark nor a note. Stumped, she picked up the brown wrapping paper and was about to screw it into a ball when she noticed a small rectangle of white card caught in the folds of one side. On it was typed:

THIS OWL IS WISE,
BUT NOT AS WISE AS YOU, ANNA BROWNE.

Anna stared at the message. These were the first words she had received from her mystery gift-giver, but they made no sense at all. She didn't feel very wise. If she were, surely she would have been able to decipher the identity of the sender? Was it an invitation to guess? Or did it hint of more conundrums to come? She remembered Ted's latest theory, that a killer was drawing her into his deadly game, but quickly dismissed the thought. People didn't do that in real life, only in TV shows and films where plausibility wasn't important.

The sparkling green eyes of the owl stared up at her as she ran her finger across its head. A previous owner must have done the same, as the textured curve between its ear tufts had been worn smooth. It was satisfying to touch and made Anna feel calm. She had always been fond of owls as creatures, and the brooch would look good on the lapel of her work jacket when she wore it next Monday. Beyond that, the mystery would have to remain unsolved – for now.

Thirteen

Ted blustered into reception the following Monday like a storm-cloud threatening rain. His usual good-morning wishes forgotten, he slapped a sheet of paper on the reception desk and jabbed at it with a thick, accusatory finger.

'*There!* I told you, girl – I told you it was coming!'

Anna looked up from the appointment diary. 'Told me what was coming?'

'It's all here: tightening belts, increasing competition, special measures . . .' He shook his head. 'Just like I warned. We'll all be for the high jump, mark my words. They don't send memos like this unless they're really up the creek.'

The sheet of paper appeared to be an internal memo, sent from Juliet Evans to the editorial team.

Anna peered at the memo. 'Where did you get this?'

'It fell off one of the desks upstairs as I was passing,' Ted replied.

'*Ted!*'

'What?'

'You can't go around stealing private memos from people's desks.'

'I didn't. It *fell* . . . If papers fall off desks and I happen to pick them up, I can't be held responsible if I *happen* to read what's on them. Besides, every desk has one. I saw the new intern putting them out before the morning shift arrived.'

Anna folded her arms. 'So you *just happened* to watch the intern delivering these and then *just happened* to walk past as one fell off the desk?'

Ted was unrepentant. 'Life is one coincidence after another.'

'Hmm.' Anna read the memo. It called for a meeting of the editorial team that afternoon, at which both Juliet and the senior Board members would be present. She had to admit, it didn't look promising. There had been rumours for months now that the *Messenger* was in trouble, but this was the first tangible indication that they were anything other than the product of wild speculation and Ted's gossip-mongering. It was common knowledge that the *Messenger* had been trailing its three biggest national rivals in popularity for a couple of years, its fortunes dictated – as were those of other national newspapers – by changing readership values, and not helped by its tardiness in embracing the digital age. But even this hadn't dented the fierce ambition of the paper's editor, who regularly circulated defiant news briefings to her staff, boasting of the paper's innovative strategies and stable circulation figures.

'See what I mean? Dragon Evans wouldn't call a meeting

like that unless pushed.' Ted sucked air in through the sizeable gap in his front teeth. 'Bad news, if the big boys are crashing her party.'

'We don't know that,' Anna replied, careful to keep her voice steady despite her concern. 'And you should know better than to steal other people's property. This meeting could be anything. Ms Evans talks about new strategies in her weekly staff bulletin all the time.'

'But she doesn't usually have the Board to babysit her, does she? Admit it, Anna, you're worried now.'

Anna was, but Ted Blaskiewicz was the last person on the planet she would ever admit it to. Her concern would be broadcast across the building in a heartbeat: *It must be bad, if even* Anna Browne *on reception is worried* . . . Involuntarily, her fingers rose to her left lapel to stroke the smooth metal head of the owl brooch, its coolness soothing. 'We'll be fine, I'm sure of it. Now go and put that memo back where you found it, before the team arrive.'

Sheniece spotted Anna's brooch as soon as she joined her at reception. 'Cute owl. Is it real gold?'

'I don't think so. It looks like brass to me.'

'Is it new? I haven't seen you wearing it before.'

'It arrived on Friday.'

Sheniece's charcoal-lidded eyes widened. 'Is that what was in your parcel?'

Forgetting the worrying staff memo, Anna smiled. Her colleague's excitement at her latest gift matched her own, and she liked having something to share at last. 'I think it's possibly a piece of 1950s costume jewellery.'

'They're slipping, after last time.' Sheniece made a closer inspection of the owl. 'That scarf was proper money. You'd think they'd have gone for gold for this one.'

'I like him. He makes me smile. And if the brooch was really expensive, I wouldn't have worn it for work.'

'You wore the scarf. And look what happened when you did that: people noticed.'

'You noticed the owl,' Anna returned.

'You're right, I did. I like his eyes.'

Anna couldn't help sharing the details of her latest gift. 'There was a note too, this time.'

'No! So who's your secret admirer?'

'I have no idea. It was just a message: "This owl is wise, but not as wise as you . . . "'

Sheniece wrinkled her nose. 'What's that supposed to mean?'

'Search me. I've been trying to work it out all weekend, but it just doesn't make any sense.'

'Weird. Although, you are quite wise actually. I've always thought that.'

It was a casual remark, but its impact on Anna was considerable. Firstly, she never imagined herself to be wise, and secondly, her endearing but self-obsessed colleague noticing anything about Anna was practically a miracle in itself. 'Really?'

Sheniece was inspecting a scuff on one of her painted fingernails. 'Mm-hmm. Wiser than me, anyhow. Not that that's setting the bar high or anything. I mean, you always know what to say when morons come to the desk. You

114

don't answer back or tell them to get stuffed, like I want to. I like that. I envy it, a bit.'

'That's a lovely thing to say—' Anna began, but Sheniece was already heading off to the kitchen behind reception for her early-morning caffeine shot. Alone again, Anna considered the revelation. Of all the people she knew, Sheniece Wilson was the last she expected to hear that from. *Was* she wise?

As the week passed, the difference that Anna had felt wearing the scarf returned. She was more aware of her reactions; as if she were granted more time to think before speaking. The message from the parcel still confused her, but the faith professed in her good judgement by whoever had sent it meant a great deal. Of course people had complimented her character before – she remembered the regulars in the Blue Peter Inn congratulating her for being 'nothing like your mother, God save her,' and her friends in the city seemed to value her opinion. But to receive an endorsement from someone she didn't know was a new experience.

It had all happened since she had received the second parcel. And, as with the first, Anna was amazed at the change she felt. She had never considered herself remarkable before: could an anonymous note and a quirky brooch really change that?

Fourteen

Seamus Flatley had been the caretaker of Walton Tower for fifteen years and nothing surprised him. It was a source of great pride to him, and a fact he guarded jealously. His mother had scolded him for it, many moons ago, in the grey-green kitchen of his County Clare childhood home: *There's no surprising you, is there, Seamus Flatley?* Seamus didn't mind. Better a life lived with no surprises than one derailed by bad ones. Take his eldest brother Colm, for example, now almost fifty, with three failed marriages behind him and nothing but the bottle for consolation. Poor beggar hadn't seen any of the divorces coming. Colm had been the one who wanted surprises as a kid: given the nasty shocks life had thrown into his path, what good had surprises ever done him?

And so it was with some consternation that Seamus discovered his long-held assumption was wrong.

It was the fault of that young woman in 16B. Seamus thought he'd got the measure of her – quiet, pleasant girl from out of town, who never played her music too loudly or complained to him about the state of Walton Tower's faded amenities, like many of its other tenants. The kind of person you notice for her ordinariness.

But that Friday evening, everything changed.

He was mopping the brown-and-white tiles of the apartment-block entrance lobby, one ear on the angry man shouting from a talk radio station on the small portable propped on a bank of post-boxes, the other listening out for the sound of approaching footsteps from the staircase rising above his head. It paid to be aware of movement in and out of the building, especially when several of the tenants owed his boss money. Seamus considered himself something of an expert in deducing which tenants would appear next on the chase-list scrawled in the building owner's heavy hand: it was amazing how fleet-footed even the most naturally cumbersome could become when rent was owed.

A few minutes after six o'clock the front door creaked open and the Nice Girl from 16B entered. She was carrying a brown package in her arms, but this wasn't what made Seamus Flatley stop mopping and stare at her. It was her face. He'd seen it often enough during the years she had occupied 16B and had to admit it was very pleasant indeed. A little shy, to be sure, but welcoming – not like the professional business people, who were locked-and-bolted doors as far as any human interaction was concerned. But today it was different. She was glowing, as if a golden spotlight were pooling over her as she walked across the lobby.

'Hi, Seamus,' she called out, before he'd had the chance to wish her a good evening.

'Hello, Anna.'

She didn't just pause on the stairs as she usually did. She came bounding over to him – as bold as brass – a delighted smile on her pretty face. 'Don't you think life is wonderful, sometimes?'

'I . . . well, I hadn't really thought of it,' he stuttered.

'It is. You never know what's around the corner, do you?'

'I suppose not.' Like poor Colm and his three ex-missuses . . . 'You seem happy.'

'I am. And not only because it's Friday.' She hugged the parcel as if it was a small puppy. 'Have a lovely weekend.'

Then she smiled at him and he was struck by a sudden sense of someone so completely happy they could melt into air before him. Seamus was transfixed as she passed him and ascended the stairs. He had always thought of Anna Browne as shy and sweet, but steady. She had never given any indication that she had the ability to be forthright. But this evening she had been like a completely different woman.

It was only when she had disappeared from view that Seamus realised his long-held belief in his ability never to be surprised had crumbled like the plasterwork on the lobby walls.

'*Another* parcel? Your secret admirer's keen, isn't he?' Sheniece had rushed to Anna's side like a wasp to a jam jar as soon as the courier left reception, earlier that day.

Exactly a week since the owl brooch was delivered, a third parcel now lay before Anna – and she could hardly believe it.

'It could be anything,' Anna had replied, but her heart was pounding. Even after two parcels had arrived for her, she hadn't expected a third. Who was her mysterious benefactor? Would their identity be revealed within the brown-paper packaging of the new parcel?

Of course, the new delivery *could* be anything. But the coincidence of three courier-delivered parcels arriving, each with no sender details and all addressed to her, was too delicious to ignore. Was it possible that her extraordinary adventure wasn't over yet?

'So open it.' Sheniece had grinned at her, the too-white enamel on her teeth glinting in the reception-desk spotlights.

'I'll do it when I get home.'

'Do it now!'

'I can't. Sorry.'

'Oh, come on, Anna. It's a Friday. The only exciting thing that happens here on a Friday is when my shift's over. We *need* excitement – you owe it to all of us.'

This never happens to me, Anna had said to herself. But in her hands was the newly arrived evidence that she was wrong.

Sheniece had groaned and click-clacked off to find Friday-morning entertainment elsewhere. Relieved to be released from the scrutiny, Anna had carefully stashed the parcel in the locked drawer beneath the reception desk for which only she had a key. It could stay there safely until she went home.

Within ten minutes the eager eyes of the *Daily Messenger*'s chief of security were boring into her back as she signed three visitors in for a high-level meeting taking place with directors, editors and shareholders on the top floor.

'Ms Browne,' he intoned.

'I'm busy, Ted.'

'Not too busy to be receiving a *third* mystery delivery, I hear.'

Anna handed passes to the visitors and turned to face Ted. 'I might've known Sheniece would go running to you.'

Ted frowned. 'I haven't seen Sheniece. Murray Something-Double-Barrelled from the news-desk told me.'

'Murray Henderson-Vitt? How does he know?'

'He's on the news-desk, Anna. It's kind of his job . . .'

'Very funny. But the parcel only arrived ten minutes ago.'

Ted tapped his nose. 'I have my spies, girl. So, are you gonna open it?'

'Yes,' Anna replied, seeing triumph register on Ted's face, '*when* I get home.'

'Charming, that.' Ted kicked at an invisible stone at his feet. 'You can go off people, you know.'

When Anna opened her apartment door she noticed a folded piece of blue notepaper lying on the doormat. Placing the precious parcel on the kitchen counter, she bent to retrieve the note:

Hey, stranger
   I've emerged from post-Spain hibernation and have
a bit of good news I want to share with you.
   Bottle of wine this evening? About 7 p.m.?
   Jonah x

She looked at the parcel and considered hiding in her apartment, pretending she hadn't received the note. But Jonah would know. And she liked Jonah. Besides, with three parcels now arrived, it was high time she told him. During their trip out to the Hampshire countryside a fortnight ago she had only spoken to him about her work-shadowing, thinking then that her scarf from the parcel-sender was a singular surprise. Since then, the owl had arrived, and now this parcel – and Anna wanted to talk about it. Jonah would have a good take on the situation, where Tish and her work colleagues still maintained their suspicion over the sender's motives. She looked at the kitchen clock: half-past six already, barely time to shower and change from her work clothes before heading across to her friend's apartment, let alone open her parcel. It would have to wait. But then half the fun of the previous delivery had been the anticipation – this delay would only add to her excitement.

Twenty-five minutes later, Anna took one last, longing look at the brown-paper-wrapped box, now in the middle of her dining table, before she deliberately turned her back on it and left the apartment.

Fifteen

Jonah Rawdon had lived across the hall from Anna for five years and liked to think he knew her well. He too was an outsider – a native Yorkshireman uprooted and transplanted down south to follow his chosen career. The first time he met Anna he was trying to work the anti-quated intercom system in his flat. After an hour of fiddling, he stepped out into the hallway in sheer exasperation and bumped into Anna, who was passing his door. Her residency in the building for eight months instantly qualified her to solve his problem, and as a thank-you he invited her in for a pot of tea and some Betty's Fat Rascals, sent as a care-package by his mother in Ilkley. Whether it was the tea, the conversation or the delectable cake that endeared him to Anna, Jonah wasn't sure, but their friendship began that day and quickly grew.

What Jonah liked most about his neighbour – apart from her enormous blue eyes and smile, which made you feel better about everything just by seeing it – was her ability to appear fascinated about aspects of his life, even if he suspected she wasn't really that interested. Being a TV cameraman often drew excited questions at dinner parties, but once it was established that he met very few celebrities the initial interest waned. Not so with Anna. He could talk to her about the technical requirements of his job for hours and her eyes would never drift away. She was always willing to head out on location-scouting trips with him, regardless of how muddy or remote they were. Jonah liked that. Recently he'd noted that Anna seemed almost happier discussing his life than her own. He hadn't encountered many people like this, especially not in the city, where what you did, who you were and what you thought were the currency by which you moved ahead.

Of course Jonah asked Anna about her life – it would have been rude not to – but her job as a receptionist at the national newspaper didn't appear to change much from week to week, thus diminishing the conversational possibilities considerably. She talked little of her former life in Cornwall, preferring instead to discuss the stunning landscape of her home county, which Jonah, a keen weekend surfer, was only too happy to indulge her in.

He had wondered on several occasions whether to ask Anna out on a proper date, but had, until recently, always felt an immediate reticence when the moment presented itself. Why this was he couldn't say: they were both attractive young singles who had already established a great deal in common with one another. In the beginning he put it down to his need for a good friend being greater than his need of a relationship. But in recent months his feelings had started to change. She'd hugged him tightly before he left for his assignment in Spain and he'd been drawn to the scent of her hair as he'd held her. Filming a colony of blue rock thrushes in the sultry heat of the Tabernas Desert, he'd missed her – *really* missed her – as if a part of him had been left behind. And then their trip out to a remote lake that he'd been scouting for a wildlife documentary had made up his mind. He'd been struck by how beautiful Anna was, as she'd gazed out across the stillness of the lake, an air of complete contentment surrounding her. It was as if every quality she possessed was magnified in that moment, and Jonah was transfixed. Anna was beautiful, generous and fun to spend time with – why *wouldn't* he want to be with her?

He *had* to do something . . .

'I'm telling you, Anna, five hours in that soggy field had me longing for a desk job . . .'

Anna smiled as Jonah recounted his latest work assignment – a piece for *Countryfile* on a new biodiversity project in deepest Kent. Instead of the forecast spring sunshine, the production crew had been hit with torrential rain, transforming what should have been lush pastureland into a near-impassable quagmire. 'You'd go mad working at a desk.'

'I pretty much went mad in that field. I think the director was scared of me.'

'I can picture that. All part of the showbiz magic of your job.'

'Oh aye. The glamour is *unbearable*.' He grinned as he passed her a glass of wine in his kitchen, Bennett making happy doggy circles around his feet. 'Actually, that was my bit of good news I wanted to tell you. I've been taken on as regular crew.'

'Oh, Jonah, that's great! Are you happy about it?'

'I am. Means I'll have to invest in new wellies, if the last assignment was anything to go by, but it makes money a little more certain for the next four months at least. And, chances are, if the director likes what he sees, I might be called up for other stuff. So, I bought us cake to celebrate –' He hesitated, as he often did when concerned he might be appearing presumptuous. Anna liked his slightly bumbling nature and deeply rooted politeness. '– that is, if you don't object to celebrating with me?'

'Not at all. And I could never object to cake, you know that.'

Jonah beamed brightly. 'That's what I hoped. It's proper fancy and owt.' He opened a large white cake-box and started to cut slices of opulent-looking *Sachertorte*. 'So, how was your day?'

A well of happiness rose within Anna. 'Good. Amazing, actually.'

'Oh? How so?'

She thought of her latest delivery, the new package wrapped in its carefully folded brown paper and waiting for her in her apartment. It was a delicious torture, knowing of its existence as she sat just across the hall and yet unable to touch it.

Jonah was staring at her, almost as if seeing something

new in his neighbour. 'What aren't you telling me?' he asked, sharp as a button.

Patting Bennett's head, Anna smiled. 'Can you keep a secret?'

He frowned. 'Why?'

'I mean it, Jonah. If I tell you, I need to know you won't pass it on.'

'Are you in trouble?'

'No – of course not. Promise you won't tell anyone.'

Jonah raised his eyes heavenwards. 'Fine. Scout's honour.'

'I've been getting parcels at work. For me. I don't know who they are from or why I'm receiving them, but they're wonderful.'

'How many have you had?'

'Three. The latest one arrived this morning.'

'There's no note with them?'

'Not with the first one. With the second there was an unsigned riddle. But no sender's name or address.'

Jonah's eyebrows lifted. 'And you're not worried about that? It seems odd, someone going to so much trouble and not wanting to be known.'

Not Jonah as well! Anna had hoped his response would be more down-to-earth. Was it a mistake telling him? 'Should I be worried?'

'I don't know. If it was me, I'd want to find out who was sending me parcels and why.'

The truth was, Anna wanted to know too. Each gift had increased her curiosity. But she was annoyed by Jonah's readiness to jump to the same conclusion as everyone else.

'Isn't it enough that someone is taking the trouble to send me gorgeous things?'

'I suppose it's a nice thought.' He shook his head. 'How come, Anna Browne, you've lived in the city for five-and-a-half years and *not* become inherently cynical?'

'I can be as cynical as the rest of them, when I want to be,' she returned, annoyed by his inference that she was some sweet, naive West Country bumpkin. 'But I happen to think it's a beautiful thing for someone to do.'

'That's as may be. But it's still odd. It could be anyone.'

'Yes, it could.'

'I mean *anyone*, Anna! Don't you want to know?'

She considered the question. Yes, she was curious. It didn't make sense for someone to invest so much time and thought (not to mention expense) without wanting to be known for it. She liked surprising her friends with gifts, but even she enjoyed taking credit for them. It was one of the best aspects of gift-giving. Another thought occurred: would she like what she discovered, if she pursued it? 'Maybe. Okay, yes, I do. I suppose I'll discover who they are when they decide to tell me. But part of me likes the *not knowing*, if that makes sense at all?'

Jonah's smile was reassuring. 'Perfect sense. If it comes from a good place, it's a lovely gesture. Just promise me you'll be careful, eh? One thing I've learned, living in this city, is folk rarely do something just for the heck of it.'

'Thanks for the warning. I'll let you know if the parcels turn nasty.'

Later that evening Anna turned the new package over in her hands as she sat at the table. Why was everyone's

127

first inclination to suspect the worst? She wasn't naive enough to think the sender didn't have an agenda of some kind; but she didn't *need* to know now. That consideration could wait a while.

Tonight, all she wanted to do was indulge herself in the luxury of a third mystery gift. Feeling the same thrill as before, Anna carefully opened the brown-paper wrapping to reveal a long, thin red box tied with wide satin ribbon, the colour of clotted-cream ice cream. As the loops of the bow slid away in her hands, she could swear she caught a waft of vanilla. Living by the sea as a child had meant she was surrounded by the scent of ice cream, fudge and freshly baked scones from the cafés, shops and bakeries that supplied the tourist hordes during the summer months. Her favourite thing back then was to buy a sugar wafer-cone with a double scoop of home-made ice cream from Mrs Godolphin's tiny shop by the harbour with her pocket money, scrambling up the steps at the side of the Blue Peter Inn to eat it on the cliffs overlooking the perfect Cornish ocean. Once Mrs Godolphin learned whose daughter little Anna Browne was, she often refused payment and gave her young customer free cones. At the time, it was the most wonderfully kind gesture Anna had ever witnessed; many years later she understood that Mrs Godolphin, like many of her fellow villagers, was attempting to redress the imbalance of kindness in Anna's life. Bags of 'broken biscuits' from the grocer's, which on inspection appeared remarkably intact; bottles of tart lemonade left beside the milk bottles on their doorstep, yet never charged for; lengths of 'leftover' fabric miraculously found by Laura Duckett, the resident dressmaker, when Anna was invited to her first senior school disco – all of these gifts had been her neighbours' way of ensuring that Senara Browne's eldest didn't go without.

Was the same motivation at work now, Anna wondered? She stared at the box, the untied ribbon curling around it like eddies of cream satin. Did someone think she needed gifts? Did they consider her lacking in attention? If so, was this parcel a pity-gift? For the poor, quiet girl on the *Messenger*'s reception, who had so little of a life that she needed such a mystery?

Anna shook the thought away. She didn't want to think like that – especially when everyone else around her was so ready to view her gift-giver with cynicism. *It's a kind thought*, she reminded herself. *I shouldn't be questioning it.*

Inside the box, layers of wafer-thin black tissue paper were folded around an object. The tissue had a cinnamon-spiciness to it as it crumpled between her fingers. Anna gently unfurled it to reveal a necklace made of delicate white-gold daisies. Each charm had a tiny sparkling yellow stone at its centre; on closer inspection, she thought these might be yellow diamonds. It was beautiful – understated, yet exquisitely made. When she held it up to the light, the daisies shimmered and shone.

The daisies were cool as they rested against her collar-bone, and when Anna saw her reflection in the living-room mirror, it looked as if the necklace had been made to fit her. She had loved all of the gifts, but this was by far the most special. Drawing her fingers along the silvery charms, she noticed that her eyes sparkled like the tiny diamonds at each daisy's heart. Tears she had held at bay for many years broke free of their restraints.

In the heady Cornish summers of her early childhood, Anna and Ruari had whiled away hours with Grandma Morwenna. She would travel by bus to Polperro and take the children for long walks along the cliffs while their mother was otherwise occupied by work, or other activities not suited to their eyes. In the lush pasturelands bordering the cliff path they would sit on a threadbare travel rug and eat pork pies, cheese sandwiches and slices of home-made lemon-cake produced from Morwenna's ancient creaking wicker picnic basket, lying back against the warm wool as bees and dragonflies buzzed and danced over their heads. Anna could still recall the smell of sun-warmed grass, wicker and sweet lemon, the tang of salty sea air on her lips. After they had eaten, she and Morwenna would pick and weave daisies into delicate chains as Ruari chased butterflies in the long, yellow-green grass. It was as vivid a memory today as it had ever been, a rare care-free moment, its vibrancy and warmth framed by time. Young Anna had assumed these days would be never-ending. She was wrong.

In the years following the breakdown of Senara's relationship with her mother, Anna would often find herself picking daisies when she saw them, slowly twisting their hopeful green stems together, as her grandmother had shown her. But the summers were never as warm or bathed in sunlight as they had been when Morwenna had crowned her with daisy chains, her fingers lingering on

130

Anna's hazelnut-brown hair. The separation had been swift and cruel – Anna and Ruari dragged from their beds in the St Agnes cottage at midnight, Senara screaming damnations at her mother as she pushed the sobbing children into the back seat of her rusting Volvo. Anna's last glimpse of Morwenna was the dumbstruck woman staring after them, torrential rain soaking through her dressing gown and slippers.

Senara never told Anna the reason why Morwenna was banished from their lives, or the details of the argument that tore them apart. Anna wasn't sure she wanted to know now: the truth might be too much to bear. When Anna reached eighteen and went in search of Morwenna, she discovered she was too late. Her grandmother had died of a stroke four years before, with neither her daughter nor her grandchildren beside her as she slipped away. Anna's Uncle Jabez had emigrated to Australia by then and, since he was no longer on speaking terms with his sister, hadn't thought to pass on the news. It was unclear whether Senara knew from Morwenna's former neighbours that this had happened, but Anna never asked. The daisy chains she had made since Morwenna's death brought her some comfort – an abiding memory of her beloved grandmother in all her vibrant glory, woven between the fresh green stems and brave flowers.

How could the person who sent this have known what it would mean to me?

If it was a guess, it was a remarkable one. The daisy-chain necklace sparkled and gleamed at her neck as she wiped her tears away. It was as if her perfect summer memory had been captured and cast in white-gold and diamonds – a permanent reminder of someone she had loved with all her heart.

How had the parcel-sender known to send this? Nobody knew much about her life. Had she mentioned it to Jonah? Anna couldn't remember. Tish barely knew where Anna had grown up, let alone was aware of the finer details of her childhood. Ruari certainly didn't have the disposable income to buy such a gift, either. If Morwenna hadn't been long dead, Anna could almost have believed her grandmother had sent the daisy chain. A shiver passed across her shoulders.

I can't think like that, she decided. *It* must *be a coincidence.*

Sixteen

Walking through the huge chrome-and-glass doors of the *Messenger* building the following Monday, Anna touched the daisy-chain necklace and smiled. Its arrival had brought back many happy memories of her grandmother over the weekend, and its cool presence on her skin now made her feel as if Morwenna was beside her, keeping step with her favourite granddaughter through the city streets. What would her grandmother have made of Anna's new life, she wondered? Would she have gazed up at the many-windowed buildings rising above her and been impressed? Morwenna had once lived in Chicago, back in her late teens, working as a nanny for a wealthy Plymouth family who moved there on a six-month secondment and took her with them. Anna remembered her grandmother talking about the 'grand buildings and elegant streets'. As a child, she had found it hard to imagine Grandma Morwenna living anywhere but her small white cottage in St Agnes, but now she understood the lure of city-living after a rural upbringing. Morwenna was a fan of life – as large and as exciting as possible; the constant noise and bustle of the city would have suited her down to the ground.

Babs Braithwaite was rubbing at a stubborn stain on the smooth wood of the reception desk, tutting loudly, when Anna arrived.

'Bloomin' city types,' she muttered, not looking up. 'Stick their too-expensive coffee cups anywhere they damn well please, without so much as a thought for the poor beggar who'll be cleaning up their mess.'

'Anything I can do to help?' Anna offered.

Babs blinked at her. 'Not unless you're willing to bump a few of 'em off for me, to lessen the load?'

'I can't promise that, sorry. I could always make you a cuppa, if that would help?'

'No need, flower. Coffee's what got us into this mess in the first place, ain't it?' Her pale-grey eyes narrowed. 'Nice necklace. New, is it?'

'Yes. It—'

'Another gift from your secret admirer, I s'pose?'

'Ah, I see you've heard.' Ted Blaskiewicz was certainly getting his money's worth out of Anna's parcels.

'Whole of the building's heard, more like! We've not had anything as exciting as this happen for a long time.' Babs grinned, her gold teeth glinting. 'Now don't you look so worried, pet. It's just human curiosity. We don't get much that isn't staged or faked these days, so it's nice when something real comes along. Mind if I take a closer look?'

She didn't wait for an answer, hurrying up to Anna and

inspecting the silver daisies with nicotine-stained fingers. Anna giggled at the inappropriate closeness, turning her face away slightly to avoid the smell of stale tobacco on Babs' breath.

'Well, I'll say this for him: he's got a good eye for quality. And a large wallet, too, by the looks of it.'

This assumption intrigued Anna. 'What makes you think it's a "him"?'

Babs stared up at her. 'Well, it has to be, don't it? I can't see a woman going to that kind of trouble, not unless she's – you know – the *other way inclined*.' A frown furrowed her brow. 'Not that it's a bad thing if she were . . . If it was all right with you . . .'

In a brave new world of political correctness, it was touching to see a woman of her years attempting such inclusivity. Anna was quick to save her. 'I'd be flattered if a woman had sent it to me as an admirer, but I wouldn't take her up on the offer.'

Babs' relief was palpable. 'That's all well and good, then. But I still say a fella bought this for you. And, if you'll pardon my saying so, he might well be worth taking up, if he's offering *that* good a gift.'

It seemed that the *Messenger*'s Head of Clean Team was not alone in her assumptions.

Ted, his eyes wider than saucers, took great delight in profiling the personality of the potential parcel-sending suspect: 'White, male, early forties, good job, own home, *shrine to Anna Browne in his kinky punishment dungeon . . .*'

Joe Adams heartily agreed: 'I'd send you jewellery if I

135

wanted to get your attention, Anna. But I'd always go for *gold*.'

When Rea Sinfield from the newsroom saw the necklace, her advice was straight to the point. 'As soon as he tells you who he is, *marry him*. I've been dating in this city for four years and, until your parcels arrived, I'd all but given up on the possibility of generous, genuine men existing.'

Sheniece was very excited when she discovered that Orin Wallasey, wealthy business tycoon and a regular on the Most Eligible Bachelor lists, had visited the *Messenger* building three times, each visit occurring a day before Anna's parcels had arrived. 'It's like kismet, karma and fate all rolled into one, Anna!' she yelled, brandishing the sign-in book as irrefutable evidence of her theory.

'But I don't think I even spoke to him,' Anna protested. 'Why would he send me gifts?'

'He's a multi-millionaire! Why wouldn't he?'

While Anna's curiosity over the sender of her gifts was growing, the question of their gender had hardly arisen. As far as she was concerned, the thought was what mattered: if or when the sender revealed their identity, she would discover that detail. But she was taken aback by the interest everyone at the *Messenger* had in her gifts. It seemed that everyone who passed by reception made a beeline for Anna Browne, unwilling to leave until they had gleaned the details of her latest delivery. Anna found their attention flattering, even if several of them were intent on declaring her the target of a sinister campaign. In the past she would have shied away from being the centre of attention, but she was surprised to discover she was enjoying it. Perhaps it was because the delicate daisies around her neck were a tangible reminder of her feisty grandmother and the unshakeable love she had lavished on Anna.

So, when the much-revered editor of the *Daily Messenger*, Juliet Evans, made a point of chatting with Anna, the miracle of the gift was confirmed to her colleagues.

'Good morning, Anna,' Juliet said, resting the pile of papers she carried on the reception desk. 'I hope you had a good weekend?'

'I did, thank you,' Anna replied, the memory of Juliet's singling her out in the editorial meeting a few weeks back still sitting uncomfortably. 'Did you?'

Sheniece's ruby-lined lips pressed together as if suppressing a squeal, her eyes alive with scandal.

'Can't complain,' Juliet replied. Was that a *smile* she was attempting? The gesture was so alien, when applied to her steely expression, that Anna couldn't be sure. And then, as quickly as it had materialised, it vanished. 'There is an important meeting in the boardroom this afternoon. I will have one of my team bring you a list of attendees, to save signing them all in. Time is of the essence, as I'm sure you'll appreciate.'

'Yes, of course.'

'Good. Pandora,' she turned to an impossibly young, reed-thin intern who had scuttled to her side and looked as if she was permanently on the edge of throwing up, 'have the list drawn up and on Anna's desk by ten. Yes?'

137

'*Yes-Ms-Evans*,' Pandora rushed, as if an invisible force had sucker-punched the air out of her.

Juliet leaned a little way over the reception desk. 'If you haven't received it by 10.05 a.m., Anna, call my office and I will *find someone capable instead*.' Her emphasis was not lost on her young assistant, who paled.

And with that, Juliet was gone, the sound of her scurrying entourage fading from earshot.

Anna turned to Ted, whose jaw was hanging open. 'It's okay, Ted, you can breathe now.'

'She *spoke* to you! Again! You had an actual conversation this time! I saw it with my own eyes, but I don't think I believe it. That woman never talks to *anyone*, girl. You'd better hope she isn't adding you to the list of redundancies.'

Sheniece gripped Ted's sleeve. 'Redundancies? What redundancies?'

'I told you. That memo I – *found*.' He smiled innocently at Anna. 'The shareholders are baying for her blood, I heard. If this paper doesn't turn around soon, Dragon Evans'll be out on her designer bum, you'll see.'

'Well, she'd better up her game.' Sheniece picked at her cuticles. 'I need this job, especially if me and Darren are going to get that house in Hatfield.'

'Who's Darren?' Anna asked.

'Footballer I met in town, last Saturday night,' Sheniece informed her, brightening considerably. 'I think he's a keeper.'

'Goalkeeper? Who for?' Ted asked, missing the point entirely.

If the Botox had allowed it, Sheniece's forehead would have furrowed. 'What are you on about, Ted?'

'Nice necklace.' A deep, male voice made Anna turn, her stomach performing a small flip when she saw the man standing at her desk. It was the first time Ben had spoken to her since the end of her time in the newsroom with him, and she had been hurt by his radio silence. But he looked *good* – as he'd always done – and he was here now. Was that enough?

Sheniece, who was well aware of her colleague's un-requited crush and had mercilessly bombarded her with questions when she'd returned to her normal job, jabbed Anna in the ribs as she passed her, giggling loudly on her way to the work kitchen.

'Thanks.' Anna could feel a hot blush prickling across her cheeks. *Why haven't you talked to me lately?*

Ben smiled. 'Ted reckons you have a psycho-stalker.'

'Yes, well, Ted reckons Babs from Clean Team is a secret agent for MI5. I wouldn't trust his judgement.' The joke seemed to warm the air between them.

'Fair enough. It's a beautiful gift, though. I hear there have been several gifts now. Any idea who sent them?'

'No.' Anna was all too aware of her own awkwardness returning. She thought of the daisy-chain necklace and imagined Grandma Morwenna's encouraging smiles.

'Right. Look, Anna, I—'

'I do hope you enjoyed having *our Anna* in your news-room,' Ted interjected, a little too pointedly, taking care to look down his nose at Ben.

Ben stared back. 'Yes, of course.'

'Only I thought it odd you hadn't come to see her at all, since we got her back. Seeing as I heard the pair of you got on so famously.'

Anna felt the ground undulate a little beneath her feet. *Not now, Ted* . . .

'Ah. Well . . . I've been busy.' Ben sounded as if he had yet to convince himself.

'She did well, though?'

Ben shifted uneasily. 'Anna was great.'

Ted was now observing Ben like a pushy parent grilling their child's teacher. 'I heard she saved your biggest story.'

'*Ted*,' Anna barked, turning quickly to Ben. 'I never said . . .'

'Chap I chatted with on your floor reckons you owe her.' Ted delivered his killer-blow.

Anna saw the accusation register on the journalist's expression.

'I offered her billing – did the *chap* tell you that, too?' Ben's mobile phone buzzed in his hand and he seemed relieved by the excuse to leave. 'Looks like I'm being summoned. Anna, it really is good to see you. You look . . . good.' Was there a slight reddening across his cheekbones?

Encouraged by the unexpected sight of Ben McAra suddenly on the back foot, Anna smiled back. 'Thanks. You don't look bad yourself.'

She could hear Ted's held breath and feel Sheniece's surprise. Best of all, she saw the spark reignite in Ben's stare.

'Well . . . maybe I'll see you soon?'

140

Anna patted the mahogany of the reception desk. 'You know where to find me.'

Like a mirrored image across the smooth wood, Anna and Ben shared the same smile. 'I most definitely do.'

Watching him walk away, it was all Anna could do not to squeal out loud. Where had her confidence come from? She wasn't the only one to notice, either.

'*Ohmygoshohmygosh*, Ben-flippin'-McAra was *totally* chatting you up!' A woodpecker-like sound of tapping heels echoed around the atrium as Sheniece bobbled by Anna's side.

Anna groaned, her smile tellingly bright. 'He was not.'

'He was, Anna! And get you, all cool and give-as-good-as-you-get with him. What happened? When Ted started his Overprotective Creepy Uncle thing, I thought you were going to die of shock.'

'Charming!' Affronted, Ted harrumphed and headed off on an unannounced tour of the ground floor.

'I was just making polite conversation.' Anna's heart pounded. 'He was being nice – before Ted got on his case. He noticed my necklace . . .'

'He was being *obvious*. Men don't notice jewellery from other men.' She stared at Anna. 'Unless . . . oh, that's perfect! *He* sent it!'

Anna laughed. 'No, Shen, he didn't.'

But Sheniece was already running her new theory to test its legs. 'Think about it: he doesn't talk to you for, like, *ever* and then you happen to get three gifts, and he *happens* to notice the most expensive, most important one.'

141

'But I spent two weeks working with him. I wore my scarf several times. If he bought it for me, why didn't he tell me then?'

Sheniece waggled a recently tanned finger. 'Ah, but he didn't see the work-shadowing coming, did he? I reckon this is what happened: he sent you the scarf, then he was getting ready to ask you out, only he found out who he'd been paired with, so he had to rethink. Instead, what better way to get to know you than work with you for a fortnight and *then* send the gifts? Hmm? You've got to admit, Anna, it's possible.'

It was a preposterous theory – wasn't it? Anna tried to recall everything they had talked about, but the sheer volume of questions Ben had fired at her made it impossible. Could she have given clues away that led him to buy the owl, and now the daisy-chain necklace? 'I don't know, Shen . . .'

'Think about it: why would your necklace be the first thing he commented on, if he hadn't sent it, eh?' She snapped her fingers. 'Too obvious. He was trying to find out what you thought about it. Classic male strategy. Send an anonymous gift, then ask so many flippin' questions it's blindingly obvious he sent it. My last guy was like that on Valentine's Day. Sent me a dozen red roses, then asked me if I got anything, if I thought roses were overpriced on Valentine's, and ended up asking me if I'd heard of the florist's who delivered it. He might as well have carried a six-foot-high placard with I SENT YOU THE ROSES written on it. That settles it. Ben McAra is your secret admirer!'

Laughing, Anna dismissed her colleague's wild theory and returned to the list of tasks in the work diary. But Sheniece's words kept returning to her as the day passed. At five-thirty-five, squeezed into a seat on the bus heading home, Anna finally allowed herself to consider the possibility. Could Ben McAra be sending her parcels? It made no sense: why would he single her out for such a lavish scheme? If the parcels were from him, why not let her see his name on the sender's details, or claim responsibility when she was working with him? Ben didn't strike her as the kind of man who hid behind gifts. If he did something, Ben McAra wanted the world to know. Everything he did was designed to draw attention to himself; he had worked hard to establish his name and reputation in Fleet Street and was known for being quick to claim naming rights on breaking news stories. Would someone who had made a career out of being recognised for his work be likely to send anonymous gifts? Anna didn't think so.

But if Ben hadn't sent the parcels, why choose today to comment on her necklace? Anna had to admit Sheniece had a point – it was an intriguing coincidence that he had noticed the most expensive gift Anna had received so far. Plenty of other people had complimented her on the scarf and the owl brooch (although, admittedly, most of these were women). What was it about the necklace that had caught Ben's attention, where nothing else had?

Perhaps he wanted to make amends for not talking to me recently, she surmised. *He needed a conversation-opener and my necklace was there.* That was plausible enough.

It made her feel good to think this might have been his motivation.

Resolved not to question it any more, Anna hunkered down in the cramped bus seat and allowed herself to simply enjoy the memory of chatting with the handsome journalist. More than just the thrill of his having spoken to her again, she was amazed by her own confidence. Ben's apparent snub of recent weeks had knocked her and she'd assumed that, if he decided to speak to her again, conversation would be awkward between them. But today her confidence returned – welling up within her, without thought or effort. Had she even been flirty?

Her shock at her own response was as welcome a surprise as the beautiful daisy chain around her neck. The gifts in the parcels were bringing about tiny changes in Anna Browne. And she liked what she saw.

Seventeen

Murray Henderson-Vitt was having a Slow News Day. That it coincided with a Wednesday – and his longest shift of the week – wasn't helping matters. He stared at the greying dregs of his fifth cup of coffee as if inspiration might be floating there amid the sludge of coffee grounds.

No such luck.

Groaning, he lifted his head to peer across the newsroom over the annoyingly positive red desk partition. Journalists milled around, some deep in conversation, some hard at work, while others were staring wide-eyed back at him, equally lost. Ben McAra was at his desk as usual, head bowed, tapping furiously on his computer keyboard. *Smug git*, Murray thought, wishing a sudden, unfathomable fault to occur that would render the star journalist's Mac useless for the rest of the week. *Give some of us poor beggars a chance.* McAra was the kind of person whose feet were seemingly gilded by the gods; he was guaranteed to land on them, no matter what occurred. Murray, on the other hand, was an old-fashioned hack through and through: destined to trudge unaccredited through the dross of fifth-, sixth- and seventh-page stories while blue-eyed boys like Ben McAra took all the plaudits.

If only he could find a story worthy of the front page. Or even the second – he didn't mind. To see his name under the headline, and the smirk wiped off McAra's irritatingly chiselled face, would be all of his Christmases come at once. Just one major scoop to send him on his way. It wasn't much to ask, was it?

Claire Connors from Features passed his desk, looking as if she hadn't slept in a month. *That's what you get for being cited in divorce papers*, Murray chuckled to himself, looking over to the empty Obituaries desk, where her erstwhile lover should have been. If the *Messenger* could mine its own office scandals for news stories, its fortunes would be reversed in seconds. The meeting with Juliet Evans and the stony-faced shareholders last week had not been pretty. Bring the *Messenger* into the Big Three national tabloid titles and you have a hope of keeping your job, they'd stated. A six-month deadline now cast a dark, impenetrable shadow across the newsroom and everyone was feeling the pressure. Even Sanjay and Claire's indiscretions weren't enough to lift it.

'Did you hear?' Ali, the perennially sunny junior reporter, chirped, handing Murray a steaming mug of newsroom rocket-fuel.

'Hear what?' He accepted it. At least she'd brought him coffee. Perhaps today was looking up . . .

'Anna Browne in reception's just received another parcel.'

Now *this* was something. Not that Murray had thought so initially, even after Ted the security officer's frequent updates for anyone who would listen. So the receptionist had a secret admirer. So what? That was, until Murray had mentioned it to his wife last week, just after Anna's third parcel had arrived. *That* was when he realised the potential.

His wife had *cried*. Actually shed real tears. The way he'd only seen her cry on the day they got married, and a year later when their son Kieran was born. To Murray's shock, Leah Henderson-Vitt had stood in their too-expensive new kitchen and sobbed over parcels sent to a woman she neither knew nor cared about.

'That's . . . so . . . *lovely*,' she had struggled, wiping her eyes on her sleeve. 'You never hear about selfless things like that happening nowadays. It's straight out of a classic novel.'

Fast on his feet, Murray had declared *he* would do something like that for her in a heartbeat. And although Leah's tears had then become uncontrollable laughter, it had still earned him a place in her good books and a night of really quite decent lovemaking. In that sense, he already had much to thank Anna Browne for . . .

'That's four parcels now,' Ali said. 'They seem to be arriving pretty regularly. And still no indication of who is sending them – or why.'

'Interesting. Has she said anything about it, do you know?'

'Not to me, but I don't really know her that well. Ted Blaskiewicz is all over it, of course.'

'No surprise there.' A thought occurred to him. 'I might – you know – pop down to reception and . . . er . . .'

'Check if we've had any deliveries?' Ali's smile was the picture of conspiracy.

'Exactly.' Murray cast a cursory glance towards Ben McAra's desk. There was a chance McAra was too wrapped up in whatever glory-seeking news item he was beavering away at to have heard yet about the receptionist's latest mystery parcel. If he was quick, he might just be able to get the jump on him.

Grabbing his Dictaphone, Murray headed for the lift.

'Sign here,' the courier said, handing his electronic device to Anna. It was the same courier who had delivered the previous two parcels – a man with a cheeky smile and an impressive arsenal of flirty one-liners. Only the first had come via UPS, the subsequent parcels being delivered by a local company. The courier's name badge read: NARINDER RANA. 'Looks like you're a lady in demand.'

Anna smiled brightly as she signed her name. For the first time since the parcels began arriving she'd dared to hope that the daisy-chain necklace was not the last gift she would receive. Now, in her hands, was evidence of that wish granted. 'It's definitely making work more exciting.'

'I'll bet. Nice gifts, are they?'

Anna nodded, patting the silver daisies at her neck. 'This was in last week's parcel.'

Narinder leaned a little closer. 'Very impressive. Your boyfriend has good taste.'

'But I don't – oh, no, it isn't from my boyfriend. I don't have one.'

'Oh, really?' The courier's eyebrow made a bid for the glass ceiling.

'I don't know who they're from.' Anna watched as Narinder added a check to the device screen. 'Do you have any record of the sender there?'

'Not on this, mate. There might be paperwork back at the depot, but I just get a delivery code. Maybe there's a note inside the parcel?'

'Maybe. There's only ever been one note before, but that didn't mention a name.'

'Very mysterious. Enjoy it, anyway. I guess I'll be seeing you next week?'

Anna hugged her latest delivery. 'Hope so.'

The parcel was around six inches square and made no sound when Anna shook it. She turned it over, to find only the depot number in the sender details. Was she hoping to see something different there this time? Her curiosity had grown with the arrival of each new parcel and, while the possibility of each one being the last was always at the back of her mind, she wondered who had singled her out for such generosity – and why.

'Seems to be getting keener, your chap.' Ted Blaskiewicz was on top form as usual. 'Couldn't even wait till Friday this week.'

'If it is a guy – and I'm not saying it is – he's definitely not mine,' Anna returned, slipping the parcel into her usual hiding place beneath the reception desk and locking it, before her colleague could get a closer look.

'Ah, but I'm betting he will be, if he carries on at this rate. Be daft not to take him up on his offer.'

'Ted, you're impossible. And whoever sent my parcels hasn't offered me anything.'

'*Yet.*'

Anna groaned. 'Don't you have things to do, places to be, rumours to start?'

Ted clamped a hand to his heart. 'Less of your filthy accusations, girl! Any information I may or may not disclose to other members of staff is merely in the course of my job.'

It seemed that news of Anna's parcels was spreading throughout the *Messenger* building. Now, when journalists arrived to sign in and collect their post, their first question was, 'What did you get this week, Anna?' And so when Ben's competitive colleague arrived in reception later that morning, Anna anticipated his question as he was still lolloping across the polished marble floor towards her.

'Anna Browne, how the devil are you?' Murray Henderson-Vitt was all smiles and winks.

'Very good, thank you. And you?'

'Me? Always happy.' Murray laughed a little too loudly and rested an arm on the reception desk. '*So* – anything interesting arrive today?'

'I take it you've heard.'

'*Everyone*'s heard, Anna. You, my dear, are the talk of the newsroom. My wife thinks you should marry him.'

Anna shook her head. Why did everyone in the building

now assume that her gifts had come from a man? 'I have no idea who is sending the parcels – male or female.'

'Really?' Murray seemed to be fiddling with something in his suit-jacket pocket. After a few seconds he was leering at her again. 'So, you have *no clue* as to the sender's identity?' His question appeared to be louder than before.

'No – I just said that.'

'Still no notes? No indication of their address? Did you ask the courier?'

Anna stared back. 'Not that it's any of your business, but I did actually.'

Murray's fingers left sweaty smudges on the polished mahogany as he leaned closer. 'And?'

'He didn't have any details, either.'

Murray frowned. 'Do you think he might know more than he's letting on? Is he trying to protect someone? Could there be a sinister motive behind your parcels?'

Not this again. Murray was talking in print-worthy headlines now. Which could only mean . . . Anna glanced down at his pocket, her suspicions confirmed by a badly concealed bulge that was the wrong shape for a cigarette packet. 'You're recording this, aren't you?'

Murray threw up his hands, but the colour drained from his face. 'No . . .'

For a journalist, Murray had all the covert information-gathering skills of a sledgehammer, Anna mused. Staring at him, she held out her hand. 'Hand it over.'

'What? No – I'm not . . .'

'Murray. The recorder, please?'

The journalist's shoulders drooped and he reluctantly

fished his Dictaphone from his pocket, putting it into her hand like a sullen teenager handing over illicit bubble-gum to a teacher. 'Can't blame a chap for trying.'

'I work in a national newspaper building,' Anna said, inspecting the recorder. 'I know how journalists work.' Checking that the device was still recording, she held it to her lips. 'I am Anna Browne, receptionist at the *Daily Messenger*, and I have been receiving mystery parcels at work. They are anonymously sent and are simply a lovely, kind gesture that I have no intention of questioning.' She clicked the Stop button on the recorder and handed it back to the dejected hack. 'Was there anything else?'

Murray loosened his tie and leaned a little more heavily on the reception desk. 'OK, I'll level with you, Anna. I need this story. I'm dying on my ass up there, and if I don't get something interesting soon I might as well chuck in the towel. Would you just promise me one thing? If you hear anything more, or get any idea of who is sending you the parcels, you'll talk to me first? And if Ben McAra starts sniffing around, don't tell him anything.'

Ah, so *that* was what Murray's ham-fisted attempt at espionage was about . . . Anna folded her arms and fixed the journalist with what she hoped was a reprimanding stare, secretly feeling sorry for him. It must be awful to be in a job where your reputation hung on how good your most recent story was. She was glad of her chosen profession, where all she had to concern herself with was being polite to everyone who arrived in reception, regardless of how pleasant they were in return. She had seen too many casualties of the cut-throat newspaper business during her time there to ever wish such a career for herself. 'Ben's already asked me about it, I'm afraid. And I told him exactly what I told you. That's the end of the story. I'm sorry, Murray.'

'Right, then. But if you change your mind . . . ?'

'You'll be the first to know.'

'Blimey, Anna, get you,' Sheniece remarked, as Anna watched Murray Henderson-Vitt slump back in the lift up to the newsroom.

'Sorry?'

'You totally called him out! What's happened to you?'

Anna shrugged. 'I didn't want to be taken advantage of.'

'You were amazing! I was watching how you spoke to him. It's like you went to sleep as Minnie Mouse and woke up as Beyoncé! Girl's got attitude now!'

Anna giggled as Sheniece turned to the reception screen. She *had* stood up to Murray, hadn't she? Usually, she would have found a way to accommodate his request, not wanting to hurt his feelings. But the parcels were *her* gifts, and hers alone. Why should she have to share them with anyone else? She was experiencing a strength of will that she'd often longed to feel; it was only since the parcels began arriving that this had happened. How strange that four neatly wrapped packages had made such change possible! Did the sender know the effect their generosity was having on her? Anna couldn't tell. But she made a promise to herself that she would thank the parcel-giver, if their identity were ever revealed.

*

153

Once again, Anna made herself wait to open the new parcel, taking time to shower and prepare her evening meal, before curling up on the sofa with it. Steeling herself, she began to peel back the perfect folds of brown paper, feeling her excitement build. A black-and-gold-striped box filled with shreds of gold tissue paper held a small canvas on a tiny easel. On it was painted the most exquisite scarlet heart, edged with skilful gold brushstrokes. An aubergine ribbon with scrolled ends stretched across the heart, bearing a single word in gold paint:

HOPE

As Anna lifted the canvas from the box, she discovered a card underneath. Turning it over, she found a typed message:

What do you hope for, Anna?

Her heart skipped a beat. It was a beautiful gift and sentiment – but what *did* she hope for? Leaning back into the comfort of the sofa cushions, Anna considered the message. Why did the sender want to know about her hopes? Did they really care, or was the question rhetorical? For the first time, she wished she knew who had sent her this gift. There was so much she wanted to express – not just gratitude, but also how changed she felt by the experience. And what that change meant to her. The parcels had already been more than she could ever have hoped for: was this the answer to the question? They had brought her a new confidence, the ability to flirt with the handsome journalist she had admired from a distance, and had made other people notice her. Dare she hope for more?

I hope to be happy . . . I hope to keep my job . . . I hope I keep changing . . . None of the hopes Anna listed to herself seemed to quite fit. Holding the hope-heart canvas, she frowned. This was a question she needed more time to consider.

Eighteen

Dear Staff Member

This is a gentle reminder that the annual Messenger *Charity Fair and Auction takes place at St Vincent's Children's Hospice, Esher, Surrey, this Saturday.*

Please remember that your willing participation in this event is <u>required</u> *under the terms of your employment. All staff should report for duty at 8 a.m. sharp, dress code CIRCUS PERFORMER. Please also bring your* <u>smiles</u> *with you.*

Yours sincerely

Juliet Evans

Editor

'It's a freakin' *joke*,' Sheniece protested, adjusting the plastic bow tie at her neck as the train from Waterloo sped through the Surrey countryside. 'Never mind that we have to give up a Saturday to "volunteer" for this every year, or get up at the crack of dawn, but to have to do it in ridiculous fancy dress is asking too much. Look at me! No wonder Darren the footballer dumped me! How am I ever going to pull wearing this?'

'You think *you* have problems,' retorted Rea, trying in vain to pull down the hem of her too-short pink ballet tutu. 'At least you went for the safe clown option. This pony-rider's costume is practically obscene.'

'Very much in the spirit of the occasion, if you ask me, girl.' Ted – dressed as a ringmaster, naturally – was making a too enthusiastic survey of Rea's costume. 'Those legs of yours bring a smile to my face.'

'Eeurgh, you old letch!' Rea made a swipe for the lascivious security officer and grabbed her coat to drape modestly over her knees.

Anna patted her baggy charity-shop trousers and congratulated herself for taking Tish's suggestion of going to the charity event as a down-and-out clown.

'Think Judy Garland singing "A Couple of Swells" in *Easter Parade*,' she'd said, finding a yellow-and-blue-striped T-shirt for Anna to borrow. They had found the grey tweed trousers, several sizes too big for Anna, and a pair of braces in a charity shop down the street from their apartment building; a felt bowler hat from a party-supplies warehouse had been decorated with a huge daisy on a bendy green wire that Seamus, the caretaker of Walton Tower, had inexplicably found in his lost-property box; and the outfit had been completed with Jonah's 'one and only' burgundy tie, which he kept for job interviews and so rarely wore. Anna remembered her old pair of bright-yellow Doc

Martens boots stashed at the back of her wardrobe, that she'd practically lived in at university, when the initial boost of being away from home had prompted her to adopt a daringly confident image for a year. To give herself a suitably clownlike look, she'd bought some children's face paints, drawing white ovals across her eyes, a black-outlined red circle on the end of her nose and a comical, curvy red mouth over her lip-line.

She had attended every *Messenger* charity day while she'd worked at the newspaper, but this was the first time she felt excited about it. Last year she had hidden her fancy dress (an ill-fitting superhero costume that was the last one available in the costume shop) beneath her raincoat and hoped against hope that nobody in the train noticed her. Today, her coat had been left at home.

'I'm looking forward to it,' she said, eliciting the moans of her colleagues. 'No, I am. It's a lovely sunny day, we're going to raise money for an excellent cause and it's going to be fun.'

'Speak for yourself,' Sheniece muttered. 'You sound like bloody Dragon Evans. "Please bring your smiles with you!" Patronising or what?! Yeah, *Ms Evans*, I'll bring my smiles – if you'll pay me for the Saturday I'm wasting on your event.'

'Ah, another willing volunteer, I see,' Murray chuckled from the seat opposite. 'Don't worry, Sheniece, I brought a *little something* to help the day go faster.' He wiggled a silver hipflask as the junior receptionist's eyes lit up. 'Genuine Kentucky Bourbon. The kind of smoothness Jack Daniel's would kill for.'

'You know, a girl could get to like you, Murray. Do you fancy pairing up with me to run a stall?'

As her colleagues colluded, Anna turned her head to watch the lush Surrey fields flying past the train window. If Murray and Sheniece were already paired up, it saved her from the prospect of being grilled by him about her latest parcel. She thought of the hope-heart painting on her coffee table at home and smiled to herself. What did she hope for today? She had considered the question a great deal since Wednesday evening and had still not found a definitive answer.

I hope the sun stays out . . . I hope we raise a lot of money for the hospice . . .

Sighing, she dismissed the question for the time being. The answer would come when it was ready.

A coach was waiting at Esher station to ferry the *Messenger* employees to St Vincent's Children's Hospice, which lay a few miles out of town. A uniformly grumpy troupe of unwilling circus performers shuffled onto it, the sight of grumbling clowns, acrobats, jugglers and a particularly cheesed-off stiltwalker struggling onto a luxury coach garnering laughter from weekend commuters. Anna waved back at a small boy who was staring in open-mouthed joy at the brightly dressed line of people filing past his pushchair. *Last year I couldn't wait to hide on the coach*, she thought, performing a comedic bow to the delight of the young onlooker and his parents. This year she found she was loving every minute.

'Love the hat.'

Anna turned to see Ben McAra standing next to her.

He was wearing a dark-blue one-piece cycling suit with an enormous blue-and-white-spotted bow tie and looked a little self-conscious. 'Nice – erm – *bow tie*.'

Ben laughed. 'I know, the suit seemed like a good idea at the time. Now I feel a little too *exposed*.'

'You wear it well,' Anna replied before she thought better of it. 'I mean—'

'Anna Browne! Are you checking me out?'

Mortified, Anna stared down at her yellow Doc Martens. 'No.'

He nudged her. 'It's okay. Makes a nice change from Claire Connors' unwarranted attention on my groin. I swear she was trying to strike up a conversation with it, all the way here.'

'Does Sanjay know?' Anna giggled, the blush on her cheeks thankfully hidden behind the ruby-red face-paint circles.

'Sanjay's been signed off for three months. *Work-related stress*, apparently. So Ms Connors is officially back on the prowl.' He shuddered. 'She's trying to get me to pair up for a stall today. Don't suppose you fancy rescuing a poor, practically naked journalist, do you?'

What do you hope for, Anna?

Anna suppressed a smile. 'Well, when you put it like that . . .'

There it was again – the confidence she'd discovered lately, as natural as breathing. She thought of the daisy-chain necklace and the owl brooch lying on her bedside table, of the scarf in her wardrobe and the hope-heart painting in her living room. Four unrelated items – save for the person who had sent them – and yet the reason for the brand-new boldness she felt. Each gift had lifted her, filled her with courage and caused her to dare to wish for more.

If I ever get to speak to the sender face-to-face, I'll tell them how wonderful their gifts have been, she promised silently, stealing a sideways glance at Ben on the seat beside her as the coach headed towards St Vincent's.

The unseasonably warm April day bathed the hospice buildings and grounds with pale golden light, as teams of *Messenger* employees set up trestle tables on the wide, manicured lawn and laid out goods and games for the Charity Fair. Tombola stalls, funfair games and a coconut shy gradually took shape, with stalls selling home-made lemonade, cakes and jars of jams and chutneys dotted in between. At one end of the arc of tables a red-and-white-striped Punch and Judy stand was being erected, while yard upon yard of rainbow bunting was suspended over the stalls from two large pine trees that framed the Charity Fair site. Juliet Evans had called in favours from everyone she knew, bringing Shetland-pony rides, a Throw-and-Dunk cage and Florence, a beautifully restored 1966-vintage VW ice-cream van painted in pale-pink and light-brown stripes, to add to the delights on offer. It reminded Anna of the church fetes she and Ruari would visit in Polperro and Looe with various extended family members – usually Uncle Jabez or Aunt Zelda, Senara's brother and sister, who took pity on the children after they were forbidden from seeing Morwenna. She remembered cake stalls heaving with home-made scones, Victoria sponges and fairy cakes – and the thrill of scrambling onto the cool grass beneath the gingham-covered tables with her fellow schoolfriends to eat their pocket-money purchases.

'Names,' an officious employee nobody recognised barked, as Anna and Ben stepped off the coach.

Ben answered before Anna could give her name. 'Ben McAra and Anna Browne. We're paired up to man a stall.'

The unsmiling jobsworth twitched in his yellow high-vis vest. 'We've already allotted teams for stalls.'

'Well, *un-allot* us from whoever you have on your list.' Ben straightened to give the marshal the benefit of his full six feet, three inches of height, making a point of reading the plastic ID badge swinging from his official lanyard. 'You see, *Keith*, Ms Browne and I are working together today.'

The marshal looked up from his clipboard and attempted to outstare the journalist, resorting to a pained sigh when it became apparent he wasn't going to win. 'I wish you people would stop pairing up on the coach. It took me *hours* to write this list.'

'And the poor, needy children of St Vincent's thank you for your commitment.' Ben slapped Keith on the back. 'So, which stall?'

'Splat the Rat,' he glowered. 'Between Guess the Name of the Teddy and the ice-cream van.'

'Could he have said that with any more contempt?' Anna giggled as they made their way across the lawn to their stall. 'I don't think I've heard the words "ice-cream van" delivered with such venom before. Who is he, anyway? I've only ever seen him with a clipboard at this event each year, but never at work.'

'You want my theory? He's Juliet's love-slave, only allowed outside for one day of the year.'

'Ben . . .'

'Look at him – you don't get that pasty white complexion from regular exposure to the open air. If you ask me, our Keith Sutton spends most of his time on his knees in a gimp mask.'

'Stop it!'

'You might not believe me, but I tell you, more scandals exist within the walls of the *Daily Messenger* than will ever fill its pages.'

They had reached their stall – a bare trestle table next to a length of grey drainpipe with a hole cut halfway along its length. A sausage-shaped cylinder of brown fur fabric with a knotted string attached to one end made for a make-shift rat. Ben picked up a wooden rounders bat from the table and swung it like a baseball pro preparing for a pitcher's lob.

'I'm glad we got the passive-aggressive stall,' he winked. 'There's enough collective angst here today to send this little furry fella to Stuffed Rat Heaven. Mind you, I hear the competition for Guess the Name of the Teddy could be *fierce* this year.'

Anna inspected the pathetic excuse for a rat. 'I feel a little sorry for him.' She stroked its synthetic fur. 'Doesn't even have a face, to see what's coming.'

'Oh, great, I get to work with a pacifist.' Ben nodded at the owner of the vintage ice-cream van as she laid out candy-coloured tables and chairs in front of the serving hatch. 'I bet you don't have this trouble.'

'Have *you* ever faced the wrath of a queue of customers impatient for ice cream?' she smiled back. 'Maybe I should be worried that there's a bat within easy grabbing distance of Florence.' She patted the paintwork of the VW van as she walked behind it.

Anna picked up a tablecloth from the folding chair behind the trestle and unfurled it. 'What do people win, if they Splat the Rat?' She noticed a box of sealed yellow paper bags beneath the table. 'These?'

Ben bent down to look. 'It looks like someone's been burning the midnight oil making pick'n'mix prizes. Maybe that was *Keith*'s punishment in the dungeon . . . Okay, I won't mention it again. I suppose the point is that everyone's fifty pence to play the game goes to the hospice. The prizes are irrelevant.'

The fair had its official opening at noon, Juliet giving a proud speech about her long-standing commitment to St Vincent's and how much money her charity initiatives had raised to date. Anna couldn't help thinking the *Messenger*'s assertive editor was a little too focussed on her own benevolence, rather than the work of the hospice in whose grounds she stood. But Juliet Evans was nothing if not ready to trumpet her own achievements – it was what set her apart in Fleet Street, characterising her career and making her one of the leading names in the newspaper business. The *Messenger* employees applauded politely, although Anna caught sight of Sheniece and Murray

164

making vomit-impressions from behind the safety of the crowd.

Compared with previous years, Anna's stall was simple to run, but required far more energy. With so many stalls clamouring for attention (not to mention the irresistible delights of artisan ice cream next door), Anna and Ben had to fight to be noticed. Surprised again at how much fun she was having, Anna happily shouted to passers-by, trying to persuade them to have a go.

'Roll up, roll up! Fancy your chances against Ricky the Rat, sir? He's fast, but you might be faster . . . Madam, can I tempt you to take up the Splat-the-Rat challenge? It's all for an excellent cause.'

Last year she would have hidden behind the drainpipe, never daring to raise her voice above the crowd's hubbub. And she would have hated every minute, feeling exposed and ridiculous, as she had felt every year before. But Anna Browne was different this year – laughing at her own forthrightness, playing up to the smiles of the people passing the stall. Did the parcel-sender know their gifts would have this effect, she wondered? Were they here, today, seeing the once-timid and softly spoken receptionist yelling her invitation to a field full of people she had never met before?

She remembered Sheniece's suggestion when the third parcel had arrived: *Ben McAra is your secret admirer!*

Of course he wasn't.

But what if he was?

He certainly appeared to be enjoying her performance, laughing with Anna whenever she successfully persuaded

165

someone to play the game. Their playful banter had danced as easily as the cotton-wool clouds across the perfectly blue April Saturday sky and Anna felt as if they had been friends forever. But before today Ben had practically ignored her following their work-shadowing fortnight. What had changed? And might Ben have engineered the change by sending more parcels to her?

'I brought you a reward for your excellent work.' He handed her a waffle cone filled with three scoops of pastel-hued ice cream, halting her train of thought. 'It's Butter-scotch Chip, Rhubarb-and-Custard and Toffee Fudge. I wasn't sure what you liked, so I chose my favourites and hoped for the best.'

What else did you choose for me, Ben?

Anna stopped herself. Far better to enjoy the day without questioning any of it. 'It looks wonderful. Thank you.'

'Don't thank me, thank Polly.' Ben nodded in the direction of the smiling lady serving ice cream to a long line of customers. 'She's been so impressed with our stallholder skills she gave us these for free. She said we deserved them after all our yelling.'

They sat on the folding chairs as a family took turns to catch the furry rat. Anna looked up to the bunting fluttering in the breeze overhead. 'I'm exhausted.' It was a good tiredness, though; breathless, like the aftermath of a giggling fit.

'You can't tell me you've never done that before. You're a pro.'

'I've had fun,' Anna replied, savouring the taste of ice

cream and still-new calmness in her spirit. If time were to freeze right now, locking this moment into eternity, she couldn't be more content. 'But I don't think I'll have much of a voice left tomorrow.'

'I'll be dreaming of stuffed rats all night, I think.' He turned his head to her, squinting in the sun. 'You surprise me, Anna.'

'Why?'

'I just never pictured you as the gobby type.'

Anna laughed. 'Neither did I, before today.' She accepted the rat from the family who had completed their game. 'I must have Ricky to thank.'

'Yeah, about that: what's with *Ricky* the Rat?'

'It's a great name.'

'It is not.'

Anna turned the rat towards Ben. 'He looks like a Ricky.'

'He looks like a furry poo.'

'Great way to put me off my ice cream, McAra.'

'Sorry. Although, if you're sure?' He made a grab for Anna's ice-cream cone, but she snatched it away.

'Hands off! I've earned this.'

Ben's smile was earnest. 'Yes, you have.'

It was only much later that day, as the sun dipped down behind the Surrey countryside through the train windows, that Anna realised Ben hadn't once asked her about the parcels. Murray Henderson-Vitt had implied that Ben would be after her story, yet he hadn't mentioned Anna's mysterious deliveries, or even alluded to her gifts today. If Sheniece's theory that Ben sent the parcels was correct,

167

why hadn't he seized the opportunity to gauge her reaction to them?

Sheniece is wrong, Anna concluded, letting the warm afterglow of a fun day flood her weary body. *Ben couldn't be the sender.*

Nineteen

Ted Blaskiewicz was at Anna's side faster than a moth to a light bulb on Monday morning.

'Pretty cosy with our star reporter, weren't you, girl?'

Anna had expected as much, having seen the not-so-concealed glances of her colleagues during the Charity Fair on Saturday. She had deliberately chosen a different carriage for the train back to Waterloo to avoid the inevitable grilling, but was well prepared to face it this morning. That Ted had been able to contain himself until eleven o'clock was a minor miracle. 'Maybe I was, Ted.'

Ted's bushy eyebrows rose. 'What's with you? Last year you wouldn't have said "boo" to a goose. Now here you are, all flirty.'

'I had fun,' Anna replied, handing him a mug of coffee. 'Now drink that and stop picking on me.'

'Ah no, you don't get away that easy. Considering as I heard our Mr McAra talking about you in the newsroom this morning when I went up.'

Anna couldn't hide her surprise. 'Ben was talking about me?'

'See, you're interested now, aren't you? I knew you would be.'

'What happened?'

'I was up there – doing my rounds, you know, all part of the job – and as I was coming round the corner from the picture desk, I see our famous friend holding court with the other reporters. He was at his desk, with them lot gathered around him like flies round . . . Well, you get the idea. Mouthing off about you, he was. Stopped pretty smartish when he saw me, mind.'

Never sure how much store to set by Ted's stories, Anna approached with caution. 'What was he saying?'

'He was warning them off your story.' Ted's eyes shone with pride at his bombshell delivery. 'He "found" you, apparently, so everyone else could back right off. Said that if anyone was going to write about your mystery parcels, it would be him. What do you think of *that*, hmm?'

Is that true?

It seemed unlikely, but why would Ted concoct such a story otherwise? He had never passed judgement on Ben before; why start now?

'I'm sure you misheard him. That doesn't sound like something Ben would do.'

'Doesn't it? Tell me, how many hacks have you encountered over the years, eh? You're greener than I thought! Fact is, Anna, your handsome reporter isn't as pearly-white as you think he is.'

Whether it was true or not, the suggestion hit Anna like a lead weight. 'It's *lily-white*, Ted. And he's not *my* reporter.'

'Your face says different, girl. Must say, it surprised me, after seeing the two of you together at the fair. But, at the end of the day, journalists are all the same. Nice as pie to your face, sell your granny to the paparazzi as soon as your back's turned. McAra's the worst sort. You think he got where he is without stamping over people? Trust me, Anna, you don't get a star reporter's job by being nice. He's a shark, that one.' He saw Anna's expression and lowered his voice a little. 'I'm sorry, though. You looked happy on Saturday.'

'I was.' *And all weekend, too*, Anna added to herself, feeling the floor beginning to crumble away beneath her.

She had been so happy that Jonah had remarked on it yesterday when they passed in the corridor between their homes.

'That's a nice smile you're wearing,' he'd said, as Bennett jumped up to have his ears scratched. 'You look happy.'

'I am,' she had replied, her heart light, despite the gravel in her throat and the aches in her limbs from working at the fair.

'It's a good thing to see. You're a bit pretty when you smile,' he had said, instantly wrinkling his nose. 'And that were just about the cheesiest line I could've said. What I meant was . . .'

Anna was quick to rescue the blushing Yorkshireman. 'I know what you meant. And I appreciate the compliment.'

As she'd turned the key in her front-door lock, she

could feel Jonah's eyes on her as his dog nagged him for his walk.

I've been stupid, she thought now, the obvious regret on the security officer's face scarce comfort to her. Maybe that would teach Ted Blaskiewicz not to be so liberal with his gossip, seeing the damage it could cause. But Anna knew that the hurt Ted now saw in her expression had nothing to do with him.

'Ben said that?' Tish's expression was pure horror. 'What was he thinking?'

'That I'm a story waiting to be picked, I suppose.' Anna pushed aside the pillowy cinnamon roll Tish had bought for her. She'd lost her appetite since this morning and it showed no sign of returning.

'*Eat*, Anna.'

'I'm not hungry.'

'Then take it home and *promise me* you'll eat it later.' Tish frowned. 'My mother always insisted I ate something when a crisis hit. Though in her case it was usually half a ton of pasta. Be thankful I'm only pressing a pastry on you.'

'Thank you.'

'I don't like seeing you like this, sweetie. You've been so up lately.'

'I'll be fine, don't worry.' Anna made herself drink some coffee, baulking at its bitterness. 'This is strong.'

'Triple-shot. I thought you needed it.' She flicked a sugar packet across the coffee-shop table to her. 'Use that. It'll help.'

Anna doubted very much that the too-strong beverage could be helped by a small packet of sugar, but she did as Tish suggested. 'I've gone over and over what Ted told me all day,' she confessed, 'and I can't make sense of it. If Ben was only interested in the parcels, how come we spent the best part of six hours together and he never mentioned it? He's too busy to waste that amount of time for a story.'

'And you didn't feel he was building up to it?' Tish asked.

'Not at all. As far as I was concerned, I thought we were having fun.'

'Could've been trying to get on your good side, I guess? Building up your trust before jabbing the knife in?'

Tish Gornick was a woman blessed with a killer line in questioning.

'He could have been. But it's hardly a groundbreaking story, is it? Not his usual column-fodder. A receptionist receiving gifts from an unknown sender doesn't fit the pattern. It's a small, human-interest piece. That isn't going to bother a star reporter. When I was shadowing Ben, I saw the junior reporters in the newsroom handing down those kind of stories to the interns to write.'

And why would Ben have wasted all day pretending to like her, if all he wanted to do was tell her story? If he *was* pretending, that is. Anna considered herself a good judge of character, but if Ben had been feigning friendship, he'd had her completely fooled. There had been nothing in their exchanges at the fair to suggest he wanted anything from her other than the pleasure of her company. How could she have been so mistaken?

'Unless he sent them.'

Anna looked up at her friend. 'That's what some people at work think. But surely that would give him even greater reason to talk about the parcels when he had the chance? And it wouldn't benefit him to engineer a story just for the sake of a few lines. I just don't understand, Tish. I keep telling myself it's just Ted stirring, as usual – or that he was trying to protect me.'

'There is that, I guess.' Tish wasn't convinced. 'Do you want to know who's sending you the parcels?'

At the very beginning Anna's answer would have been a definite no. But too much had happened – both to her and *in* her – for this to remain so. The question kept returning to her thoughts. Who was behind the anonymous gifts and, more importantly, why was she receiving them?

'Yes,' Anna replied. 'I think I do.'

Twenty

Narinder Rana was not a bad man. Maybe he was a little cheekier than his fellow deliverymen at the central-London courier firm, perhaps a tad braver when it came to bantering with customers. But his intentions were as pure as the driven snow.

Almost always . . .

But this was too good an opportunity to miss.

For the last three weeks he had delivered parcels to a pretty brunette receptionist in the *Daily Messenger*'s impressive building and had struck up a line of friendly conversation, during which he had learned that she had no idea who was sending them. This, unsurprisingly, he rarely encountered in the course of his work. She was very attractive – more so each time he saw her – single, as far as he knew, and clearly intrigued by the parcels he delivered. As were several of her colleagues, whom he noticed scurrying to her side as he left the building. The younger receptionist – about whom he had been well warned by his workmates – appeared particularly keen to inspect each new parcel. So keen that she hadn't tried it on with him for a month now, which was a blessed relief. Narinder didn't like her sort: too eager to thrust everything they had under your nose. The brunette was far more intriguing.

And now Narinder was walking into the *Daily Messenger* building with another parcel addressed to Miss Anna Browne. No sender details, wrapped in brown paper and smaller than the last. Another delivery to intrigue the pretty young lady. And the perfect opportunity to make his move . . .

'Surprise!' the courier smiled, sliding a small parcel across the reception desk to Anna.

This was just what she needed. After a few days mulling over the events of the weekend, and Ted's supposed revelation about Ben, she had been hoping that another parcel might arrive and turn her mind to more positive things.

'Am I glad to see you,' she smiled at Narinder, welcoming the thrill that returned as she accepted the parcel.

'I'll say this for him: your mystery chap's a dab hand at parcel-wrapping. Shame you don't know who he is, though.'

Anna checked that none of her colleagues were within earshot and leaned a little closer to the courier. She had been toying with an idea for a while, and now seemed like the perfect time to pursue it. Of course Narinder might say no – it could breach the terms of his employment and land him in trouble. But unless she asked, she would never know. 'Actually, I was meaning to ask you about that . . .'

'Oh?'

'The thing is, I've had quite a few parcels now – five, including this one – and you've delivered all but one of them. Which means whoever is sending them has settled on your company as their preferred courier.'

There was a definite twinkle in Narinder's eye. 'Our rates are very competitive.'

'Of course. But what it *also* means is that the sender probably has an account with you?'

'What *are* you suggesting?'

Anna hoped he wasn't offended by her suggestion, but she had come too far to back out. 'That you might be able to check for me? Last time you mentioned something about paperwork back at the depot? I realise it's a big ask, but I really want to know who to thank for these wonderful gifts.'

Narinder rubbed his chin. 'I don't know. Stuff like that we're not supposed to share . . .'

Anna's heart sank. 'I understand.'

'That's not to say there isn't a way round these things.' He lowered his voice. 'Fact is, I *might* know something.'

'You do?'

'Possibly. Don't suppose you're free for a drink Saturday night? About seven?'

Anna considered this. From what Sheniece had told her about the courier, he wasn't averse to a bit of wheeling and dealing, so he might be bluffing to get a date. On the other hand, if he *did* know something, surely it was worth one drink on a Saturday evening to find out?

'I might be . . .'

A few years had passed since the end of Anna's last relationship – a junior architect called Tom, who, it transpired, was more in love with his burgeoning career than with the idea of settling down. At the time she had been blindsided by the break-up, not least because Tom had pushed for them to move in together and plan for the future. Years of seeing her mother rush into new relationships and get hurt had made Anna wary of pursuing her own relationships in the same way, but she loved Tom and everything he said indicated his full commitment. But a little over a month after Anna finally relented and agreed to move in with him, Tom changed his mind, accepting a year-long posting to an architects' firm in New York and moving out of her life. Since then she had dated, but she had yet to find anyone she wanted anything more with. This was one drink with a good-looking, single man who might just be able to shed light on the identity of the mystery gift-sender. It was a small risk for a potentially large reward.

I can do this, she told herself. *It's not a big deal.*

Her colleagues, however, disagreed.

'You're going on a *date* with him?' Sheniece's jaw had dropped low enough to grant Anna a clear view of the chewing gum wrapped around her molars. 'Narinder Rana – the wide-boy from CityServe Couriers?'

'It's just a drink . . .'

'It is *never* just a drink with that bloke. Jenny from Classifieds went out with him last year. She said he's out for whatever he can get.'

'Which, as I've said, will be one drink.' Anna rolled her

eyes. 'I don't know why you're so shocked, Shen. I do go on dates, you know.'

'Not with anyone who matters, and definitely not with people like Narinder Rana.'

'This is about that McAra chap, isn't it?' Ted nodded sagely. 'Rebound.'

Anna ignored him. 'It's one drink, in a pub that will be packed with other people. And I'll be fine.'

'No, you won't. This is a really bad idea . . .'

'Now, you heard her, Sheniece,' Ted said as he passed the fuming junior receptionist. 'If Anna thinks she can handle it, that's good enough. You're just sore he isn't interested in *you*.'

'No, I'm not. I might have flirted with him once or twice, but that's just to entertain myself. And why can't I be worried about my friend? *You* seem willing to butt into her business at the drop of a hat. Maybe *you're* the one who's jealous!'

Leaving her colleagues to battle it out, Anna dismissed their concern. She was going to be *fine*.

The unknown promise of Anna's fifth parcel sustained her through the day and all the way home, but unlike before, she couldn't prolong the anticipation once she arrived home. Her raincoat, umbrella and handbag were discarded on the breakfast bar as she headed to her sofa with the precious item. This time she didn't even pause to look for sender details, knowing that she would find none, her fingers sliding quickly beneath the perfect points of brown paper. Lifting them up, she pulled out a cube of cardboard the colour of clementine oranges, constructed of a series of triangular folds fastened with a vivid blue bow. When opened, the triangles parted to reveal a slender glass vial of liquid decorated with a single swirl of silver paint, nestling in a padded dark-grey velvet cushion. A curl of cream vellum paper had been wrapped around it, upon which was written:

A signature scent for Miss Anna Browne

She cradled the delicate glass atomiser in her fingers as she slowly prised open its frosted stopper. The moment it was removed, the most wonderful aroma filled the air. Anna closed her eyes and let the fragrance surround her. It was the sea and powdered sugar; tiny violets that grew wild in between weathered stone walls across clifftop fields; and chamomile warmed by the sun in Grandma Morwenna's garden. It was a scent designed to stand out, confident and heady, and Anna immediately understood why it had arrived now. At the beginning of her extraordinary adventure she wouldn't have considered herself brave enough to wear it; now, she was eager to discover the effect it might have.

And tomorrow night would be the perfect opportunity to find out.

Twenty-One

The city-centre pub was as busy as Anna expected it to be, crammed with city workers keen to put the past week behind them and enjoy the weekend. It was loud and boisterous, the general buzz punctuated by sharp barks of laughter. Drinkers occupied every available inch of floor space, propped against pillars and leaning almost back-to-back with perfect strangers without acknowledging their existence – a phenomenon unique to the city. It had been alien to Anna when she arrived from Cornwall, where it was always best to assume you knew someone regardless of how unfamiliar they looked, but now the carefully observed splendid isolation suited her. Far safer to pretend you were invisible than risk awkward, unwanted communication. It clothed her in a blanket of anonymity, giving her mental space even when her personal space was compromised – a much better way to be than living under the scrutiny of a small seaside community.

Her new scent surrounded her, its aroma warmed and

deepened by the contact with her skin. The daisy-chain necklace was cool against her collarbone, the owl brooch pinned to her jacket. With her gifts for company, Anna felt strong, ready for whatever this evening might bring.

Bracing herself, she squeezed between the wall of bodies towards the bar. As she reached it she saw a hand rise above the heads of the drinkers and wave in greeting. Narinder was at the far end of the bar, his pint already half-empty.

'We finish early on Saturday shifts,' he said by way of explanation. 'What'll you have?'

'White wine, please.'

Narinder raised a five-pound note to attract the barman's attention, turning to Anna while he waited. 'I like this place. Your local, is it?'

'No. But I've been here a few times with people from work. I like it.' Anna had been careful to choose a pub far from her own home. It was a personal policy formed from bad experience. When she first began dating after Tom left for New York she once made the mistake of meeting a graphic designer from Shoreditch in the pub across the road from Walton Tower. While it was immediately obvious to her that he wasn't what she was looking for, he unfortunately failed to reach the same conclusion, which led to several awkward meetings in the pub afterwards and, eventually, Anna finding a different pub to patronise.

'It's a cool place. Busy, though.' Narinder slid the glass of wine to Anna, who was careful to take a small sip. She needed to keep her wits about her this evening, to gather the information she needed.

'Isn't everywhere in the city on a Saturday evening?'

'Good point.'

For a while they passed the time with non-contentious subjects: their jobs, the weather, what they both enjoyed in their spare time – nothing that might provide a stumbling point during the early awkwardness of their meeting. But after an hour the time inevitably arrived to address the real reason they were there. By then, they had happened to spot a table away from the bar and had settled against the dark-brown leather of the bench seats. Narinder had refreshed his pint while Anna's wine glass remained half-full. She seized the opportunity when a lull appeared.

'So . . . I was wondering: have you been able to find out anything about the sender of my parcels?'

Her pulse began to pad against the silver daisies at her neck. The moment suddenly assumed a significance she had not anticipated: depending on the courier's answer, the next few minutes could change everything. Anna would know more about the sender than before – briefly she wondered if some of the magic would disappear with the mystery. Did she *really* want to know?

Of course she did. It had been all she'd thought about since the fifth parcel arrived and, as Saturday evening approached, her excitement had been building. It seemed the next stage in the journey she had unwittingly embarked upon: the next logical step. What was the alternative? If the sender of the parcels chose not to reveal their identity, where would Anna go from there? Part of her wondered if the mystery might be the point of the gifts. But perhaps it was her responsibility to take control now. Until this point she had been content to receive the generosity of the unknown person without question, a passive player in an adventure she had not written. That had to change eventually; now was as good a time as any.

Besides, Anna Browne was experiencing the strongest surge of confidence in her life, driven, she was certain, by the mysterious gifts. She wanted to know who had sent them and discover why.

Narinder glanced to the side, secret agent-like, which – given that he had to raise his voice to be heard over the noise of the pub – was a somewhat futile gesture. 'I have.'

Anna's heart skipped a beat. 'And?'

'Are you *sure* you want to know?' It was as if he knew what she was thinking. 'Because, you know, once I tell you, there's no going back.'

'I'm prepared for that. What have you found out?'

Narinder swigged a mouthful of beer. 'I *think* I know who it is.'

'You think you know?'

'No, I'm pretty sure.' Why had eye contact become a challenge for him?

'Okay, so who do you think it is?'

'I haven't got a name yet. But it's definitely a bloke.'

'Definitely?'

'I think.'

Confused, Anna stared at him. 'How can you *think* it's a bloke? Surely it is or it isn't?'

'Yeah. What you said.'

184

He was making no sense at all and Anna began to feel the moment slipping away. 'Who do you think it is, Narinder?'

'Bloke started coming into the depot about a month ago. I didn't catch his name – the reception guys deal with orders; I'm just in the unit behind the office. But I hadn't seen him before that.'

'What does he look like?'

Narinder looked at Anna like a mechanic who doesn't want to give a reason for expensive car repairs. 'Didn't get a very clear view, to be honest.'

'Is he tall? Short? Young? Middle-aged? What colour hair does he have?' Frustration was building as she squared him.

'About our age. Couldn't make out hair colour. But tall, I'd say. Not as tall as me, but taller than you.' Pleased with his summary, he rewarded himself with the last of his beer.

Considering the difference between their heights was at least a foot, this didn't provide much insight. Anna took a breath and adopted a different approach. 'Okay. So it's a man, who started sending parcels about a month ago, and he's around thirty years old. Can you tell me anything else about him? Anything at all?'

'Not right now, no. But if we did this again – say, next Saturday – I could have more details for you.'

And then, the penny dropped for Anna. 'You don't know who it is, do you?'

'Yes, I do! Tallish guy, our age, comes in once a week . . .' He was flailing now. 'It's like I said . . .'

'What you said was what you thought I wanted to hear. Which was enough to keep me hanging on without giving me any concrete facts. Am I right?' Her heart hammered in her chest, her skin clammy from the atmosphere in the pub.

His defiance only remained as long as it took to meet her stare. Then his shoulders dropped. 'Yeah, all right. Can't blame a guy for trying, eh? How about I buy you dinner next Saturday night to apologise?'

Numb on the bus rumbling home, Anna allowed herself to see the funny side. She'd had a wasted evening and her hope of finding her parcel-sender had suffered a setback. But that was all it was. In the grand scheme of things, it was less of a blow than it might have been. Narinder was an opportunist, but harmless otherwise. At least he'd admitted that he lied. As the lights of the city moved slowly along the misted bus windows, Anna realised the courier's deception had inadvertently given her a new gift: a greater determination to unravel the mystery of her parcels. Before this evening, the question had intrigued her; now she knew she needed to seek out the truth.

And she was no longer afraid of what she might find . . .

Twenty-Two

For Mrs Isadora Smedley, Sunday afternoons were made for high tea and scandal. A widow for more years now than she had been a wife, these days she lived for moments when tantalising mouthfuls of food were accompanied by delicious morsels of gossip. For many years her closest friend, Sheila, had provided both delicacies, always the first to know the inside track on their friends and acquaintances. But last year a sudden stroke had taken her first to hospital and then to a hospice in Bracknell, leaving Isadora alone for the first time in her eighty-four years.

Crushed by this but determined to carry on, Isadora had made a valiant effort to keep all of the dates the two friends had established: Monday afternoons playing bridge at the local Age UK day-centre, Tuesdays and Wednesdays walking to the park and having tea at the small café by the duck-pond, Thursdays collecting their pensions at the post office and doing their shopping, Fridays catching up on the papers and sharing their findings over a phone call,

Saturdays for resting and Sunday afternoons meeting for high tea at the Pleasance Hotel, just around the corner from the Victoria and Albert Museum.

Until a hidden threat appeared, which changed it all . . .

Walking home from the supermarket one Thursday afternoon in November, as the weak daylight began to fade and street lights fizzed into life, Isadora had become aware of someone walking quickly behind her. When she slowed to check her handbag for her front-door key, the footsteps slowed, too. She had glanced over one shoulder and caught a glimpse of a hooded figure moving towards her. It was enough to make her hurry towards the lobby light of Walton Tower's entrance, spilling out across the darkened pavement just ahead. It was close, but still too far away – and as she ran, her aged knees smarting in protest, all she could think of was the horror of being caught, of the unknown shadow reaching out and grabbing her shoulder . . .

The fright had changed her overnight from a woman who had feared nothing to a virtual recluse. She had retreated to the small confines of her apartment, refusing to leave and ordering food by telephone to be delivered to her door. Gone was her prized routine, replaced by a frightened loneliness that clung to her skin and dragged at her heart.

Until she met Miss Anna Browne from 16B.

The delightful young woman's kindness and help had transformed Isadora's life. Now, more than twelve months since her neighbour had conspired to gain entrance to her

188

home and win her trust, Isadora was enjoying what she often referred to as 'my second youth'. Visits to the theatre, galleries, cafés and exhibitions and strolls in the park on pleasant days – all accompanied by her new friends: Anna, Seamus the caretaker, Jonah the *rather* handsome Northern chap from 16D and Tish, the amusing American lady from the floor below. Isadora's social calendar now sparkled, as it hadn't done in over thirty-five years. Darling Anna had arranged it all and, even more surprisingly, appeared to enjoy Isadora's company.

In return, Isadora did what she did best: Sunday high tea with lavish helpings of gossip in her home, for Anna and any of her friends who were free. But the times she liked best were when she and Anna were alone. She had never been granted children or grandchildren of her own, but the lovely girl fitted the bill perfectly. Sweet and attentive, she possessed a quick wit well concealed from the outside world. And recently Isadora had seen Anna begin to bloom, like the blousy pink 'Albertine' roses Mrs Smedley remembered growing in the garden of her childhood home. The girl had splendid potential. With the right encouragement – in ways both open and covert – she could make a better purveyor of gossip than Sheila herself, given time . . .

The day after her date with Narinder, Anna enjoyed high tea with her elderly neighbour, Mrs Smedley. Jonah joined them midway through the elegant feast Isadora had spread out for them on her best tablecloth and soon the topic of conversation moved to Anna's parcels.

'It's all most exciting,' Isadora beamed. 'Beautiful gifts from a secret admirer – how wonderful!'

'Are you going to find out who it is?' Jonah asked, brushing petits-fours crumbs self-consciously from his T-shirt. 'I mean, you do want to solve the mystery, right?'

'I do. In fact I've already started to investigate.' Amused now by her own situation, Anna confessed about her date with Narinder.

Jonah's chin made a bid for Isadora's prized parquet floor. 'Blimey, Anna, I'd never have thought you willing to do that. Did he know anything?'

'No. And I'm a bit thick for not realising what he was up to. I'm flattered in a way.'

'And yet no further to unveiling the culprit,' Isadora noted. 'But what fun!'

At 7 p.m. Anna and Jonah waited in Isadora's living room while she prepared for their night out together.

'I can't believe you two are dragging me to the theatre,' Jonah groaned. '*Again.*'

Anna chuckled. 'You liked the last play we went to see.'

'Well, anything by Willy Russell is fine by me. But I've never heard of this one.'

'Never heard of *Hobson's Choice*? It's the classic Northern comedy! Gosh, I thought I'd led a sheltered life in the Duchy. You'll love it, I promise.'

Jonah muttered something unintelligible, his gruff expression brightening as Isadora returned. 'So, Miss Smedley, ready for your theatre premiere?'

Isadora Smedley shook her head, her lilac-washed curls

never moving as she did so. 'Always the joker, Jonah. I am well aware it is a *community-theatre* production.' She enunciated the words as if describing something pitiful. 'In my youth, the premieres I attended were glittering in every sense. For my first theatre visit I wore my grandmama's ermine and pearls.'

'And I'll bet you were the star attraction,' Anna smiled, placing a discreet hand against the old lady's back to steady her as she stepped into the hall.

'You flatter me, darling,' Isadora replied, her powdered cheeks blushing all the same. 'But I dare say I was.'

Jonah offered his arm, which Isadora gracefully received, and together they made a stately progress towards the lift.

Taking Mrs Isadora Smedley out to various London events was something Anna – and Jonah, for all his comedy grumbling – had come to enjoy, brought about after a chance remark from Seamus, who said he hadn't seen the fiercely independent pensioner for a few weeks and was beginning to worry for her well-being. Anna had mentioned this to Jonah, who left a parcel outside her door, knocked, and hurried back to his flat while Anna waited. When Isadora finally opened the door to collect the gift, Anna was able to catch her.

Even now, the memory of what Anna had seen in Isadora's apartment when the old lady invited her in shocked her. Bags of discarded takeaway containers were strewn across the kitchen, the detritus of home deliveries, which didn't require the old lady to leave her home.

The thought of the elegant old lady being too scared

to set foot outside her home horrified Anna. She remembered her own much-loved, much-missed grandmother and thought how different it had been for her. While living in a tiny Cornish fishing community had its downsides – not least that everybody and their cat knew your business – at least the elderly residents were looked out for and called in on regularly. Here in London's perennially busy sprawl it was too easy for souls to be forgotten. What had been an oasis of freedom for Anna had become a prison of loneliness for Isadora. It broke Anna's heart and she sprang into action, enlisting the help of Seamus, Jonah, Tish and anyone else in Walton Tower she could recruit to draw up a rota of volunteers to escort Isadora out into the city that she now feared to walk alone. Over a year later, the rota was still in place, firm friendships having been forged and much fun having been had.

And so it was that the small party of Walton Tower residents now took their seats in the compact studio theatre above a pub in the West End to watch a much pared-down performance of Harold Brighouse's famous play. Anna giggled as she saw Jonah wincing at each wrongly pronounced Northern word, and pretended not to see Isadora raising a carefully ironed handkerchief to her eyes when Maggie led Willy Mossop to their wedding bed. At the end of the play they all rose to their feet to applaud the community-theatre cast and made their way downstairs to the packed bar. Tish secured a bench table and guarded it with typical New Yorker venom until Jonah returned with drinks.

Isadora sipped her cream sherry like a duchess holding court. 'What did you make of the production, Jonah?'

'I doubt any of them have ever been north of Watford Gap, but they made a fair pass,' he replied. 'Although the actor playing Willy was about as Northern as Donald Trump.'

'According to the programme, that young man hails from Connecticut,' Isadora smiled, patting Tish's arm. 'So, your neck of the woods, dear. But God bless the Yanks. They *try*.'

Tish took the half-compliment with good humour. 'Glad you appreciate my nation's effort, ma'am.'

Anna smiled as her friends exchanged anecdotes about the play, and Isadora regaled them with stories of glamorous theatre visits of years gone by. While spending the evening with two friends and an elderly doyenne might not be everyone's idea of a great night out – Anna could only imagine the look on Sheniece's face at the prospect – she loved every minute of it. Taking Isadora out had long since stopped being a Good Samaritan task and was now something she looked forward to immensely.

She patted the smooth head of the owl brooch on her jacket lapel as she watched her friends laughing together and felt a strong sense of peace wash over her. Having friends who enjoyed her company, and someone out in the world who was thinking of her, made Anna feel very loved. Again, she caught herself wondering about the identity of the sender of her gifts. Was it someone close to her? Could they be here, tonight? She cast a glance around the busy pub interior. It could be anyone in the pub, she thought. Or anyone in London. Or maybe anyone in the country. It could even be Mrs Smedley, no stranger to the extraordinary in life, if her tales of her youth were anything to go by. Anna relaxed in the company of her friends and enjoyed the possibility of what she might find.

Twenty-Three

For the next four weeks, no new parcels arrived.

It led Sheniece to declare that Narinder from the courier company had obviously been the mystery sender and that, failing in his chance to come clean during his date with Anna, he was now in hiding. Ted attempted to console Anna by suggesting that her life would be 'less sticky' without the anonymous gifts, while Babs was characteristically blunt.

'If he only sent you five things, he wasn't worth having anyway. You deserve someone who'll shower you with gifts, flower.'

Anna was disappointed that the parcels had ended. It had been a wonderful adventure and she'd started to rely on the deliveries to inject excitement into each week. But she wanted to know *why* they had been sent – and was even more determined to unravel the mystery.

I will find out who you are, she vowed, casting her eyes across the wide atrium floor of the *Messenger* building, as if hoping for a glimpse of them.

One new gift recently arrived in Anna's life was making a difference, however. An opportunist courier from City-Serve didn't deliver it; neither was it wrapped in perfectly folded brown paper. But it boosted Anna's confidence more than any of her parcels had.

It began one Monday morning when Anna, having arrived in the city centre an hour early for work, decided to treat herself to breakfast at Freya & Georgie's – a chic, independent coffee house recently opened just down the street from the *Daily Messenger* building. She had been a passive observer to the steady creation of the coffee shop during the last month, noting the changes in its interior as the weeks passed, and had decided to visit when it opened. Inside, the warm wood panelling and smooth, purple-grey slate floors offered a contrast to the monochrome concrete-and-steel buildings on the street. Large wing-backed armchairs snuggled next to low coffee tables and dusky-red fabric sofas, while tall, rustic stools stood, sentry-like, against a polished wooden bar in the window. Quotes from famous books hung around the walls in rococo-style frames of burnished gold and silver, and order numbers were given out painted silver on tiny black canvases attached to easels, like that which held Anna's hope-heart painting at home. Service was efficient and inevitably brusque – perfect for the largely business clientele who prized speed over civility – but for a city-centre coffee shop the atmosphere was pleasantly relaxed.

As she waited to order, a sudden tap on her shoulder caused her to turn – bringing her face to face with Ben McAra.

'Hi, Anna. I didn't know you came here,' he grinned.

'I didn't, before today.'

'Are you taking out or staying in?'

'Staying in.'

'Mind if I join you?'

Since the weekend of the Charity Fair Ben had made no effort to speak to Anna again. According to Ted (a questionable source at the best of times, but all Anna had to go on), Ben was working on an exclusive story and had been holed up in an Edinburgh hotel while he put it together. Anna suspected her colleague of making this up, to make Ben's absence easier for her to take, but she didn't tell Ted.

Ben McAra was annoying and Anna wasn't at all sure whether she could trust him, but facing him now, she realised she'd missed his smile. And that was as good a reason as any to offer him the spare chair at her table.

He asked what she'd been up to since the fair and, noticeably, didn't mention the parcels. Anna, who had no intention of talking about them anyway, told him about the new furnishings from Tish's beloved Marylebone boutique that she was planning to buy for her apartment, and the insider gossip she'd been given by Jonah about certain TV programmes.

'I suppose cameramen see it all,' Ben remarked. 'Is he ever tempted to film the scandals behind the scenes, instead of the countryside? I'd watch that over *Countryfile* any day.'

He let Anna steer the conversation and she never once felt as if he was waiting for the parcels to be mentioned.

In return, she asked him about his job and latest assignment.

'Ted tells me you've been in Edinburgh?'

Ben laughed. 'I might have known Bloodhound Blaskiewicz would be on my trail. I just got back, actually.'

'How was it?'

'Awful. Long and frustrating.' Seeing Anna's surprise, he continued. 'I love Edinburgh – it's just annoying to be bound by work and unable to explore the city. I spent most of the time holed up in a hotel room, trying to arrange interviews, with, it has to be said, little success.' He stirred another lump of sugar into his black coffee. 'I promised myself I'll go back there for fun, maybe later in the year.'

Anna tried to imagine what it would be like to have a job that entailed travelling to other cities and working out of hotels. The notion was appealing, but she suspected the reality would be very different. Tom had once bemoaned his job's requirement for him to work out of hotels in Rome, New York, Madrid and Berlin. 'Once you've seen one hotel room, you've seen them all,' he complained. 'Mini-bars and expense accounts are all very well, but they're nothing compared to a decent cup of tea and bath in your own home.'

And yet it transpired that Tom had found something about New York hotels to love: the last time Anna heard from him, he had been living in a hotel in TriBeCa for six months.

'So, are you planning a holiday this year?' Ben's question

brought Anna's attention back to the cool comfort of the coffee house.

'Maybe. I haven't decided yet.'

'You said you were from Cornwall? Must be great to go back there when you get the chance.'

Anna's shoulders bristled. 'I don't – go back. Not often. Not for the last six years, anyway.'

'Really? I'd be back like a *shot*. All those glorious beaches, Cornish cream teas and sea fishing; if I even slightly knew anyone who lived there, I'd be camped on their doorstep at every opportunity.'

'It's a beautiful place,' she conceded, despite all the other baggage her home county carried with it for her. 'Just not much of a holiday for me to go back there.'

'I sense a story there . . .'

'Occupational hazard for you, I suppose.'

The edge of steel in her reply made him sit back a little. Clearly rethinking his next comment, he lifted his head to scan the interior of Freya & Georgie's. 'I like it here. Know what I think?'

Relieved to be excused from discussing Cornwall any further, Anna smiled. 'What do you think?'

'I think we should do this regularly. Same time next week? What do you think?'

With that, the one gift Anna had least expected arrived: the opportunity to know Ben McAra better.

Twenty-Four

Megan Milliken never intended to be a barista. But, like much in her life, her optimistic childhood ambitions had been diverted by reality. She had come to the city seeking fame as an actress, attended nine months of auditions and then, with no work forthcoming and her landlord threatening strong-arm tactics, reluctantly accepted a waitress job in the café down the street from her cramped bedroom in a shared house. That was five years ago; and while her acting career had progressed no further, she had discovered a natural talent for making outstanding coffee.

It was this skill that saw her win the assistant manager's job at the shiny new flagship Fleet Street location of a successful coffee-house chain – Freya & Georgie's, named after the owner's two nieces. The man who hired her was Gabe, a smooth-talking entrepreneur whose rise to prominence in the business world was far removed from his humble beginnings in a small town just outside Glasgow.

And the man who, if his current persistence paid off, Megan *might* just accept a date with . . .

While she prided herself on her expert barista skills, what Megan loved most about her job was people-watching. The clientele in Freya & Georgie's was a different breed from the customers she'd served in her last job – busy city types with no time for small talk, but plenty to while away on the café's free Wi-Fi in important-looking meetings. An occasional group of well-heeled women in their early twenties came for lunch on Wednesdays, made up, it transpired, of ambitious young PAs who met to share experience and plan their eventual world domination. But, unlike her previous job, she found that the customers largely merged into grey stereotypes, devoid of variety in age, social standing and employment.

Which is why the young couple stood out.

She had first noticed them during Freya & Georgie's opening week. It had been a busy morning with particularly irascible customers and she was beginning to wish for something to break the monotony of unsmiling faces. Though dressed similarly to the other customers, the couple were remarkable for one thing: their unmistakable chemistry. It was as evident to Megan as the smiles they both wore, and she couldn't take her eyes off them. And so she was delighted when they returned twice again – and then every Monday morning, not long after the coffee house opened for trading. To Megan, a diehard fan of rom-coms, it was as if a movie plot was unfolding before her very eyes, the two romantic leads moving closer to one another with each meeting.

201

'I can see them falling in love and it's the most beautiful thing,' she told her sister after work one day. 'And the thing is, I don't think either of them realises what's happening. I feel privileged to see it, like I'm their hidden audience.'

'Maybe he'll propose in the coffee shop?' her sister suggested. 'And then you could be a witness at their wedding!'

Watching the couple this morning, their faces flushed from laughter, Megan made a decision. She would take her inspiration from them and turn the tables on Gabe. She'd take the initiative and ask *him* out. Maybe she'd do it tonight . . .

'The coffee's good here, but the soundtrack's completely up the duff,' Ben smirked one morning. 'Dire Straits and Toto? Are they trying to kill our ears?'

'I quite like it,' Anna smiled. 'It's the music my Uncle Jabez used to play in his pub band. "Money for Nothing" was his personal favourite.' She had come to love the random conversation topics they shared at each coffee meeting.

'Seriously?'

'Oh yes. Dire Straits songs went down a treat in our local pubs.'

'No, I mean you seriously have an Uncle Jabez?'

'And an Auntie Zelda. My mum's called Senara and my brother is Ruari. And my grandma's name was Morwenna.' Her throat caught slightly at the mention of it. 'We like our unusual names in Cornwall.'

'Then how did you escape with *Anna*?' Ben laughed, but stopped himself immediately. 'Not that I mean it's a bad name or anything.'

'I'm not offended. I like it.'

It was a good question. Growing up, Anna had often wondered why her mother, who in all other respects was as far from sensible as it was possible to be, had settled on such a common-sense name for her firstborn. Senara had never given a satisfactory answer, either, despite Anna asking many times about what had inspired her name. The closest she came to an explanation was one night after a large jar of local scrumpy loosened Senara's resolve: 'It sounded like a good name for a girl, is all.'

Strange that a name regarded by most people as boring and commonplace should be considered remarkable, but in Anna's childhood home this was so. It set her apart from her schoolmates, her neighbours and her family, just as her sensitivity and sweet nature contrasted so sharply with that of her mother. To Anna, the ordinariness of her name gave the distance she craved from Senara's too-public behaviour and allowed her to be different. In a village where it was often assumed children would follow their parents in temperament, lifestyle and employment, Anna Browne was granted immunity. It alleviated the biggest fear of her formative years – that she was destined to be tarred with the same brush as her mother – and ultimately fuelled her decision to leave Cornwall and carve out her own life.

'Do you have a middle name?'

'I don't have one. You?'

Ben grimaced. 'Leonard. It was my granddad's name. But if you tell anyone, I will hunt you down.'

'Your secret is safe.' Anna stifled a giggle. '*Leonard.*'

If Ben had been seeking out Anna's story at the Charity Fair, he made no further attempts during the following weeks, as he shared coffee with her. *Ted must have made a mistake*, Anna reasoned, glad that the heavy suggestion of an ulterior motive had been lifted. Without it, she could enjoy their chats over coffee for what they really were: enjoyable time spent with a man she liked very much. And was liking more as time passed . . .

The last thing Anna was expecting that weekend was a house-guest. Especially not in the earliest hours of Saturday morning, summoning her from her bed. But the sight of Tish Gornick, pale-faced with dripping wet hair, clutching an overnight bag to her chest as if it contained all her worldly goods, was enough to make Anna forget her annoyance.

'Oh, Tish, what happened?'

'I was taking a shower and the water vanished,' she sniffed. 'I told Seamus about the pressure falling three weeks ago, but he never came up to see it. Now look where I am!' For a woman unaccustomed to requesting help, the next words from her lips were clearly a struggle to form. 'Please. I have nowhere else to go. All I need is a hairdryer and a couch for the night.'

It would mark a significant step in their friendship and one that, had it happened in daylight hours, Anna might have hesitated to make. But she was already ushering her friend in, all propriety set aside in the wake of the crisis. Within ten minutes Tish had a makeshift bed made for her on Anna's sofa, a hot, sweet mug of tea to calm her nerves and the promise of a hairdryer to follow.

'I really can't thank you enough.' Tish was attempting to wrap her entire body around the mug. 'I'll call Seamus at 8 a.m. and demand he fixes it.'

While Tish dried her hair, Anna made hot buttered toast, remembering Morwenna's favoured remedy for night terrors. 'This will help, trust me. My grandma used to say, "There's not much can't be solved by a bit of toast and butter."'

'Your grandma was a wise woman.' She sniffed. 'I'm sorry, Anna.'

'What for?'

'Turning up at your door in the middle of the night, demanding your hospitality.'

Anna shook her head. 'You had a crisis, Tish. I'm glad you came here for help.'

The first sounds of a stirring city filtered into the flat beyond the windows, the distant burr of a road-sweeper van and the shrill reversing siren of a bin-lorry reverberating as the sky began to lighten from ink-black to royal blue. Though weary from the events of the last hour, neither Anna nor Tish seemed ready to sleep yet.

'So, you get any more parcels lately?' Tish asked.

Anna sat, cross-legged, in the armchair opposite her friend. 'No. Not for a month now.' Her heart sank. Plenty had happened since the last parcel, but she secretly missed the anticipation she'd felt, wondering if another gift might arrive.

Tish nodded. 'Really? They just stopped?'

'Looks like it.'

'That's sad.'

'It is, in a way. I liked looking forward to them.'

'Like I said before, things like that don't happen often. Not in this city, anyway.'

Silence settled between them as they considered this. Tish tied her silver-threaded black hair into a knot at the nape of her neck. Anna inspected her nails. Outside the rumble of wheelie bins joined the urban symphony.

'I was a little jealous of you.' Tish looked at Anna, her eyes wide in confession.

In the years Anna and Tish had known each other there had never been an admission this personal before. Anna hugged her knees tighter to her body. 'You were?'

She nodded. 'For a long time, actually. You're such a sweet girl, Anna. It irritated me when we first met.' She held up her hands. 'It's true – not that I'm proud of it. But then I got to know you better and, I don't know, I realised you were the genuine article. *Then* I got jealous.'

'I don't think anyone's ever been jealous of me.'

Anna was stunned by what she heard. Tish was the self-assured, no-nonsense American who, aside from her complaints, never allowed anyone within her carefully constructed defences. Anna, by comparison, was the person who willingly assumed a supporting role, never imagining that anyone would wish for her life. If anything, people had congratulated themselves for *not* being her, especially

206

during her Cornwall years. *Thank heaven we don't have to be part of* that *family*, she would hear her neighbours whisper, as the latest Browne saga raged in plain view of the village – usually involving a drunken Senara causing havoc, as her two children hid in the doorway of their cottage: *Thank your lucky stars you're not poor Anna Browne . . .*

'I meant what I said: those parcels have changed you, Anna. You've a spring in your step. You smile without realising. It was like you were in love – only not with anyone but yourself.' Tish laughed. 'Listen to me! I sound like Oprah. What I mean is that whoever sent those things to you did more than just give you nice surprises. Although I guess you'll never know who sent them now. Or why. Did you suspect anyone you knew?'

'No.' That wasn't true. Looking at her friend, she smiled. 'Well, not really. Of course, people at work all had their own ideas.'

'Oh?'

'Most of them thought the sender was a psycho-killing stalker drawing me into a deadly game. I think they were disappointed when dead rats and severed limbs didn't show up.'

'Was there anyone you were hoping it was?'

The question caught Anna off-guard, the heat of a blush creeping along her cheekbones. 'No.'

'Liar! Anyway, who's to say the deliveries have stopped for good? Maybe they just took a vacation.'

'For a month?'

'Some people do. My boss did last year: a whole month

jammed onto a cruise ship with rich jerks who wanted to take his money at poker every night. He practically needed rehab when he returned.'

Anna could think of nothing worse than a cruise: trapped in confined spaces with people you would never spend time with in real life, unable to escape. 'I'm not surprised. In one way, I'm glad there haven't been any more parcels. They were starting to cause problems at work.'

'What kind of problems?'

'A lot of speculation, random accusations – that kind of thing. I didn't want to be in the middle of all that, no matter how lovely the gifts were.'

'Surely you miss them?'

Anna had to concede she did. She thought about what Tish had said, later as she lay in bed, the unfamiliar sounds of someone else in her home bringing back ghosts of her former life with Tom, mingling with the thoughts she'd dared not entertain about a certain star journalist who seemed intent on moving closer to her. If Tish, who hardly ever noticed anyone unless they annoyed her, had noticed a change in Anna, might Ben have seen it, too?

And why *had* the parcels stopped arriving? If the perfume really was the final parcel, why didn't the sender give a clue to their identity? Or reveal it completely? It made no sense when she thought about it. Why go to all that trouble, if you had no intention of letting the recipient know who you were?

Unless . . . What if the sender had found another way to summon her attention? If that someone had found a way to spend more time with her, for instance, wouldn't that make any future parcels needless?

Ben McAra had started to meet Anna for coffee the week the parcels disappeared. And there had been no more deliveries since. Could he be waiting for the right moment to tell her . . . ?

And then a new thought struck. *Wait – do I want Ben to have sent me those things?*

If she did, would that mean their growing friendship was just part of a plan Ben had cooked up to get her attention? What she'd loved about getting to know him was how easily they were getting on. It seemed spontaneous and it felt the most natural thing to do. She liked the serendipity of it. But if Ben had planned this all along, was her confidence in their friendship mistaken? She liked to think it was as much her decision to be Ben's friend as it was his to befriend her. But a premeditated plan on his part would mean that she was just being played. That thought made her stomach twist.

Sheniece would probably argue that Ben plotting to get close to Anna was romantic. And maybe it was. Certainly Anna felt closer to him each time they met. She was comfortable with the flow of their conversation, enjoying the way they danced verbally around one another, each time edging a little further over the boundaries of friendship. Anna knew she was falling for Ben. He already meant a great deal to her – and she was scared that he now had the potential to break her heart, if he turned out not to be the person she thought.

If Ben was the parcel-sender, it also raised another issue:

had he sent her gifts because of who she was, or because of the person he hoped the packages might change her into? There was no doubt that Anna's confidence had grown since she'd started receiving the gifts. Everyone had noticed; and, more importantly, Anna knew it herself. She had done things lately that she'd scarcely have believed possible before. Having the courage to feel an equal to Ben in their friendship was one of the biggest achievements. But if Ben had planned it all beforehand, was she being manipulated? She was reminded of Professor Henry Higgins working out his scheme on poor, unsuspecting Eliza Doolittle in *Pygmalion* and felt the temperature drop in her body at the suggestion.

I don't want to be anyone's project. I want to be myself and discover what else I can do . . .

A crash and a curse from the living room snapped Anna back into the present. Throwing aside her duvet, she hurried through, to find Tish sprawled across the rug by the coffee table, rubbing her ankle.

'I guess that answers the question of whether I sleep-walk,' she said as Anna helped her up. 'Did I wake you?'

'No, I was getting up anyway. Cup of tea?'

Later that morning, with Tish back in her apartment barking orders at a very apologetic Seamus Flatley, Anna left Walton Tower and walked to her local park. Her head ached from lack of sleep and she needed fresh air and exercise to help her make sense of everything. As city parks go, Loveage Gardens was unremarkable, being not much more than a field edged with oak and beech trees, but it was a popular place for city residents to run, walk, exercise their dogs and escape the relentless concrete grey of their surroundings. Anna liked walking here: once through the large, swirling patterned cast-iron gates it was as if the city noise was muted by birdsong, dog barks and laughter. What it lacked in wildness it more than made up for in welcome.

The sun had retreated behind a white cloud blanket, making the green leaves stand out against the sky. Anna pulled a cardigan from her bag, slipping it around her shoulders to block the chill of the breeze that had sprung up. She felt dizzy from a disturbed night, but the wind in her hair took her back to morning walks she'd taken years before, on rough-hewn pathways snaking around the cliff edges, when she wanted to escape the constant drama of home. Now the escape was gentler, but she carried the drama in her mind.

If Ben was the sender, was this all a romantic gesture to get her attention? Did he even like her? The tingle in her toes suggested she liked the possibility. Perhaps she should just ask him, to make sure?

She bought a tea from the tiny wooden refreshment hut in the middle of Loveage Gardens and sat on a nearby bench to think. Blowing the steam from the cardboard cup, she gazed out across the park. High-rise buildings from the city beyond peered over treetops on all four sides of the green space, like nosy neighbours on tiptoe over garden fences. It was busy, even for a Saturday, with people taking advantage of the wide green lawns despite the lack of sun. As children and dogs raced across the green expanse, couples reclined on picnic blankets, lost in either their partner's eyes or the weight of weekend papers, while groups of friends laughed together beneath oak-tree boughs. There was a relaxed friendliness to the park, as if everyone was off-duty.

What do you want, Anna Browne?

The question was simple enough, but Anna had no answer this morning. There were plenty of things she would *like*: the opportunity to see where her newfound confidence could take her; the space to explore her friendship with Ben, free from suspicions; and the possibility of doing this away from the spotlight of her friends' and colleagues' opinions. But what did she want? And did her dearest wish have the potential to hurt her? Was she willing to take that risk?

For years all she had really wanted was to live out of her mother's shadow, to be in a place where she was known as Anna Browne, instead of 'Senara Browne's daughter'. She had never harboured particularly materialistic ambitions, and even though her new life in the city allowed her to build a home she was proud of, she still valued friendship and freedom over all else. Now that she had a job in which she was happy, a small but close group of friends and a life that felt like hers, not much remained unfulfilled.

Except . . . Anna had to concede that the parcels had been exciting and that their arrival had caused an itch, hidden way beneath the layers of contentment. She had enjoyed extraordinary generosity and had no right to wish for more. But she *did* wish for more – and felt the loss more keenly than she would tell anyone. For a while she

212

had experienced what it was like to be the centre of attention for the right reasons. And she had liked it immensely.

I can't think like this, she scolded herself, the hot tang of tea scalding her throat. *The experience was wonderful, but it's over now.*

As for Ben McAra, she resolved to put any suspicions to rest and simply enjoy spending time with him. The parcels had brought about their meeting, in a roundabout way, and this would be their lasting legacy in Anna's life: the final gift of a brief adventure she had loved. Wherever that led her next, she was keen to go.

Twenty-Five

If Anna thought her adventure was over, she was wrong.

The following Tuesday afternoon, a sixth parcel arrived. Anna had just returned from her lunch break and was checking the afternoon schedule when the sheepish smile of Narinder Rana appeared above her computer screen.

'Hey, Anna.'

'Hello.'

Her heart was racing and the building's glass-and-steel atrium seemed to wobble a little. Could this really be happening? The beautifully folded brown-paper covering and carefully omitted sender information suggested it was, and yet Anna could hardly believe it was real.

Narinder tapped the parcel as he laid it on the reception counter. 'So your guy came in again.' He shrugged a little, knowing that his previous claims had been rumbled and he had no more an idea of the sender than Anna did. 'I assume.'

'Ah, no sightings of shady blokes through the office

window this time, then?' When all was said and done, Anna couldn't be angry with the courier. He had seen an opportunity and taken it, and while at the time it had felt like an almighty waste of a Saturday evening, she had to admit the trouble he'd taken to date her had been flattering.

Realising she was joking, the courier's shoulders relaxed. 'Funnily enough, no. Sorry about . . . you know. Can't blame a fella for trying, eh?'

'You're forgiven. And thanks for the drink. I think I left without saying that.'

'Least I could do, given the circumstances. So, have you any idea who it's really from? The lads in the depot reckoned it was me sending them. They thought I'd roped one of my cousins into posing as a customer, so I could bring you parcels and score a date.' He shook his head. 'I mean, I won't lie: I was keen. But not enough to work that hard, just to ask a girl out. Who does that?'

Who, indeed?

Anna signed the delivery sheet and took the parcel in her hands. It was wide, flat and square, but surprisingly heavy, given its size and shape. Part of her wanted to run home and rip it open, but she still had half of her shift to complete and a set of prying eyes to quickly hide it from. The weeks since the last parcel's arrival had given her breathing space from the intrusive interest of Ted, Sheniece and half the *Messenger* employees. Anna wanted to keep it that way for as long as possible.

By the time Sheniece arrived back from her extended lunch break (caused by a queue in the bank, allegedly, although the thought of Sheniece queuing for anything

215

other than a club or a clothing sale was implausible at best), she was too abuzz with gossip to notice anything different about Anna.

'We are *so* in trouble,' she hissed, the urgency in her tone accentuated by the scrape of her acrylic nails as she gripped the edge of the reception desk. 'Kyle Chambers from the *Post* told me. Says the *Messenger*'s in trouble, and the whole of Fleet Street knows it. The rumour is they're looking for an emergency buyer. An *emergency*! That's never good news for our jobs, is it?'

'Calm down and think about it, Shen. A journalist from one of our biggest rivals tells you our paper's in trouble. Don't you think that's a little convenient?'

Sheniece jutted her chin out. 'He told me *off* the record, Anna! He was doing me a favour. Face it: we're never told anything here until it's already happening. Remember when they sold the New York office? Everyone had been handed pink slips before we found out about it. Forewarned is forearmed, in my opinion.'

Anna remembered the furore caused by that move, which happened practically overnight. She had learned about it by reading the *Metro* on the bus in to work. The *Messenger* lost several key employees following that, mostly editors shaken by the sudden exit of their transatlantic colleagues. 'I'm sure things aren't as bad as we're thinking here.'

'You say that now, but just you wait until—'

'Have you heard?' For a portly gentleman, Ted Blaskiewicz could move like a cheetah when fuelled by scandal.

'I *told* you this was happening! First the shareholders' meeting, now *this*.'

Anna stared at the puffing chief of security as he leaned against the reception desk. 'You've been talking with Mr Chambers too, I see?'

'Eh? No – what's Kyle Chambers been saying? I heard from Dave Draycott, security chief at the *Mail*. Everyone's saying it: the *Messenger*'s in deep trouble. Better start scouring the Positions Vacant pages, ladies. We could be jobless by Christmas.'

'You should ask your *new friend*, Anna.' The weight of Sheniece's implication was heavier than Ted's large belly. 'If anything's going on, I bet Ben McAra's all over it.'

Anna reddened. 'Well, I don't know what you mean . . .'

'We saw you. Yesterday morning. Me and Rea from the newsroom were walking past that new coffee place and there you both were, body language screaming through the windows at us. Don't give me that look, Anna Browne, you *know* what I'm talking about.'

'And you never told me?' Ted reddened at this revelation. 'Tsk, have I taught you *nothing* about news, girl?'

If it were possible to wither a human being using only the power of a stare, Ted Blaskiewicz would have melted like the Wicked Witch of the West in front of Sheniece at that moment. 'Nobody said you had to be the first port of call, Ted.'

His mouth flapping like a talkative goldfish, Ted pulled at the security badge on his uniform jacket. 'Head. Of. Security, Sheniece. It's my *job* to be informed of things like that – *immediately*.'

217

Anna's hopes of being relieved of her colleagues' scrutiny crumbled as the receptionist and security officer bickered over the pertinent details of her personal life. She left them to it, carrying a stack of post to the mailroom on the lower ground floor. Their discovery of her coffee-house meetings with Ben aside, the rumoured trouble that the *Daily Messenger* faced was worrying. This wasn't the first time it had been mentioned and, regardless of how much truth existed in the speculation, the number of people talking about it was surely a cause for concern. It was a tough time for any publication, what with more titles opting for digital-only editions and the well-documented fall in print sales. Rolling twenty-four-hour news and the speed of social media trumped newspapers time after time, as people simply weren't prepared to wait for a publication that would be out of date before it even hit the news-stands. But other national tabloids were just about keeping their heads above water: why should it be any different for the *Messenger*?

Anna hadn't feared for the future of her job before, but now the suggestion hung heavily over her. What would she do, if redundancies happened? She didn't relish the prospect of job-hunting: the endless hours of interviews and queues of identically qualified candidates were depressing in the extreme. Even if rumours of the *Messenger*'s days being numbered were exaggerated, they already knew a meeting had taken place to discuss the dreaded 'cost-cutting measures'. Currently reception had four full-time members of staff, one of whom covered the night shift and was more of a security guard than a receptionist. What happened if they decided only two staff members were necessary? Of the remaining three, Anna was the most senior, but also most expensive. If the *Messenger* wanted to save money, presenting the job to Sheniece or Ashraf would make better financial sense. Or they could simply add manning the reception desk to the existing security guards' remit and save even more money . . .

She pushed through the double doors to the small but busy mailroom and handed a stack of outgoing post left at reception to Vincent Allsop, the grey-haired, splendidly bearded veteran of the department who had worked there for as long as anyone could remember. There was a rumour that he had once trodden the boards in a travelling Shakespeare theatre company, but this was just as likely to be an urban myth supported by his deep baritone voice that reverberated through the *Messenger* building as it was to be true. Vincent's broad smile was more welcome today than usual.

'Ah, the lovely Miss Browne! How goes life in the great sparkling atrium?'

'Same as ever.' Anna was glad of the opportunity to talk about something else. 'You know what these newspaper types are like.'

'That I do, Anna, that I do.' He inspected the pile of letters and parcels, his nose wrinkling beneath the gold-rimmed glasses he wore. 'I see we have nothing exciting to report about these latest offerings, either. Ah well. We shall have to console ourselves with scandal and intrigue instead.' His green-grey eyes sparkled. 'So, do you think we are all to be turfed out on the street next week?'

By the time Anna arrived home at Walton Tower, her concern had become real. The only brightness in her afternoon of rumour, speculation and doom-laden forecasting was the new parcel, hidden from Ted's beady eyes in her handbag. Its promise had served as a reminder that life could surprise as well as ambush, and now all she wanted to do was lock herself away with it.

'You're in a hurry.'

Jonah was leaning against the doorframe of his front door, watching her as she approached along the corridor from the lift. Anna placed her hand protectively on her handbag and slowed her pace as she neared him.

'I've had one of those days,' she replied, feeling better for seeing his wry smile. 'I just need a cup of tea and a quiet night in.'

'There's plenty of tea at mine,' he suggested, nodding over his shoulder at the interior of his flat, which, like Jonah himself, was delightfully unkempt. Anna often pictured Jonah living in the midst of his own private hurricane, far too busy being whirled and spun by his life to worry about the tidiness of his environment. It gave him and his home a relaxed air and was something Anna liked immensely. There was no standing on ceremony with Jonah Rawdon: like the plain-talking Yorkshireman he was, what you saw was what you got. There was much to be said for the comfort of straightforwardness . . . 'Besides, I gave Bennett a bit of Thornton's toffee half an hour ago and he's still trying to lick it off his teeth. It's hilarious – you have to come and see.'

For a moment Anna was tempted – despite wondering if the sight of a dog tormented by toffee was a particularly ethical form of entertainment. It would be good to relax after the brooding conspiracies that had surrounded her day. But waiting in her bag was the sixth parcel – the one she never thought she would receive. To delay it any further would frustrate her just as much as the buttery confectionery was frustrating Jonah's canine companion.

'Would you mind if I didn't? I just need to be quiet for a while.'

Had it been Tish she was asking, the answer might have persuaded her to reconsider. But Jonah understood Anna's need for solitude, a topic on which they had often spoken. He required no further explanation.

'Gotcha. But, hey, my door's open if you need to chat later. I've a couple of days off before the next location job, so feel free to pop over any time.'

Alone at last, Anna let the excitement of the new parcel wash over her completely. What prompted its arrival – and why there had been such a hiatus between this and the previous parcel – suddenly weren't important. What mattered was that it was here and she could simply be excited about opening it.

Within the brown paper she found an old 78 r.p.m. record in a greying black-paper sleeve. The label in the middle of the ink-black shellac read:

'Ain't She Sweet'
(Music by Milton Ager, Words by Jack Yellen)
Harry Richman
Brunswick Records 1927

The record smelled of dust and time, the ridges cut into its glossy surface catching the light as she inspected it. Tucked inside the paper record sleeve was a cream envelope bearing Anna's name, a folded map and printed directions to an address in Notting Hill. With these items was a note, printed as the previous notes had been:

~ Anna ~
*Follow the map to a place where time stands still
and ask Alfie to help you hear the music.
(He'll be expecting you.)
This song is as true today as it ever was.*

The map and directions only indicated a street number in Cornwall Crescent, at the junction of St Mark's Road. Anna wasn't familiar with the area, save for the famous market on Portobello Road. She stared at the address. Was Cornwall Crescent a hint at her South-western roots, or pure coincidence? And who was Alfie?

She was already familiar with the song, if not the version on the record. It was a song Uncle Jabez used to sing to her and her cousin Elowen, when they played together on Sunday afternoons at her aunt and uncle's house in Looe. It didn't strike Anna as a song of great significance, being just a cute ditty about a girl whom the singer admires, but it did bring back a happy memory from her childhood: perhaps that was significant enough?

Anna was curious about following the directions, but was struck by a desire not to go alone. She was excited by what she might find and, now that her friends were fully aware of what was happening, she wanted to share the experience. But which of her friends should she ask to go with her? If she asked Tish, she would be subjected to an overblown lecture on the perils of going to strange places in the city. Tish believed every new corner of the metropolis harboured a waiting attacker and, given her tough New York upbringing in the depths of the Bronx, it wasn't difficult to see why.

There was only one person she could ask to help her.

But did she dare?

Twenty-Six

'It's a den of iniquity and Alfie is the heavily tattooed, multi-pierced ringleader . . .'

'In leafy Notting Hill?' Anna observed Jonah with a wry smile as the Underground train sped through the darkness towards West London.

'Ah, you mock, Anna, but think about it: where better to hide a house of ill repute than in the aspirational expensiveness of Richard Curtis country, hmm?'

She laughed. 'Jonah, stop it! I asked you to come with me because I thought you were the most sensible of my friends.'

'More fool you then,' Jonah smirked. 'Dafter than Bennett, I am. So,' his eyes narrowed as if anticipating her answer before he'd asked his question, 'they've started up again? The parcels?'

'Looks like it.' The return of the mystery packages had lifted her from the still-circulating speculation over the future of her employer, and she loved having something to smile about.

'Was there still no indication of a name in the parcel?'

'No clues at all. But I'm hoping this Alfie bloke knows something. The note says he's expecting my visit, which means he must have met the person who sent the record. It could be a roundabout way of revealing their identity.'

'You hope.'

'I do.'

'I still think Alfie will be a modern-day Bill Sikes. With his little white dog . . .' He ducked as Anna threw a well-read copy of the *Metro* at him. 'Okay, I'll stop now.'

'Thank you. And thank you for coming with me, Jonah. I don't think I would have done it alone.'

'My pleasure. I'm letting you buy me cake as my reward, of course. Just so you don't think I'm a soft touch.'

'I wouldn't have expected anything less.'

They joined the slow-moving crowd of tourists spilling out of Notting Hill Gate Tube station and turned up Pembridge Road, where the shop fronts became brighter, the shops more bespoke and their offerings quirkier. Buildings painted in candy colours lined the street as the surroundings became more familiar, captured in famous films and a million and one tourist photographs. The palette of pastel shades on the vintage stucco-covered buildings reminded Anna of a school trip she once took to Dartmouth – to her mother's utter disgust, *over the border* in neighbouring South Devon: 'What kind of heresy are they teaching kids at that school?' she had raged, on discovering the destination. 'I've half a mind to pull you and Ruari

225

out of there and teach you myself!' Thankfully she had never made good her threat, which might have had more to do with a brief, ill-advised fling with the school's married headmaster than any sensible rethink on her part.

They passed the sunflower-yellow exterior of The Sun in Splendour pub, which marked the beginning of Portobello Road, and watched most of the crowd around them heading off to sample the famous market's many delights. Anna promised Jonah they would return via the market to pick up huge slices of cake from Jonah's favourite stall. Cake could wait today; Anna's mystery mission could not.

Walking on through the heart of the exclusive London district, they arrived at last at Cornwall Crescent, which appeared to consist mostly of gorgeous townhouses far out of the price range of the average city-dweller. Anna checked the map and directions again while Jonah raised a hand to shield his eyes from the Saturday-afternoon sun to stare up the street.

'I suppose Alfie's house must be one of those,' Anna offered, feeling her stomach tighten. What if the address didn't exist, or if Alfie wasn't at home? There was no phone number to call ahead of her visit: how could the sender have been certain Alfie would be where he was supposed to be?

They wandered slowly around the crescent, stopping to peer at house numbers and then, just as Anna was about to give up, Jonah called out, 'There it is!'

Anna followed his pointing finger to see a shop wrapped around the corner between the crescent and the head of St Mark's Road. In contrast to the elegant residences on either side, the shop-front had been painted a deep burgundy, its windows filled with huge paper lanterns in bold primary colours and a selection of objects from the 1930s and 1940s. Outside, a couple of tables had been placed on the pavement, at which sat a man and a woman in impeccable Thirties outfits, the woman smoking a cigarette from a long, slender holder. It was as if a 1930s café had been transported through time to modern-day Notting Hill, coming to rest on the corner of two residential streets. Swing tunes drifted out from the shop and Anna couldn't help smiling as she and Jonah approached. The man at the table, in wide slacks with braces, a baggy white shirt and half-loosened tie, tipped his tweed trilby hat when they reached him.

'Lovely afternoon,' he said.

'It is . . .' Butterflies began to flutter in Anna's stomach. 'We're looking for Alfie?'

'Alfie?' The man exchanged a smile with his companion. 'Is he expecting you?'

Anna caught Jonah's smirk and discreetly elbowed him in the ribs. 'I think so.'

The woman stubbed out her cigarette. 'You'll find Alfie inside.'

Anna thanked them and, ignoring Jonah's whispered comment of 'Alfie is Al Capone! We're walking into a scene straight out of *The Untouchables*!', went up the steps at the entrance.

Inside, they found not only a café but a whole vintage store, filled with retro classics from huge Bakelite radios to furniture, stacks of old records, crockery and linens.

Authentic clothes hung on wooden rails around the walls, which were papered with sheets of old newspapers and pages from vintage magazines. Behind a glass counter beside a bulbous Frigidaire stood a tall, gangly man with jet-black, Brylcreemed hair, dressed almost identically to the smiling customer outside. His sea-blue eyes sparkled as he raised a hand in greeting.

'Hey, kids.'

'Hi – um . . . Alfie?' Anna held out her hand.

The man frowned. 'Sorry?'

We've made a mistake. This isn't him. Anna swallowed her rising panic and took another step towards the man, as Jonah followed suit. 'Are you Alfie? I have directions to meet Alfie, and I understand he's expecting me?' She held up the Harry Richman 78, by way of explanation. 'The man sitting outside said . . .'

The shop owner's expression became one of amusement, quickly transforming into a hearty laugh. 'Oh, so *you're* the girl. Anna Browne, right?'

He knew her name? 'Um, yes, but I don't understand. *Are* you Alfie?'

'Me? No, love, I'm Fred.' He shook her hand and Jonah's, and then reached across to pat the polished green-and-gold brass horn of a gramophone next to the glass food counter. '*This* is Alfie.'

Of course! Alfie would '*help you hear the music*'. It made perfect sense now.

Fred motioned for Anna to give him the record and placed it with great care on the antique gadget's turntable. The gramophone crackled into life and the undulating

228

strains of Harry Richman drifted into the shop. A customer browsing the racks of Forties dresses nodded appreciatively in time as 'Ain't She Sweet' played.

'Original, 1927 gramophone record,' Fred said, his eyes misting over a little, the way Jonah's did when talking about his latest bit of camera equipment. 'Gorgeous sound. Can't do that with an MP3 now, can you?' He studied Anna for a while. 'Know anything about this song, Anna?'

'Only that my uncle used to sing it to my cousin and me, when we were little.'

'Classic Tin Pan Alley tune. There's a story that Milton Ager composed it, inspired by his daughter Shana, but you don't want to believe everything Wikipedia tells you. It's someone who's proud of his girl and wants the world to agree. Sentiment like that never goes out of fashion.' Fred laughed again. 'Hark at me, eh? My wife would die laughing if she heard me getting all emotional over a song. I'd say my kids would disown me, too, if they knew, but they flew the nest years ago.'

He invited them to sit at one of the three tables in the shop while he made a pot of tea and brought over a plate of home-made scones with a jar of strawberry jam. 'There you go. On the house, that is. I had a bet with my business partner that you'd never show.'

As Jonah quickly descended on the unexpected afternoon tea, Fred pulled up a chair and sat next to Anna, who took a fortifying sip of hot tea and broached the question she hoped with all her heart the retro-shop owner could answer.

'Can I ask you about the person who told you to expect

me? They've been incredibly kind to me, but I don't know their name. Anything you can tell me would be a great help.' She noticed that Jonah had put down the scone half he was eating, leaning forward a little to hear Fred's reply.

Fred's shoulders rose in a shrug. 'Sorry, love. I never met the bloke.'

'So, it's definitely a man?' Anna glanced at Jonah, who raised an eyebrow.

'Well, I'm assuming it is, given the lyrics of that song.'

Anna felt the possibility of an answer slipping from her fingers. 'I don't understand . . .'

'Ah, got you on a bit of wild goose chase, has he?' Fred's expression softened. 'Look, all I know is that last Monday I got an email asking if the shop would be open this week and, if so, would I look out for a young woman called Anna Browne, who had an old 78 record she wanted Alfie to play. I replied to say that was fine, but never heard back. So Ernie – he owns this place with me – bet me fifty quid it was some idiot playing a prank.'

This amused Jonah no end. 'You have email? Whatever would your customers think?'

The shop owner chuckled. 'Don't worry, we keep the computer well hidden. Fact is, without the blasted Internet we wouldn't have any customers. It's the irony of the vintage market today: your goods have to be authentic, but if you aren't on the Internet or social media sites, people won't find you.'

'They didn't give a name? In the email, I mean.' She knew she was grasping at straws, but this was the closest she had come to meeting someone who'd had actual contact with the mystery gift-giver.

'Not apart from yours, love.'

The wind left Anna's sails as the last scraps of promise drifted away like a kite string let go in the breeze. She had been so sure that Alfie – or, as it turned out, Fred – would be able to give her more information on the parcel-sender. But now she had nothing more than another tantalising detail that meant nothing on its own. And then, as the stylus came to a scratching halt in the centre of the record, a tiny ray of hope emerged from the clouds in Anna's mind.

'Wait – could I see the email?'

'No problem. Follow me.'

Fred led Anna through the beaded curtain behind the counter to a small storeroom where a shiny aluminium laptop looked incredibly out of place amid boxes of vintage stock. He fiddled with the keys until the email screen appeared, stepping back to let Anna see. The email read as he'd described, and Anna scrolled upwards to the last place she could hope to find a clue: the sender line.

Her heart dropped like a rock in the sea:

Sender2006@me.mail.com

What kind of email address was that? Fighting the urge to cry, she thanked Fred and hurried back through to Jonah, who was enjoying a second cup of tea.

'Let's go,' she said, taking the record from the gramophone and slipping it back into its sleeve, not daring to look him in the eyes.

'What's up?'

Now she was pulling at his elbow, lifting his arm and his cup away from his lips. '*Please*, Jonah . . .'

'Can a chap not finish his tea?' he complained, but Anna was already urging him out of the shop and onto the street.

All she wanted to do was run home as soon as she could, hurt and disappointment crowding in on her as she hurried down Cornwall Crescent, away from the shop and the owner and the stupid old gramophone . . . *Who names a gramophone 'Alfie', anyway?*

It was only when Jonah caught her sleeve, yanking her to a halt, that Anna turned to look at him, burgeoning tears on the verge of completing her embarrassment.

'Anna, stop! What happened in there? Did he do something to you? If he did, I'll—'

'No, it wasn't anything like that. It's – *nothing* . . .' How could she explain to Jonah how she felt? None of it made sense. It *was* nothing, when you looked at it. She had hung her hopes on a possibility so gossamer thin that it would never have held any weight. It mattered to her to know who the sender was, and what had just happened confirmed that beyond doubt. How was she ever going to know, if even the most promising clues led to dead-ends?

Jonah's hand was warm on her arm, eyes full of concern. 'Something obviously upset you. Talk to me. I can't help if I don't know what's up.'

'You can't help, Jonah.' Her sigh echoed around the elegant stillness of the street. 'I hoped the email address on the message would give me a name.'

Jonah frowned. 'And?'

' . . . "*Sender2006 at me-dot-mail-dot-com.*" It's hopeless!'

'No, it isn't.'

'I thought Alfie could help me. He couldn't – because he was an inanimate object and I'm an idiot for not guessing that. I thought the shop owner would know who sent me the parcel, but he didn't know anything. And even the stupid email address was no help to me. I don't have a name. I don't know who's sending me things. So tell me, *why* isn't this whole thing hopeless?'

Jonah moved his hand from Anna's elbow, raising it to brush a tear from her cheek. It was a small, deliberate movement that instantly brought Morwenna's hands to Anna's mind and opened the floodgates. As she crumpled against her friend's broad chest, his heart beating comfortingly against her ear, she finally let go of the frustration that had been steadily building with the lack of – and the sudden return of – the parcels.

Jonah held her until her tears began to subside and her breathing returned to normal. Then, as she stepped back from him, flushed from the display of emotion and unexpected physical contact, she saw his hesitant smile.

'It *isn't* hopeless, Anna. You have a contact now. You can email whoever it is and say thank you – ask your questions, demand a name. If . . . *if* that's what you want?'

Anna stared up at the Yorkshireman's soothing grey eyes. 'It is.'

'Only I thought you said you weren't interested in

233

finding out who they are? That the gifts were more important than who sent them.'

I did say that, didn't I, in the beginning?

So much had changed since the initial surprise of the gifts. Now she cared about who it was – because she wanted to know *why*. 'It's different. Now I want to know: who they are, why they chose me, what they hoped the parcels would achieve – all of it.'

'Does it matter?'

'It matters to me.'

'Then send them an email. And demand answers.'

I will, Anna promised herself as she and Jonah wandered back towards Portobello Road, her friend unusually quiet as he walked by her side. *I'll do it tonight.*

Twenty-Seven

FROM: AnnaBrowne8@gmail.com
TO: Sender2006@me.mail.com
SUBJECT: Thank you so much!

Anna's brow furrowed. That was wrong. Too friendly.

SUBJECT: Parcels

That didn't work, either. Too businesslike. She let out a
sigh. It had taken her the better part of an hour to get
this far: how long could one email conceivably take to
write? Perhaps she was overthinking this. There had to be
a simpler way . . .

SUBJECT: Alfie says hello!

Who was she talking to, a seven-year-old? Tired and
annoyed, she pushed her chair back from the dining table

and walked stiffly to the kitchen for a glass of water. The blank email form glowed accusingly at her across the living room.

This should be easy. Say hello, thank them for the gifts and ask for their name. It's hardly rocket science.

So why did every word seem weighted with importance?

The blue digital-clock display on her oven winked *11.49 p.m.* at her repeatedly. It was too late to call anyone, even Jonah, who had an early start for his next filming assignment in the morning. Not that he'd specifically offered his help this time, which Anna found odd, considering his enthusiasm for seeking out Alfie earlier today. In fact he had spoken very little on their way back to Walton Tower, receiving Anna's thanks in the corridor outside their apartments with a muttered 'No problem', and walking to his door without looking back. Had he been embarrassed by Anna's outburst? Even now, hours afterwards, she wished Jonah hadn't seen her cry. Was it a step too far in their friendship – or the embrace that followed? Perhaps he wished that hadn't happened, too?

A heavy sense of unease settled over her, as unwilling to leave her mind as the frustratingly blank email form on her computer. The parcel's arrival had been so welcome, so exhilarating after the weeks without: how had that suddenly changed? While the thought behind the old record and the trip to the vintage shop had been well meant, what did it achieve? Like all her gifts to date, what did it mean? Instead of an adventure, the parcels were leading her up dead-end alleys; and, for the first time, Anna found herself wondering if the mysterious gifts were a good thing for her. All she wanted was a quiet life. She liked the changes she had seen in herself, but perhaps they were enough for now. The *not knowing* and her building frustration weren't fun at all.

It was late and she knew she wouldn't be able to sleep until she'd sent her message. *I'm thinking about this too much. I'm just going to send the email and stop worrying . . .*

FROM: AnnaBrowne8@gmail.com
TO: Sender2006@me.mail.com
SUBJECT: Hello

I'd like to thank you for the very kind and thoughtful gifts you have sent me. I don't know who you are, or why you decided to give me these things, but I want you to know that they have meant a great deal.

I don't understand why you haven't given your name, but I suppose you have your reasons for doing this. I'd like to be able to thank you in person – is that something you would be happy to do? If so, you know where I work already, and now you have my email address. If not, thank you for your generosity and for thinking of me.

I hope to hear from you soon.
Best wishes
Anna Browne

Satisfied, she sat back in her chair. Asking the sender to meet her in person was a bold move, especially for her.

But she *had* to know. Maybe her invitation would persuade whoever it was to come forward. Maybe then her questions would be answered and she could get on with her life. Until the mystery was solved, she was stuck. It scared her, but it was the only way.

Taking a deep breath, she hit Send.

Twenty-Eight

Juliet Evans was not a woman to be trifled with. Not by anybody – and least of all by some jumped-up businessman playing newspapers on the Board of DayBreak Corp, owner of the *Daily Messenger*. She glanced around her large top-floor office, with its wraparound view of the city skyline and huge glass desk. When she had first assumed ownership of this room she had felt like the world was literally at her feet. This morning she felt the city calling for her to jump.

The stack of flattened boxes against her desk needed to be filled, to escort her down the corridor to the former deputy editor's office. Since Bev Holder had been promoted in a blaze of glory to editor-in-chief of the *Daily Post* – the *Messenger*'s biggest rival – the office had remained empty. Now Juliet's name had been hastily stuck to its door. *I taught that woman everything she knows*, Juliet glowered, throwing a handful of papers into a box and already wishing she'd had coffee before embarking on this joyless task. *She's brilliant – but so am I. So much for gratitude . . .*

But gratitude was in short supply in this building. Never mind that she had worked impossible hours against mountainous odds to turn the paper into one of the Big Four nationally. Never mind that she had single-handedly launched the careers of many of Britain's brightest and boldest journalists. None of that carried any weight against the measure of the mighty buck. The bottom line was always money.

She would never get this done before eleven. Her two assistants were busy briefing the team on the imminent arrival of Damien Kendal – the crass, overfed, ego-inflated Board director whose gargantuan backside would soon be irrevocably denting the expensive Italian leather of Juliet's office chair. Clearly, she needed help. She could make a call from her desk phone (while it remained hers), but the sight of her beloved office in disarray was too much. She needed to be away from it. Discarding the half-filled box of papers, she grabbed her handbag and headed for the lift.

Any of the interns or assistants close to Juliet, or working in the newsroom, would be likely to add fuel to the whispered wildfires of gossip already spreading through the building. Juliet needed someone she could trust. The person she had in mind to help her was where she should be, thank heaven, smiling behind the desk at reception. The two junior receptionists were alongside her, which meant that Anna Browne could be spared for the morning.

Excellent, Juliet thought. Perhaps today wouldn't be a complete disaster after all.

'So?'

Sheniece and Ashraf flanked Anna like a pair of demanding meerkats. Anna marvelled at how quickly the latest addition to the reception team had been brought up to speed on the happenings in her life. Ashraf, it had quickly become apparent, was as much a purveyor of quality gossip as Sheniece and Ted, and almost as fast at sniffing it out.

Anna gritted her teeth into a smile. She didn't need a day of interrogation after the sleepless weekend she'd endured. 'I'm not talking about it, okay?'

'He never replied!' Ashraf clamped a hand to his heart as Sheniece shook her head.

'I didn't say that.'

'You didn't need to, babe. It's all over your face. Are you all right, Anna? I mean, *rejection* is a hard burden to bear . . .'

'Shut up, Ash! She doesn't want to be reminded of it, does she? I mean, when my Steve did the dirty on me and disappeared, I was mortified for *weeks* . . .'

Ashraf frowned. 'Which one was Steve again?'

'The footballer.'

'I thought that was Darren?'

'Oh. My. Gosh. Ash, I swear you never listen to me. Steve was the one with the dodgy kneecaps? Supposed to sign for Dagenham and Redbridge, but left after a season on loan to another club? I *told* you about him.'

'So what happened to Darren?'

'That's a story for sharing only when I have a large gin in my hand, Ash . . .' Something caught Sheniece's eye and she quickly straightened her jacket. 'Quick, look efficient – the Dragon's coming!'

Anna looked over to the far end of the atrium, where Juliet Evans was marching from the lift. It occurred to her that the *Messenger*'s editor always appeared to be sailing a few feet from the ground, as if propelled by the force of a wave. Juliet carried the air of someone who expected the world to turn on her bidding, and walls to crumble in her path. Ordinarily Anna would have been in awe of her. This morning, however, she was simply glad of the interruption to her unwanted questioning that the powerful editor's arrival brought.

'Anna,' Juliet stated rather than asked, the briefest of smiles gone as soon as it had appeared. 'I have a job for you. Follow me.'

Without pausing for her reply, Juliet turned on her Louboutin heels and headed back across the atrium floor. Anna scrambled from behind reception and followed, quickly tucking the stray strands of her hair back into her ponytail as she ran.

The lift was impossibly quiet as it rose to the top floor. Juliet said nothing and Anna felt as if the sound of her thudding heart was reverberating around the glass walls. She was nervous of what lay in store for her, but it was good to be away from reception. She didn't want to pick over the details of the email she'd sent – or the radio silence that followed – any further with her colleagues. She already felt bad enough about it. After the hours spent

242

agonising over the right mix of words, it had all been a waste of time.

And why had Anna expected any different? If the parcel-sender had wanted her to know their identity, they would have already provided their name. That they hadn't, and that her email had been ignored, should come as no surprise.

And yet, she had hoped for more. None of it made any sense.

The lift doors slid open to reveal the deep-piled cream carpet of the top floor. Anna could feel her heels sinking satisfactorily into it as she followed Juliet to her executive office – the one with the breathtaking view that everyone in the building wished they had. As she reached the doorway, her heart dropped when she saw the cardboard boxes and half-packed book crates.

'Are you . . . ?' Realising she was speaking out of turn, Anna stopped. 'I'm sorry. What would you like me to do?'

Juliet raised an eyebrow. 'Oh, don't worry, they won't get rid of me that easily. I've just –' she cleared her throat, '– *elected* to take Bev Holder's office down the hall, for a while. Damien Kendal from the DayBreak Corp Board will be occupying this one for the time being. Don't look concerned. I know what they're trying to do. He's been sent to "keep an eye" on me. It's happened before: I'm not intimidated. Besides, a change of scene is always good for the mind. This view can get a little old, you know.'

Anna couldn't believe that – and the sight of the all-powerful editor packing her belongings into cardboard boxes was alarming. What if Ted had been right all along?

What if Kyle Chambers from the *Post* was simply relaying the truth about the *Messenger*'s fate? Why would anyone dare to keep tabs on Juliet Evans – and was it a precursor to worse news? She was so synonymous with the newspaper now that her leaving would be tantamount to the ravens deserting the Tower of London. And what did this mean for Anna's own job security?

Juliet was observing her from the other side of the great glass desk. 'I need you to help me put the papers, books and equipment I've collected here into these boxes and carry them down to the other office, please. Think you can handle that?'

Pushing her concerns to the back of her mind, Anna managed to smile. 'Of course.'

'Then we'd better get started. Must be done by eleven.'

They worked for an hour, not speaking, the task at hand commanding their attention. A couple of times Anna wondered if she should make polite small talk, but what did you say to a woman who had made her fortune from the most important news stories across the world? Juliet was about as inclined to chat as Ted was to keep a secret. Anna had remarked on it to Ben that morning in Freya & Georgie's, when the subject of their boss had arisen.

'She's a pussycat,' he'd insisted.

'She's terrifying. I can't imagine she ever relaxes.'

'Oh, I've seen the old Dragon kick back once or twice,' Ben had smiled.

'I don't believe you.'

'Believe what you like. Juliet Evans keeps her cards very

close to her chest, but there's more to her than most people think. They only see the power. I see the woman.'

The memory of Ben's headline-style summation of his boss made Anna smile now, as she carried the last of the heavy book crates filled with files to Juliet's temporary office. There was no doubt he was a tabloid journalist to the core: lines as cheesy as that took years to perfect. He had admitted his shame over what he'd said when Anna almost choked on her coffee laughing, but his response had only made her like him more. She wished she had told him about the record and her email, but he had so carefully avoided the subject that she didn't want to raise it with him. What would he think if he knew the parcels had started again, or that she had tried to contact the sender for the first time? She hoped he wouldn't care about it. Believing that Ben McAra was interested in her for her own sake was wonderful: she didn't want to change that.

'I think that's everything,' Anna said, returning to the ominously empty executive suite.

Juliet was staring out across the city as if attempting to burn the view into her mind. She turned. 'Excellent.'

Unsure what to do next, Anna waited in the doorway.

As if snapping out of a trance, Juliet nodded. 'Thank you. You've been a great help.'

'My pleasure.'

'Needless to say I'm relying on your discretion about what you've seen here.' It wasn't a question.

Anna nodded. 'Of course. I won't say anything.' Taking Juliet's non-reply as her cue to leave, she took a step back, but froze when Juliet raised her hand.

'Are you happy here?'

The question hit Anna squarely. 'Excuse me?'

The editor rounded the desk and perched on the end of it. 'It's a simple enough question, Miss Browne.'

'Oh . . . sorry . . . Yes, I'm very happy here.' *Please don't fire me. I need this job.*

'I was impressed by your suggestion in our editorial meeting while you were shadowing Ben.'

'Um, thank you.' The muscles along Anna's shoulders tensed.

'Look, I've been in this business more years than I care to count and I've learned to value talent wherever I find it. There's a great deal more to you than you think, Anna. You should think about that.'

Where was this leading? Anna shifted her feet uncomfortably on the too-soft luxury carpet and tried to think of a suitable response.

'I got to where I am today by taking risks. You took a risk in that meeting – and if what I hear from the newsroom is to be believed, it was your quick thinking that saved the Vanessa Milburn exclusive. I value that.' She rubbed a finger along her chin and sighed, her eyes drifting back to the view of London's skyline that in ten minutes wouldn't belong to her. 'What I'm trying to say is that I saw what you did. It took guts and I like that in a person. Keep taking risks, Ms Browne. Your life will be all the better for it.'

'Oh. I'll do my best to.' The last thing Anna expected when Juliet requested her help this morning was life advice. To hear it from a woman who clearly found it difficult to give compliments made the advice even stranger. She knew she should be flattered, but the situation made her feel uneasy.

There was a pause as the two women faced each other. With a disinterested smile, Juliet waved her hand. 'You can go now.'

Anna was down the corridor and almost at the lift before the door to Juliet's former office shut.

'I don't think it's anything to worry about.' Jonah threw a handful of mixed seeds to the rabble of swans and ducks at the water's edge.

'Then why mention it at all? It was just *odd*.'

Jonah chuckled. 'Classic boss behaviour, that's all it is. Make out you're the great, omnipotent, omnipresent entity who knows everything. Keeps the little people in line and the business rivals at bay. Every director I've ever worked for has it. God-complex, every one of them. I wouldn't worry.'

But Anna was worried. So worried that she had arrived at Jonah's door after work that day, needing to talk about it. The more she'd considered Juliet's words, the more she'd convinced herself that 'taking risks' was a round-about way of warning her that her remaining time at the *Daily Messenger* was short. Seeing how upset she was, Jonah had suggested they head to Loveage Gardens and 'consult the oracles' – in this case, the collected waterfowl that graced the park's modestly sized lake. He brought a large bag of wild bird food – 'as an offering' – and while

Bennett dashed after a tennis ball, they fed the seed mix to the birds and talked.

'I can't help feeling she was trying to tell me something.'

'She was. That you're capable of more than you think you are. I could've told you that – anyone could.'

'No, something bad.'

'It's an endorsement, sweetheart, not a harbinger of doom. Only you could take a bit of advice and turn it into a P45.' He cast a glance at her from beneath the brim of his butterscotch-brown beanie hat. 'This is about that email, isn't it?'

Anna didn't bother to deny it. 'I don't understand why they didn't reply.'

'Maybe it wasn't the right time. Maybe it wasn't their usual email address. You'll drive yourself mad going over it, when there's no answers yet.'

Kicking at a stone, Anna sighed. 'Will there ever be?'

'I wish I could tell you. But this I know: whoever sent you those things did it because they wanted to make you happy. And they have, haven't they – I mean, aside from the most recent development? Part of the reason you're upset now is that it matters to you, doesn't it?'

'Yes.'

His smile was reassuring. 'Then I'm sure you'll have your answers soon.'

Twenty-Nine

Sheniece Wilson wasn't often jealous of people – unless they had a handbag, shoes or a boyfriend she wanted. But even then it wasn't the deep-seated, gnawing jealousy that ate away at your insides until you had to do something about it. She had only experienced that on two occasions in her life so far.

And this was one of them.

It wasn't the parcels her colleague was receiving that caused it, although they had certainly brightened her working week lately. Nor was it that the gifts were quality items (apart from the mangy old record: why anyone thought *that* was a good present was beyond her). The reason for the biting, churning jealousy assaulting Sheniece Wilson's insides was the recipient herself.

Anna Browne.

Sheniece had liked her from the moment they met, Anna's friendliness and sense of humour immediately appealing. She was a non-threatening presence, unlike many of the women Sheniece had worked with in previous jobs. There wasn't a hint of competition between them – Anna's personal style and choice of men differing greatly from her own. Sheniece liked that. Maintaining the upper hand with workmates could be exhausting.

But Anna Browne had something Sheniece coveted more than anything else: a good reputation. It was the one thing that had eluded her all her life, yet Anna had it without knowing.

Sheniece didn't set out to ruffle feathers or create a name for herself. But things just *happened* that way. Growing up as the eldest of five children in a council house designed for two people had been hard enough; being the unofficial third parent in the family caused irreparable rifts between her and her siblings. Neither a kid nor a grown-up, she'd existed in a strange limbo between the two, being the target of abuse from both sides. When Social Services threatened to separate the family, it had fallen to sixteen-year-old Sheniece to hold it all together, her parents being too busy drinking themselves into oblivion to notice. She should have been recognised for her actions, but instead she was looked down on, patronised and hated from all sides of her family. Craving the attention her parents never gave, she set out to gain favour amongst the shaven-headed, over-sexed young men on her estate, who were only too happy to assist her.

Despite her extracurricular activities (of being an un-official carer and an official bedroom legend), Sheniece did well at school, moving on to college and away from the rhetoric of the estate. She moved in higher circles, dating more successful men with equally liberal views on sex. She did well for herself – good job, good flat, regular holidays and occasionally semi-famous boyfriends – but a good reputation never followed.

Respect for Anna Browne was spreading through the *Messenger* building. She was kind-hearted and fun to be around, but now there was something else, too. She seemed to have found a new confident attitude that wasn't pushy or brass or loud (accusations Sheniece often faced). She was *queenly* – there was no other word for it. Like Grace Kelly mixed with Beyoncé. Sheniece envied that more than anything. Ben McAra had definitely noticed – and while Sheniece wasn't interested in the reporter, she envied the way he and Anna had looked together, when she and Rea had seen them in Freya & Georgie's. Ben couldn't keep his eyes from hers, his expression that of a child let loose in a sweet shop. People at work were noticing Anna, too: even the great Juliet Evans, who walked with her nose so high in the air she barely acknowledged anyone's existence but her own.

I want to be like that, Sheniece thought, watching Anna laughing with a gaggle of journalists at reception, who all seemed fascinated by her. *Maybe, if I stick close to Anna Browne, some of what she's got will rub off on me.*

'Parcel for Anna Browne?'

The courier was new, his uniform a different colour from the one Narinder and the CityServe couriers wore.

Anna felt the weight of Sheniece's stare on her as she signed for the parcel. 'Thank you. Um, which courier company are you from?'

The courier observed her with disdain. 'Xpress Direct. We don't deliver much to this street.' Without a goodbye, he walked away.

'Great customer service there.' Sheniece sniffed, peering at the delivery. 'Whoa, Anna, your chap must have been in a hurry.'

This parcel appeared to have been wrapped during a hurricane, its roughly cut edges uneven and badly taped. The contents rattled, and Anna half-wondered if the gift might have broken in transit. Certainly the courier's disinterest for his job suggested he didn't much care what state the packages arrived in. In contrast to the previous parcels, the sender information box had been filled with a single word, handwritten in slanting, primitive capital letters:

LONDON

'I suppose that's something . . .' Anna's stomach was heavy, as though filled with a spade's worth of shingle. She had hoped for another parcel to take away the disappointment of the previous delivery; but, if anything, the new arrival made her feel worse.

Sheniece tugged at her sleeve. 'Open it.'

'I think I'll wait.'

'Oh, go on, Anna! I'd just like to see you open one parcel, that's all. And this one's so badly stuck together it's practically unwrapping itself.'

She should have waited until she got home. She *should* have refused, as she had every time before. But this time

252

Anna's curiosity wasn't going to let her wait until the end of the day. 'Fine. But just this one, okay?'

Her colleague squeaked and clapped her hands together like an over-excited American cheerleader. 'Do it, do it!'

'What's she doing?' As if from thin air, the *Messenger*'s chief of security materialised, accompanied by Rea from the newsroom and two young people Anna only recognised as part of the latest intake of interns.

She had not anticipated a crowd, but it was too late to change her mind now. With all eyes on her, she began to unwrap the parcel . . .

'I reckon it's jewellery,' one of the interns said, instantly shushed by another.

'She's had that already,' Sheniece replied, nodding as one in possession of superior knowledge. 'A brooch and a necklace. He'd be dumb to repeat that.'

Rea clamped a hand to her heart. 'Could be a *ring*, though. Imagine that! A proposal in a parcel, for the woman he's wooed through couriers!'

Ted and the male intern laughed, but Sheniece silenced them by raising her hand. 'No, Rea has a point. Maybe the bad wrapping on this one was because he was in a hurry *and* nervous about the proposal!'

'Bit pointless him proposing, when Anna doesn't know him from Adam.' Ted shook his head. 'I still think it's a severed limb . . .'

His gruesome suggestion was met by a chorus of 'eeuuww's, some onlookers visibly shuddering while others mimed being sick.

'A severed limb that *rattles*?' Sheniece raised a pitying eyebrow.

'Could be,' Ted insisted. 'Could be sticking-out *bones* . . .'

Anna had heard enough. Gathering the half-unwrapped parcel and paper up, she faced them. 'If that's the kind of conversation you want to have, I'm going to open this somewhere else.'

'No, Anna, don't!' Rea pleaded. 'Ignore Ted. He's a *psycho* . . .'

'*I'm* the psycho? You should throw that accusation to the chap sending Anna dodgy parcels, girl!'

'Please, Anna?' Sheniece's hand on Anna's arm made her stop. 'Just one parcel and then I'll never ask again. Promise.'

With a sigh, Anna returned the parcel to the desk and pulled away the ragged-edged brown paper.

Inside was a plain white cardboard box. There was no ribbon or aroma, just a small square of sticky tape that appeared to have been bitten off the roll and stuck on at an impatient angle. It took the top layer of cardboard from the box as Anna peeled it off. Carefully, she lifted the lid.

There was a rumble of discontent around her as the contents were revealed. No tissue paper surrounded them, just a transparent ziplock plastic bag, which looked suspiciously like a sandwich bag. Instead of containing the selection of shells and sea-glass beads inside the box, it had been laid on top of them like a blanket. Each of the shells had been drilled with a small hole and the sea-glass beads were looped with thin silver jewellers' wire, with a small silver hanging ring attached to each one. A length of narrow black leather thong had been wound into a circle secured by an equally dog-eared scrap of tape. In the bottom of the box was a rectangle of white card, upon which was typed:

Make of this what you will
xx

'He's slipping.' Sheniece's disgust was immediate.

Rea, searching for positives, gave Anna a weak smile. 'At least he put kisses?'

'I thought you said the parcels were amazing?' an intern whispered to Rea, loud enough for everyone to hear.

One by one the onlookers quietly dispersed, no doubt in a hurry to share the latest instalment of the Anna Browne parcel story with anyone who would listen. Only Ted and Sheniece remained, as Anna stared at the box's contents.

'He was bound to run out of ideas sometime,' Sheniece offered, glancing at Ted for support. 'I mean, that dodgy old record and map-thing last time were pretty lame.'

No matter how long Anna regarded the gift, she couldn't make out the reasoning behind it. The shells and sea-glass beads were pretty in their own way, but what *was* she supposed to 'make of' them? She had never been what she would call a 'crafty' person. Weaving daisy chains with Grandma Morwenna had been the closest she'd come to making anything – and now she was grown-up she preferred to buy beautifully crafted items rather than make them herself. So why would the sender think this gift suited her?

She pondered this throughout the day without finding answers. When the bus dropped her outside Walton Tower, she headed to the floor below hers instead of going home. Another pair of eyes was required to help her see what had been invisible to her.

Tish sucked a mouthful of air through her veneers. 'This is disappointing. But I guess there's only so much imagination a guy can have. Soon it'll be IOUs and gift certificates.'

'It is as bad as I thought, isn't it?' Anna had hoped her straight-talking friend might be able to offer a ray of hope. Her shoulders dropping, she slumped into the dragging squashiness of Tish's oversized sofa and wished she hadn't opened the parcel at work. 'Do I look like a crafty person?'

Tish's expression clouded. 'You couldn't be devious if you tried. But what does that have to do with the beads?'

'What I mean is that I've never been a creative person. I like handmade things, but I've never wanted to make them myself. I don't know what to do with these shells and beads.'

'I guess you're meant to thread them onto the leather string. Weird that there's no instructions.'

'Other than "Make of this what you will".' Anna groaned. 'The worst of it is that I chose to open this one at work. And now everyone is talking about how disappointing the parcel was to open – at least, if Ted is to be believed.'

'You just wanted to share it with your workmates, Anna. It was a sweet thought.'

'But this parcel doesn't fit the profile of the others. And I don't ever want to sound ungrateful, but I'm beginning to wish the sender hadn't bothered.' It was a dreadful admission, but after hours of confusion over the parcel, this was the feeling she had been left with.

Until today, Anna had liked the changes wrought in her by each new gift. But this parcel had unearthed an emotion that she didn't like. She had never considered herself ungrateful before despite the accusation being repeatedly levelled at her by Senara over the years. And yet, she felt it now: a churning, razor-edged disquiet within her that refused to leave. Why had the sender wrapped the parcel so badly, when every other present had been given such painstaking attention to detail? Why had a different courier delivered it this morning? And why did they expect her to make her own gift?

And then a thought occurred to her. 'Tish, you don't think they're annoyed I tried to contact them, do you? Was this parcel meant to show me I'd upset them?' Even as the words came out, they sounded preposterous. But what else was she supposed to think?

Tish was noncommittal. 'Who knows? Maybe just take this one as a slip-up, and hope the guy smartens his act next time . . .'

The answer did nothing to reassure Anna.

That evening, the contents of the box spread out across her dining table, she looked again at the note:

Make of this what you will
xx

The shells and sea-glass beads told her nothing. Frustrated, Anna pushed them away and cradled her head in her hands. If there were answers to be found, they hadn't been included in this delivery. From feeling on the verge of solving the mystery, she was now further away than she had ever been. She would have to wait for the sender's next move – if there was one . . .

Thirty

For the next week a stubborn bank of rain lodged itself over the city, magnifying its greyness with unrelenting gloom. Sheets of water lashed down, turning the pavements into leaden glass and the roads into car parks – journeys halted by the inclement conditions. Famous red double-decker buses dragged through congested streets in a sea of stationary black cabs, a slow-moving slash of scarlet in the unremitting monochrome. It seemed to mirror Anna's mood, which had not been improved by seven days of mulling over her latest parcel. This morning the bus ride into work was slower than ever, its driver making no attempt to disguise his frustration with the traffic or his bad-tempered passengers.

'Thirty-five minutes we waited for you,' a sour-faced woman snarled at him as she flashed her Oyster card like a middle finger. 'Call this service?'

'You want I should make this bus fly?' he snapped back,

his Eastern European accent deepened by anger. 'You don't like it, lady? Then *walk*.'

By the time the bus arrived at the stop outside Freya & Georgie's Anna barely had enough time to grab a take-away cup before work. Ben was waiting by the counter, checking his watch, when Anna hurried inside, brushing rain from her coat sleeves.

'You made it!' he grinned, a sight even more welcoming to Anna than the large coffee cup he held out to her. 'I took the liberty of ordering for you, given the time. Hope you don't mind?'

'Not in the slightest.' Anna glanced at her watch. 'I have to be on reception in twenty minutes.'

Ben indicated the bar stools in the window. 'So, sit with me for ten?'

On any other day Anna would have headed straight to the *Messenger* building, not wanting to risk being late, but today she needed a friend. The rumours surrounding her most recent parcel had raged around the floors at work, causing her to answer a torrent of questions as unremitting as the rain that pounded the streets of the city. She was tired of being the centre of attention – and at least with Ben she knew she was safe from questions that she had no answers for.

'You look tired,' he observed, taking the lid off his coffee cup and stirring in two packets of brown sugar.

'I feel tired. I think it's this weather. It's so depressing – it's meant to be summer, for heaven's sake, not winter.'

'Unfortunately, nobody's told the clouds that. Still, it adds to efficiency at work. Nobody's interested in extended

260

lunch breaks when they have to dodge the rain. I've never seen the interns in the newsroom so keen to work in-house before. Usually they're begging me to take them out on assignment. Not this week.' He smiled and then, without warning or invitation, took hold of Anna's hand.

Surprised, Anna looked down, but she didn't pull away The sight of Ben's fingers cradling hers was beautiful – and in that moment she forgot the parcel and the questions and her own dark mood. None of it mattered. The warmth of his skin against hers made her aware of her own heart-beat; and when she raised her eyes to his, she realised she was smiling.

'Is this – okay?' he asked, his tone low and uncertain.
'Yes. It is.'

For a while neither spoke, their smiles and touch surrounded by the noise and activity of the coffee house. Anna was pleased by the silence between them, because at that precise moment words failed her. She saw neither the rain pelting on the window nor the second hand on the clock above the counter, marking the time passing. All she could think about was Ben. She wanted to tell him what this meant to her, what *he* had come to mean to her as they had talked here for weeks. Had she found the words she was searching for, she could have expressed how *this* moment was more profound, more heartfelt and more of a gift than any of her mystery parcels – and how differently he made her feel about her own life . . .

And then Ben spoke. 'I want to ask you something, but I'm not sure how you'll react.'

Anything, Ben. Ask me anything . . . 'Go ahead.'

261

Was this what she thought it might be? Did he feel the attraction between them, too? Anna held her breath and waited for his reply.

'The last parcel upset you, didn't it?'

For a moment Anna wavered, her thoughts everywhere and nowhere at once. She saw Ben's smile fade away and realised she had snatched her hand from his. The last words he had spoken replayed in her mind, a scrambled anagram that wouldn't let her solve it.

'What did you say?'

'The shells and the beads . . . ?' He had moved away from her a little, his tone cautious.

'I know what was in it.' The sharpness of her reply surprised her more than him.

'Of course . . . I – I just wanted to say I'm sorry you didn't like it.'

Why would Ben McAra be sorry? Unless . . .

'Did you send it?' The question was immediate, and for once Anna didn't pause to consider whether she should be asking. 'Were the parcels from you?' She had relied on Ben being the only person who didn't want to know about them, but his question changed everything. 'Have you been sending them?'

His eyes widened and Anna couldn't make out if it was guilt at his secret being revealed or shock that she would even accuse him. He caught her coat sleeve as she made to leave. 'Please, Anna, just listen. I didn't mean to freak you out. I know I haven't asked before. It's just . . .' His eyes darted left and right across the wooden countertop as if he might find the right words etched in its polished grain. 'People were talking about it this week: about how you opened the parcel with an audience, and how you've been quiet ever since. And – I don't know – I wanted to check you're all right. The other gifts were so kind and genuine . . .'

So Ben knew it all. Anna kicked herself for not guessing he would be on top of the *Messenger* gossip. Of course he would be: it was his job to know what was happening. 'I'm fine.'

'Are you?'

Anna stared at him. Why did he care? Wasn't the office gossip enough?

'You don't look fine to me. I've watched you on reception since that parcel arrived and you looked so different. I miss your smile, Anna, and I think you do, too. I realise it's none of my business, even if half of the *Daily Messenger* staff seem to think what's happening to you is public property. And the irony of a tabloid journalist making that statement is not lost on me. I think this parcel was a blip. I believe the next one will be better. *Far* better. Listen, what I'm saying is that I'm here if you'd like to talk about it – or *not* talk about it?' His eyes drifted to the rain-battered street. 'That's all I wanted to say.'

She had been blindsided by Ben's question, but what he'd said struck a chord. After the disappointing seventh parcel, everyone around her had returned to their favoured pessimistic theories about the sender. It was definitely a man, Sheniece and her friends claimed, because men always defaulted to disappointing with their gifts. Perhaps the sender was getting bored, others like Tish argued, and maybe the game they had started was running out of appeal. Jonah being away and unreachable on location didn't help, either. Meanwhile, Ted and several of his gossip merchants repeated their darker assumptions: that the sender's plan had taken a sinister turn, leading Anna down the path they had always intended for her.

But nobody – not a single person in Anna's life – had attempted to comfort her, or offer a positive perspective.

Until now.

He might have raised the issue in a clumsy manner, but Ben's heartfelt words were soothing. There were many things Anna didn't need, but Ben stepping back from her – when his was the only encouraging voice amidst the doomsayers – wasn't one of them.

'You really think there will be more?' she asked.

'I do. And when they arrive, talk to me about them. Because I'm interested.'

The interior of Freya & Georgie's seemed to brighten a little despite the unchanging greyness outside, as Anna smiled at the journalist. 'I'd like that.'

Having an ally in Ben was the tonic Anna needed. That day she hardly noticed when the same half-baked suppositions swirled around her, laughing away the doubters. She was confident once more, daring to hope for better things. As the week passed, she began to look objectively on the sixth and seventh parcels. The old record and her trip out to Notting Hill with Jonah had caused more questions than they'd answered, but the gift had given her two things: firstly, the story behind 'Ain't She Sweet', which, true or not, hinted at someone observing a woman they were so proud of that they wanted others to look at her; and, secondly, the chance to say thank you to the person who had sent the gifts. That they had chosen not to reply was immaterial. Finding a lead of any kind felt like a step forward, bringing Anna back into control. She remembered something her brother Ruari had said a few months ago, when a potentially lucrative sponsor for his surf school had pulled the plug at the last minute: 'I can't waste time worrying about slammed doors. This is just one closer to finding an open one.'

The sea-glass and shells were harder to rationalise, with the bruises of recent disappointment still smarting. But the pieces had a beauty of their own, even in their unfinished state. The sender wasn't to know that Anna wouldn't know what to do with them. If Ben was right and this was a blip, maybe she would understand better when the next parcel arrived.

'You've got that posh scarf on again, I see.' Babs nodded approvingly as she dusted the reception counter.

Anna was almost an hour early for work, but she had come in anyway, relishing the space and quiet before her colleagues arrived. As she had been leaving home she was struck by a sudden urge to wear the silk scarf with the yellow rose-print again. It rested like a lover's whisper against her skin now and reminded her of how everything had started to change with its arrival. Too many questions had crowded her lately; she needed to return to the breathless optimism the parcels had unearthed in her – to reconnect to the sense of magic and wonder. Maybe then she would find a new clue to unveiling the sender.

'It is lovely, isn't it? And it feels fantastic on, too.'

'I'll bet.' Babs coughed through the cloud of spray polish and scowled accusingly at the aerosol can. 'Oh, this stuff is abysmal! I swear management has started shopping for cleaning products at one of them pound-shops,' she said, showing it to Anna. '*Mr Shiny Polish?* Never heard of it! And it's not just this, either. These dusters would tear in a summer breeze. And the floor-cleaner is so thin I need half a bottle to do one bucket.' She gave a loud, disapproving tut. 'Cost-cutting, that's what this is. You take my advice, flower: find the chap who could afford to send you that scarf and *marry him.* Better to be a kept woman, if you're going to be next on the list for the chop.'

Anna touched the gossamer-soft silk at her neck and tried her best to discount the cleaner's suggestion. Every business had to cut costs, she assured herself; better that it be in cleaning products and printer paper than in personnel.

But still, it was worrying. She thought back to Ted's reaction after she'd helped Juliet move office and he'd found out, despite Anna's best attempts to keep the editor's secret. 'I *told* you this place was going up the Swanny. If Dragon Evans is giving up her lair, it can only mean one thing: bad news.'

Anna had argued back. 'It means nothing of the sort, Ted. People move offices all the time.'

'All smoke and mirrors, ain't it? Make us all think it's

business as usual and then – *whammo!* – four hundred employees out on their sweet backsides!'

As Babs shuffled her duster around the atrium, Anna lifted her fingers again to the reassuring coolness of her scarf. What if her job was in danger? Was it the worst thing that could happen? Juliet's words from her starkly empty office came back to Anna's mind: *Keep taking risks, Ms Browne. Your life will be all the better for it.*

What if losing her job at the newspaper allowed Anna to take a risk? She considered what else she could be doing, if not working on reception. She liked working with people and got a kick out of solving other people's problems. She'd enjoyed organising the rota among her friends to help Isadora last year – and she'd been surprised by how much she'd liked working out business plans for Ruari and Gary her dentist. Perhaps she could revisit what she'd learned at university – maybe working with other entrepreneurs to make their business dreams happen. It was something she'd never considered before, but in the early-morning stillness of the atrium the idea began to take shape.

Thirty-One

Ben McAra stared at his shoes, hoping his ordeal would soon end.

He had endured twenty minutes of Juliet Evans' wrath already and was beginning to wish he'd listened to his hangover this morning and called in sick. A late-night meeting with a civil servant from the Ministry of Education whose tongue famously loosened when given alcohol had led Ben to share a bottle of obscenely expensive single malt last night, in exchange for what turned out to be not very useful gossip. And now his head was shouting at him almost as loudly as his editor.

'I don't need your excuses, McAra! I need you to do your job! We need something big – something that will wipe the smug grins off the faces of the *Post* and the *Mail*. They've beaten us to the punch too many times this year – and our readership knows it.'

'I'm working on it, Juliet . . .'

'And I'm not talking about your corruption-in-schools exposé.'

'I'm almost there. My source is *this* close to breaking . . .'
Don't you dare call time on me, Ben silently threatened. *I've been working my ass off to get this story . . .*

'From what I hear, your *source* has been happily spilling his guts to the highest bidder for months. Kyle Chambers from the *Post* was bragging about it in the Members' Club *two weeks* ago.' Juliet Evans ran a hand through her razor-edged blonde bob and paced the office that wasn't hers. She seemed smaller in the former assistant editor's office, but her wrath, if anything, was amplified. 'You're forgetting why I hired you, McAra. Anyone can write about corruption. Anyone can find a bent MP, a dodgy police chief, a High Court judge with a weekend name. We have to find a story that will capture our readership's imagination and kick the competition to the kerb. I want you to find me *that* story.'

I don't know any other stories, Ben retorted in his head, needing caffeine or, possibly, a full frontal lobotomy to ease the hammering in his brain. Caffeine would be easier to come by, if decidedly more temporary than the latter solution. He promised himself an unscheduled visit to Freya & Georgie's as soon as the Dragon released him from her temporary lair.

And then he thought of Anna. Of her smile and sense of humour, of her uniquely charming view of life. And *those eyes*: blue as a summer's day and sparkling like the sun on the sea. The thought of her commanded his attention as his boss raged on like a hurricane around him. He was falling for Anna – had been for some time – and now they had established a level of trust, he was ready for the next step. His plan to move closer to her was working perfectly, despite almost blowing everything a few days ago in the coffee house . . .

Wait. That's it!

A way to get what he wanted, both professionally and personally. A way to capitalise on his efforts of the past two months *and* get Juliet off his back for the time being. She'd been banging on about human-interest stories for months, 'good news' tales that might capture their dwindling readership's attention and persuade them to hang around a bit longer. Now the perfect candidate was staring him in the face. It wasn't a huge story, but it was brilliant – even with his brain's current delicate state, he had to congratulate himself on his genius.

'Actually, I might have a lead on something,' he said, cutting Dragon Evans off in the middle of her torrent. 'But I'll need four weeks.'

'You have a fortnight,' Juliet snapped. 'Make it happen.'

'So, I said to him, "I don't care if Gary Lineker said you were the Dalai Lama, you're a rubbish boyfriend!" And then I got his chauffeur to drive me home.'

'But he could be the next Rooney,' Rea insisted, her superior knowledge of the football Premiership something she liked to show off, even if it was lost on Sheniece Wilson.

'Exactly – and look what that poor Coleen has to put up with! Emile is about as useful as a fart in a hurricane when it comes to women. Good luck to whoever gets saddled with *that* as a partner.' She turned to Anna, who was trying her best to disguise her amusement. 'See, what I need is a *star journalist*, like Anna has.'

Rea gasped at Anna. 'Are you going out with Ben McAra?'

'No, I'm not. We're just friends.'

'Not what I hear,' Sheniece smirked, filing a chip from her fingernail. 'We saw you with him, remember. And my mate Megan works in Freya & Georgie's and she said you two were all over each other last week – in a body-language sense.' She winked at Rea. 'If she isn't shagging him yet, it's only a matter of time before she jumps his bones.'

Horrified, Anna hurried to her own defence. 'It's not like that. Ben's a friend.'

'What I wouldn't give for a friend *that* fit! Hang on, look lively.' Rea grabbed a pile of leaflets from the reception desk and held one out to Anna. 'So, if you can make sure these are available for people to see, that would be great . . . Oh, *hi*, Ben.'

She stepped back to reveal the smiling journalist walking towards them. Anna did her best to appear unmoved by the sight of him, but she knew she was fooling nobody. Her colleagues had hit the nail on the head, even if they'd assumed Anna and Ben were further down the road than they were. Anna knew that if Ben asked her out, she would be only too willing to accept.

'Ladies. I was just passing and wondered what the gossip was.'

Rea frowned. 'Since when were you interested in girlie gossip, McAra?'

'I'm an investigative journalist, Sinfield. It comes with the territory. So?'

Anna chuckled. 'Babs reckons there's a conspiracy by management to deny her quality cleaning products. You could investigate that.'

The sparkle in the journalist's eyes made her spine tingle. '*This* could be *huge*. Clearly we need to talk more, Anna.'

Their shared smile wasn't missed by Rea and Sheniece.

'Any excuse,' Rea muttered, loud enough to make Anna blush. 'So, Ben, what's the big breaking story that's going to save the *Daily Messenger*?'

'Apart from Babs' lack of Flash? Actually, I should make a note . . .' He grabbed a complimentary pen and sheet of *Messenger* notepaper from the reception desk. 'That would be a killer headline.'

'Well?'

'There isn't a big breaking story to save the paper because, ladies, the paper is not in trouble and therefore doesn't need saving.'

Rea folded her arms. 'Right. So sleazy Damien Kendal setting up shop in the Dragon's office is just a coincidence, is it?'

'Who understands the mind of the Board? They don't feel they're doing their job if they aren't checking up on us minions. You know that, Rea. So don't go spreading rumours that help nobody. We operate on facts alone here.'

His comment caused Rea to laugh so hard she nearly dropped her armful of papers. 'We work for a tabloid,

Ben. Facts are the *least* of our concerns!' She beckoned to Sheniece and they walked towards the exit together.

Ben grimaced. 'That sounded so much better in my head. So, Miss Browne, what time do you clock off?'

'Now, actually. I was just closing up the desk. You?'

'I'm done. The interview I was planning has fallen through. What are you up to when you leave? Anything exciting?'

Anna did her best to look unmoved, despite the rising excitement within her. 'Not really. I was planning an early night. You?'

'Forget your early night. I want to take you out for a drink.'

'You do?' She couldn't hide her smile. This was the invitation she had been hoping might follow after their heartfelt exchange earlier that week.

'Yes, I do. So what do you say? I'll give you a clue: the answer you're looking for is "Yes, Ben".'

Anna was about to answer when she caught sight of a familiar figure approaching. It was strange to see her friend and neighbour in her work environs, but she was delighted to see the scruffily dressed cameraman, with his wonky smile and attitude, completely unfazed by the smart atrium he was strolling through.

'Ey-up, lass!' He grinned, his exaggerated Yorkshire pronunciation a running joke between them. Both had commented that their regional accents became stronger when they were in unfamiliar surroundings.

'All right, my *'ansum*!' Anna replied, playing along. What brings you here?'

'I had an interview for a job in White City. Thought I'd look you up and see if you fancied a brew, a bus-ride home and a reet good natter with me?'

Ben was watching the Yorkshireman as if observing a strange and exotic animal in the wild. Anna smiled by way of explanation. 'Ben, this is Jonah, my neighbour and friend. Jonah, this is . . .'

'Ben McAra, Senior Correspondent,' he interjected, his handshake so perfunctory it was almost a sword-thrust. 'I'm good friends with Anna.'

'She has *many* friends,' Jonah returned, his smile as fleeting as Ben's handshake.

The temperature in reception seemed to plummet, so much so that Anna looked over to the entrance to see if the mechanism on the automatic doors had stuck open again. Ben and Jonah stared one another down, like lions about to do battle.

Anna was torn: part of her wanted to go for a drink with Ben to see what might happen. His invitation confirmed that he was interested in her, beyond occasional coffee-shop visits before work, and that felt good. But Jonah so rarely visited her at work that she would feel bad if he'd made the journey and she'd accepted Ben's offer instead. Added to this, the strange behaviour of the two men was making her uneasy. Not wanting to create a scene that might cause further rumour in the building, she made a quick decision.

'I'm sorry about the drink, Ben. I really could do with an early night. Mind if we make it another time? Maybe next week?'

274

'I guess so.' Ben's eyes slid from Jonah to Anna. 'Are you certain I can't tempt you? I'm happy to throw in a taxi ride to save you from the Friday-evening bus.'

'I don't mind *us* catching a cab.' When irritation pulled at the journalist's face, Jonah's smile said it all. 'It's not beyond my means, you know.'

It was definitely time to leave. Anna turned the switch-board to night service and picked up her bag. 'I'll see you in Freya & Georgie's on Monday, Ben. Have a lovely weekend.'

'Fine by me. Jonah, it was good to meet you. Anna, I'll *call* you.'

Anna wished she hadn't seen the hurt in Ben's eyes, or the smug expression Jonah now wore. What was wrong with both of them? Ben could hardly call her when she'd never given him her phone number. And why was Jonah trying to out-taxi Ben? The peace she had enjoyed barely half an hour before vanished like sea mist in the sun as Anna left the *Messenger* building, aware of Jonah's stare as they walked down the street. After a full five minutes of unwarranted scrutiny, she challenged him.

'*What* are you staring at me for?'

'I'm not.'

Anna stopped abruptly, sending irritated commuters swerving around them to avoid a collision. 'Yes, you are. And what was all that about, back there?'

'Back where?'

Anna folded her arms. 'Come on, Jonah, you know what I'm talking about. You were pretty rude to Ben.'

'I was not. I shook the man's hand. What else did you expect me to do: ask him for a dance?'

'You were staring at him like he had a gun pointed at your head.'

'Well, he started it.'

With a loud groan, Anna began to walk again. It wasn't her idea for Jonah to surprise her at work, any more than she'd anticipated Ben asking her for a post-work drink. What should have been a sweet invitation had become World War Three; she'd only agreed to go home with Jonah to stop the animosity escalating further. Now she wished she had accepted Ben's invitation and let Jonah go home, to sort out his stupid, male head . . .

'Anna! Don't be like that! I can't help it if I don't like the chap.'

'I never asked you to like him! I never asked you to meet me today, either.'

'Oh, so you'd rather I hadn't?'

He had caught up with her and Anna wished she'd brushed both of them off and done her own thing. 'Now you're being pathetic. What's your problem? Ben's a work colleague and a friend.'

'A friend who wants to get into your knickers.'

She halted again, bristling for a fight. 'And what if he does? What business is it of yours?'

'Oh. Like *that*, is it?'

'No, it isn't! But what's the point in me saying anything else? If that's what you think is happening and you won't listen to me, why should I tell you any different? You say you're my friend, but you just embarrassed me in front of my work colleagues. What gives you the right to assume anything about me?'

'Anna, stop.' Jonah was holding out his hands, realising his mistake too late. 'Maybe I overreacted, okay? Is that what you want to hear? I didn't like the look of him, that's all. But I know that isn't your problem. And I shouldn't have made it appear that way, especially not where you work. I'm sorry. Can we just go somewhere and talk? I don't want you to be angry with me.'

But Anna had heard enough. Despite his apology, Jonah clearly thought Ben was out to use her and that she was too thick to realise it. He thought she was some innocent country bumpkin who needed protecting. Which was ludicrous. Why couldn't she make up her own mind? She had always considered Jonah her closest ally – someone unaffected by the pettiness that seemed to obsess so many of her fellow city-dwellers. His no-nonsense attitude to life had been a breath of fresh air and Anna had come to rely on his ability to find humour in everything. But she'd seen a side to him today she didn't like – and that threw everything else into question.

'I'm sorry. I'm going home.'

'Then let me come with you . . .'

'No. Leave me alone.'

She didn't take the bus home, concerned that Jonah would use the excuse to travel with her regardless. Instead she headed for the mind-numbing crush of the Friday early-evening Tube, not caring when she was jostled and squashed between impatient commuters. Space was the last thing she was looking for now: space to move and consider might give her too much time to think. Instead she surrendered to the anonymous jam, keen to escape, to think of nothing but finding the smallest space to be in.

An hour later, after taking a meandering route home, she arrived at her front door to find a bouquet of flowers and a note: *Sorry. I'm an idiot.*

Yes, you are, she agreed, leaving the flowers in the corridor as she shut herself into her flat.

That evening, still rattled, Anna switched off the television and listened to the muted sounds of life from the apartments above and below. Outside a police siren split the distant hum of traffic, a rush of flashing blue lights temporarily illuminating her living room. She wandered into the kitchen to flick the switch on the kettle, leaning against the countertop, her mind a tumbled mess; but when the kettle boiled she ignored it and walked away.

The box of sea-glass beads and drilled shells was still in the middle of her dining table. Taking a seat, she reached for it, letting her fingers pass over the cold glass and rough shells. How dare Jonah think it was his job to choose her friends? And Ben, squaring up to Jonah like an eighteenth-century dueller, had been no better. She might lead what others thought was a quiet life, but this gave no one the right to dictate how she should live it. She'd had more than her fair share of unwanted commentators on her life during her childhood – people who assumed they were more qualified than she to decide her path. Neighbours, supposed friends and pub regulars in Polperro had all taken it upon themselves to publicly pity her as a child, their concern often nothing more than a badly disguised excuse to gossip about the Browne family. She had hoped moving to the city and slowly carving out her own future would have ended that.

Some chance.

Irritated, she lifted the length of thin leather from the white cardboard box and took out a green-blue sea-glass bead. Carefully she threaded the leather through the silver wire hoop, pulling the bead along to the end, where a small double knot had been tied.

Jonah can't dictate my friends . . .

A tiny scalloped limpet shell followed the bead.

. . . and neither should Ben . . .

A pale-green sea-glass bead reflected the light from the pendant lamp over Anna's table as it moved along the leather.

Nobody decides that but me . . .

Soap-bubble lustre-lined shells and matt glass beads passed through her hands in an alternating pattern, as Anna mulled over her response. The meditative act renewed her perspective and, as her creation grew, her resolve began to form.

It's my life.

Sitting back, she looked at the completed length of beads, shells and leather. She draped it over her wrist, tying the two ends together to form a bracelet. It was simple but had its own beauty, reminding her of treasures lying on the Cornish beaches she'd played on years ago:

– the message had read. And, at that moment, it began to make sense. What she created was her choice; nobody else's. The more she considered this, the stronger the notion became. What she decided to do with her life was entirely her responsibility and right. She had two choices: allow others to control her choices or make her own way.

In the stillness of her home Anna made a promise to herself. It was time to stop worrying about what other people thought and follow her heart. She held her future in her own hands: successes and failures might come in equal measure, but she was determined to make the most of every decision, for better or worse.

The bracelet would remind her of that. Maybe the sender of this gift knew what they were doing after all. Peace settled over her, a welcome refreshing of her mind after the hours of frustration.

It's my life, she told herself again. *Whatever happens next is up to me . . .*

Thirty-Two

Anna didn't see Jonah for a week. She ignored his calls and refused to answer the door when he knocked. She would talk to him, of course, eventually. But she had a point to make and he needed to accept it. She wore her handmade bracelet to work, its presence reassuring, and found her fingers subconsciously reaching for it when she had decisions to make or an opinion to give. Like the daisy-chain necklace, brooch and scarf before it, Anna felt stronger when wearing the parcel-sender's gift. And, as before, people around her began to notice the change.

'You on Valium or something?' Ted asked, after she had refused to accept a delivery brought to the *Messenger* building in error and a near stand-up battle had ensued with the courier. 'Normally you'd be high-tailing it round to Hanson Holdings to take it to them. What's got into you?'

'I'm sick of doing it,' Anna replied. 'It's time the couriers realised they can't keep making the same mistake when they're short on time and expect us to do their job for them.'

'What on earth did you say to Phil Jackson from the newsroom?' Sheniece was aghast, later that day. 'I met him in the lift and his face was white . . .'

'He tried to blame me for him not booking the meeting room. His visitors were with him and he was making out I was his minion to shout at. I told him it was his fault and that reception staff aren't responsible for room reservation,' Anna told her, adrenaline still pumping from the situation that, even a week earlier, she wouldn't have answered back on.

'I hear you've been terrorising my colleagues,' Ben smirked one morning in Freya & Georgie's. Since his altercation with Jonah he had steered clear of any mention of her friend, choosing instead to pick up where he and Anna had left off. It was a safer option by far and one Anna had no intention of challenging. She was enjoying his company too much and was keen to banish Jonah's suspicions about him. This, she reminded herself, was *her* decision to make. If Jonah were proved right, at least she would have had fun in the meantime. 'What's with you, Ms Browne?'

'If you're referring to Phil Jackson, he knows full well why I said what I did. We get it at reception all the time: we're nobody's servants.'

Ben's chuckle was as warm and sweet as the pastries and smiles Megan brought to their table. 'I think the entire newsroom knows not to repeat Phil's mistake now.' His eyes narrowed. 'And I would hope, for the sake of your mystery parcel-sender, that he never upsets you again.

Talking of which,' he leaned a little closer, 'any news on that front?'

'No.'

The mention of Anna's parcels still sat uneasily within her, but she reasoned that Ben had as much right to enquire about them as anyone else.

'I'm not a betting man,' he said, popping the last piece of almond croissant into his mouth. 'But I'll bet another one arrives soon. You'll tell me, won't you, when it does?'

Anna couldn't read his expression, but was keen to draw a line under the subject this morning. 'Of course I will.'

She considered Ben's recent interest in the parcels. It bothered her a little and she couldn't quite say why. Was he a little too eager to discuss it? Or was it because he had so carefully avoided mentioning the parcels before? At least at work her colleagues' interest had faded after the disappointing seventh parcel, so she had some breathing space there. Even Ben hadn't noticed the homemade creation on her right wrist. The gifts had once again become intensely personal, the magic she'd experienced from the beginning making a magnificent return. She decided to be careful about how much she shared with Ben from now on. She'd promised she would let him know if another parcel arrived, but she'd never said *how much* she would tell him. Whoever was sending the parcels had intended them for her, not for her colleagues and certainly not an over eager (if very good-looking) journalist.

From now on, this was *her* adventure and she was determined to enjoy it.

As it turned out, she didn't have to wait long for her next gift to arrive. That Friday evening a brand-new parcel lay on her dining-room table in the light of the pendant lamp overhead. Determined to summon back the magic of the former deliveries, Anna took time to make a meal, put on her favourite music, pour a glass of wine and relax before opening the package. By the time she was ready to do so it was almost nine o'clock and a childlike excitement gripped her.

She remembered her sixteenth birthday when Henry Nancarrow, her freckle-faced first love, had planned a surprise day for them both. Much to Senara's disapproval, he had called on Anna at six o'clock in the morning, leading her, blindfolded, through Polperro and down to the harbour. When the scarf was removed from her eyes she found his father's fishing boat bedecked with bunting and bearing a picnic for them to enjoy at sea. What Anna had loved the most – and had never told Henry – was that the walk from her front door to the harbour's edge was more magical than any of the lovely things that followed. He had recognised her love of surprises and created a day with Anna at its centre – and that meant more to her than she could say. The thrill of what lay ahead that day outlasted their fledgling relationship (ended by distance, when Henry went to university in Edinburgh) and several relationships that followed; it glowed even now when she remembered it.

The parcel was rectangular and a sliding, rustling sound emerged from its depths when it moved. The perfectly judged corners had returned, together with the blank sender details, a comforting sight after the chaotic appearance of the previous delivery. As Anna peeled away the brown-paper jacket she caught a glimpse of gold and her heart leapt. The box was made from matt-gold card, tiny ridges along its surface glinting as she held it. At the centre of the lid was a raised star covered in shimmering glass glitter, its sweeping trail picked out in black ink that swooped over the edge and down one side. Anna's breath caught – and any doubts about the sender that she'd had after the last gift vanished – as she carefully lifted the lid.

Inside, a layer of black tissue paper embedded with tiny gold stars hid the contents from view. Attached to the fold at the top was a square of white card, upon which was printed:

★

★　★

~ Handmade for Miss Anna Browne ~
A gift to dance under the stars in

★　★

★

A delicious rustle filled the air as the tissue paper parted, joined by an aroma that reminded Anna of her very first pair of ballet shoes, bought for her by Grandma Morwenna when she was seven years old. Within the starry tissue folds lay the most beautiful pair of midnight-blue, high-heeled velvet shoes, tied in the middle with a length of silver satin ribbon. A cluster of four glittering silver stars were positioned on the outer edge of each shoe and a tiny silver star had been hand-painted onto the top of each heel. They were quite unlike anything she had seen before and her fingers fumbled to remove them from the box. When she slipped them onto her feet they fitted perfectly, leading her to wonder how the sender had known her size. She rose and moved around, the comfort of the new shoes surprising her. Giggling, she gave a twirl on the polished floorboards of her apartment floor, feeling like a child let loose on a dressing-up box. Her sixth-floor flat was as close to the stars as she could be for now, but for the way the shoes made her feel she might as well have been dancing through the atmosphere at the edge of space. The gift was a magnificent return to form – and with it came a rush of awe that lifted Anna from her questions and concerns. The night hours melted away as she whirled and wheeled around the furniture, finally collapsing, breathless, in the early hours of the morning.

Just as she was drifting to sleep, still clothed and wearing the beautiful shoes, she remembered Ben's request to be told about the next parcel when it arrived. The only way she could know for sure whether he was the sender was to say nothing. One way or another, the truth would be revealed . . .

Thirty-Three

Rea Sinfield had worked for the *Daily Messenger* for four years, rising from the lowly rank of unpaid intern to become one of the staff writers who tackled everything from breaking news to celebrity gossip. She had established a reputation as a solid writer – an 'all-rounder' who could turn her pen to any given subject. Last week she had written a stellar article on the environmental implications of a proposed rail link; the week before her assignment entailed her enduring the endless chauvinism (not to mention dodging the roving hands) of a leading City stockbroker for a behind-the-scenes look at the London Stock Exchange. Today she had been given the task of carving a two-hundred-word story from a photo of a fake-tanned former reality-TV star emerging from a club a little worse for wear. Versatility was her secret weapon. Even if it meant most of her working week was taken up with wading through mind-numbingly boring reams of research, much of which would be cut by the sub-editor's virtual pen.

The advantage of such professional boredom was that it afforded her the opportunity to note the far more interesting goings-on of the newspaper itself. And, lately, life at the *Daily Messenger* had provided rich pickings. Vomit-inducing Damien Kendal, for instance, holed up in Juliet Evans' office – and the Dragon ominously compliant with it all. The aftermath of Sanjay from Obits' affair had lost much of its lustre, but the further exploits of his former lover were at least continuing to entertain. Claire Connors, the new rumour in the newsroom had it, was desperate for a baby as her forty-fourth year approached, making anything remotely male and virile fair game. The latest male interns were so terrified of the resident cougar's passes that they regularly dived into cupboards, toilets and adjoining offices when she swept in.

But what intrigued Rea more than all of these attractions was the suspicious chemistry clearly forming between her colleague Ben McAra and Anna Browne from reception. The hidden rumour-mongers of the newsroom were divided on whether McAra had any involvement with the strange, anonymous parcels the receptionist had been receiving for a few months, but all agreed that it was only a matter of time before the mysterious deliveries were overshadowed by the budding romance.

Secretly, Rea hoped Ben and Anna would act on the attraction between them. If her fellow hard-bitten journalists knew this, she would be laughed off Fleet Street, but the fact remained that Rea longed to witness a real romance within the walls of the nation's fourth-biggest tabloid. Not the sordid fumblings of Claire Connors et al., but something honest and authentic that would restore her faith in the existence of love. She had seen precious little of the latter in four years of journalism; even the love-life of her best friend Sheniece was more akin to a car crash than a beautiful journey. And as for her own dating hell – the less said about that, the better. If Ben and Anna fell in love, there was hope for Rea.

And so, as she conjured journalistic eloquence from thin air, she watched and waited . . .

'Have you forgiven your friend yet?' Ben asked, handing Anna an oversized cup of frothy cappuccino.

'Which friend?'

'The rude Yorkshireman.'

Anna ignored the bait. This morning nothing could challenge her mood. In reality she might have been whiling away an hour before the start of her shift, but in her head she was still traversing her apartment in the magical heels. 'I've nothing to forgive him for.'

'Didn't look that way in the street after you left.' Seeing her reaction, he held up his hand. 'What? I *might* have followed you both out.'

'You're impossible! Like I said, I wanted an early night, so I decided to go home alone. There's no scandal here.'

Denied the information he was after, Ben sank a little further into the coffee house's leather armchair. 'Spoilsport. Okay, next question: has he always been *just* a friend?'

'Really?'

'It's an innocent question.'

'It isn't.'

'So – indulge me.'

Anna raised her eyes to the industrial silver air-conditioning pipes in the high ceiling of Freya & Georgie's. 'You want to know if I'm sleeping with Jonah Rawdon? Well, not that it's any of your business, but I'm not. He's my friend. That's all.'

Mischief played in Ben's smile. 'I hear you. So, there isn't anyone . . . I should know about?'

'Well, I was considering an illicit affair with Babs the cleaner.' Anna joked, her expression deadpan.

'You're not . . . are you?'

'Serves you right, for asking personal questions.'

A little rattled, Ben turned his attention to the wedge of biscotti beside his flat white. Anna smiled at the pretty blonde barista collecting coffee mugs from a nearby table.

'Nice day, isn't it?' Megan nodded at the sunlight flooding the front half of the coffee shop. 'Looks like we might actually get a summer this year.'

'I hope so,' Anna replied. 'We need a bit of sunshine after all that rain.'

'How's your coffee this morning?'

'*Intrusive*,' Ben muttered under his breath.

Anna's smile widened in response. 'Really good, thanks. Best coffee in the city, I think.'

Megan's face lit up. 'That's a lovely thing to say, thank you.'

'You shouldn't encourage strangers,' Ben said, when the young woman had returned to the counter. 'Next thing you know she'll be sharing a bus ride home with you and buying identical outfits.'

'Don't be so cynical. You're sounding dangerously like Ted Blaskiewicz. Where I come from, people talk to other people. It's called being polite.'

'In this city, we ignore people. It's called being *safe*.'

'*You* spoke to me when I hardly knew you. Should I be worried?' Anna laughed. 'You're a pest this morning. What's up?'

'I'm sorry, just work stuff. Ignore me.'

'I will. It will be good practice for *being safe* in this city, apparently.'

Ben laughed. 'Go out with me?'

The question was fast, unexpected. Anna blinked. 'Excuse me?'

'Forget the dubious attractions of Babs and Jonah, and whoever else might ask. Let me take you to dinner?'

She'd been pleased with the invitation of a drink last week. Dinner was *far* better. Had it been a month ago, or back when she first noticed him, Anna would have been too nervous to accept. But her life had changed irrevocably since then. Without hesitation, she accepted.

'I'd like that.'

They walked in delighted silence to work, their hands deliciously close to touching, and when they parted ways beneath the grand glass-and-steel atrium their smiles promised more – soon, but not yet. Anna moved on air to her workplace, Ben's sudden invitation still playing in her mind. His questions about Jonah now made sense at least. The thought of the Yorkshireman made Anna wish she could share the news with him. She had missed his opinion, although she didn't regret the silence she'd initiated. But given what had happened this morning, perhaps the time for reconciliation had arrived. Still smiling at the thought of what might await her and Ben, she decided to answer Jonah's next call. It was time to move on.

Thirty-Four

Camden Lock was a writhing, bubbling mass of bodies when Anna stepped off the bus on Saturday morning. But for once she didn't see the crowds of global tourists or the clumps of sullen teens blocking the paths around the market. The sun peeked fleetingly through gaps in the banks of white cloud like a coquettish game of hide-and-seek, flirting with the world below. It gave the day a playful air, helped in no small way by the promise of Anna's first date with Ben that evening.

Anna had come to find a dress to match her starlight-dancing shoes, which were the obvious choice to wear. It had been a while since she had treated herself to anything, the parcels fulfilling that need until today, and she was looking forward to finding something new. She wandered around the stands with the scent of Vietnamese noodles, fresh-baked French crêpes and coffee wafting up from the food stalls around the lock. Garments of all colours and fabrics passed under her fingers, but none quite fitted the quality of the parcel-sender's latest gift. An hour of leisurely browsing passed and then she saw it: a simple, bias-cut dress with a full skirt at mid-calf length, its hue identical to the midnight-blue shoes. Congratulating herself on the match, Anna bought the dress and wandered over to the crêpe stand to reward herself.

'Anna! Um, hi.'

Jonah Rawdon's hesitant smile and respectful distance contrasted sharply with the shoulder-to-shoulder bodies surrounding him. 'Don't leave, Anna. I want to apologise. Again.'

Anna had no intention of going anywhere, but waited for him to say more.

'Can I . . . buy you coffee, or lunch, or something? I've been a complete idiot and I've missed you.'

As apologies went, it was far from the most eloquent. But Anna had known Jonah for long enough to understand how much effort it required. Granting him a smile, she nodded. 'Lunch would be good. I've missed you, too.'

In a canalside restaurant near the market, Jonah raised his glass. 'Friends again?'

'Friends.' Their glasses clinked. 'You were an idiot, though. If there was anything going on with Ben, you know I'd tell you.'

'I know.'

Anna's pulse quickened as her eyes met his. He should be the first to know – just in case this evening was the start of something significant. 'Um, which is why . . .'

Jonah's shoulders visibly fell. 'Ah. When?'

'He's taking me to dinner tonight.' She indicated the

294

string-handled orange paper bag beside the table in which her new dress lay. 'That's why I was shopping.'

'Right.'

'Why don't you like him?'

Jonah appeared taken aback by her question. 'I never said I didn't.'

'You know what I mean.'

He shrugged. 'Sometimes I get a gut feeling about somebody.'

'He's a good man.'

'Is he?'

'I think he is. I've wanted to date him for a while and I'm really happy.'

Jonah pushed a piece of steak around his plate with no intention of eating it. 'I can see that. Everyone can see it. I even had the caretaker asking me yesterday what had happened to make you smile so much. It's got to be plain as day if Seamus sees it. He thought it was me who'd made you smile, mind, but . . . You're happier than I've seen you before and, well, I might not like the chap, but I don't want to rain on your parade.'

'Thank you. And it's just a date. I'm not eloping with him or anything.'

'Yet, eh?' He made a sound like a laugh, which was instantly at odds with his grave expression. 'Just be careful, lass. You deserve the best.'

Jonah's tacit acceptance of the situation both comforted and confused Anna as she prepared for her evening with Ben. He hadn't really elaborated on his reasons for disliking the journalist, but it was obvious Jonah didn't trust him. How was it possible for him to reach such a conclusion based on a single, brief meeting? She had never seen him make a snap judgement about anyone before, preferring the wait-and-see approach to most things in his life. He was apparently famous for it in his family, his own mother describing him as being 'so laid-back you're in the middle of last week'.

Anna knew she was far from being objective on the subject. Coming from a tiny village where instant opinion was the main currency, she had learned how divisive that could be; and having a mother whose behaviour invited such judgement had made her avoid it at all costs in her own life. Jonah didn't say he thought Anna was mistaken in Ben, but had been noticeably quieter during lunch and their journey home. For Anna, this felt more damning than the loud, uninvited opinions directed at her in her youth, as her mother went increasingly off the rails:

She's a mess, your mother. You should be ashamed of her . . .

Senara Browne is a waste of good air . . .

I pity you, girl. What hope is there for you?

Accusing eyes in the street. Undisguised discussions behind her back in the post-office queue. Reported indiscretions repeated to her face. Year after year of judgement and criticism, while Anna did her best to rise above and shield her brother from it all. The worst thing was that deep down she had agreed with every comment. Senara was a nightmare, less of a mother than their next-door neighbour who sometimes left mercy parcels on the family's doorstep. When Anna left the family home, the relief at being released from it all was stronger than any emotion she had known. It was the reason for her quiet life in London, for blending into the blessed anonymity of the city and her firm belief in finding the good in people.

Jonah could think what he liked: in Ben, Anna saw a man who could be trusted – and she was looking forward to getting to know him more.

At eight o'clock Anna stepped out of the black cab at the address Ben had given. She looked up at the elegant Georgian townhouse lit by white floodlights and breathed in the midsummer night air. Set in a leafy suburb of the city overlooking the Thames, the restaurant within the building had been recommended by the *Daily Messenger*'s food-and-wine writer, according to Ben. Anna wasn't certain whether this meant her date had told everyone they were going out, but tonight she didn't care. No doubt she would discover on Monday morning how many people at work knew.

A waiter led her through the restaurant, with its pale wooden chairs and tables, white tablecloths and Wedgwood blue walls, on through an open set of French doors to a river terrace. Bright paper lanterns suspended overhead cast a magical glow across the candlelit outdoor tables, as the smooth notes of a jazz quartet drifted up from the lawn beyond. Couples at the tables sat close, heads inclined towards each other, lost in the understated romance of the setting. It was perfect – and in the centre of it all was Ben. He stood as she approached, a quick readjustment of his jacket the only indication that he might be as nervous as Anna felt.

'Hi.' His eyes made an appreciative sweep of her. 'You look amazing.'

The waiter left and Ben leaned in to kiss Anna's cheek. Feeling a blush rise to where his lips had brushed, she sat down and let her gaze drift across the lantern-framed lawn to the inky blackness of the river. 'This place is gorgeous.'

'Miles said we'd like it. He was very interested to know who I was bringing here. Of course I was the perfect gentleman.'

Anna smiled. For tonight, at least, she could enjoy Ben's company without the scrutiny of others. He seemed more relaxed here than in the city centre, his hair a little less styled and his shirt collar open. The light from the candle in the centre of the table framed the contours of his face and danced in his eyes. His warm laughter and eager talk betrayed a hint of nerves, which was impossibly endearing – and Anna was drawn to him in a way she hadn't allowed herself to be before. Here she felt sure of herself, able to talk and flirt a little, confident of his acceptance. She had often wondered what a night out with Ben would be like; this evening surpassed any of her imaginings.

'If only people at the *Messenger* could see us now,' he smiled, as they finished eating. 'The news would be all over London in seconds.' He looked over his shoulder. 'Just checking we haven't been tailed here by Ted. Knowing his security connections, I suspect he has eyes everywhere.'

'He'll be furious when he discovers I met you without telling him.'

'He'll survive.' Ben took a sip of wine, his eyes smiling. 'Would you mind if he knew?'

'Not at all.' Her voice was light and carefree – and Anna loved the new sound of it. 'I don't care who does.'

'Are you glad you came?'

'I am, thank you.'

'I hoped you would be.' His fingers gently met hers, the easy touch a gift in the warm summer air. 'You're lovely, Anna. I've thought so for a long time. But I wanted to wait for the right moment to say it.'

'I think you're lovely, too . . .' Her breath stopped as he raised her hand to his lips and planted a gentle kiss on her fingers.

The jazz quartet on the lawn began to play 'Someone to Watch Over Me'. Anna closed her eyes and tried to capture this moment in her mind. It was as close to perfect as it was possible to be and she longed to exist forever only here and now. The certainty of Ben's affection for her was a wonderful gift and made the midsummer night sparkle with possibility she'd never dared to consider.

'Would you like to dance?' He laughed at his own question. 'That sounds like the worst line from a film – I'm sorry.'

'I'd love to.' Anna rose from her chair. 'It would be a shame to waste a good band.'

Ben took her hand and they walked down the terrace steps to the makeshift dance floor marked out by a square of star-shaped paper lanterns suspended over the lawn. Anna had never danced like this with anyone before – far removed from the awkward shuffles of clubs and parties she'd shared with previous dates. In Ben's arms she felt safe and, when he lowered his head to kiss her, she accepted as easily as breathing. The restaurant, the river and the diners floated away as they kissed, music softly embracing them as their bodies moved in time. She was aware of the long grass brushing against the midnight-blue velvet of her shoes – and when their kiss ended, her gaze dropped to the shimmering stars at her feet.

Did the person who sent the shoes know this night would happen? The glow of the city blocked any view of celestial bodies, but the star lanterns around them swung gently in the breeze – *A gift to dance under the stars in . . .*

Laughing, they made their way back to their table, hand-in-hand. Happiness coursed through Anna and she was struck by a desire to share everything with Ben.

'I had another parcel,' she confessed.

'You did? When?'

'Last week. I didn't tell anyone because . . .' She paused, realising an excuse wasn't necessary. It was her gift and her decision. 'Well, I didn't want to.'

'Can I ask what was in it?'

She pointed to her shoes. 'These.'

'Lovely! But how did they know your size?'

'I have no idea. But I don't care. They're gorgeous and I adore them.'

'Do you want to know who sent them? I mean, are you curious?'

'Of course I am. But whoever sent them doesn't seem interested in telling me who they are. I never had a reply to my email.'

Ben's eyes widened. 'Email?'

She had said too much not to explain. As she had broken her promise not to tell Ben any more than the basic details of the parcels, she might as well share it all now. 'The sixth parcel had an old record and directions to a vintage shop in Notting Hill. The owner showed me the email from the person who arranged it, and I sent a message to that address. But they never replied.'

'I didn't know you'd tried to make contact . . . How do you feel about them ignoring you?'

'They aren't ignoring me – they've sent two more parcels after my email, so they can't have been offended. I don't understand their reason for remaining anonymous, but I have to respect it, I guess.'

'What did the email say – if you don't mind me asking?'

Anna shrugged. 'I thanked them and suggested I'd like to say it in person, but said I would respect their wishes if they didn't want that to happen.'

He sat back as the waiter returned with coffee. When the waiter left, Ben looked at Anna, his expression still. 'What would you say to the sender if they were here with you, now?'

Anna's heart began to beat faster. 'Ben, are you saying . . . ?'

His voice was low, insistent. 'What would you say?'

She kept her eyes on his, feeling the warmth of his skin as their fingers locked together. 'I'd say thank you, again. I'd tell him that the gifts have changed the way I see myself, the way I see the world. He couldn't know what some of them meant to me, but they have brought back memories I thought were lost and people I've missed.'

Was Ben the sender after all? Anna couldn't tell from the way he looked at her, but why else ask the question and be so intent on receiving her answer? 'And I'd tell him that I don't want him to be anonymous any longer . . .'

'Great.' Without warning, Ben's hand left hers and he stirred a spoonful of brown sugar into his coffee. 'I think that's great, Anna. I mean, if you get the chance to say that to him, I bet he'd be over the moon. So, what's the plan now?'

Confused, Anna stared at him. 'I'm sorry?'

'Are you going to try to contact the sender again?'

'I tried already. Were you listening to me?'

'Of course I was.' Misreading her confusion as embarrassment, he gave her a reassuring smile. 'The sender clearly has a good reason for not revealing their identity right now. Maybe more needs to happen before they do. But I think you shouldn't give up hope of finding out. Have you told anyone else about this – anyone at work?'

Pushing her reservations away, Anna looked down at her coffee cup. 'Ted, Sheniece and Ashraf know about the first six parcels. Murray Henderson-Vitt and Rea Sinfield have asked me a couple of questions. But only Jonah knew about the email. Anyway, can we talk about something else?' She was confused by Ben's about-turn. Was he confessing? Asking her to wait a little longer before he told her? Or had she read too much into his reply? Feeling hemmed in by the bank of unanswerable questions, she forced them away. She wanted to return to the simple pleasure of Ben's company. Of that, she could be certain tonight.

'I'm sorry, blame the journalistic instinct. Forget I mentioned it. What I really want to know is: would you like to do this again, sometime soon?'

This was the easiest question of the night to answer. 'I'd love to.'

They shared a taxi home, stealing kisses as they snuggled together. It was more than Anna could have anticipated, but as natural as if they had always been this close. When the cab pulled up outside Walton Tower, Anna turned to Ben. There was so much more she wanted to say and she was surprised to find herself considering asking him to join her. But before she asked, Ben kissed her.

It was a beautiful kiss, soft and tender, promising more. Anna let herself get lost in the loveliness of it.

When they pulled apart, Ben's fingers remained locked with hers, as if he didn't want to let her go. 'Thank you for tonight. It's been fantastic. So, I'll see you in F & G's on Monday?'

'You will.' Anna kissed him again, delighted by how easy it felt to make the first move and loving the warmth of his skin beneath her fingertips as they brushed his cheek. Audaciously, she dared to think of what might follow soon . . . 'Goodnight.'

She hardly noticed the judders of the lift as it rose to her floor and she was at her front door before she'd even realised she'd been walking along the corridor. It was as if her velvet-clad feet were still dancing on pockets of air, her heart still pressed against Ben's under a canopy of swinging stars. She felt alive, as if energy was fizzing and coursing through her veins – and at that moment she had no other cares in the world. All she could see was Ben McAra and the promise of many more nights like this one. The shoes that had carried her to his side now spun her around the room as she giggled and danced and wished for the night to be endless. It had to end, of course: Sunday would bring time to reflect, while Monday morning would bring a return to work and the analysis that always follows a wonderful experience. Ben's strange questions, and the possibility that he was her mystery benefactor, still skulked in the shadows of her consciousness. But they could wait – it could all wait.

For now, Anna Browne was happy. And that was all she cared about.

Thirty-Five

'I *knew* it!'

Ted Blaskiewicz was *not* impressed. He was sore that he'd only learned of Anna's date after the event, but his main bone of contention appeared to be that Ashraf had blurted it out over coffee that morning. 'Why wasn't I informed of this?'

'Because it's none of your business?' Sheniece shot back, clearly happy that she'd been party to the news before the chief of security. 'Anna doesn't have to tell you everything, Ted.'

'She told you. And Ashraf. Apparently everyone who didn't need to know first, unlike me. The point is, I *should* know as a matter of urgency if it could affect the security of this building,' he blustered. 'It could have . . . *ramifications.*'

'How, exactly? They met outside of work. So your pokey old nose can stay out of it.'

Anna found their verbal battle amusing. The memory

of Saturday night still burned brightly within her and her colleagues' war couldn't extinguish it. 'I had a lovely evening, Ted. Thanks for asking.'

Ted folded his arms. 'And are you planning on doing it again, girl?'

'Maybe.' Her comment had its desired effect on the rotund security guard, whose expression simmered with beetroot rage.

'Impossible, the lot of you,' he stormed, huffing away to his room.

'Was it amazing?' Sheniece was eager to know every detail. 'I heard you went to Riverside One. My mate knows someone who works there, and they said celebrities turn up to eat there all the time. Peter Andre, the love-rat from *Made in Chelsea* and that woman from *Geordie Shore* were spotted just last month, apparently.' She let out a sigh. 'Maybe if this place goes under I should go for a job there. You never know who I might bump into . . .'

While Sheniece drifted away to her own reality-TV fantasy, Anna sorted passes for the next expected visitors. 'I didn't see anyone famous, if that's what you want to know, but the food was fantastic.'

'So, did he stay the night?'

Even for the liberal-minded junior receptionist, this was direct. Anna stared at her colleague. 'I can't believe you asked me that!'

'That's a yes then.' Rea Sinfield – summoned no doubt by the gossip searing through the building – grinned as she joined them. 'You should see McAra this morning.

Typing like a demon with a great big, dopey smile on his face.'

'Not that either of you deserves an answer, but no, actually. He was the perfect gentleman.'

'Oh, bore *off*. Trust Ben McAra to change the habits of a lifetime just when things were getting interesting.' Scandal denied her, Sheniece headed for the kitchen.

Rea leaned closer. 'Have you seen Ben yet this morning?'

'We had coffee before work, but he was in a hurry so we didn't stay long. Why?'

'I've been watching him upstairs. He looks really happy, Anna. And now I see you do, too.' Checking that they were alone, Rea lowered her voice. 'Don't tell anyone but . . . I was hoping you two would get together.'

'You were?' The journalist's sudden confession surprised Anna.

'We're not all cynics in the newsroom, you know. I've seen far too many sordid office flings lately. It makes a nice change to see the real thing happen for someone. Makes me believe it's possible.'

'Anything is possible.' *But before our date I couldn't have known how wonderful it would be*, Anna added to herself, her heart growing warm at the thought.

'I was beginning to think that wasn't true.' Sadness passed across Rea's eyes. 'Everyone has an agenda in this city. Especially in the media. You take my advice, Anna: if this is the real thing, hang on to it and never let go.'

News of Anna and Ben's date surged through the *Messenger* building, bringing people Anna had barely shared two words with before down to reception. Each

307

arrived armed with a threadbare excuse: visitors that mysteriously hadn't shown for appointments; water-cooler bottles that needed replacing immediately; enquiries after expected parcels not yet delivered. Anna calmly and politely answered them, knowing that a question about Ben would surely follow. In return, she heard more reports of his good mood and increased focus, all of which were assumed to be down to her influence.

'He's spent the whole morning at his desk. McAra *never* does that . . .'

'I heard him *humming* to himself . . .'

'He's like a different man, Anna. What did you *do* to him on Saturday night?'

She wondered if the reporters, picture editors and interns who visited her would return to Ben with similar tales of Anna. Did she look different? Were her answers more confident than before? On the inside she felt as if a spotlight had been pointed at her and a raised stage planted beneath her feet. As her visitors kept arriving and the questions continued, she drifted back to the gorgeous memory of Ben's hand holding hers, of their kisses that she'd never wanted to end.

Ted, still smarting from being the last to know, sidled up to her at the end of the day. 'For what it's worth, girl, I'm happy for you. McAra might be a pesky hack, but if he makes you smile like that, more power to you both.'

Anna patted his arm. 'Aw, thanks, Ted.'

'I'm still watching him, mind,' he added quickly, in case Anna thought he was turning sentimental. 'Wouldn't be doing my job if I didn't.'

'I'd expect nothing less. Thanks for watching out for me.'

Reddening, he tipped the brim of his guard's hat and hurried away.

Tish was agog with the news when Anna met her in the coffee shop beneath Walton Tower, later that afternoon.

'You've liked the guy for so long – was it what you'd hoped?'

'Better.' A small squeal of pure joy escaped from Anna's lips before she could stop it. 'Honestly, Tish, he was a complete sweetheart. It was like we'd been together for years and I felt so comfortable in his company. I thought we'd have a good time, but Saturday night was incredible.'

'Ugh, spare me the details,' Tish grimaced. 'I don't need to know my friends are getting it, when I'm not.'

'Tish! I wasn't "getting" anything, apart from a really great night out.' Anna's face had begun to ache deliciously from smiling all day. 'I think this could be something that lasts, though. I *hope* it is . . .'

Her friend's frown softened. 'I can tell: it's written all over your face, Anna. Believe me, I'll be first to the hat store when the wedding invitation arrives.'

Anna laughed off the insinuation, but it struck her how differently she felt about Ben compared with other men she had dated in the past. The last time she had been so at ease and so certain of her partner's feelings was with Tom; when he left she'd wondered if she would ever feel that way again. She had never questioned Tom's love for her – until the end of their relationship – but he'd always maintained a distance that she never managed to breach. It meant that even when she was by his side, as close as two people could be, Tom could feel as if he w. 's a hundred miles away. He had protected his heart too much, and Anna realised after he'd ended their relationship that he'd never really opened up to her in the way she had to him.

But it was as if Ben had already closed the emotional distance between them, long before the physical gap narrowed. Being with him, first as a friend and now as – well, whatever they were becoming – felt more grown-up from the beginning, and Anna knew her hopes were soaring sky-high for where that might take them.

In her apartment she caught sight of the star-studded shoes beside the table. All this had happened since their arrival. Was it possible that one had brought about the other? It was fantastical to consider, but that the two had happened so close together – if a coincidence – was intriguing. But then her life had taken an extraordinary road this year, turning on its head her idea of who she was and what her life looked like. She liked the difference immensely.

Life is beautiful, she thought, pouring a glass of wine and sinking into her sofa to consider it all.

Thirty-Six

Lucy Goodliffe wished that real life could be as wonderful as the life she had created online. A cashier in a pound-shop by day, by night she transformed into a social-media magpie – her blog and Twitter feeds filled with exciting, beautiful things she'd discovered. On the Internet she was a queen, followed by a faithful army of subjects who liked, re-tweeted and commented on her every word. Seven-and-a-half thousand people she had never met in person, who nightly flocked to her virtual side to view her latest treasures. Even as she served the unsmiling, uncommunicative and occasionally unwashed masses of Wolverhampton in PoundUniverse by day, she was dreaming of the next post for *Lucy_Hearts*, her blog, which only last year had been hailed as a 'Blog to Watch' by one of the many blogger collectives she belonged to.

Today had been a particularly challenging day IRL (*In Real Life*), her pockmark-faced boss Derek accusing her of not keeping her mind on the job, in plain sight of the queue of shoppers lining up at her till. He'd called her thick, too! Did he *know* who she was? And how much of her brain did she really require, to ring up baskets of items with an identical price, anyway? She was hardly likely to have to query anything, other than the sanity of the people choosing to shop there.

Honestly. If it wasn't that her rent was due and the prospect of moving back home with her dad and his horrible chavvy girlfriend was worse than death itself, she would have told Dodgy Derek to stick his job, right then and there. But until she could save enough to support her blog full-time, she was stuck in her loo-cleaner-blue tabard and would have to put up with it.

But her shift was over for tonight – and she'd taken tomorrow off as holiday to schedule in a raft of new blog posts to sate the appetite of her faithful followers. Snuggled up in her favourite PJs with a large glass of white wine provided by her flatmate, she began to surf her favourite sites for sparkling titbits of loveliness. As usual, the hours melted away as Lucy lost herself in the virtual world. When she eventually looked at the clock at the top of her computer screen, she was surprised to find it was midnight.

And that's when she saw the story on the *Daily Messenger*'s website. It popped up at 12.05 a.m. – and it stopped Lucy in her tracks.

Oh.

My.

Goodness!

An ordinary girl, just like her, receiving mysterious parcels from a secret admirer! It was like the plot of a

312

rom-com, only it hadn't been dreamed up by a team of Hollywood writers: this was *actually* happening! She quickly checked the news postings to see if any other eagle-eyed blogger had reposted the story. Half an hour later, she was satisfied nobody had.

This was *perfect*! A real-life fairy-tale mystery – and a blog exclusive, to boot!

Sleep could wait. Clamping a hand across her mouth to suppress a squeal of delight, Lucy set to work . . .

Within an hour, the story was flashing up on blogs and Twitter timelines across the UK, an army of late-night and early-morning bloggers seizing it with all the vigour Lucy had. Within six hours, social-media commentators had picked up the story in the US and Australian bloggers were quick to follow suit. Across the world, people who longed for good-news stories and tales of real-life romance devoured the details of ordinary Englishwoman Anna Browne, her secret admirer and the gorgeous gifts delivered in brown-paper parcels.

It must be a man, the unseen speculators asserted. *The love of her life she doesn't know yet – how romantic is that?*

It restores your faith in happy-ever-afters, others said, their own secret dreams of a mystery benefactor and sublime gifts being fired by the news of it happening to someone, somewhere in the world.

Hundreds, then thousands, then tens of thousands of bloggers, tweeters and Facebookers like Lucy Goodliffe felt the same surge of hope that the story offered as they read it in bedrooms, on buses and trains and from behind

313

official work documents when their bosses weren't looking – passing it on with the click of a mouse.

By 8.30 a.m. the story was a full-blown viral sensation . . .

Ben wasn't in Freya & Georgie's next morning. Anna checked her phone for messages, but found none. She was sure he'd mentioned meeting, although in her blissful mood it was entirely possible she was mistaken. Unconcerned, she bought herself breakfast and enjoyed a conversation with Megan, the friendly barista, who was overjoyed to hear that the young couple she'd placed so much hope in had finally acted on their chemistry. Anna noticed that she blushed profusely when her good-looking boss walked by.

'Is there anything happening with you two?'

The barista shook her head, but her expression belied the truth. When he was out of earshot, she confided in her customer. 'You have to *swear* not to tell anyone, but we kissed last night! We were closing up and the other girls had gone home. I'd arranged to go on a date with my sister's friend's brother and was just about to leave, when Gabe suddenly blurted out that he liked me. He begged me not to go on the date and go out with him instead! Turns out he'd been so jealous all day and couldn't stand the thought of me meeting someone else. Then we kissed and . . . well, safe to say he doesn't have to be jealous any more.'

Perhaps there was something in the air today, Anna mused. As she looked around the coffee house she saw couples and soon-to-be couples emerging from the sea of city suits. The hum of conversation even carried a different tone – warmer and more convivial than she'd noticed before. The sight of smiles in the heart of the city was new and extraordinary, mirroring the optimism Anna felt.

Positive vibes seemed to be at work in the *Messenger* building, too. The atrium, much busier than usual, was buzzing with an energy all of its own, as people turned to smile at Anna as she entered. She glanced up at the large chrome clock above reception to make sure she wasn't late, but the time was identical to that on her watch.

Strange, she thought, lifting the hatch to move behind the reception desk. *Maybe there's a meeting this morning that I've missed in the diary . . .*

No sooner had she taken her place at reception than the first group of *Messenger* employees approached.

'Great morning, Ms Browne,' one of them said.

'Is it?'

'Indeed. Great for us, great for the paper – and especially great for *you* . . .'

Anna stared back. Were the people here so starved for news that her date with Ben was cause for such celebration? 'This is about Ben McAra, isn't it?'

The group nodded, their identical smiles a little unnerving.

'Well, I'm delighted, obviously. But, you know, taking each day as it comes and all.' Her answer did nothing to end the conversation, and the undiminished scrutiny made her shift uneasily behind the desk. 'I'm sorry – is there anything I can help you with?'

315

'You've done enough already,' a woman said. 'It might just be you've saved us.'

Anna could feel her hackles rising. 'I don't know what you mean. And, with the greatest respect, if you don't need anything, can I ask you to leave the desk, please? We're likely to be busy today and we need visitors to be able to sign in.'

The group shuffled away, but Anna heard, 'Oh, she'll be busy in here all right' as they left. Gradually the crowd in the atrium dispersed, but Anna still felt as if she were being watched as the morning shift began. More strangeness soon followed.

'Excuse me, are you Anna Browne?' a smiling woman asked as she signed in.

That's what it says on my name badge, Anna thought, smiling at the visitor. 'Yes, I am.'

'I think it's wonderful,' the woman rushed as she picked up her briefcase and began to walk from the counter. 'Just wonderful!'

Frowning, Anna watched the visitor hurry across to the lift, still waving and smiling towards reception. What was wrong with everybody today?

It was only when Sheniece arrived for work that Anna's questions were answered.

'Oh. My. *Life*. Anna, are you okay?' she asked, gathering a stunned Anna into her arms before she had even taken off her coat.

'I'm fine,' Anna coughed back, prising herself free of Sheniece's too-tight hug. 'Everyone else is acting oddly, though.'

316

'No surprises there.' Sheniece slapped a folded copy of the *Messenger* on the reception desk. 'I expect they think you're the saviour of the paper. But if you ask me, it's sneaky, using you like that.'

Utterly bewildered, Anna followed Sheniece's stabbing acrylic nail to the newsprint – and her heart hit the floor:

SIGNED, SEALED, DELIVERED – BUT WHO BY?

*'My Mystery Parcels Changed
My Life,' Says City Worker*

A mystery is unfolding within the walls of the *Daily Messenger*, reports CHIEF CORRESPONDENT, BEN MCARA.

An anonymous benefactor is showering a young receptionist with gifts that, she claims, are having a profound effect upon her life.

Parcels began arriving at DMHQ two months ago for receptionist Anna Browne, 31. Wrapped in brown paper and bearing no details of the sender, they have sparked a conundrum that has employees of the leading national paper befuddled.

The pretty brunette, described by colleagues as 'charming' and 'sweet', was practically unknown at the newspaper until the deliveries began. But it appears someone has been watching Ms Browne and has singled her out – making her the talk of the town.

It is unclear what the stranger's intentions are towards the young woman, with some suggesting a sinister purpose. A senior source at the *Daily Messenger* confirmed that internal security is keeping tabs on the situation. 'It could be anyone – with any motive. We believe in protecting our staff,' he said.

Ms Browne refutes this. 'It's very kind. I'd like to thank the sender in person.'

Gifts have included perfume, jewellery, a treasure-hunt-style jaunt to a Notting Hill vintage store and, most recently, a sumptuous pair of handmade shoes.
More on this EXCLUSIVE story follows TOMORROW.

'He's a *dog*!' Sheniece proclaimed. 'Ben McAra is not worth your time.'

'I – can't believe it . . .' Anna felt sick as anger, betrayal and fury churned inside her. She wanted to run, but couldn't move, forced to stare the horrible truth in the face: Ben had lied to her. It was all a lie. The friendship, the date, the kisses that had meant the world to her – all just a part of . . . what exactly? Just another story? A plan to set her up? Was he laughing at her now? How had she been so blind?

'You look like death, sweets. Here, sit down. Shall I get you some tea?'

'Tea isn't what she needs,' Ted said, pushing Sheniece out of the way and looming large into Anna's view. 'Anna needs a bloody big sledgehammer to brain that *bas*— Pardon my French, girl, but that McAra's the lowest of the low.'

Sheniece groaned and pressed a glass of water into Anna's hands. 'It's just a story. It'll pass.'

'Don't bank on it, girl. It's *everywhere*. Story broke online this morning and it's all over Twitter. Reg in Security over at the *Daily Post* says they're kicking themselves for missing it. Reckons they'll be heading this way, trying to steal you for an exclusive story.'

'*Ted!* You're not helping . . . Anna, say something. Do

you want me to go up there and give McAra a piece of my mind?'

But Anna couldn't think, let alone answer. The space around her undulated, as Ted and Sheniece's voices echoed far in the distance. The words of the article tumbled around her, Ben's name in the byline refusing to leave her sight. Everything she had placed her trust in – their growing friendship, the wonderful night at the riverside restaurant, and all the hopes she had dared to entertain since – were now revealed as nothing but elements of a cold, cynical scheme. How had she missed it?

She had wanted it to be true – and perhaps that was where her mistake had been made. She had allowed herself to trust Ben, when plenty of others questioned his integrity – including Jonah. Now her fingernails carved ugly half-moon marks into her palms as she clenched her fists in her lap. She didn't look at anyone, not wanting to see the pity on their faces for the too-sweet girl so easily taken advantage of.

And the day was about to become far worse.

By three o'clock a group of journalists from rival newspapers had arrived and were being kept from the door by a very over-excited Ted, possibly the most dramatic thing to happen to him in the twenty-six years of his security career. Sheniece and Ashraf assumed switchboard duties as incoming calls became dominated by press requests. Rea hurried down from the newsroom to report mentions of Ben's article as far afield as America and Japan; Damien Kendal was rumoured to be prowling the floor with a smile as wide as a month of Christmases, while the author

319

of the incendiary piece was conspicuous by his absence. The accepted wisdom was that Ben had been sent on assignment and wouldn't return for a week. The unofficial assertion was that he was hiding from Anna's wrath, like the coward he'd proved himself to be. All of this swirled around Anna in a blur. All she wanted to do was run home and hide. But she couldn't leave, trapped by the job she'd always loved. It was utterly hopeless and she willed the hours to pass.

A call from Juliet Evans at half-past four summoned her to the top floor. Keeping her eyes to the ground, she hurried through the open-plan offices, not wanting to see the expressions of journalists who had stopped working and were watching her pass. The coolness of the editor's temporary office was a welcome relief after the weight of scrutiny that had mugged her all day.

'Anna. Please sit.' Juliet didn't smile or make any conciliatory gesture, taking the seat opposite and folding her expensively manicured hands on the glass desk. 'I won't waste time enquiring after your health. I think I know the answer. The question is: what is the best course of action from here on in?'

Anna maintained her low gaze, fearing that eye contact might cause tears she would regret revealing. 'I don't know.'

'I would be lying if I said the reaction to Mr McAra's story hasn't lifted the load from a great number of shoulders,' Juliet stated. 'The story is performing well online and the traffic there is better than we've seen all year. It's a small beginning, but what it's done for morale today has been great. We are hoping tomorrow's follow-on story brings more people to the site. I'm sure you understand that this has come at a crucial time for the paper . . . But that isn't the issue. Scrutiny of you is only going to worsen for the next few days. So I suggest you take a leave of absence – a paid leave, naturally. We'll handle everything from here, and I'll do my best to ensure your home address isn't made available to the press. If you talk to anyone, you talk to us, okay?'

'I don't want to talk to anyone.'

'Not right now, but in time maybe you will. And an interview in the *Messenger* – perhaps with a video we can post to meet online demand – might just be the way to keep the story small but effective. For all of us. Another newspaper might not be as flattering to you as you have my word the *Messenger* will be.'

Anna was disgusted by the suggestion, but dog-tired weariness was setting in and she just wanted to leave. 'Fine, whatever,' she said, staring at the edge of Juliet's desk.

'Good. So go, take some time away from this. I'll call to advise when to come back to work, yes?'

To be away from the *Messenger*, her colleagues and a certain journalist she never wanted to set eyes on again was exactly what Anna wanted. 'Yes. Thank you.'

'My pleasure.' For a moment, Anna thought she saw a glimmer of compassion in the editor's eyes. 'It will pass. It always does.'

The news story might, Anna thought. *But the damage Ben has done won't* . . .

Thirty-Seven

Juliet's driver picked up Anna from the service entrance at the rear of the *Messenger* building. He'd been instructed to drive her wherever she wanted to go and offered to take her home, but Anna needed time to think, and the possibility that a journalist might be following the car scared her. Instead she asked to be dropped off near Covent Garden, scurrying into a café near the Royal Opera House that she'd been to once before on one of Ruari's rare visits to the city. The small link with family made the café feel like a sanctuary. She found a table near the back and ordered a large coffee, intending to take her time over it.

'I'll give you a *biscotti*, too,' the Italian-accented waiter smiled, as if guessing Anna's troubled mind. 'On the house.'

As he placed the cup and saucer on the table, Anna's mobile buzzed beside it. The heartening smile of her brother beamed up at her from the screen.

'Rua?'

'An, you all right? I saw the paper. Never expected my big sis to be a celebrity.'

'It's awful. I've been given time off work.'

'Wish I could be sent home on full pay. Sorry, An. I just wanted to check you were okay, though?'

'Not really, not at the moment. But I will be. The worst thing is, the story was written by Ben.'

She heard a sharp intake of breath at Ruari's end of the call. 'Not that journo you've been seeing? What a rat! Want me and the lads to drive up to the Smoke and sort him out?'

Anna gave a weary smile, her heart filled with love for her brother. 'Bless you. Not right now, but I might keep the Perranporth Hit-Squad on standby, if you don't mind.'

'Pleasure. We'll await your call! Look, you know if you fancy a few days down here, me and Jodie and the kids'd love to see you. Jodie was the one who spotted the story today. Vicious about it, she was! She sends her love.'

'Thanks, Rua. I'm just going to sit it out and hope the story goes away soon.'

'I imagine it'll pass quick enough. But you know where we are, yeah? Love you, Anna.'

Ruari's concern was touching and she loved that his first instinct was to call her. They might be separated by physical distance, but in many ways the Browne siblings grew closer every year.

As she ended the call, her finger inadvertently caught the phone-book icon on the screen – and she came face-to-face with Ben's number. She stared at it, the image of a cup of coffee that she'd picked for his caller ID, in lieu of his photo, reminding her of every hope she'd carried during their coffee-shop meetings. She could do nothing about his article, but she could evict him from her mobile. Without hesitation, she deleted the entry. It was a hollow victory, her heart wincing as confirmation flashed on the screen: *ENTRY DELETED*.

Not wanting any more calls, Anna switched off her mobile, picked up a discarded copy of *The Times* from a neighbouring table and tried her best to escape the endless carousel of questions in her head. Her eyes skimmed the newsprint, not really seeing the stories. She thanked heaven that the café wasn't the type to offer the *Daily Messenger* to its customers. For a few hours at least, she could be free of Ben's article.

What hurt the most was that Ben never even hinted that the story was imminent. He claimed to be a friend – and to aspire to be more than that – yet he was happy for Anna to be ambushed by his handiwork. She had expected better from him. But maybe Ted was right: once a hack, always a hack.

She was angry with Juliet Evans for being so willing to sacrifice her privacy on the altar of the paper's salvation. A ride home in her expensive Aston Martin and fully paid leave fell woefully short of an adequate apology. But then what did the high-powered editor care for a receptionist she barely knew, when faced with losing her own job? And how bad *was* the situation at the newspaper, if Anna's story could be its salvation?

She had no answers because none existed. It was cruel and unfair – and Anna was the unwitting collateral damage. At the end of it, the paper might be granted a reprieve and Ben would emerge unscathed, save for a dip in popularity at work. But Anna's heart had been broken – and she didn't know if it would recover.

A horrible thought reared up in her mind: maybe the parcels had just been part of a plan to create a story. Could that be true? In her heart she felt it was unlikely, but not knowing who had sent them meant she didn't understand why they had been sent to her. That was the worst thing. The question *why* was what she most wanted answered. Why had she been chosen? Ben hadn't confirmed he was the sender on Saturday night, but he hadn't denied it either, had he? There had been a moment before his kiss that swept Anna's questions aside, when she'd almost believed he was trying to tell her something.

But would Ben have gone to all the trouble of sending eight parcels just for a small story that *might* have helped the newspaper's fortunes for a couple of days?

She considered the midnight-blue shoes and how they had made her feel. Regardless of whether Ben had sent them or not, Anna couldn't bring herself to write off the gift. Discovering the shoes and their gold box in the brown paper had been a magical, heart-stopping experience of deep personal significance. Whatever the sender's motives, she couldn't discount what she'd felt.

And then a new, defiant voice appeared in her head. Why *should* she have to dismiss the parcels? She hadn't asked for them, or used them to draw attention to herself, but their arrival in her life had sparked something profound inside: changes that she and other people had noticed.

Changes for the better. Through them she had discovered her own voice, her confidence and even the beginnings of ambition. Perhaps the greatest gift had been what Anna had found within herself. Nobody could take that away from her.

The thought sparkled in her mind, casting out a little of the gloom and strengthening her resolve. She might have been betrayed by Ben and used by the *Daily Messenger*, but she still had what she'd taken from the experience. When the story had passed, what mattered was what she retained.

I'm not going to be defeated by this, she vowed as she joined the throngs of commuters heading for Leicester Square Underground station. *I'm worth more than that.*

It was almost seven o'clock when Anna arrived home. She was relieved to discover the pavement outside Walton Tower mercifully free of camped-out journalists, the street more or less empty of people as the early-evening traffic crawled past. Her post-box was empty in the lobby and the building had an air of quiet welcome. If it remained like this for the rest of her paid leave, she would be more than content.

Seamus, in the middle of a phone conversation, gave her a thumbs-up as she passed his open door, and a lady from the floor beneath Anna's apartment wished her a good evening without making extraordinary eye contact. For tonight at least, the *Daily Messenger* exclusive had seemingly yet to reach these walls.

Taking what felt like the first deep breath of the day,

Anna turned the key in her front door and inhaled the welcome scent of home. Discarding her bag, she walked into the kitchen and picked up the kettle.

'Seems my girl's a bit of a star then,' said a voice.

Slowly Anna turned, already knowing its owner before her vision confirmed it. Six years since she'd last heard it in person, but the chill of recognition was as sure as ever. The very last person Anna ever expected to see in the city was making herself comfortable on her sofa, sun-browned bare feet up on the cushions and nicotine-stained fingers picking at chipped pink varnish on the toenails.

'What are you doing here?'

Senara Browne folded leather-jacketed arms across her ample chest and gave a loud tut. 'T'ain't no way to welcome your own mother, is it?'

'And how did you get in?'

'Nice Irish bloke at the front door let me in, when I said I was your mum.'

'What do you want?'

'Less of your attitude! Not allowed to visit you, am I now? 'Gainst the law, is it?'

'No, but . . .'

Senara nodded at the kettle still swinging limply in Anna's hand. 'Cup of tea *dreckly* would be *nice*, thank you. Do you know what they tried to charge me on the train up for a cuppa? No wonder nobody smiles here. Blinkin' daylight robbery.'

Numb with shock, Anna made tea. It seemed the logical thing to do, both to fill time while she constructed a response and to prevent conversation while the kettle boiled noisily. Senara had shown no interest in Anna's life since she'd moved to the city. There had been no correspondence between them – not even a Christmas or birthday card – and only one phone call, in six years. Why change that now?

The article – that's what's brought her here.

Senara Browne didn't understand the concept of selflessness. Nothing had ever happened in her life without a perceivable benefit attached. Seeing Anna in a national tabloid must have set pound-signs floating in her vision. Ben McAra had no idea of the trouble he had caused Anna. Encouraging her mother to leave the 'blessed Duchy' and land at Anna's door was the worst possible thing he could have done.

'Why are you here?' Anna asked, ignoring the dramatic snort of disapproval Senara made when tasting her daughter's tea.

Never one for hidden motives, her case became immediately clear. 'It's all over the papers, ain't it? My Anna, gettin' gifts from a stranger. What you do to be that lucky, hmm? And how much did you get for that tale? National papers pay big, everyone knows it.'

Anna chose a seat at the table – as far away as possible from Senara. 'First of all, I didn't sell my story. Someone else wrote it without my permission. And secondly, I don't know who sent me the parcels. I have nothing to give you, Mum.'

'You'll forgive me if I don't believe you.' She abandoned her mug of tea after a second displeased sip and looked around the room. 'Nice place you got here. Fancy. You don't get that from a nine-to-five.'

'I do, actually.' *Because unlike you, Mum, I don't need to blag my way through life . . .*

'Whatever. Never think of your poor old mum, though, do you? I almost lost my home last year, no thanks to you. I don't make much, not working the bar at the Blue. And what little work I pick up here and there don't cover it, either. If it hadn't been for my Ruari, I'd be on the street by now.'

Anna shook her head. Ruari's sweet nature was a mine of rich pickings for their mother, and Senara knew it. She remembered the phone conversation with her brother last autumn that had painted a very different picture: 'She's missed a month's mortgage payment,' Ruari had told her, the weariness evident in his voice. 'I lent her money again, but I'm not convinced she'll use it for that. She'll be straight to her latest flame and it'll be gone . . .'

'Ruari has a family and a business he's worked hard for. You shouldn't keep running to him for money.'

'What choice do I 'ave, when life slings me the muck it does?'

'You seem to be looking after yourself just fine, Mum.'

'No thanks to you.'

Anna hadn't even known her mother owed money until Ruari told her, probably because Senara knew what Anna's response would be. But there was no use in arguing the point. Anna looked at her watch. 'It's getting late. What time's your train back?'

A defiant smile spread across Senara's face, the one that

329

said: *I know I'm going to win.* 'Got one of them open returns, didn't I? Thought I'd see the bright lights you're so fond of.'

'You can't stay here.' It blurted out from a far-away place; from a small child terrified of the trouble her mother was about to unleash. Anna might have to hide away from work for a week, but she was not sharing the experience with her mother.

'Giss on, Anna! You've more than enough room.' She patted the sofa. 'I'll be good on this. Very comfy. Very *expensive*.'

'No.'

'I 'spect you need support, at a time like *this*,' her mother continued, undeterred. 'Being a national laughing stock an' all. You need your mother.'

The statement was as ludicrous as it was heartbreaking. There had been countless times when Anna had needed a mother, but Senara had missed every one. Instead, Anna had learned to do without – never to call on Senara to fulfil the role she claimed to own only when it suited her. When Anna had nightmares as a child, Senara's room was out of bounds; when she fell in the playground, her teacher kissed the grazed wounds better; when her first period arrived, her best friend helped her. First break-ups, exam stress, achievements to be celebrated, fights to be settled – all went unshared and unnoticed. Besides carrying her and giving birth, Senara's maternal remit was blank.

'I appreciate your concern, but I'm fine.'

'Well, it's too late to go back tonight, so I'll have to

stay one night at least. Now, what food you got, Anna? I'm starved.'

Ambushed by her mother and dog-tired from the emotion of the day, Anna had no choice but to accept her unwelcome visitor for the night. After a meal and awkward exchanges bordering on civility, she made up a bed for Senara and retreated to the blessed peace of her own room. Finally released, she climbed fully clothed into bed, burying herself down under the duvet and sobbing soundlessly into her pillow. Ben, her mother, blurred newsprint and perfectly wrapped parcels whirled about her head in a taunting mental merry-go-round until the early hours, when sheer exhaustion dragged her to a fitful sleep.

Thirty-Eight

Next morning, with Senara's loud snores drifting through from the living room, Anna sat in bed nursing her throbbing head. There had to be a way through it all, but how would she find it? One thing was certain: she wasn't going to share her time off work with her mother. Quickly dressing, she took her purse and mobile phone and sneaked out, grateful that Senara was a famously heavy sleeper. It was only when she emerged on the street outside Walton Tower that she felt she could breathe again.

It was almost eight-thirty, but the coffee shop was surprisingly empty. Unlike Freya & Georgie's, which was packed all day with city workers, Spill the Beans did most of its business at the end of the day, when weary local residents needed to unwind before heading home.

'Hey, Anna,' Chas, the smiling owner, called out as she arrived at the counter. 'We don't usually see you this early. You okay?'

'I'm good. Just taking a little time off work,' she replied, hoping against hope that a certain copy of the *Daily Messenger* hadn't made its way here yet.

'Sounds nice.'

With her mother hanging around, this was unlikely. She settled at a table and sought out her brother's number on her phone.

'Anna? Wass gonon?' Ruari sounded sleepy, despite probably being up for hours catching waves before work.

'Sorry to call so early, but I've got a bit of a crisis.'

Her brother's chuckle brought a smile. 'Even more than yesterday? Lads on the beach were agog with it last night. Clem Wheelwright says he wished he'd dated you at school, so he'd have a story to sell on you now.'

'Charming. It's not the story that's the problem this time, but it's dragged Mum up here.'

There was a pause. Anna pictured her brother's face as he processed what he'd just heard. Anna could hear the gabbling of seagulls and the crash of waves on the beach, where Ruari would be preparing for the day's surf-school clients. 'Mum's in London? *Mum?*'

'Caught the train up the minute she read the paper, apparently. I haven't heard from her for six years and then yesterday there she was, bold as brass in my flat. I asked her to leave, but she refused last night.'

'I'm still getting over her leaving Cornwall. I always figured she'd turn into a pillar of salt the moment she crossed the Tamar.'

'I think she wants money, Rua. I can't imagine she's come to look after me.'

333

Ruari laughed – but this time Anna could hear the hollowness of experience. 'What you going to do?'

'Short of getting a restraining order, I don't know.'

'I might be able to help you out on that score. Remember Griff Grantley, the little kid who used to trail after our gang wanting to join us? He's only a Detective Inspector now! I could ask him to sort you out.' He let out a long breath. 'I wish I could come up and drag her back, An, but I'm run off my feet here. Besides, I'm not 'zackly her favourite person at the moment.'

'Oh? That isn't what she said.' Anna might have known that her mother's glowing endorsement of Ruari's behaviour was merely a stick to beat her with.

'Jodie and me are pretty much done with her now. She turned up last Saturday, drunk out of her mind, scared the kids – and that was it: Jodie threw her out and threatened to leave me if I help her again. I'm not risking my family for that woman, not any more, An. But I'm always here for you, yeah? Always. And I mean that.'

'I know.'

'Look, I'll try and call her mobile today if she's got it turned on, and talk some sense into her, yeah? But beyond that, I don't know what I can do.'

'It's okay. I just wanted to tell someone more than anything. I'll deal with her.'

'Well, be careful. You know how conniving she is. And if it gets worse, call me and I'll . . . just have to make sure Jodie don't find out.'

Anna didn't want to cause trouble between her brother and his partner, especially given the hassle they'd put up with over the last six years. Ending the call five minutes later, she sank back into the coffee shop's leather sofa and let her thoughts wash over her.

She couldn't be angry with her younger brother. While she had escaped to a place where Senara was unlikely to follow (or so she'd thought), Ruari had stayed in the county, never more than an hour's drive away from their mother's latest whim. But he had his partner and two beautiful daughters now and had worked hard to build the happy, secure home he and Anna had been denied as children. He deserved a reprieve from being the blue-eyed boy. Senara was in Anna's city now – and it was up to her to deal with it.

An hour later, with nothing else to keep her away from her apartment and the unwelcome visitor still encamped there, Anna went home. A suspicious fug of nicotine smoke hung guiltily by the window as she entered, Senara hunched over a black coffee in Anna's dressing gown, which she'd pilfered from the back of the bathroom door.

'Morning.' Gravel grated in her mother's low voice, followed by a fit of guttural coughing. 'Hope you don't mind this.' She pulled out the lapel of the dressing gown.

'Help yourself.'

'I did. So, how comes you're not at work, maid? Lost your fancy job, have you?'

'I have some time off.'

'Ah! Plenty of time to show your old mum round your swanky town then. Convince me how the 'ell you think this place beats Kernow.'

'I'm not taking you anywhere, except the station.'

Unmoved, Senara picked at her fingernail, dropping a shred of red nail varnish on the coffee table. 'Like that, is it?'

'I don't want you here. I'm sorry.' It surprised her to hear how boldly she addressed her mother. But she was furious with Senara for abusing Ruari's care, and her mother needed to hear it.

'Well, you've got me. Thing is, I thought your paper might like a character reference for their latest star. Bit of background, you know. Add a bit of colour. Course, it'll cost them. But that's how papers like that work, ain't it?'

One thing could be said for Senara Browne – she never troubled herself with pretence.

'They wouldn't be interested.'

'Your man Ben would be, I'm sure.'

'He's out of the city for work,' Anna shot back, crossing her arms as a protective shield. Senara's intention scared her more than the thought of Ben's follow-up article, which by now would have been read all over the country. There was no telling what lies Senara would weave, if she thought it would bring her more money. 'You have to go.'

And then, without warning, her mother burst into tears. 'One day, An! That's all I'm askin' for! T'ain't much to ask. Maybe I miss my girl – have you stopped to consider that? Maybe I want to make things right a'tween us. I turned fifty last week. My life's headin' towards the grave and I don't like all I see back down the road. Your brother's gone cold on me, too, now. I blame that maid he's shacked up with – never liked me, she hasn't. Oh, come on, girl! Just one day. Then I'll catch the train tomorrow

336

and you won't have to hear from me again, if you don't want to. I can make myself comfortable here – I won't need babysittin'. How about I get us something for tea, eh? You go out and do what you have to, and I'll sort it for when you get home?'

Anna stared at her mother, suddenly unsure. She knew Senara could cry crocodile tears like a pro when she needed to, but she couldn't escape the hint of desperation in her mother's voice. 'I don't know . . .'

'Please, girl? I know I ain't been a good mother – I've had enough folks tell me that over the years. I've let you down and I ain't been there when you needed a mum. It ain't much, but it might go towards tipping the balance back. I don't want us at war, Anna, despite what you might think. Let me do this, then I'll go. Promise.'

It was clear that Senara had no intention of leaving today. A little confused by her mother's emotional response, weary from lack of sleep and having no will to fight, Anna conceded defeat. 'Okay. I'll be out for most of the day, though.'

Senara's eyes lit up. 'You take all the time you need. I'll be fine, here, don't you worry. Eight o'clock tea, yeah?'

In the corridor outside, Anna turned to look back at her front door. She should be worried: when had her mother ever been sincere about anything before? Anna knew she could have stood her ground, insisted that her mother leave immediately and won the sole use of her home back, but something had stopped her. Maybe it was tiredness, or perhaps a deeper motivation. For too long she'd feared the day her mother might turn up in London – maybe facing

337

that fear with the new confidence she'd discovered in herself would help her to draw a line under the events of her childhood? This evening might be the time she could reveal who she really was, to a mother who had never taken the time to notice. And then, Anna could be free.

Still, the problem of what to do with her unwanted day off from work loomed large. Having banished herself from her own home until the evening, Anna had no choice but to keep busy – but what should she do?

On a whim, she crossed the hall and knocked on Jonah's door. He was probably out on a project somewhere, like every other self-respecting worker in the city today. Turning away as soon as she'd knocked, she jumped when the door behind her opened.

'Anna? What's up, lass?'

She turned back. 'I'm sorry, Jonah, I've nowhere else to go . . .'

Saying it out loud caused the frustration of the past twenty-four hours to flood over her. All of this had been brought about by someone she'd cared for – someone she trusted. Ben had forced a spotlight on Anna that she'd never asked for and now, across the country, readers of the *Daily Messenger* were forming opinions about her – just as the residents of Polperro had done when Senara crashed Anna's musical performance so many years ago. It might pass quickly, but what if it didn't? What if from now on she was known as 'That Girl with the Parcels', just as she'd been known as 'That Poor Anna Browne', years before? The thought terrified her. And it was all beyond her control . . .

338

Without warning, she burst into tears, her loud sobs echoing down the corridor. Frustration, weariness and the injustice of it all converged to overwhelm her; with no strength left to resist, Anna let go. Shocked, Jonah didn't wait for an invitation, wrapping his arms around her and leading her inside.

'It's okay,' he murmured against her hair. 'It'll all be okay.'

Thirty-Nine

The comforting warm chin of a concerned Border collie brought Anna's tears to an end. With a small smile, she reached down to pat Bennett's soft head.

'See? No one's allowed tears for long in this place,' Jonah smiled, handing Anna a mug of tea. 'Bennett's rules, not mine.'

'Thank you. And I'm sorry about crying all over you again. It's just been an awful time after the story went out.'

Jonah frowned as he sat beside her. 'Story?'

'It's okay – you don't have to pretend. I imagine every-one's seen it by now.'

'Anna, I haven't the foggiest what you're talking about.'

Was he doing this for her benefit? 'The article in the *Messenger* – that Ben wrote?'

'Ben wrote about you?' His frown deepened at the mention of the journalist. 'I've spent the last week filming

340

in a field, lass. Haven't seen any papers, and – no offence – the only thing I'd use your paper for is loo roll.'

Anna was relieved to find the only person in the city who hadn't read about her, but it did mean she had to relive the experience in order to enlighten him. He listened without passing comment, but his expression grew ever darker.

'And then my mother turned up,' she added, her heart dipping at the inescapable fact.

'I thought you said she never left the Duchy?'

'I didn't think she ever would. But she's at my place now, planning dinner.' Anna had told Jonah little about her relationship with Senara, but it was enough for him to understand the gravity of the event. 'I can hardly believe it.'

'So, the article kicked her into action?' He shook his head. 'Families, eh? More trouble than they're worth, sometimes.'

'So now I have time away from work while Ben's exclusives run, and I don't know what will happen. I'm just hoping the story will fade and be over by the time I go back.'

'And if it hasn't?'

She had wondered the same herself as she hid in the coffee shop this morning. But driving herself mad thinking of every possible outcome would get her nowhere. 'I'm just taking a day at a time.'

He nodded. 'I understand. Well, I've the day off myself, so let me take you out somewhere.'

'That would be fantastic. Thank you.'

'Least I can do for you, lass.' He gave a rueful smile. 'I'd offer to sort that bloody journalist out for you, but I suspect that wouldn't help. Just know that, in my mind, I'm currently pummelling his smug little head into the pavement.'

To his credit, Jonah didn't mention Ben again as he and Anna caught the Overground train to Kew and spent the day wandering around the beautifully peaceful Royal Botanical Gardens. The lushness of the scenery helped to take Anna's mind off the story and her mother, and Jonah's matter-of-fact take on it all was comforting.

'Well, I've just spent the last week watching lambs get castrated,' he grinned, as they ate ice cream in the White Peaks café, gazing out across the manicured lawns. 'And you think *you've* had it tough. Between that, spending a day-and-a-half getting eaten alive by midges in a field and filming vets with their arms up the backside of heifers, it's been delightful.'

Anna laughed, imagining Jonah trying to keep a straight face while filming it all. 'You're doing your dream job, remember?'

'Oh aye, the glamour is *exhausting.*'

'Well, at least I can say I haven't had to shove my arm up a cow yet. So, that's something.'

'I think you'll be just fine,' he said, reaching over the table to squeeze her hand. 'You have a great deal going for you.'

Surprised, Anna smiled. 'Thank you. You too.'

'Oh, don't you worry – I know what a catch I am. Seriously, though, there's no point fretting over stuff that hasn't happened yet. And stuff that *has* happened you can just deal with at the time. Standing in a field with a camera for hours on end makes you realise how much time can be chucked away beating yourself up over rubbish. I once spent two whole weeks filming foxes and regretting breaking up with a girl back home. Made me miserable as sin, but did nothing to change the situation. I just had to deal with what had happened and move on. You'll be fine, Anna.'

Jonah's faith in her was as welcome a sight as the natural beauty of the gardens soothing Anna's eyes and soul. 'That's a lovely thing to say.'

'Aye, well, I come up with profound chat every now and again,' he grinned. 'Not bad for an Ilkley lad, eh?'

All too soon the day ended, the knot in Anna's stomach twisting tighter as she neared home. Jonah said goodbye to her in the corridor and planted a hesitant kiss on her cheek, 'for luck'. Bracing herself, Anna opened her front door.

'Ah, right on time,' Senara called.

The sight that greeted Anna stopped her in the doorway. The mess of her mother's belongings, which earlier had commandeered most of her living room, was gone. An open bottle of red wine and two glasses had been placed on the coffee table, along with a couple of lit tea-lights as a centrepiece. Soft music hummed from the radio on the kitchen counter and the smell of cooking filled the air. In the centre of it all, wearing an apron that might as well have been a suit of armour for the awkward way it sat on its wearer, was Senara, stirring simmering saucepans, her stack of silver bangles jingling as she moved. Anna wondered if she had inadvertently entered an invisible portal and was now in an alternative-universe version of her apartment, facing the domestic-goddess facsimile of her mother.

'Is . . . everything okay?'

'I'm doin' well, An, as you can clearly see.' She chuckled. 'Don't look so shocked, girl! Your old ma's learned a bit of stuff since you last saw her. Chuck some wine in them glasses, yeah? It's thirsty work, this cookin' business.'

Alcohol seemed the perfect solution to make sense of what she was seeing. Anna poured two large glasses and downed half of hers in a single gulp. For Senara to find a kitchen in the first place was remarkable; for her to be cooking apparently from scratch, when her idea of 'classy food' used to be tinned spaghetti Bolognese, bordered on world-shaking significance. 'Did you find everything you needed?' Anna was careful to keep her voice steady.

'I went to the supermarket just down the street. Got everything in there, ain't they?' She indicated an empty carrier bag on the kitchen counter. 'And get your old mum, eh? Like that Nigella, only with better tits.'

It was too much for Anna to take in. She sat and watched Senara blustering around her kitchen, thinking she would wake up any second. Her phone buzzed and the screen displayed a number she didn't recognise.

'Hello?'

'Anna, it's Ben.'

She ended the call and threw the mobile onto the sofa cushions, her heart thudding. She'd deleted his number from her phone, but *why* hadn't she blocked it, too? Trust Ben to think she'd still want to hear from him. How dare he expect her to talk to him, after what he'd done? The screen lit up again, the same number appearing as the mobile vibrated itself almost full circle.

'Ain't you going to answer that?' Senara called.

'No.'

The ringing ended, then began again. 'Seems awfully keen, whoever it is.'

'I don't want to talk to him,' Anna replied, kicking herself for giving too much away.

Her mother's eyes lit up and she sashayed across the living room to pick up her wine glass. 'Ah, so it's a *man*, is it?'

'Leave it, Mum.'

'My little Anna all grown-up and breaking hearts over London,' Senara mocked, her amber eyes wide with amusement. 'Well, I never. Always thought you'd end up a spinster, if I'm honest. But nice to see you provin' me wrong.' She bent down and snatched up the phone before Anna could stop her. 'And he isn't even in your address book? You into one-nighters now, maid?'

Infuriated, Anna held out her hand. 'Give it back.'

'Who is he? No, I'm curious. What's his name?'

'I'm not telling you. Give my phone back, please, Mum.'

Senara's face lit up with scandal. '*No* – it couldn't be, could it? You've been shaggin' that journalist, haven't you?'

'I don't know what you're talking about.' The defensiveness in her tone gave the game away.

345

'I'm *right*, aren't I? Oh-ho, An, you shagged him and he did the dirty on you!'

'I didn't "shag" him . . .'

'Maybe not, but your face tells me you weren't afar off. Bloody Nora, girl, turns out you take after your old mum after all.'

This was a step too far. Anna shot to her feet and snatched her phone back. 'I am *not* like you. I will *never* be like you!'

Still laughing, Senara held her hands up and stepped away. 'Calm yourself. I was only jokin', wasn't I? Thing is, An: men are all the same, in the end. Unreliable. Liars. Crooks. Like your father and Ruari's father, and every man I've had the misfortune to care for. They take what they're after and drop you like a stone. I know, better than anyone.' She sat down and patted the sofa cushion next to her. 'Now sit. Have another tot of wine. You looks like you need it.'

Anna's phone rang for a third time. She turned it off and slumped next to Senara, her mind so conflicted over Ben that she momentarily forgot the fight with her mother. 'I wish he'd leave me alone. He's done enough damage already.'

'Like him, did you?'

Anna turned to her mother and answered truthfully. 'I thought I did.'

'Smooth-talker, was he?'

'He's a journalist, so . . .'

Senara nodded. 'Say no more. I know the type. Spun his words round you till you were dizzy, I bet.'

'Something like that.'

'Just like your dad.'

The revelation caught Anna by surprise. 'Really?'

'Mm-hmm.'

Daring to take advantage of the unexpected moment of understanding between them, Anna pushed her luck. 'In what way?'

'Beautiful words, he had. And a body to match.'

'Was he a journalist, too?'

Her mother gave a snort. '*Hardly.*'

'Tell me about him?' Anna willed her mother to speak. Her father had been the reason she'd fallen in love with London, believing him to be in the city. If Senara told her more about him now, there was a chance – however slim – that she might be able to find him.

'Oh, the stories I *could* tell about him . . .' Her voice trailed off and Anna held her breath. Was this it? All her life Anna had asked questions about him and Senara had refused to answer them. Now she felt closer to her mother breaking her silence than they had ever been before. 'He was a— *Damn it*, my pan's boiling over.'

Leaving Anna open-mouthed, Senara dashed across to the kitchen to grab the bubbling pan. And while the possibility could have remained for her to elaborate, Anna knew the moment had passed. She eyed the half-empty bottle of red wine and a thought began to form: perhaps if she kept the wine flowing this evening, Senara would relax enough to answer some of the questions Anna had carried all her life. She had relented once, on only a few sips of wine this evening – surely it could happen again?

As her mother crashed and clattered over her kitchen creation, Anna sneaked into her bedroom to pull two bottles of red from the small wine rack in the bottom of her coat cupboard. The wine rack had been a gift three Christmases ago from Jonah, after Anna admitted she had nowhere to store wine. The bottles were various Christmas, birthday and thank-you gifts from friends and at work, left in the wine rack for an opportunity to share with someone, as Anna rarely drank alone. Tonight presented a perfect occasion to break into her collection.

She returned to her living room and placed the bottles on the table.

'Where'd you magic those from?' Senara called, her internal alcohol-locating radar as sharp as ever.

'I just thought we might need them,' Anna smiled back, formulating her plan. *Eat, let the wine flow and get Mum talking . . .*

Senara's culinary creation was revealed to be a slightly overcooked pasta bake, heavy on the cheese and light on seasoning, but as it was the most complicated recipe Anna had ever seen her attempt, it was as impressive as a highly technical dish. Just as Anna expected, her mother relaxed as the wine disappeared. After dinner they left the table and sat at opposite ends of the sofa, Anna trying her best to pace her drinking and not mind Senara propping her feet up on the coffee table. Eventually, just after eleven o'clock, Anna sensed the time was right to begin her questions.

'So, you were saying about Dad?' She hoped it was leading enough to coax her mother's reply.

'Was I?' Senara replied, yawning.

'Mm-hmm. You said he was good with words.'

Her mother leered towards her. 'T'ain't all he was good with, neither. Oh, don't look so disapprovin'. Did you think you were an immaculate conception?' She rested her head against the back of the sofa and closed her eyes. 'Tall, he was. And broad. Little wiry curls all over his chest – colour of your hair. I thought the world revolved around him . . .'

'What was his name?'

'. . . And the thing was, I never could say no when he asked me over. More fool me, course.'

'Mum? His *name*?'

Senara's eyes screwed up. 'Can't recall.'

'Yes, you can. *Tell* me, Mum. Just his name.'

'*Can't*, An. Wasn't mine, was he? Another woman had his name. Had to keep it quiet, we did. Sneaking around like a couple of guilty kids. 'S what made it exciting, though. Till he went back – to *her*. And those screamin' brats . . .'

The revelation sobered Anna in a second, as a sick chill took hold of her. So her father was married, with a family of his own, too? No wonder he wanted nothing to do with his daughter – the product of an illicit affair. She'd considered the possibility, of course, over the years; and it explained why her grandmother couldn't tell her much about her father. But having it confirmed so casually crushed Anna. Feeling numb, she pressed on.

'Just give me his name, please?' Grasping at straws, Anna made a bid for the only thing she could think of.

349

Even if her father had written her off, even if he'd want nothing to do with her now, somehow hearing his name would give her a connection to who she was. It wasn't much to ask of her mother, but her heart beat rapidly as she awaited Senara's reply.

Senara stared at her daughter and for a moment appeared to be battling with the question. Anna almost swore she saw a flicker of compassion pass across the swarthy features. And then –

'Whose name?'

'My father's.'

'*Liar*, that's the only name I know him by now.'

Heart sinking, Anna knew her chance had gone. It was time to try a different angle. Leaning over to fill Senara's glass, she forced a smile. 'And Grandma? You said you'd tell me about her.'

Her mother shook her head. '*Bitch!*'

'Mum . . .'

'Always tellin' me I wasn't good enough, that I didn't deserve two kids like you and Ruari. Said I was an unfit mother, did you know that? But oh no, 's far as what you and he are concerned, that woman could do no wrong.'

'Is that why you stopped us seeing her? Because she said that?'

Her mother's laugh was sharp and bitter. 'You'd think.'

'It wasn't?'

She shook her head. 'No. In the end it was a tiny straw that broke *that* camel's back.'

Having been denied the information she'd longed for about her father, Anna was determined to hold out for this. She didn't know her father, and now wasn't sure she wanted to any more; but Morwenna was an entirely different case. She had been the closest thing to a mother Anna had known, a strong presence in her formative years and the one whose loss she felt more keenly than any other. Since the last night she saw her grandmother alive, one question had evaded her: *why*?

Senara's kohl-smudged eyes were closed and her wine-stained lips had begun to droop open as she drifted to sleep. The wine glass tipped at a dangerous angle, but Anna wasn't concerned for her sofa. Covers could be easily replaced, but she may never have the chance to ask this again.

'*Mum*,' she prompted, watching her mother jump back to consciousness, saving her wine before it spilled out.

'Mmm-whaa?'

'Tell me what you and Grandma were fighting about, the night you came to get Ruari and me.'

'It doesn't matter now. *Bitch* is long dead . . .'

The word smacked Anna as hard as a physical blow again, but she refused to give up. 'It matters to me, Mum. What caused the fight?'

Senara's eyes flicked open and she stared at her daughter. 'You don't want to know, girl. There's a reason I never told you.'

'I do want to know.'

'I'm sayin' nothin'.'

'Then I'll keep asking.'

Senara's groan was long and pained. 'Leave it, An!'

'*Tell* me.'

351

Her mother threw up her hands in frustration. 'She wanted *you*, yeah? Happy now?'

What was that supposed to mean? Adrenaline pumping, Anna moved in. 'But she had us. What are you saying?'

'She wanted to have you herself, and not me . . . She was going to take you and your brother. Thought I didn't know about it, didn't she? Well, she was wrong.'

'Take us? Take us where?'

'*Away* . . .' Senara moaned, fat tears suddenly falling. 'And I couldn't let her do that. I might not be the best mother – and Lord knows she told me that often enough – but my own mother wanted to steal my flesh and blood away from me. *Bitch!*'

Was it true, or another figment of Senara Browne's twisted imagination? Anna had always known there was little love lost between her mother and grandmother, but had Morwenna really threatened to take Senara's children? 'Are you sure? Maybe you were mistaken? Got the wrong end of the stick? I can't believe Grandma would have done that to you.'

'I might have known you'd think no ill of her,' Senara spit back, swatting salt water from her cheeks. 'Morwenna Browne, the untouchable saint! Well, I know different. You want the truth, girl? Your precious bloody grandma went to a solicitor to have the courts take you two off of me for good! She was plannin' on taking you off that weekend – to Devon, would you believe? Steal my kids from me and call me an unfit mother!'

'I don't believe you – you're lying . . .'

'That's what you want to believe, ain't it: your lyin',

cheatin' mum accusing a dead-woman-saint? Shows what you know, Anna Browne. She planned it all right – only I found out, didn't I? Bitch from Social Services called me; somethin' your grandma didn't count on. So I drove straight over there and took back what was mine. I see it all over your face: you think I'm wrong. But I remember what that woman said to me. She called me a filthy drunk and a whore – to my face! I'll bet you don't remember *that*, do you?'

Tears were streaming from Anna's eyes now, the truth ripping into her. All she had known of her grandmother – save for that final night – was a dear, sweet woman, whose smiles and embraces made everything right with the world. Senara had made many mistakes as a mother, but could Anna's grandmother have really planned to take custody of her children? She was torn between shock at Morwenna's actions and grief over the life she and Ruari might have had. Would she have been a different person, growing up away from the constant rollercoaster of Senara's life? Or would her problems have grown worse without her mother?

'Call me what you like, An, but I never – not in all the time I've had you and Rua – stopped lovin' you. You're my *blood*. You're the only two things I've done successful in my life.' Senara looked straight into Anna's eyes and, for the first time, Anna saw a glimpse of something resembling love. 'Lord knows I'm a mess. I stuff up everythin'. When I met your dad I was young and I fell for his lies. Folks said nothin' good could come from it. But look at you two! Ruari with that business of his; you in your swanky flat with your secret admirer . . . I look at you both and I think maybe I didn't too bad after all. Your grandma, she never saw that. Had me pegged as a bad apple from the start. When she found out 'bout you and where you'd come from, she nigh on disowned me. 'Twas only cos she saw you in your pram that she ever changed her mind. You and Rua are the reason she ever talked to me again. And then I found out what she was plannin' – and it broke my heart. I thought she'd see me as good, cos of you pair, but all she wanted was to steal you away . . .'

Anna had waited for this for so many years; yet when it finally arrived, amid a mother and daughter's drunken tears, it failed to bring the peace she'd longed for. With Morwenna gone, she would never know the whole truth, but what she had learned tonight would stay with her forever. Moved by emotion and wine, she found herself wrapping her arms around her still-sobbing mother – their first embrace in over a decade. It wasn't a reconciliation, but a truce. And given the tumultuous waters under the bridge between them, that was perhaps the best outcome.

'I s'pose I'll be gettin' the train back to the Duchy tomorrow then,' Senara sniffed when they were side-by-side once more.

The wine and the strange events of the night conspired to mellow Anna's mood. 'I don't mind if you want to stay another day,' she said, scarcely believing her own words. 'You haven't seen London yet. Seems a shame to come all that way and not do some of the sights.'

'Really?' Senara's hesitant smile looked alien on a face

that was more used to snarling. 'I wouldn't need you to babysit me. I could head out on my own. Thing is, I quite fancied a trip on that big wheel. Nance from the Blue went on it for her fiftieth last year and said it was proper stunnin'.'

'I tell you what, I'll phone to book you in on the London Eye in the morning and call you a taxi to take you there.'

'You'd do that for your old mum?'

'You made dinner. Call it my contribution to your trip.'

Anna was slowly finding her feet in this new territory and still wasn't sure what to make of it all. But Senara's obvious surprise set a tiny spark alight in her daughter, far beneath the layers of protection and disappointment. For the first time Anna felt as if she'd made her mother happy. She'd longed to feel that as a child, but never had. Tonight, a hurt that had stung all her life was healed.

'Then I accept. Right, I'm to bed.' Senara reached out and ruffled Anna's hair as she rose. 'You're a good girl, An. Always was. Better 'n I deserved, anyhow.'

In the early hours of the morning Anna lay in her room, her eyes and body aching. It had been a remarkable night, even if some of her precious memories of Morwenna had been forever altered. Questions still remained unanswered; perhaps they always would. She would still ask Senara to leave – she had to, for the sake of her own sanity – but maybe one more day together wouldn't hurt. Her mother had unwittingly moved closer to her than ever before this evening, and Anna wondered if they might have reached a turning point.

They would never be close, of that much she was certain. Too much had been said and done over the years to make any kind of normal relationship possible. But as the sky began to lighten beyond her window, Anna felt a curious new hope dawning.

Forty

London was too busy, too dirty and too loud. As a tourist, Senara Browne was yet to be impressed. Traffic moved slower here than the tractors on Cornish country lanes and smelled about as bad as the muck-spreaders they towed. She would be glad to get home – whenever that happened. To add to it all, the taxi driver had a roving eye and when he dropped her off at the entrance to a swanky Mayfair hotel the only tip she gave him was, 'Keep your eyes on the road and stop pervin' on your passengers.'

Inside the sumptuous lobby her thong sandals sank into thick carpets that felt as if they were made of money – making her smile for the first time since Anna had waved her off in the black cab that morning. This was more like it: light and spacious; not like that horrible poky flat of Anna's. Here, the soothing tones of a grand piano drifted through the opulent interior, where people with more cash than brains moved in slow motion as if weighed down by the wealth in their pockets. Chandeliers the Queen herself would envy shimmered expensively overhead and every inch of the sculpted pillars and ceiling appeared to be crafted out of apricot and cream-coloured royal icing, like the fancy wedding cakes her dumb-headed girlfriends all insisted on having.

Shame I didn't book in here instead, Senara mused. *I might've liked this city a whole lot better . . .*

She passed the sharp-suited men and women in reception and headed for the hotel bar. Once in its polished mahogany and brass surrounds, she scanned the room until she saw him.

The man by the bar was as shifty-looking as she'd expected. But Senara Browne wasn't looking for a date. What the overweight reporter with his three-day-old stubble and sleazy leer was offering her was better than sex. Sex always led to trouble; money solved it.

Maybe she should feel bad about lying to her daughter – and about what she was here to do. But Senara had her reasons. Having the whole of the village buzzing about Anna on the day the news story broke had prompted her into action. There was only one Browne who ought to be in the Polperro spotlight. What made it worse were the things her neighbours said – how *nice* Anna was, how polite and how pretty – every compliment a backhanded jibe at the mother who, in their opinion, didn't deserve credit for the way her daughter had turned out.

'She'll be famous now,' she overheard Doreen Rees in the post office saying, 'and this time for the *right* reasons.'

Oh, my girl'll be famous all right . . .

It was time the world knew the truth about Miss I'm-So-Perfect Anna Browne . . .

The man raised his hand as she entered. At first Senara wondered how he'd recognised her. But one look at her old leather jacket, long green embroidered skirt and jangling silver at her wrists and ankles confirmed she wasn't a London local.

'Mrs Browne,' he gurned, sincerity obviously not part of his job description.

'Ms,' she corrected him, her long eyelashes giving a coquettish flutter. 'No man's been lucky enough to turn me into a *missus* yet.' It was an old line, one that had got her under more than a few covers before, but it still had the desired effect. Senara congratulated herself when she saw the telltale shudder of delight pass across his portly frame. Poor beggar was in the palm of her hand and didn't even know it.

'Their loss, I'm sure. Drink?'

She eyed his empty glass on the bar. Match him drink for drink – making him think he was getting her drunk – and the meeting would no doubt turn in her favour. She had honed the skill over many years and it never failed her. 'Whisky would be good,' she purred.

'Ah – a lady after my own heart. And before midday, too? Well, well. I think you and I are going to get on *famously.*'

This was too easy. Following a long-practised routine, Senara coiled a strand of silver-black hair lazily around one finger, passing it slowly along her bottom lip. 'Oh, I *hope so*, my 'ansum.'

One glance at his eager smile told her she'd already won . . .

With her mother off sightseeing and her home returned to her sole use – if only temporarily for now – Anna settled in her armchair with a book. She was enjoying the silence when her phone rang.

'Hi, Anna, I've got news.' Sheniece sounded more excited than usual. 'Is now a good time to chat? I've managed to sneak out for five minutes. Ashraf thinks I'm smoking again.'

'You have my full and undivided attention,' Anna smiled, despite the dull headache from too much wine and emotion with her mother last night.

'I wanted to call you the moment I found out. It looks as if the paper's saved!'

Anna's book tumbled to the floor as she sat upright. 'What? Are you sure?'

'We had it confirmed this morning. It's a management buyout, apparently. Damien Kendal and a couple of the cronies from the Board made DayBreak Corp an offer and it was accepted last night. Can you believe it? The Dragon reckons there'll still be some job cuts – streamlining, they call it. But it's better than us all being shown the door.'

'That's amazing! Everyone must be so relieved.'

'We are. Didn't take Ted long to start his conspiracy theories again, of course. He upset Babs by suggesting the oldest will be the first out, if jobs go. Babs is due her golden handshake next year and now she's convinced management will chuck her out before it happens.'

Anna could picture Ted snatching defeat from the jaws of victory. Poor Babs. But the news was incredibly welcome, especially after the events of recent days. To know her job was – if not completely safe – *safer* than it had been was a huge relief. 'Tell Ted to stop stirring and be happy for a change. And give Babs a hug from me.'

'I will. We're all missing you. How does it feel to be a viral Internet sensation? Oops, sorry, don't answer that. My little sis found a story about you on a *Malaysian* blog today. How mad is that?'

Anna shuddered at the thought. 'Please don't tell me any more. It's scary enough as it is. I haven't dared to look online since it happened.'

'So you won't have seen Ben's other stories, then?'

'*Stories?*' Anna closed her eyes. She had hoped the follow-up would be the last word on it. 'There were more?'

'Oh, yeah, they've been in all week. Newsroom's buzzing with it.' She paused and Anna could hear the squeak of an acrylic nail being chewed. 'Actually it's been nice stuff. I know you probably don't want to hear it, but Ben's been really complimentary. If I didn't know better, I'd say he's still holding a torch for you.'

Anna's headache deepened with the mention of Ben. 'You're right: I don't want to hear it. Did you know he's been trying to call me from different phone numbers? I'm ignoring the calls.'

'Today's the first time I've seen him and he looks dreadful, honey.'

'Perhaps the burden of being the *Messenger*'s saving grace is too heavy.' Anna baulked at the bitterness she heard in her own words. But she had no energy for diplomacy this morning.

'I totally get why you're mad at him. And I'll give him a piece of my mind if he tries to talk to me. He lied to you and that's awful. But the thing is, I've seen Ben McAra when he's bragging about his work and this isn't it. You'd think he'd be crowing from the top of the building about writing a story that's gone around the world. But he doesn't look very victorious to me.'

'It's probably an act. I wouldn't trust him now as far as I could throw him.' Anna rubbed her eyes. 'I appreciate you telling me, but there's no one in the world I want less to hear about.'

'I know. And I'm sorry. It's just that, if I didn't think he was such a dick – which I do – I'd almost say he didn't plan for this to happen.'

Anna didn't answer, staring out at the buildings across the street. If Ben was regretting anything, it was most likely getting caught. His article had showed no remorse; if later pieces indicated regret, it was only for effect. Also, knowing that the reception staff and overprotective security chief were gunning for him, Ben's demeanour could be as much for protection as it was any genuine indicator of his mood.

Anna's silence had the desired effect on Sheniece. 'I'm sorry. I shouldn't have said anything. I just thought you'd want to know. Hurry back soon, okay? We miss you.'

In the stillness of her home Anna mulled over what she'd heard. Did Ben feel anything at all? She didn't want to consider he might have motives beyond those that had

362

caused him to lie to her – because that was the point, wasn't it? Whether he had planned for events to progress as they had or not, he had still engineered a friendship to get a story. That was not the action of someone who truly cared about her.

And yet, it *had* seemed out of character when the story broke . . .

As if seeking answers, she opened one of the five voice messages Ben had left after his unanswered calls.

'Anna, please, let me explain. I know you're hurt and I know you hate me, but there's a reason I did what I did . . .'

She couldn't listen to any more. There was no remorse in his voice, only wounded pride and the panic of being revealed for the liar he was. Angry and annoyed for even entertaining the idea, she deleted all the voice messages and switched off her phone. For today, she wanted to forget Ben McAra ever existed.

Forty-One

'Hello, Anna? This is Piers Langley, Juliet's PA. She wishes to inform you that she expects you to return to work on Monday morning, if that is acceptable to you?'

Anna exchanged glances with Tish, who mouthed 'What?' over the rim of her coffee cup. She couldn't help thinking that Juliet's PA had added the last line for politeness: she couldn't imagine the Dragon concerning herself with the personal opinions of her employees. 'That's fine, thanks for letting me know.' She had missed the comfort of her work routine, but a concern remained. 'Can I ask, has the – um – *situation* changed, regarding rival reporters?'

Piers' laugh was kind. 'Oh, you're old news now, Anna. I shouldn't worry if I were you.'

'Was that work?' Tish demanded, as soon as Anna ended the call. 'Do they expect you to go back so soon? It's barely been a week.'

'I don't mind, actually. I'm running out of things to do

to kill time and I could do with the excuse to ask Mum to leave.'

Her friend chuckled. 'Is she *still* at your place? Wow, Anna, you're a better woman than me. If I had to breathe the same *air* as my mother longer than twenty-four hours I'd go insane. There's a good reason we keep an ocean between us. How's it going with the Browne family reunion?'

The truce between mother and daughter was still stilted, but they had settled into a rhythm of cordiality – a phenomenon that surprised nobody more than Anna. For the price of a cab fare and a lunch out, she had secured the majority of each day on her own, the pair meeting for dinner when Senara returned from her day's sightseeing. 'My mother seems quite taken with London, which is a minor miracle.'

'What's she been doing in the city?'

'The tourist hot spots, from what she tells me. London Eye first, Tower of London yesterday and today she's visiting Madame Tussaud's and shopping on Oxford Street. She goes out all day and comes back about six.' Anna was treading this brave new soil with caution. 'But it's high time she left. If I'm back at work on Monday, it makes sense for her to go.'

Senara appeared nonplussed that evening when Anna suggested she return to Cornwall the next day. She arrived home suspiciously short of shopping bags, but definitely the worse for wear, leading Anna to suspect she was enjoying the spirits of the city far more than its sights.

'Fair enough. 'S about time I went back to civilisation anyhow.'

'Have you had a good time?' It seemed strange to be exchanging pleasantries with her mother, but Anna had asked before she could think better of it.

Senara reached out and cupped her daughter's cheek. 'The best, An. And you made it all possible.'

Anna watched her mother saunter away to the bathroom, feeling inexplicably uneasy.

The sensation still hung over her on Monday morning as the glass doors of the *Messenger* building slid open to herald Anna's return. She had parted on good terms with her mother before she left for work, handing her several twenty-pound notes for food and drink on her train journey.

'This is good – us, I mean,' Senara had grinned. 'Can't believe what a tiger my little Anna's turned into. Suits you, girl. Don't you let no one walk all over you, yeah? Now, I'd say I'll call when I get home, but you know that won't happen. I'll be seeing you sometime, I s'pose.'

Despite the melting of ice between them this week, Anna strongly suspected it would be several years before she and Senara stood in the same room again. It was just the way things would always be between them. She was grateful for the seeming calm in their relationship, but she wasn't expecting Senara to become Mother of the Year. She hadn't discovered her father's name, but she understood a little more why he hadn't been in her life. Learning of Morwenna's foiled plan for her and Ruari was difficult, but the story had brought a surprising declaration of love from her mum. With some ghosts laid to rest, Anna felt stronger in Senara's company. At the end of the day, this

366

was more of a positive thing than she could ever have expected. At least she could focus on the future now.

'Anna! You're back!' Sheniece's embrace nearly knocked Anna off her feet.

'I certainly am. Did I miss much?'

'Only the paper being saved, Damien Kendal getting slapped by Lucy in Accounts for a sexist remark, and a certain male reporter looking like someone barfed in his pint. Oh, and Ted had a *date* . . .'

'He did?'

'Just the one. Someone persuaded him to try a dating website and he met a woman who turned out to be nine-tenths psycho.' She giggled. 'Seriously, ask him about it – his reaction is hilarious! Only Ted could have an innocent date turn into an episode of *CSI*.'

It was a relief to find the internal *Messenger* gossip-spotlight had moved on. Settling back into her familiar routine, Anna took her place behind the desk and revelled in the comforting monotony of her day's tasks.

'Mornin', love,' Murray Henderson-Vitt grinned, as he arrived in reception to collect his visitors. 'You recovered from being our resident star yet?'

Knowing this wouldn't be the only time she was asked today, Anna braved it out. 'Just happy to be back at work, Murray.'

'You should've spoken to me first, like I said.'

'Oh? And you would have written the story any differently from your colleague?'

'Probably not.' He gave a rueful smile. 'Journalists, eh? Bunch of con artists, the lot of us. Tell you what, though,

I would've looked a damn sight happier about it than McAra does right now.'

'You're all heart.'

Murray's mention of Ben's mood was interesting, especially after Sheniece had remarked on it days before. It could be part of a plan, she supposed, a damage-limitation exercise by newsroom colleagues to smooth over rough edges left by the stories. But Anna knew there was little love lost between Murray and Ben; he had no reason to make life easier for his colleague.

She discovered the truth when she first caught sight of Ben at lunchtime. He was hollow-eyed and pale as he waited for the lift; four-day-growth cloaked his chin and his clothes were creased, as if he hadn't changed them for a week. Seeing Anna, he changed course and began to walk towards her desk.

'Anna . . .' he called, but she had already hurried into the staff toilet, one door along from the work kitchen, her place behind the desk assumed by an unsmiling Ashraf.

She could hear their exchange as she hid, Ashraf refusing to fetch Anna for Ben. After a few minutes of wrangling, her colleague knocked on the toilet door.

'It's okay. He's gone.'

Anna slid back the bolt and opened the door. 'What did he say?'

'He wanted to speak to you. He said he wouldn't give up. So I told him I know jiu-jitsu.' Ashraf was clearly proud of himself. 'He didn't hang around after that.'

'Thanks. I appreciate it.'

368

'You'll have to speak to him sometime, though, Anna. Unless you get another job. Ben's always going to be here.'

Anna knew he was right. At home, it had been easier to block Ben from her life, but here – where the unexpected reaction his story had caused around the world was being cited as the reason the Board had changed its mind and saved the newspaper – it would be impossible to avoid him forever. Anna desperately wanted never to see him again, but she was also angry and wanted answers. The battle between the two raged within her. She knew, eventually, she would have to face Ben.

But not today. I'm not ready to go there today.

Assured that the coast was clear, she returned to the desk, smiling as a grey-uniformed courier approached.

'Parcel that needs signing for?'

'No problem. Who is it for?'

The courier checked the label. 'Anna Browne?'

Anna hesitated. Was this an attempt by Ben to get her attention? She didn't know for sure whether Ben had been the sender of her previous parcels, but she wasn't expecting another one in the light of everything that had happened. 'That's me.'

As she took the parcel, the courier pulled a camera from his bag, clicking furiously as Anna blinked in horror at the flashes. Ashraf vaulted the desk and dragged the photographer to the ground, yelling for Ted while rendering the paparazzo immobile with a swift upper cut to his jaw. The security chief puffed his way across the atrium, joined by a couple of passing journalists, and together they ejected the intruder from the building. In the middle of the commotion,

Anna couldn't move. She remained, frozen to the spot with the parcel in her hands, while Sheniece tried her best to comfort her.

'Piers Langley said this was all over,' she managed, her body numb. 'He said the story had passed.'

Gently her colleague guided her to a chair. 'Take some deep breaths, Anna. You're white as a sheet.'

'I wouldn't have come back if I knew this would happen . . .'

'I know, lovely. Is there anything in the parcel?'

Anna stared at it. The corners were wrong – but then, they had been once before. No sender address appeared on the brown packaging, but a faint rustling sound came from inside. It wasn't one of her parcels, so what did it matter if she opened it here? Still shaking, she tore open the paper and lifted the old sports-shoebox lid. The box was filled with balls of newspaper and a white postcard sat on top.

Sheniece unrolled a paper ball. 'It's the *Daily Post*.' Disgusted, she dropped it.

A message and phone number had been scrawled across the postcard:

A story will appear in tomorrow's Daily Post, *claiming you concocted the 'secret parcel' story with your lover, Ben McAra, to fool the public and save the* Daily Messenger *from extinction. It will also claim that you are an attention-seeker and compulsive liar. We have reliable information confirming this from a source close to you, and we will print it in full.*

However, if you grant us an exclusive interview, we will run this instead.

Call Mike Hennessy (Chief Reporter) on 07957 . . .

'Hennessy's a shark,' Joe Adams from the newsroom commented as a group of onlookers crowded around Anna. 'If he says he has a story, he means it.'

'Is there any way of finding out who his source is?' Ashraf asked.

Joe shook his head. 'Not unless Anna asks him.'

Rea had arrived, summoned to the ground floor by the speed of the *Messenger* grapevine. 'Or someone who *says* she's Anna,' she winked.

'Great idea!' Sheniece said, squeezing Anna's shoulder. 'You see, Anna? We've totally got your back.'

'No – let me do it.'

The *Daily Messenger* employees turned as one to stare at Anna, who was breathing heavily, white-hot anger searing through her limbs.

'I can pretend to be you,' Rea argued. 'Get enough information to hang him and then drop the bomb. Hennessy's a total git: it would be my pleasure to get one over on him.'

'I want to speak to him. Tell me how best to do it, to get the information you want, and I'll do it.'

'Right, call him.' Joe nodded. 'We'll record it and find out what he has. It's possible he's bluffing about his information, to get you to discredit the paper. Anna, try not to worry. We'll tell you exactly what to do.'

But Anna was worried. The details could have been a

lucky punt – plenty of people knew she and Ben were close, a few even knew of their date; the *Daily Messenger*'s precarious financial position was well known in Fleet Street. It would have been easy to concoct a tale from these facts. But the claims about a source close to her were troubling. Had Hennessy invented this, too – or had he tried to target her friends?

Half an hour later Joe Adams called her to the news-room floor. A group of journalists, including Rea and a few Anna recognised from the news team, were waiting for her in a small office just off the main newsroom. Ben was conspicuous by his absence – but nobody in the room was willing to refer to it. Anna would have refused to go ahead if he had been there – and the journalists knew it. Joe quickly ran through how the conversation should go, sliding a prompt-sheet across the desk to Anna. Ashen-faced, he and his colleagues surrounded Anna as they made the call on a conference phone.

Mike Hennessy's tone was as self-satisfied and appalling as his note had suggested. It sounded as if he was constantly chewing when he spoke and Anna imagined that he wore an identical snarl to the one she heard in his voice. 'Miss Browne, I'm glad to hear from you.'

'I want to know who's sold a story on me,' Anna replied, following Joe's scripted lines from the sheet of paper.

'Of course. But first I need to know we have an under-standing.'

'What do you mean?'

'Well, our readers have a right to the truth. And we have a choice, Anna: either I print what I already have, or you tell me what really happened. I can make it worth your while, naturally.'

'And what if I tell you it's none of your business?' She could feel her blood boiling.

'Means nothing to me, pet. Fact is, one way or another you're starring in the *Post* tomorrow. Whether that's as an angel or a villain is up to you.'

Anna felt sick, but kept her eyes on the handwritten lines. 'What's in it for me, if I give you what you want?'

'A considerable sum. Much more than that crappy job pays you.'

'How much?'

'We're straying from the point, Anna. Do we have a deal? Exclusive story for the *Post* and no last-minute running to your bosses?'

'On one condition.'

'Name it.'

'Tell me who's talked to you.'

'Time is money, Anna. I'm going to need an answer.'

'I don't think you have anything on me, Mr Hennessy. I think you've made it all up.'

'I assure you we haven't.'

'I don't know that. You could have put two and two together. I've had one date with Ben. Our newspaper's troubles are well known. I reckon you're lying about the rest. You don't have anything on me . . .'

'Question is, Anna: are you willing to take that risk?'

'I don't think you have a story, Mr Hennessy. My parcels were real and I didn't make them up. I'm an honest person and I avoid being the centre of attention – why would I lie and bring all this on myself?'

And then, with all her lines performed and as she was looking up helplessly at Joe Adams, Hennessy suddenly took the bait.

'You think you're supported by your friends and family? You think they weren't only too happy to sell you up the river?'

'I don't have any enemies. I have friends and people who love me.'

'Oh, they do, do they? You poor deluded woman.' His nicotine-heavy cough reverberated around the office walls from the conference-phone speaker. Anna saw the grave expressions of the journalists around the room and wondered if they felt as nauseous as she did.

'You're making this up so I'll talk to you. You have no evidence.'

'I assure you I do. I recorded the entire conversation and will be only too happy to publish that on our website.'

Was Mike Hennessy winding Anna up now? If not, who had he spoken to? Fear clung to her heart as she answered, 'Then you must have bribed someone – blackmailed them . . .'

'Spare me the melodramatics, Miss Browne. The *Messenger* might resort to tactics like that, but the *Post* doesn't have to. Fact is, our source came to us.'

'WHO WAS IT?' The shout came from deep within her, making her ears buzz with its force.

'Your own mother, Anna! She walked, bold as brass, into my office and spilled her guts for a nice fat cheque!'

Horrified, Anna slammed her hand down on the Call button. Silence filled the interview room. 'I'm sorry – I'm so sorry,' she rushed, as Hennessy's words seared into her soul: *Your own mother, Anna!*

And then the grotesque fact hit her full-on: Senara Browne had come to London not for an emotional reunion, but to sell her daughter to the highest bidder. The un-accompanied tours of the city were revealed for what they truly were. How many newspapers had her mother visited, when she was supposed to be treading the tourist trail? Cold, sticky bile rushed up Anna's throat and a watching journalist thrust a waste-paper bin into her hands in time to catch the torrent, while other hands scrambled to hold back her hair.

Nobody spoke. All eyes remained on the receptionist as she slowly sat back. She was handed a tissue and wiped her mouth, too distraught to care about being violently sick in front of her colleagues. Taking a breath, she stood, the journalists parting as she made her way to the door.

'Do you want me to come with you?' Rea offered. 'We could go and get some fresh air.'

'No. Thank you . . .'

'Someone needs to tell Juliet,' she heard one of them say, as she fled to the waiting lift.

Anna held her tears at bay until the doors closed, then sank heavily against the steel wall as the lift descended, dragging her heart with it.

Forty-Two

Mike Hennessy, it appeared, didn't need Anna's words in order to quote her. Next day the *Daily Post* printed its story, complete with posed photographs of Senara playing the wronged-mother card with thoughtless ease, and Anna holding the fake parcel, trapped in the flashbulb glare, her shocked expression passing well for rumbled guilt. But at its centre, in bold newsprint, was a supposed quote from Anna, bragging about the money paid to her by the *Messenger* in exchange for her 'story'.

'"I'm just a simple Cornish girl and when my employer offered me so much money, what was I supposed to do? I've earned more for one story than I would working there for five years!" . . . Oh, Anna, what bollocks!' Ted shook his head as he pored over the offending double-page spread on the reception desk.

'It's such a mess.' Anna had debated not coming to work today. She hadn't slept all night, pacing the floor of her home and chastising herself for believing Senara. But in the early hours of the morning her mood had passed through a sea change. Why should she hide at home, as if the lies in the rival rag were true? She had nothing to hide and had done nothing wrong. Ben's article had been bad enough, but at least it had painted her in a favourable light compared to the vitriol coming her way from the *Daily Post*. She would not give Mike Hennessy the satisfaction. Holding her head high, she had caught her usual bus and was now standing at her post, determined not to back down.

'I think you're so brave for coming in,' Ashraf soothed, handing Anna a mug of tea. 'Especially with *that lot* out there.' He nodded towards the *Messenger* building's entrance, where a line of uniformly disgruntled paparazzi were kicking the pavement.

'Don't you worry about that shower,' Ted replied. 'Me and the boys are keeping them in check. One wrong move and they're history.'

'I'm sorry, Anna, but your mother's a prize *b-i-t-c-h*.' Ashraf pointed at the smirking woman in the centre of the article. 'Look at that photo: she's loving it! What kind of a mother sells a story on her kid?'

'The *worst* kind, that's what. Families – load of bother, the lot of them.' Ted patted Anna's shoulder. 'What you need right now is friends like us, girl. We'll see you right.'

As her colleagues continued their uninvited autopsy of the life Anna thought she knew, she did her best to keep busy. What she couldn't fathom was how her life – the quiet, happy existence she had safely cultivated, away from scandal, disappointment and hurt – had become *this*.

I never asked for any of this: not the parcels, not my mother, not Ben. So how has it all happened to me?

An hour later news reached reception of a follow-up story on the *Post*'s website, with Anna allegedly slating the *Daily Messenger* – criticising DayBreak Corp and accusing Juliet Evans of company fraud.

And then discontented rumours began to seep through the building . . .

Ashraf was the first to hear them, having overheard a conversation in the post room. His uncharacteristic silence when he returned to reception was followed by hushed conversations with Ted and Sheniece. When others in the atrium followed suit, Anna cornered Ted.

'What's going on?'

'Nothing.'

Anna folded her arms. 'You're a pathetic actor, Ted. I've seen everyone looking this way. I know that if anyone in this place knows what's happening, it's you.'

Ted flushed from the compliment. 'I like to think I do.'

'So?'

Resignation spread across his face. 'I'm sorry, girl. It ain't good. People – *some* people – are saying the *Post* has reason for printing that stuff about you.'

'They think I made this all up? Why would they think that?'

'Well, what your ma said . . .'

How could anyone believe Senara's lies – in a tabloid headquarters, too? Surely everyone knew how these stories worked? Or did they know Anna so little they couldn't see how ridiculous the rival paper's claims were? 'They don't know my mother – they don't know what she's capable of.'

'You and I know that, but . . .' Ted let out a long breath. 'Look, all the uncertainty there's been about the paper lately has rattled everyone. They're ready to think anything's possible – and not the good stuff, either. Plus, McAra's been shouting his mouth off upstairs and they're saying he's protesting too much.'

What was Anna meant to do? She couldn't stop opinion any more than she could halt the tide, yet her inability to answer the accusations levelled at her made her feel a failure. 'Then I can't win.'

The internal line lit up on the switchboard and Anna answered.

'Anna? Piers Langley. Juliet wishes to see you in her office. Immediately, please.'

The call ended abruptly. Anna turned to Ted, the blood rushing from her head. 'This day really can't get any worse.'

The sympathetic smile of Juliet's PA did nothing to reassure her when she arrived in the editor's office.

'Go right in,' Piers said, his perfectly honed professional calm reminding Anna of the secretary at her primary school, who sent naughty children to their punishment in the headmistress' office with a chillingly placid smile.

Juliet didn't smile when Anna sat opposite, her green eyes unblinking as they bore into her.

'This is unfortunate,' she said, her choice of word designed to instil fear.

'I never asked for any of this—' Anna began, halted by the sudden rise of Juliet's hand.

'Frankly, I don't care. What I want to know is how the hell your mother got involved? I've been told she was staying with you recently?'

'I didn't know she was selling her story.'

'Blatantly. And you had no idea of her true intention?'

A crushing weight dropped in Anna's stomach. Of all the people in the world, she should have been the first to suspect Senara Browne's real reason for getting on her good side. How had she been so stupid? 'No, I didn't.' *More fool me.*

'I have to say, I'm not happy about this. Your mother is making us look like complete idiots. Whatever possessed the woman?'

Anna's hands clenched in her lap. Why should she be made liable for Senara's actions? 'If I could answer that, I could have saved myself years of heartache.'

'Don't be cute, Anna.'

'I wasn't trying to be.'

Juliet pushed her chair from the desk and walked to the window. 'I should have expected it, of course. The *Post* and the *Mercury* are hopping mad that we found a story with such appeal. Despite their *lame* attempts at discrediting us, our online click rates are still high. But the *Messenger* is in a precarious position, with the new management structure still being finalised – any knock in our fortunes could be catastrophic.'

'Can I say something?' The rush of righteous indignation rising inside Anna forced the words from her lips. It wouldn't be stopped by anyone – not Juliet Evans and not Anna's own better judgement. She was sick and tired of being made responsible for the newspaper's future and angry that nobody seemed to understand her point of view. Juliet was going to hear it, whether it was a good idea in the end or not.

Juliet turned to face her, surprised. 'It seems you already are.'

A steel-strong resolve fired along Anna's spine as she faced the editor. 'I didn't ask to receive parcels. I certainly didn't ask to be used by one of your journalists for the sake of a story. I object to my life being sacrificed in order to save this newspaper.'

'Is that so?'

'Yes, it is.' Anna ignored Juliet's ominously darkening expression, the fire too strong to extinguish. 'Yesterday I discovered that my mother – the woman who is meant to love me – had sold lies about me to the highest bidder. Do you have any idea how that makes me feel? I am not my mother's keeper. I have been hurt beyond words by her actions – not that I imagine you care at all . . .'

'That's enough, Miss Browne.'

Anna rose to her feet, the pain and frustration tumbling out of her. 'I will not be accused of something I haven't done – not by you, not by my mother and certainly not by the *Daily Post*!'

'Enough, Anna!'

A sudden urge to cry pushed the air from her lungs as she stared helplessly back.

'Sit down, Anna. *Please*.' When she didn't move, the editor took a step towards her. 'You're not in trouble, you have my word.'

Anna resumed her seat, tears stinging her eyes.

'I've heard the rumblings in the newsroom and I will deal with them. As for the bleatings of our rivals, we will counteract with the threat of legal action, if necessary.' She picked up a pen and rapped it on the desk. 'I'm sorry you've been hurt. It was never my intention – or that of anyone here. Have you heard from your mother?'

'No. She went home yesterday and I hope I never see her again.'

Juliet nodded, her stern expression softened by concern in her eyes. 'Personally I don't subscribe to the universal sainthood attributed to all mothers. But I would advise that you don't share any more information with her.'

'I don't intend to.' A heavy weariness descended upon Anna as her adrenaline subsided. 'I – I didn't mean to shout.'

'You didn't. Compared to the volume this office has witnessed of late, you weren't even close.'

'Thank you.'

'I wonder if perhaps I called you back too soon.'

'I like working. I have nothing to hide.'

'I understand. But given the current state of play, I suggest a few more days' leave would be appropriate. For your peace of mind, as much as anything. It will allow me to handle the situation and keep the press pack at bay.'

Anna was certain that her peace of mind would be better preserved by a return to her normal routine, but she was too brow-beaten by the day's events to argue. 'I just want this all to be over.' She thanked Juliet and made to leave the office.

'Miss Browne: one more thing . . .'

'Yes?'

'It can be easy, at times like these, to lose sight of the good. Not everything you've encountered is negative. Try to remember that.'

The editor's words played on Anna's mind as she walked along the carpeted corridor towards the lift. It was an odd thing to say; stranger still that it should come from a woman so famously devoid of compassion. She pressed the Call button and waited. Juliet had a point, of course: the gifts in the parcels had meant a great deal to Anna, as had Ben's attentions. But if the two were linked and therefore part of a plan for a story, what did they mean now?

The lift doors slid open and Anna walked inside. She stared down at the shell and sea-glass bracelet, which she had subconsciously chosen to wear today. Out of all her gifts, this had been the one she understood the least, but her memory of piecing it together gave it a significance its component parts lacked. Maybe that was the point: the parcels had been a starting point, but what she did with them mattered more.

A chime sounded above her head and the lift shuddered to a halt. Jolted from her thoughts, Anna looked up at the display to see that she had reached the third floor. She stepped back as the doors parted, expecting a crowd of people to enter from the newsroom floor, but only one person was revealed.

The *worst* person it could have been.

'Anna! I—'

Instinctively she hit the button to close the doors, but Ben's hand prevented their progress. He jumped into the lift as the doors sealed them inside.

'No, I'm sorry. Not this time. We need to talk.'

Trapped, Anna stood her ground. 'We don't.'

'Anna, please – I've been going out of my mind . . .'

'And I haven't?'

'I never anticipated this.'

'I'll bet you didn't.' She rounded on him. 'I'll bet you expected it to go without a hitch. Only you didn't count on my mother turning up and spoiling the party.'

Sheniece's description of the journalist proved accurate, his pale skin and darkened eyes almost spectral in the blue-white lift lighting. 'That isn't fair. I couldn't have known . . .'

'No, you couldn't. Not in the paltry amount of time you spent getting to know me before you printed your story. Because, Ben, if you'd taken the time to find out about my life, you might have found out what my mother was capable of. But that wasn't important to you, was it?'

The lift reached the second floor, but Ben slammed his hand against the door control button, closing the doors before anyone could enter. 'I know you're angry with me, and I'm sorry the story came out when it did. But I didn't get to know you because of a cheap article. I spent time with you because I wanted to.'

'I can't hear this now.'

'Listen to me! The timing sucked, but it wasn't my call. Everything I said to you was true, Anna. You trusted me and you were right to – okay, I know you can't see it like that now, but it's the truth!' As the lift continued its steady descent, he spoke again, quieter than before. 'I made a mistake: a monumental one. I'm not proud of what's happened. Just – please – don't hate me. There's so much more I can give you. I can make this right, Anna . . .'

'I don't think you can.' Her heart broke with the admission; saying it aloud made it horribly real. 'You hurt me and betrayed my trust. I can't get past that.'

With nothing more to be said, neither Ben nor Anna spoke again as the lift dropped the final few feet to the ground floor. When the doors opened, Anna hurried out. She didn't look back – she couldn't. Ben didn't follow her or call her name. In silence she collected her belongings and left. Rounding the corner from the obscured service entrance, she could see the press pack still encamped by the front door, Ted distracting them to assist her escape.

It's over, Anna told herself as she hurried away. *Ben is out of my life for good.*

Forty-Three

The journey home through building afternoon traffic passed in a blur, Anna neither seeing nor caring about the crawling lines of vehicles at either side of the bus, or the blaring horns of impatient drivers that split the air. Time seemed to move frame-by-frame, snapshots of her fellow passengers permeating the fog in her mind as street sounds muted to a distant mumble. Her head hurt, the fury she'd unleashed on Ben leaving bruises where thoughts should have been.

Weary-limbed, she stood as the bus slowed, shuffling behind the small group of alighting passengers onto her street. She paused outside Spill the Beans, debating whether or not to go in; deciding against it, she walked into Walton Tower. Her bed was calling – and Anna suspected that, once in its blissful surrounds, she might remain there for the rest of her enforced leave.

I don't need to see anyone today. I just want to hide . . .

But someone was waiting for Anna Browne: slumped

against her front door, half-empty bottle of Jameson's whiskey swinging with the silver bangles from her hand.

'H-h-here, she is! My little *A-nna* . . .'

There were no words. Anna stared at her mother in numb shock.

'It's all gone *wrong*, An!' she whined, her nose leaving a slug-trail along the sleeve of her leather jacket as she wiped it. 'I just needed a little more cash, but they wouldn't budge. They called me a bad mother – did you see? Written all over their paper this morning, like it was the truth. Shows what *they* know.'

'You should be in Cornwall.'

'Reckon I should now. Thought I could do better, though, didn't I? More f-f-fool me.'

'I put you in a taxi to the station – why didn't you get on the train?'

'Fancied a stop in that swanky hotel. Should've seen their faces when I paid in cash!' Her shoulders shook with a snot-rattling snigger. 'I made them bring me champagne and caviar on room service. Like a queen, I was.'

Unbelievable woman! Not content with betraying her daughter and tearing her world apart, Senara Browne had come back to gloat over the damage.

'Go *home*.'

'Can't.'

'You can't stay here. I don't want you here, do you understand?'

'Always shoutin' at me, ain't you, girl?'

'You sold lies to a national newspaper, Mum! I think that gives me the right to shout.'

Senara pulled a face and made mocking crocodile-mouths with her hands, like Anna's brother used to do when teasing her for speaking too much. Fury rising, Anna shoved her mother out of the way and moved to open the door.

'N-n-no, Anna,' Senara protested, swinging her body across the frame and blocking Anna's way. 'I just need a bit of help.' Her cold fingers clamped across her daughter's cheek. 'You're a good girl, everyone says it. You won't let your poor old mum freeze on the street.'

'You're not poor. You've made a fortune out of me. Cash your cheque and move into that hotel – you can afford it now.'

She elbowed her swaying mother out of the way, sliding the key into the Yale lock, but Senara fell forward, pushing both women to the floor as the door swung open. Anna scrambled to her feet, standing over her mother's sprawled, drunken body that now appeared to be attempting to swim across the floor.

'You're pathetic,' she shouted. 'Look at you!'

Senara's body began to shake and convulse and Anna slowly recognised the dirty, retching sound it emitted as laughter. She looked down at the wreck that was once her mother and felt *nothing* – no anger, no sadness, not even pity for the woman who cared so little for her. She thought of the many years she had fought this woman's battles, buried her own hurts and pushed away the shame. In the end, what had it all been for?

'I can't do this any more,' she said, her voice cold and steady.

388

Her mother rolled onto her back, her laughter veering between amusement and tears. 'Good old Anna Browne,' she spit out, raising the whiskey bottle towards her. 'Too good for her mother. Too good to come from *here* – ' she slapped a hand on her abdomen, a sound like a gravel-coated sob blurting out. 'I should've *got rid* when I had the chance . . . When your *father* gave me *money for it.*'

Before, Senara's cruel insults would have crushed her daughter – but things had changed. None of it mattered now. Anna Browne knew her mother would only ever live to serve herself – she had been right about her from the start.

'All my life I've tried to protect you. I've fought battles that weren't mine and I've rescued you so many times, when it had nothing to do with me. But today I realised: you don't *want* rescuing, do you?'

'My life was *ruined* when I had you! I was happy and free and did what I liked. And then you came along and stuffed it all up. Some bloody life I've had, 'cause of you, Anna . . .'

It was as if both women were talking through a glass wall, years of trapped bitterness and rage finally breaking free. Anna knew that if she didn't say this now, she never would.

'I hoped you'd see what I did – what Ruari and I have both done for you. But you can only see yourself.'

'Always Miss High-and-Mighty, always ashamed of me. Well, I went and got what I was *owed*, that's all. Payment for years of puttin' up with you and Ruari, for *no bloody thanks* . . .'

Anna stepped back from Senara as if avoiding rubbish. 'I'm done, Mum. *We're* done. Get your stuff and get out of my home.'

Senara blinked upwards, her laughter gone. 'You don't mean it.'

'I said, get out.'

'You'll be runnin' back, girl. Always do, in the end. You're more like me than you think, Anna Browne.'

Blocking out her mother's words, Anna stood firm. 'Get out, *now*!'

'Aw, come on, *An* . . .' Senara was on her knees, reaching out for her.

With every last scrap of strength in her body, Anna grabbed her mother's arm and pushed her bodily out of her apartment. 'We are done. *Get – OUT!*'

'Everything all right here?' Seamus called, summoned to the corridor by the commotion.

'She needs to leave. She has a train ticket.'

Seamus nodded, immediately understanding the seriousness of the situation. 'I'll put her in a taxi, shall I? You come with me, Miss . . .'

'I'm going *nowhere*,' Senara shouted, but Seamus had already locked an arm through hers and was pulling her away from Anna's door. 'Take your hands off of me! No! *An!* You can't do this.'

Anna said nothing, felt nothing.

'But I *need* you! *Anna* . . . !'

The last she saw of Senara Browne was her mother's look of horror as Seamus dragged her out of view.

'Lass? What's up?' Jonah was standing in his doorway.

As Anna's knees gave way, he caught her, half-carrying her into her apartment. Her body felt completely drained and, as she lay back on the sofa, she closed her eyes and let her tears flow. Beneath the pain, she felt free – as if an oppressive weight that she had carried all her life had been finally lifted.

Jonah knelt by her side, maintaining a respectful distance, his hand hesitant on her shoulder. When she opened her eyes, he dug in his jeans pocket for a cotton handkerchief and handed it to her.

'Was that your mother?'

Anna nodded.

'Seamus said she sold a story about you.' Jonah frowned. 'He saw it in the paper. I take it you sent her packing?'

'She won't be back.'

'I thought you were back at work now. Things not go well?'

'No.' She held the creased cotton to her eyes and inhaled deeply. 'The story Mum sold caused problems, so the editor sent me home again. I just didn't think my mother would try to come back here.'

'I heard you shouting before you even opened your door. I've never heard you shout like that, Anna.'

She laughed in spite of herself. 'I don't think I have, either.'

'Sometimes, it's what's necessary.' He sat beside her as Anna lifted herself up. 'You know what you need?'

'Triple vodka?'

'Aye, well, we can definitely arrange that. What I'm talking about lasts a bit longer and is a damn sight less painful next day. I've temporarily loaned Bennett to a pal of mine so his kids can practise looking after a dog, so I'm heading off in my van to catch some waves for a couple of days. Fancy tagging along?'

'Where are you going?'

'Cornwall.'

'I'll pass.' She shook her head, the thought of sharing a county with her mother too close for comfort.

'But I'll be miles away from Polperro. T'other side of the county, as a matter of fact.'

'Where?'

'Godrevy, near St Ives. I take it you have no oddly-named relatives in the area?'

Anna smiled. 'None that I know of.'

'Well, there y'are. This place is special, Anna. It's wild and away from the tourist bustle. You can be there a whole weekend and never see anyone you know. Beautiful beaches, a lighthouse and walks along the cliff path that take your breath away. It's the only place I picture when I think of Cornwall – and it's perfect for getting your head together. Which, pardon me for saying, looks like what you need.'

Anna considered his invitation. It was lovely of Jonah to offer and Godrevy sounded like a wonderful place, but she was tired. More than anything, she just wanted to sleep.

'I don't think I can. I'm sorry.'

'That's okay. I'll pop th'kettle on.' He headed for Anna's kitchen. 'You don't have to decide right away, of course. I'm not leaving till eight. I drive through the night to be there when the sun comes up. So, rest now and have a think, yeah?'

Jonah stayed for an hour, then left as Anna thanked him and climbed into bed. When she woke, it was dark in her room. Disoriented, she clicked the bedside light switch and squinted at her watch.

Five to eight . . .

Recalling Jonah's invitation, she suddenly changed her mind. She didn't want to stay hiding in her apartment as the *Daily Post* and *Daily Messenger* waged a war in her name. It was time she did what she wanted, not wait for life to push her helplessly into the next drama. At that moment she was desperate to leave. Stuffing a change of clothes and a few essentials into a bag, she hurried out of her flat and dashed across the corridor. The door swung open as she raised her hand to knock, sending Jonah stumbling a step back when unexpectedly faced with her fist.

'Is your offer still open?' she rushed, her head dizzy from her sudden awakening.

Jonah kissed her cheek. 'You're just in time.'

Forty-Four

Anna awoke to the muffled sounds of the sea. She ached from her awkward sleeping position on the back seat of Jonah's Volkswagen camper-van and her head felt stuffed with wire wool. She pulled back a blanket she didn't remember lying underneath and rubbed her eyes. Early-morning light streamed through the camper-van windows, the sky a glow of pinks, reds and golds against the dark-ened hulks of grass-crowned sand dunes. She was alone – the front seat empty where her friend had stoically sat as he'd driven through the night hours.

Gaining her bearings, she looked around the vehicle's interior, catching sight of a note propped up against a stainless-steel flask on the small melamine counter in the rear, next to a folded slate-grey garment:

Anna –
  Gone surfing!

*Tea in the flask for you, chocolate bars under the
sink.
    You might need the hoodie – it's a bit parky out!
    Back about 9 a.m.
    Jonah* ☺

Smiling, Anna scrambled over the back seat and opened
a small cupboard door beneath the sink, to reveal a Tupper-
ware box stuffed with chocolate bars of all varieties. Jonah
was certainly prepared for sugar-based emergencies, she
thought to herself. Her hunger surprised her: in recent
days she had struggled to find enthusiasm for food. Helping
herself to a couple of bars, she unfolded Jonah's hooded
sweatshirt and pulled it over her head, laughing at how
big it was on her. Most importantly, it was warm, blocking
out the damp dawn chill permeating through the thin
T-shirt and jeans she had thrown on in haste last night.
She stuffed the chocolate into the hoodie's pouch pocket,
took the flask and blanket and slid open the side door of
the camper-van.

    A rush of cold, salt air met her as she stepped out. The
grass beneath her feet was dew-damp and sand-strewn,
bringing a thousand memories to her mind of early Cornish
mornings on deserted cliffs and beaches. She could almost
picture her younger self and even younger Ruari whooping
as they skidded down sand dunes, racing onto the beach.
When she looked out across the still-dark sand, she could
just make out black-suited bodies weaving and spinning
through sunrise-painted waves, the shouts and calls of her

memories morphing into those of the early-morning surfers.

Godrevy was beautiful. Anna spread out the blanket and sat down, pulling her knees up into the oversized sweatshirt and drinking in the view. She had never been here before, yet it seemed to sound a chord inside her, recalling something long forgotten. It was the call of home-land – although it surprised her to feel it. Her mother's insistence of an irresistible pull to home that existed within every Cornish heart had become little more than a panto-mime act, causing Anna to dismiss the notion. Suddenly, she understood. The wild, untameable beauty of her birth-place stole her heart and, for the first time in her life, Anna felt she belonged.

Breathing in the new sensation, she smiled. What would her mother think if she knew Anna was back in her home county again, six years since she'd left? The thought of Senara dropped like a pebble into a rock-pool, sending disquieting ripples through her mind. She didn't have to think about the woman ever again, certainly not after the finality of her dismissal yesterday. Godrevy contained no memory of Senara to tarnish its beauty, and for that Anna was exceedingly grateful. Banishing thoughts of her mother, she focused on being present in this moment. It didn't matter what the papers said about her, what the rumour-mill accused her of or what lay in store for her when she returned to London. She had faced off Mike Hennessy. She had stood up to her mother. She had told Ben exactly how she felt. And she had taken back ownership of her own life. From today, she could be whoever she wanted to be, no longer bound by what others thought. She had the company of a good friend and the unbelievable beauty of this tiny corner of Cornwall: what more did she need?

She caught sight of the sea-glass and shell bracelet on her wrist, which she had grabbed as she left her home. The delicate beads shone in the pink-gold glow of sunlight breaking where sky met sea. They looked at home here, too. Anna had thought nothing of bringing the bracelet with her last night, but it seemed to acquire a new meaning at Godrevy. She had made it herself, despite thinking she couldn't make anything of the beads when they'd first arrived; now she was watching white-crested waves breaking in a place she had decided to visit, surprised by how spontaneous she had been. Both actions seemed to represent the change in her life – small but significant.

The tea from the flask was strong, perfect for warding off the autumnal bite in the air. Jonah's sweatshirt smelled of his aftershave – warm cinnamon and spiced wood. It was comforting and friendly, as its owner had been during their drive down. As soon as they had left the city last night Anna had relaxed, the miles of darkened motorway carriageways soothing as they chatted for hours about unimportant things. Jonah knew what Anna had been through and this was enough to avoid the subject. Anna loved him for this: his unflappability and perennial steadiness were a gift after the wild histrionics of her mother and those at the *Messenger*. Jonah Rawdon was a good friend and Anna chided herself again for not listening to his views on Ben. Had she taken notice, it might have prevented what followed. She reminded herself that he deserved an apology while they were here.

With each new breath of perfect sea air, each bite of sweet chocolate and each sip of amber-rich tea she felt renewed, as if being in this place was healing wounds long forgotten. The power of the sea and the devastating beauty of the landscape gave her mind space to wander, her resolve room to grow. Like waking up from a troubled dream, Anna felt alive, rejuvenated. Coming here was the perfect decision. Trusting her gut had paid dividends.

Things will be different when I go home, she promised herself. She was going to stand up for herself, like she had with Juliet, with the rival *Daily Post* journalist and with her mother. She might look into her earlier idea of helping small businesses – perhaps even consider a career change. Anything seemed possible in the early-morning light.

'Morning, you,' Jonah called as he sprinted up the dune from the beach, a weather-beaten surfboard under one arm. 'Making yourself comfy?'

'I am.' Anna smiled up at him. 'How's the surf?'

'Awesome.' He slid the camper-van door open, threw his board inside and brought out a towel. 'I needed it, I can tell you. I've been dreaming of that swell for months.'

'Do you come here a lot?'

'Aye. There's a couple of lads I know from freelancing who surf, so we tend to take turns driving down on weekends and in between jobs.' He rubbed his hair with the towel. 'It's the best therapy. You should try it.'

Anna handed him the flask. 'No thanks. My brother

used to surf a lot in his teens, but I was always more of a swimmer. I'm quite happy with the view, to be honest.'

'It's pretty grand, isn't it?' He smiled over the steel cup as he blew away steam. 'I've been all over and never found a place like it. Godrevy always pulls me back. I'll live here one day, if the work keeps coming in. Can't exist in London forever.'

He clambered into the van and emerged a few minutes later wearing a dark-blue hooded sweatshirt and long khaki cargo shorts. Flopping down onto the blanket beside Anna, he handed her a pair of binoculars.

'I spotted a group of Arctic terns diving just off the shoreline. If you aim those over there you might still see them.'

Anna followed his pointing finger to the edge of the beach and scanned across the water until she spotted tiny white shapes plunging headlong into the waves. 'Oh, wow . . .' She studied the sea birds' flight for a while; when she took the binoculars from her eyes, Jonah was smiling at her. 'Something amusing you?'

'I love watching folk when they see nature. That's what I feel every time, even though it's my job. You'd think it'd get old, but it never does. I used to watch Arctic terns off the coast in Scarborough, where my family went on holiday every year. My dad and me spent hours birdwatching. I suppose that's where the camera stuff started.'

'Do you see your family much?' Anna asked. 'I don't think you've told me before.'

'Aye, we get together when we can. Dad remarried after Mum passed, so he's mostly in Spain these days, and my brothers are pretty spread out – Edinburgh, York and Sussex – so when the Rawdons meet up it's a red-letter day.' He smiled. 'And now I know you aren't that close to your mum.'

Anna gave a grudging smile. She had never been, and now never would be. 'Ruari and I are close, though, so at least there's that.'

'Families, eh? Complicated animals.' He nodded towards the sea. 'Simpler to watch those fellas diving into the sea than trying to make sense of humans, I reckon.'

It was strange to be laughing about her relatives with Jonah, but now that he'd seen her mother at her worst, it really didn't matter what else he knew. It felt good to be talking about her family and her background with him. It seemed like the change of scenery encouraged her to share new things with him – and he with her.

'My dad nearly disowned me when I said I wanted to be a cameraman,' he admitted, as they set off for a walk along the beach. 'It was odd. We'd always been close, too, so it came as a bit of shock.'

'What happened?'

'I beat him into submission,' Jonah grinned. 'No, I made a film about him and Mum for their wedding anniversary, using some of their wedding photographs and old cine film. Did it like a documentary and sat them both down to watch it. Dad was a wreck by the end of it.'

'At least you were able to convince them. I think, deep down, I always knew Mum would never fully accept me, even though I spent most of my childhood trying to get her attention. Now I know not to expect her to ever be able to do that. She can only see her little world, which revolves around how she feels, what she wants. She'll never change.'

Jonah picked up a smooth, flat stone and skimmed it out across the shore-lapping waves. 'She could change. People do.'

Anna appreciated his suggestion, even though she didn't believe it would ever happen. 'Maybe. The point is, I no longer need her to.'

As they spent the day together, walking and putting the world to rights, it occurred to Anna that Jonah had become more than a casual friend. He had been there when she'd needed support and he seemed closer to her than before. Where she'd once guarded details of her life, she now felt at ease sharing them; it felt good to know she had a friend who cared enough to listen. So when Jonah broached the subject of Ben that evening, as they ate fish and chips overlooking the sea, Anna didn't hold back.

'I should have listened to you when you said you didn't trust him.'

'You liked the chap. There's nothing wrong with that.'

'Except he used me.'

'Aye, well. I take it he's still hiding from you?'

Anna remembered her last conversation with Ben and the haunted look she hadn't quite managed to forget. 'He tried to apologise.'

Jonah raised an eyebrow. 'Oh?'

'I didn't want to hear it.' She watched the steam rising from her chips. 'He looked awful.'

'I should hope he did. Better off without him, eh?'

401

Anna nodded, but her heart felt heavier than the boulders at the base of the cliffs far below them. She shouldn't feel anything for Ben, apart from anger and relief that she'd found out who he really was before she got too involved. But secretly she still wished things had been different.

'Cool bracelet, by the way. One of your parcel gifts?'

Pleased to move on from the subject of Ben, Anna smiled. 'It was. Although it threw me for a while, because it didn't seem to fit the pattern of the others.'

'It didn't? How come?'

When she looked up at her friend she noticed he had stopped eating. 'It wasn't wrapped in the same way, and the message with the beads and shells didn't make sense. But then I put the bracelet together and understood.'

The last sliver of evening sun slipped below the water at the horizon and its dying glow illuminated the sky. In the bay below a few hardy adventurers rode the waves, wringing every last drop of time out of the day before nightfall. Anna watched their progress, the shore becoming darker as the light faded.

'It's beautiful here. Thanks for bringing me.'

'I'm sorry it isn't for longer.'

'When do we go home?'

Jonah wrapped up the remainder of his meal and stretched out his legs on the blanket. 'We'll head off about this time tomorrow, when the light goes. May as well make the most of the day. I have to say, it's been nice to have your company. Maybe you'd like to escape with me again sometime?'

Surrounded by the beauty of Godrevy, with more peace within than she had felt for months, Anna's answer was easy. 'Any time.'

That night, gazing through the camper-van windows at the blanket of stars shimmering over the darkened bay from the warmth of her makeshift bed, Anna thought about her parcels. If Ben had sent them, the adventure was surely over now. After what she'd said to him in the lift, he knew exactly what she felt about him. It saddened her to think that what had begun as a thing of wonder and joy had ended as little more than a plot to further his career. His friendship and the mystery gifts had been unexpected and beautiful; now, what were they?

One thing confused her: a throwaway comment Jonah had made that evening that stuck in her mind.

'Don't discount everything, just because McAra was an idiot.'

'What do you mean?'

'Those gifts – they were well meant. And they made you happy. I reckon that's all you need to know about them. Trying to analyse why they were sent, and who sent them, will drive you mad and take a bit away from the experience. Best to have some things in life we don't question, don't you think?'

The comment had come from nowhere, yet it echoed Juliet Evans' words. It was strange that two such unconnected people in her life had offered the same thought. Were they right? Was Anna missing out by wanting answers?

With the sound of Jonah's slumbering breath drifting

403

over from the front seat, Anna's eyes grew heavy. *They might be right*, her thoughts concluded, as sleep began to pull her away from them. *But I still want to know who sent the parcels. And why . . .*

Forty-Five

Snuggled up in Jonah's hoodie again on the beach next morning, watching him and his fellow surfers chasing waves, Anna dared to switch on her phone. She was surprised when it found a signal: the last time she came back to Cornwall the only place anyone found reception was on the heights of Bodmin Moor. But much had changed since that ill-fated Christmas visit to her childhood home, six years ago. The row she'd witnessed between Senara and half the village in the pub had sounded the death-knell for her travels back to Cornwall, Anna vowing never to attempt a Browne family reunion again. Today, having spent twenty-four hours back in her home county, she could see return visits in her future.

Tish had sent three messages, each one progressively more concerned for her well-being. Anna replied, simply stating she had gone away for a few days and would be in touch soon. Sheniece's single voicemail message instructed Anna to 'Call me when you can, yeah?' Anna wondered what new gossip her younger colleague had to share, but was in no hurry to think about it here. She was determined to enjoy her last day at Godrevy; there would be plenty of time later to face whatever awaited her.

'A day away from civilisation and you're having to check that thing?' Jonah chided, pushing his surfboard into the sand beside her. 'You're more of a townie than I thought.'

'It's good that I did. Tish was at the point of sending Scotland Yard out on a manhunt. You could have been hauled in by MI5 for questioning.'

'Tish Gornick is the biggest drama-queen this side of the Atlantic.' He flopped down on the sand. 'No wonder America was happy to let her go.'

'She loves you, too.'

'There's a scary thought. You hungry?'

Anna was: the sea air and sanctuary of this break from her regular life had reignited her appetite. They headed across to the small café nestled between the dunes and ordered full English breakfasts and huge mugs of coffee. It was still early and Gordon, the café owner, joked that any earlier and they would have had to cook their own fry-ups. Anna watched as Jonah and Gordon ribbed each other, enjoying being in the middle of their easy banter. Jonah possessed an uncanny knack of knowing people in the most unlikely places. Gordon, it transpired, was a retired assistant director who had worked with Jonah on many of his early filming jobs for the BBC. At the age of forty-four he'd suffered a minor heart attack, an experience that brought about a decision to completely change his life. He'd sold his London home for a typically ridiculous sum, bought what was then a rundown beach bar and turned it into the chic café it was today.

'This place changes you for the better,' he explained. 'My partner brought me to Godrevy to recuperate and I just knew this was where we belonged. Four months later we'd sold up and were camping out on the floor of this place while we renovated it. I was supposed to be taking it easy, of course, but running this business has been the making of me.'

Anna could appreciate the lure of Godrevy, but she thought it was funny that people from her adopted city saw Cornwall as a dream location, when she had spent most of her life trying to leave. Would she find somewhere other than London to escape to, she wondered? Would there come a time when roots and quality of life superseded the city's pull?

Jonah was unusually quiet as they walked onto the cliff path after breakfast. Anna put it down to tiredness caused by early hours spent battling the Godrevy surf. They followed the track past the National Trust car park, which was filling up already despite the still-early hour, and on through the shivering grass that cloaked the cliff edge. The bright white beacon of the lighthouse stood out against the greying sky as foaming white breakers crashed on the rocks around the little island where it stood. Gulls chattered noisily overhead, their calls rising over the roar of the waves pummelling the shore far below. Through Jonah's binoculars, Anna saw jet-black shadows of cormorants diving into the deep blue-green sea and the occasional bob of a seal's head in the calmer waters offered by tiny bays beneath the cliff edges. Godrevy seemed a place of gathering for all kinds of creatures – from the gaggles of tourists dotted across the rising cliffs to the swallows, swifts and sand martins swooping from cliff to sky and the wheeling, yapping selection of dogs dashing across the green expanse.

'What are you thinking?' Jonah asked, suddenly.

'What a beautiful place this is,' Anna replied. 'I can tell why you love it so much.'

'Know what I like best?'

'The surf?'

'Oh, that's grand, of course. But the best thing for me is the freedom. I might only have a number of hours here, but the time I have feels like an eternity. I don't have to think about anything, or I can consider the world in minute detail. I have no responsibilities, no pressing engagements or crazy schedule, but I can be as busy as I want to be. Sometimes I surf from sun up to sun down. Other times, I just sit and take it all in. There's no expectation of me here, no one telling me where I should be or what I should be doing. It's just me, the ocean and this beauty.' He chuckled. 'And if you didn't already know I was daft, you do now.'

Anna smiled back. 'I don't think you're daft at all. Well, not apart from spending hours in the freezing cold sea for fun.'

'Aye, there is that.'

'I think it's a good thing. I've never had anywhere I could go to feel like that. Maybe I should find a place.'

Jonah nudged her. 'I'll let you share this one with me, if you like.'

'Deal.' Anna offered her hand and he shook it.

As they walked on, Anna could feel her spirits brightening as if the sun had broken free from the clouds and was shining directly on her. While stubborn greyness remained in the sky, inside she was glowing.

Later that afternoon, sheltering from the strengthening wind in the camper-van's cosy interior, Anna considered her future. It lay wide open like the green fields rolling across the clifftops of Godrevy. Part of her wanted to stay here, where nobody knew her, but that wasn't the answer. Nothing could hold her back now: what she did with what she had discovered about herself would define what happened next.

She wondered if Ben was happy with himself. Had he just been pretending to regret the story, to smooth things over with her? Was he now back to boasting about writing a story that had attracted such attention? Had he even stopped for a moment to wonder how Anna was? Strangely, a part of her still couldn't quite believe that Ben had used her just to save his own skin. Everything he had said and done before the story broke had seemed real. His kisses definitely had. She was annoyed that she still felt anything for him, but the feeling wouldn't go away.

She gazed out through misting camper-van windows at the windswept cliffs and beach. This much beauty would be wasted on Ben McAra. If he couldn't profit from it, he wouldn't be interested. It felt good to be here with Jonah, who understood her perfectly. The time she had spent with him confirmed that he was a much closer friend than she'd realised before.

I'm lucky to have such a good friend, she thought, sipping her second mug of tea and snuggling further beneath the warm woollen blanket as the wind buffeted the body of the camper-van. The vehicle rocked gently in the breeze, a satisfying creak from its springs sounding like the groaning of an old ship's timbers. Inside, Anna felt completely at peace – moved by the force of the gusts, but not troubled by them. She took a mental snapshot of this moment and promised herself she would return to it back at home, whenever she needed a picture of serenity under pressure.

She must have fallen asleep because when Jonah returned it was a little before five o'clock.

'Nice day?'

Anna smiled happily. 'The best.'

He handed her a bag of still-warm, golden-brown Cornish pasties he'd bought from Gordon's café. 'I thought these would sustain us on the long journey home. Fancy saying goodbye to the beach with me?'

They walked back along the path that skirted the sand dunes and led down to the wide, fudge-coloured sand. Surfers still revelled in the ocean swell, the thunder of breaking waves causing Anna and Jonah to shout in order to be heard. The wind whipped at Anna's hair and salt spray stung her cheeks. In the distance the lighthouse stood, alabastrine and proud, keeping watch over them.

'You look at home here,' Jonah said. 'I'm glad you came.'

'Me too. I think you may have restored my faith in Cornwall.'

'That so?' He laughed and slung his arm around her shoulders. 'I reckon we make a good team.'

'How, exactly?'

'I surf and you watch. Perfect!'

Anna jabbed him in the ribs and when he yelped she sprinted from him, giggling at the sheer freedom she felt, her feet kicking up showers of sand behind her as she ran. Jonah gave chase, his laughter rising above the crash of the surf, until he cornered her and, wrapping his arms around her waist, yanked her with him to the sand.

Before she knew it, Jonah's lips were on hers, his hands pulling her closer to him. The suddenness of it rendered her immobile for a moment, but then she was pushing and kicking him away, scrambling to her feet and gawping down at him in sheer horror.

'What – was *that*?' she demanded, the intrusion still smarting.

Aghast, he stared up at her. 'I thought you wanted—'

'I didn't!'

'But . . .'

Anger was surging up within her. 'I *never* asked you to do that! What were you thinking?' She stumbled back and began to walk quickly away from him. She had nowhere to go, but was compelled by a need to be as far as possible from the man she'd wrongly thought was just her friend.

'Anna, stop!'

411

'No!' Her feet stamped angry holes in the beach as she pressed on.

Jonah's voice grew nearer as he followed her tracks. 'What was I supposed to think? You changed your mind and came with me at the last minute. We've done nothing but flirt with each other since we got here. And you were wearing the bracelet . . .'

She skidded to a halt on the sand and turned back. 'What about the bracelet?'

He stopped too, a little way from her. She could see his chest rising and falling as he caught his breath. 'I thought you'd guessed. When you talked about the parcels yesterday . . .'

Was this a confession?

'It was *you*?'

Jonah hung his head. 'I thought you knew.'

'Knew what? That you were the one sending me gifts I didn't understand, and setting me up to be disappointed when I tried to find the sender? How cruel was that, Jonah?'

'I didn't mean . . .'

'You set the whole thing up, with the old record and the fake email address – why? Did you think it would make me fall for you?'

His grey eyes flicked up. 'Eh? Now hang on . . .'

'What else am I supposed to think, Jonah? When you knew how much I wanted to find the sender, how could you not tell me you'd sent the parcels?'

He was shaking his head now, his hands held up to halt Anna's accusations. '*One* parcel, lass. That's all I sent you.'

Bewildered, Anna didn't reply.

Jonah flushed red. 'You were so upset after that record jaunt, and I didn't know if your mystery chap would send you any more packages. I hoped you'd remember me saying another parcel would come soon and work out I'd sent it. I just wanted to make you smile.'

Anna held up the sea-glass and shell bracelet on her wrist. 'You sent this?'

'Aye.'

And then it made sense. The gift that didn't seem to fit the pattern of the others was never meant to, because it didn't come from the same person. Thinking of the words on the card that had accompanied the beads and shells, she could hear Jonah's Yorkshire dialect: *Make of this what you will* . . .

'And what about the other parcels?'

'I don't know who sent them.'

'But you were happy to let me think you had?'

'If it meant you wanted to be with me, yes. I'm sorry, lass. But the fact is, I like you. I've liked you for a very long time, only I was too dumb to say owt. I wish I had now. I . . . I didn't mean to scare you.'

It was all wrong. Jonah was a friend – and Anna counted on him to stay a friend. It was what she needed and she couldn't consider him as anything else. What she'd thought was an invitation for her benefit was actually for his: to get her alone, in order to move their friendship in a direction Anna wasn't prepared to go. Suddenly the beauty around her meant nothing; she wanted to leave.

'Can we just go, please? I want to go home.'

413

He said nothing, his resigned expression the only assent he could convey. In silence they retraced their steps away from the churning, angry ocean, the purposeful distance they kept from each other a cold, unyielding reminder of the divide that now existed between them.

The journey home was the longest – and most awkward – Anna had ever experienced. They hardly spoke for the entire five hours, her gaze fixed determinedly on the road ahead as Jonah stole glances at her. Roadworks and tail-backs dragged the motorway traffic to a near-halt for almost twenty miles, the camper-van's speedometer barely registering above five miles an hour for what felt like forever. The sight of city lights had never been so welcome for Anna – and she suspected for Jonah, too, who gave an audible sigh of relief as he parked in Walton Tower's underground car park. With the rasp of the VW engine gone, he turned to her.

'Home, then.'

'Thank you for the trip.'

'I – suppose I'll see you around?' From his look of defeat he obviously held out little hope for this.

'Yes.' Her answer was necessary to facilitate her escape, but Anna was too tired and emotionally drained to be able to give a definite reply. Taking her bag, she fled from the camper-van across the pale-grey concrete of the car park and ran up the stairs to Walton Tower's lobby. Not wanting to take the lift, she carried on ascending the steps to hurry into the blessed peace of her flat, slamming the door and locking it.

It was only when she was alone, in the middle of her darkened home, that she realised she was still wearing Jonah's hoodie. She struggled out of it, tossed the oversized garment into a heap and burst into tears.

Forty-Six

Nothing was turning out the way Anna had expected. Work had become tarnished by the unwanted articles; her relationship with her mother had died a spectacular death; Ben had been revealed as a plotting cheat; and now she had lost Jonah – whom she'd considered her closest friend. Even her parcels, which had started as kind, anonymous gifts but had become something entirely dearer, had been tainted. Twenty-four hours ago she'd thought she was turning a corner in understanding who she was and where she could be going. Today, as she stared into the depths of her black coffee, she felt lost.

When her phone began to buzz beside her, Anna was tempted not to answer. She peered at the display and saw Sheniece's name. Relieved the caller wasn't a grovelling journalist or a mortified cameraman, she answered the call.

'Anna! How are you? More importantly, *where* have you been? I kept getting your answerphone.'

'I had a couple of days away.' *Please don't ask me for details.*

'But you're back now, yeah? Good. I need to see you – are you free for brunch?'

They arranged to meet at a chain restaurant in Kensington High Street, where Sheniece was enjoying her day off from work, 'spending money while it's there' on the new credit card her latest flame had given her.

'We've missed you at work,' she said, hauling a handful of shopping bags onto the leather bench seat and sitting next to them. 'It's been so boring, you wouldn't believe.'

'No armies of rival hacks camping outside the building? No more Ben McAra exclusives?' It felt good to be able to joke about recent events, Anna being confident that Sheniece was the best audience for it.

'Don't take this the wrong way, sweet, but you're *old news* now.'

'I've heard that before.' Anna remembered Juliet's PA assuring her of the same, before Senara's story broke.

'Ah, but this time they've run out of things to say. Rea reckons Ben's refused to write any more about you, but I think the Dragon's got what she wanted with this buyout deal – and taking the *Post* down a peg or two into the bargain.' She buffed her nails with a linen napkin. 'So you're surplus to requirements.'

'I'm relieved to hear it. So, what else did I miss?'

With a conspiratorial smile, Sheniece reached into her pink leather bag. 'Only *this*,' she said, lifting out a parcel wrapped in brown paper. 'It arrived yesterday morning, but I signed for it before anyone else saw. Nobody knows, apart from Narinder, me – and now you.'

Anna accepted the parcel, inspecting it carefully. The corners of the wrapping had been folded with precision, the sender's details absent once more. Knowing the seventh parcel had been from Jonah, this had to be from the original sender. It was the last thing she'd expected to happen – but she was surprisingly happy to see it.

'I don't suppose you fancy opening it here?' Sheniece ventured. 'Seeing as I kept it a secret for you.'

'Thank you. For not telling anyone else.'

Her colleague's shoulders drooped. 'So that's a no, then?'

Anna considered the parcel in her hands. It represented a new adventure after the confusion and disappointment she'd experienced recently. And, really, what did it matter who witnessed its opening? She appreciated Sheniece's thoughtfulness: without it, she could have faced more scrutiny over the delivery when she returned to work. This way she could enjoy whatever she'd been sent, away from the glare of *Messenger* interest; involving Sheniece would ensure it remained that way.

'Okay, I'll open it here.'

Sheniece clapped her hands, causing diners to peer over. 'Result!'

'But on one condition: whatever is inside remains a secret between us. Agreed?'

'Yes, of course. Open it, open it!'

Enjoying her friend's excitement, Anna lifted the two perfectly creased corners of the wrapping paper. Sheniece leaned over the table for a better view as Anna pulled out a purple box tied with a black bow.

'This is like a fairy tale!' Sheniece squeaked, unable to contain herself.

Anna smiled and untied the black satin ribbon, lifting the lid to reveal pale-lilac tissue paper. Within the folds she found a beautiful hardback book, its edges gilded and its title embossed in swirling silver and gold.

Her companion was a little disappointed. 'A book?'

'It's a lovely book.'

'Yeah, but . . . don't get me wrong, An, I like to read sometimes, but a book isn't a patch on expensive clothes or jewellery. Which book is it?'

'*I Capture the Castle* by Dodie Smith.' A memory of her Aunt Zelda gifting her a dog-eared copy of the famous coming-of-age story warmed Anna's heart. 'I read this when I was thirteen. It was my aunt's favourite book and she gave it to me like a rite of passage. It's a beautiful story.' As she flicked through the pages, a square of white card fell onto the tablecloth. 'Oh.'

'Is that a message? What does it say?'

Printed on the card were words Anna immediately recognised:

. . . because life is too exciting to sit still for long

'I don't get it.' Sheniece frowned at the card. 'Sounds like a strap-line from a shampoo advert.'

Anna laughed. 'It's a quote from the book.'

Sheniece shrugged. 'I still don't get it.' She let out a sigh.

419

'I'm glad this means something to you. If I got this through the post I'd be demanding a name, or a phone number at least. Especially after the wringer whoever sent the parcels has put you through. Cryptic messages would annoy the hell out of me.'

Anna hugged the book as she read the note again. 'I wanted to be Cassandra Mortmain for a year after reading this. She expects the best out of life, all the time, even though the circumstances she finds herself in aren't what she'd hoped.' The protagonist's irrepressible optimism had struck a chord with the young Anna, who was just beginning to understand how far from perfect life as Senara Browne's daughter was.

'Right.' Sheniece was observing her as if Anna was attempting to explain string theory. 'Well, as long as you're happy . . .'

To her surprise, Anna was. Happier than she had been for a while, and certainly happier than she thought she would be after the ill-fated trip with Jonah. The book had reminded her of a time when she'd believed the best was possible: it was that belief that had led her to dream of a better life in London. It had been a long and difficult journey, in reality only ending when she'd finally stood up to her mother. But she had made it, had never stopped believing her freedom was attainable; and now – who could say what was possible?

On her journey back across the city, Anna felt a welcome calm returning, as if the book she carried was a long-lost friend, returned from too many years away. She changed Underground lines at Green Park, dodging packs of foreign tourists heading for Buckingham Palace, and as she waited on the platform for the next train a new thought occurred: *what if Ben sent this parcel?*

How would she feel if the journalist wasn't ready to give up? Could it be another ploy to extend his recent run of attention-grabbing news stories? She couldn't imagine he had ever read *I Capture the Castle*; even if he had, the thought of him identifying with Cassandra Mortmain as much as she had was crazy. He didn't strike her as the hopeless romantic type. She'd made it clear she didn't want to see him again last time they had spoken. But what if Ben wasn't willing to let it end like this?

So many details of the parcels had put Ben in the frame as the sender before he'd written the newspaper story. The coincidence of the midnight blue shoes arriving close to their first date when they'd danced beneath the stars was too significant to ignore. But back then Anna knew she had wanted Ben to be her mystery benefactor. She'd wanted to believe he'd done it out of love, to win her heart. But if the parcels had been sent just for the sake of a story, why send another gift when he'd been found out?

Is this an apology?

It was a strange choice, if so. He couldn't have known about Anna's love for *I Capture the Castle*. She couldn't remember specifically mentioning the book to him during their early-morning coffee-house visits. Maybe it was just a lucky guess?

She was still angry with Ben. But since Jonah kissed her, she had been slowly growing aware of a truth that she didn't know what to do with. What had forced her away from her friend with such definite action hadn't been anger because Jonah had crossed a line. It was because, in that moment, it galvanised her feelings for Ben. Pointless feelings – feelings that couldn't be acted upon after what she had said to him the last time they met.

How did I find myself here?

She looked back at the quote on the card:

. . . because life is too exciting to sit still for long

Is my life exciting?

She had never considered it as such, before the parcels arrived. But back then 'exciting' wasn't at the top of her requirement list for a happy life. Safe, secure and '*mine*' were. Had she ever craved excitement? It was difficult to say. Her life in Cornwall had been anything but dull, but Anna longed to live away from the constant drama. Excitement became a byword for whatever car-crash relationship Senara was either lusting after, involved in or noisily exiting. That kind of excitement Anna was keen to avoid.

The memory of the optimism of Dodie Smith's story had cheered her today, when she most needed it. If Ben had sent the gift, was that his intention? She stroked the embossed cover of the leather-bound book and let her worries go. She was tired of unpicking every development and the thought behind this gift was kind, regardless of *whose* thought it was. Opening the book at the beginning of the story, she began to read. Words she had loved so much in the past rose up to meet her and Anna welcomed their return. If there was ever an important time to revisit Cassandra Mortmain's irresistibly optimistic world, it was now.

Forty-Seven

There were benefits to having water leaks in your apartment, Tish Gornick concluded, as she enjoyed the welcoming warmth of the coffee shop below her home. Firstly, she couldn't work while it was being fixed, which was always an unexpected blessing on a Friday when she usually completed the accounts from home. Plus, she didn't trust the Wi-Fi in Spill the Beans (at least, that was what she'd told her manager this morning when she'd phoned in her apology).

Secondly, she could allow herself a larger-than-usual late lunch in order to kill time, writing off the no-doubt-excessive calories against the increased emotional stress of the event. The indignity of the water situation in her apartment called for it. After having no water at all a few weeks ago, the tinkering done to fix it then had now caused the ageing pipes to give up the ghost.

But the most unexpected benefit had presented itself when Seamus, the admittedly rugged Irish caretaker of

Walton Tower, removed his shirt in the line of duty – and, inadvertently, revealed a rather deliciously toned chest that commanded her attention. She blushed thinking of it, even two hours after the event. Who knew the caretaker was hiding such an awesome body?

Her mother would be *appalled*, of course, her own deep-seated mistrust of Irishmen informed by a brief but disastrous fling with an Irish deli-owner in Harlem, not long after she divorced Tish's father in the late Seventies.

'Never trust an Irish fella,' she'd often warned her daughter. 'They whip up a tale around you so sweet you're drowning in sugar, then drop you like a hot rock.'

When Tish was still young and impressionable enough to take notice, her mother had practically locked her in their house on St Patrick's Day, forbidding her to attend the parade that passed by, for fear of Tish becoming enchanted by a Gaelic ne'er-do-well. She would be horrified to learn that her daughter was, at that precise moment, conjuring up raunchy scenarios starring the caretaker, while devouring a hunk of chocolate cake large enough to make her arteries beg for leniency.

When her daydreams offered her a moment's respite, Tish looked up and spotted her friend Anna Browne sitting on the opposite side of the coffee shop. She was practically curled around a hardback book, oblivious to everything around her. The book looked old and expensively bound, although Tish couldn't make out the title. But most noticeable was the expression Anna wore. It was wistful – a word not usually in Tish Gornick's lexicon, but the most apt for what she saw. She toyed with the idea of remaining in her seat, leaving Anna be. But who was she kidding? She *had* to know what was going on.

With thoughts of the unexpectedly delectable caretaker still sweetly glowing at the back of her mind, Tish left her table.

'Anna? I thought it was you.'

Anna looked up and reluctantly put her book down, marking her place with a coffee-shop napkin. 'Hi, Tish.'

Without waiting to be asked, Tish sat down at Anna's table. 'What happened to you? Where did you disappear to?'

'I just needed to clear my head for a couple of days.'

'You left in a hurry.'

'It was a last-minute decision.'

'Was it that crazy article about your mother? Mrs Smedley showed it to me when I looked in on her yesterday. I'm sorry you had to go through that, Anna.'

Anna shrugged. The article seemed a world away now. 'It's done. I'm moving on.'

'Okay, what aren't you telling me? What happened while you were away?'

'Nothing special.' Anna hoped her smile would be enough to curb Tish's questions. 'Anyway, I'm here now, and hopefully back to work on Monday, so I'm making the most of my long weekend.'

'Reading.' Tish's flat tone conveyed her disdain.

'Call it revisiting an old friend.'

Tish peered over at the cover. '*I Capture the Castle*? Wow, it's years since I read that. My sister was obsessed

426

with it in high school. I even caught her trying to write with her feet in the kitchen sink once.' She shook her head. 'I guess you love it, huh?'

'I do. I take it you don't?'

'Too rainbows-and-bluebirds for my taste. I was more of a John Steinbeck girl.'

'Ah.' This came as no surprise to Anna. 'Well, I love it.'

Tish sat back in her seat, observing her friend. 'Where did you get it?'

She could lie, of course. But she found she wanted to know her friend's thoughts, her own being difficult to quantify. 'It was in another parcel.'

'Another? They started up again?'

'Apparently.'

'Was there a note?'

Anna handed the card to her. Tish studied it as if close inspection would uncover the sender's DNA.

'And you're thinking it's the journalist, right?'

'I don't know what to think. The last conversation I had with Ben was pretty final. I don't know what he would gain from sending another gift.'

Tish held out her hand for the book, subjecting it to the same scrutiny. 'Could be an apology, I guess. Weird choice.'

Anna accepted the book back and stroked its cover. 'Actually, it means something to me. But Ben – or whoever else might have sent it – couldn't have known.'

'Lucky guess? Doesn't every girl love Dodie Smith?'

'You didn't.'

'Good point. So how do you feel about the new parcel?

427

I only ask because, if it was me, I'd probably wish I'd never had them at all.'

Anna stared at her friend. She had felt like that before, but spending time in Cassandra Mortmain's world again had make her think differently. 'I want to know who sent it, obviously. But I don't wish the parcels had never arrived. I haven't liked everything that's happened, but when in life do we ever get everything we want? The thing with Mum was hard and it hurt, but it also made me stand up for myself, and I would never have thought I could do that before. I thought the gifts in the parcels were changing me, but I was wrong. They gave me the courage to change myself.'

Tish's eyes narrowed. 'I guess that's one way of looking at it.'

Anna put the book on the table between them and rested her hand on its cover. 'If Ben sent the parcels – and I'm not saying he did – then regardless of everything that's happened, I'm still grateful to him. I haven't forgiven him for the story, of course. But I like the changes I've made this year. They weren't made trying to impress anyone, just to make me happy. For that, I'm grateful.'

Her friend smiled and, quite unexpectedly, leaned over and hugged Anna. 'I think that's awesome. You know, my therapist says life is a choice and a journey. It's a choice because nobody can change you without your permission, consciously or otherwise. And a journey because it's a process. I've watched you changing every week. You're more confident. You walk taller. You stood up to your mother, for heaven's sake! I've been in therapy twenty-two years, yet I still turn into a mouse when my mother walks in.'

In all the time they had been friends Anna had never heard Tish talk so personally. She had always pictured the irascible former New Yorker as too concerned by her own worldly woes to notice anything else. 'A choice and a journey. I like that.'

Back at home, Anna gathered together all of the gifts, spreading them out across the living-room floor. She knew what she'd told Tish was right. The scarf that had made people notice her – it wasn't the beautiful design or liquid-like fall of the fabric that caressed her skin; it had been the way she'd felt about herself when she was wearing it. She hadn't been respected more because of the owl brooch, but because she'd dared to believe herself wise. When she'd danced with Ben in the midnight-blue shoes or travelled back in time in Notting Hill with Jonah, it had been *her* choice, *her* journey. On their own, each gift was a kind gesture; collectively they were tools she had used without knowing it.

It was never about the parcels. It was always about me.

The gifts, the mystery and the questions – all were irrelevant in the light of the person she was allowing herself to become. Knowing this didn't solve the mystery, but it gave her a way forward. She might never know the sender's identity; what mattered now was what she did with what she'd learned.

Life is too exciting to sit still for long . . . the latest note stated. Surrounded by the parcel gifts, Anna realised she hadn't sat still for the entire journey. Now she understood that she was the person steering, she wasn't scared of what the future might hold. *Little Anna Browne* – the quiet girl with the quiet life – was no more. Anna had left her far behind without knowing it, never to retrace her steps.

On Monday she would return to work, facing whatever awaited her. But instead of going back already anticipating defeat, she would walk into the *Daily Messenger* as the Anna Browne she was choosing to become.

Smiling, she imagined her grandmother standing beside her. Morwenna might have made mistakes, but she was a woman who owned every inch of her life. Anna had assumed she could never be like her. Now she was determined to follow her example.

Whatever happens next, she decided, *is up to me.*

Forty-Eight

'You going to last more than a couple of days between paid leave this time?' Ted smirked, his fatherly nudge conveying his welcome back to Anna.

'I thought I'd give it a go.'

'I was beginning to think that psycho parcel-sender might have done away with you. Any more deliveries I should know about?'

'Only a dead rat and severed finger.' Straight-faced, Anna enjoyed Ted Blaskiewicz's look of pure horror.

He turned to Sheniece. 'Did you know about this?'

'Oh yes,' the junior receptionist played along. 'And you thought Anna was just taking a couple of days off. Scotland Yard got involved and everything.'

'It'll be on *Crimewatch* next month.'

'And *Scott & Bailey* soon after . . .'

Anna and Sheniece could maintain the joke no longer, descending into giggles. Ted's face reddened. 'Oh, I see. Like that, is it?'

'Oh, Ted, your face!' Breathless with laughter, Sheniece patted his shoulder.

'Jokes of that nature with a member of the security services could be dangerous,' he huffed.

'I had a book,' Anna said, taking pity on the security chief. '*I Capture the Castle* by Dodie Smith. It was a lovely gift.'

'I don't know why you didn't just say that in the first place, girl. You could've given me a coronary. So, it wasn't McAra then?'

'I don't know who sent it.'

'Only I heard he's been offered a job with Sky News. Thinking of taking it, too, if word in the newsroom is right. Reckon he wants to get away from here as soon as possible.'

The news stole the wind from Anna's sails. If Ben had sent the parcels, was the book quote a clue to his identity? Had he sat still at the *Messenger* for too long – and was this his way of saying goodbye?

'I heard that, too.' Sheniece shook her head. 'He's not been the same since the parcel story. A change of scene is probably what's best for him now.'

Ashraf dashed from the lift across the atrium. 'Have you seen the memo?'

'What memo?' Unsure what to make of the latest *Messenger* bombshell, Anna turned her attention to her younger colleague, who appeared to be about to expire from the excitement of conspiratorial gossip.

'Check the monitor,' he managed.

Sheniece surveyed him with disdain. 'You should go back to the gym, Ash. You're out of condition.'

'I ran all the way back. Everyone upstairs is buzzing about it.'

'Here it is.' Anna opened the email file. 'Juliet Evans has called a whole-company meeting in the newsroom at two o'clock today.'

'I told you stuff was happening.' Ted said, his thunder well and truly stolen. 'I've said it for *weeks*.'

Ashraf groaned. 'It's bad news, I know it. I've only just arrived here: guess who'll be first to go, if there's redundancies? My mum will kill me. I didn't go to college because this job came up.'

The wording of the memo was short and to the point, giving nothing away. 'It might not be bad news,' Anna suggested.

'Calling everyone together for an announcement is *always* bad news.'

'You don't know that, Ted. What about the management buyout? I thought that had saved the paper?'

'It wasn't set in stone. And even if it's gone through, there'll be redundancies. There always are.'

Ted wasn't the only one to be concerned. Every person who passed reception that morning seemed subdued, as if the expensive lights in the *Messenger* building's lobby had been dimmed. In the space of a few hours an innocuous three-line memo had become a portent of certain doom. When Babs Braithwaite and her cleaning team were asked to stay later than usual to go to the meeting, she arrived back at reception in floods of tears.

433

'It's the end, I tell you! I can kiss my retirement villa in Benidorm goodbye.'

'On your salary?' Ted remarked unhelpfully, being sent packing by a disgusted Sheniece.

'A few more years might have done it,' she sniffed, as Anna did her best to comfort her. 'Or the Clean Team syndicate might have won the lottery. A girl can dream, can't she?'

'You dream all you like, Babs,' Sheniece replied, snatching the apologetic cup of tea that Ted had made for the cleaner. 'Dreams might be all we're left with, after today . . .'

In the middle of it all, Anna wondered what this meant for her. She loved her job – always had – but since her trip to Cornwall with Jonah she'd thought more about what else she could do for a living. As her colleagues continued to depress themselves with dire possibilities of what the meeting might hold, Anna thought about the initial research she had done the night before: of business courses that would refresh what she had learned at university, possible posts in organisations that supported small businesses. She'd drawn up a tentative list, beginning with local Chambers of Commerce. She was nervous about the news the meeting might bring, but at least she had started to put contingencies into place.

The mood at the *Daily Messenger* darkened as the afternoon approached. Not wanting to continue the prospective post-mortem with her colleagues over lunch, Anna left them behind to visit Freya & Georgie's. She waited in the lunch queue, glad to be out of the pressure-cooker environment at work. Megan Milliken spotted her and waved, while fulfilling four customer orders at once.

'Hey! I haven't seen you for ages. Are you well?'

'Yes, thanks. You?'

Megan seemed to illuminate the space around her. 'Great, actually. I'm moving in with Gabe next week.'

'That was fast!'

'I know, that's what everyone says. But we're in love, so why wait?'

Anna smiled. 'Congratulations, then.'

'Thanks.' She peered over the counter. 'Your chap not with you today?'

'Afraid not. And he isn't my chap.'

'Oh. Sorry. Only the two of you looked so . . . My mistake. Haven't seen him much in here lately, come to think of it.'

To be in Freya & Georgie's without Ben was a strange, empty experience. Anna wondered what he was doing today and whether she would see him at the company meeting in less than an hour's time. Perhaps the rumours about his new job were true and he'd tendered his resignation already? There would certainly be little to keep him at the *Messenger* if a career-defining appointment was on the cards. Anna had wanted to believe he was motivated by a genuine desire to spend time with her; even at their last meeting, when her anger had obliterated his words, a part of her still longed for a different outcome. Jonah's unwanted advances had magnified how *wanted* Ben's were – even though they weren't real. For better or worse, she felt the loss of his attention.

Not wanting to dwell on it, she collected her lunch and left the coffee house.

In the *Messenger* building she entered a brooding atmosphere. Employees milled around the atrium, killing time, their expressions grave and voices low as they grouped together, heads bowed. Resignation met worry, rumours and counter-rumours circulating like vipers about to strike.

'I'd have more fun at a funeral,' Sheniece whispered, as Ted walked with practised ceremony to lock the entrance doors, every eye in the atrium following him. 'The sooner we know what the Dragon wants, the better.'

Ted returned, pausing by each group to speak and nodding solemnly as they dispersed towards stairs and lift.

'At least Ted's having fun,' Anna observed. 'Oscar-worthy performance, I reckon.'

Sheniece rolled her eyes. 'Looks like we're being summoned, too.'

They joined their colleagues in slow procession to the third floor, their muted conversations deadened as if being broadcast through cotton wool in the stairwell. The packed newsroom was ominously quiet, its computer screens dark and desks abandoned. Some commandeered chairs while others stood. The signs of anxiety were everywhere – shuffling feet, fingers twitching, necks rubbed and strands of hair chewed. It reminded Anna of the queues of nervous teens at her school waiting to be admitted to the exam rooms.

Muttered conversations began to fade and the crowd parted as Juliet Evans made her way to the front. She carried authority in her stride, her expression giving nothing away. When the newsroom was silent, she spoke.

'Ladies and gentlemen, thank you for your attendance. I appreciate you taking time out of your day and I promise you won't be kept long . . .'

'*See?*' Ted hissed, silenced from further comment by his colleagues' withering stares.

'As many of you know, we recently proposed a management buyout of the *Daily Messenger*'s assets from DayBreak Corp, masterminded by Damien Kendal and several of my esteemed colleagues on the Board of Directors. I won't lie to you: this was a hard decision and one that none of us were convinced would come to fruition.'

'Here it comes . . .'

'*Ted!*'

'But it appears our hard work has been rewarded.' Juliet glanced at Damien Kendal, who was standing far enough away so as not to steal her thunder, but visible enough to confirm his authority. 'As of midnight last night, we are now an autonomous entity.'

Applause broke out across the newsroom, four hundred employees breathing a collective sigh of relief. Even Ted Blaskiewicz appeared stunned by the news. Anna felt tension lifting like a curtain, letting light flood into the *Messenger* news floor. Juliet allowed the celebration to continue, the merest hint of a smile appearing. Then she held up her hand.

'Needless to say, while uncertainty over our future was still in place, our rivals on Fleet Street took pleasure in our supposed demise. I, for one, am tired of their jokes at our expense, their snide little comments printed week in, week out. News of our renaissance will not be received well. So, I feel a little celebration is in order. Show *certain publications* that the *Daily Messenger* is far from dead and buried, and rub salt into the wounds that our survival will inflict. On Saturday night we will throw the grandest, most lavish party London has seen. I intend it to be the talk of the town, to leave our detractors in no doubt whatsoever that we have a future and *will* succeed. Let them see that we are more than back in business.'

Ripples of approval passed through the newsroom. Anna scanned the smiling faces for one that had so far eluded her. While her colleagues applauded their leader and each other, her own relief was tempered by her search. Eventually she saw him, standing a little way from his fellow journalists, watching from the sidelines. Ben seemed to be out of place, as if he had already left the *Messenger* in all but body. Anna wanted to ask him, once and for all, if he was the parcel-sender, but she remained frozen in the midst of the celebrations. Just as she was about to leave, his head turned and he saw her. Anna held her breath. His eyes held hers, his stare wide and searching. Then his head bowed and he disappeared into the cluster of bodies as the crowd began to disperse.

Pushing against the flow of people heading out of the newsroom, Anna made for the place she had seen Ben, determined to speak to him. If she could just say thank you, tell him that his gift meant more to her than he was ever likely to know, maybe the barrier between them would break. She had been a passive participant in the parcel scheme until now. That had to change. It was her choice to confront Ben – if she could find him . . .

But when she reached the place she had last seen him, he had gone. The corridor to the other offices was fast clearing, the main newsroom was returning to normal life, but his chair was unoccupied, his desk too empty of its usual detritus. A cold chill settled on her shoulders. With nothing else to be done, she reluctantly returned to reception.

The congratulatory voices of Ted, Babs, Sheniece and Ashraf rose excitedly around her as she assumed her place in a daze, feeling that she'd missed an important opportunity. Her job was safe – for the time being at least – and things could return to normal. Of this she was undeniably glad. But the victory had a hollow edge somehow.

'Anna?' Sheniece was staring at her.

'Sorry?'

'I said, I heard the party's going to be at Kensington Palace Orangery! Can you believe it? I wonder if Prince Harry will be around . . . What do you think?'

Anna smiled back, but the question mirrored the one she was asking herself: *What do I think? I think I have to put some things right.*

Forty-Nine

Jonah Rawdon was a broken man. He had spent the days following their return from Cornwall feeling like the biggest idiot on the planet. How could he ever have mistaken Anna's kindness towards him for attraction? With no work to distract him, he was a wreck – too much time to consider his stupidity had taken its toll on his appetite and his ability to sleep. In recent days he had taken to avoiding his reflection, the sight of his unshaven face and unkempt hair doing little to help his mood. Bennett, his dog, had retreated to the safety of his basket, his mournful eyes following Jonah's directionless wanderings as his lead remained on its hook by the door.

Why had he kissed her? The moment their lips met, he could feel Anna pulling away and knew he'd made a mistake of epic proportions. The euphoria he'd experienced at sharing his favourite place with her, and seeing Anna reunited with the county she'd abandoned, must have messed with his head. It was the only explanation. But knowing what he'd done wrong and making it better were two different things. He wasn't ready to face her again – and the way he felt right now, he might never be.

Which is why he couldn't hide his shock when he found Anna Browne on his doorstep.

'Anna . . .'

Even as she'd knocked on Jonah's front door, Anna hadn't been sure if he would slam it straight back in her face again. After all, she'd rejected him and then hidden away. She couldn't help how she felt, but neither could he.

'Can we talk?'

Jonah didn't speak for a moment. He had every right to refuse, of course, given the awkwardness of the situation, but Anna hoped he would listen to her. He was a good friend – too good to lose for the sake of an embarrassing misunderstanding.

'Sure. Come in.'

Anna could see a pile of empty pizza boxes just visible on the edge of his kitchen counter and clothes strewn across the floor behind him. 'Not here. Let's go out.'

'I look like a tramp,' he protested. 'Can you give me five minutes to have a shave? You can wait here, or I'll knock on your door when I'm ready.'

'How about I wait for you downstairs?' Her nerves had been building since she'd made the decision to visit Jonah after work and she needed to feel in control to see it through.

'Fine. Won't be long.'

In the early-evening sunshine Anna waited outside Walton Tower's entrance. She had rehearsed what she wanted to say on her commute home, a speech she hoped would navigate the emotional minefield between them. And she hoped Jonah would listen. Whether their friendship could return to what it had been before hung in the balance. He might decide to back away. That was his choice. But her choice was to try.

He joined her on the street ten minutes later, clean-shaven and wearing clothes that didn't look as if they had been slept in. Bennett fussed about his feet, a black-and-white blur of pure canine joy at the prospect of a walk at last.

'Hey. Where are we going?'

'It's a nice evening. I thought we could head to the park?'

Anna was glad of the good weather: talking to Jonah in the confines of a room would have magnified the awkwardness. The autumnal palette of Loveage Gardens was soothing, the sounds of the park far better than the silence of either of their homes. They reached a green cast-iron bench and sat down. Jonah kept his eyes trained on the wide verdant expanse. Anna's nerves flipped up a gear. Bennett raced off after a tennis ball, but was soon meeting up with other dogs in the centre of the park.

'Busy this evening,' he said suddenly.

'Yes – I suppose . . .'

'Bennett's happy as Larry. I think he thought he'd never get another walk.'

Steeling herself, Anna bit the bullet. 'Jonah, I want to say—'

He raised a hand to his forehead. 'Don't. Okay? Don't say sorry. I should be the one apologising.'

'I feel awful about what happened.'

'Believe me, you're not the only one.' He turned to her. 'I was an idiot . . .'

'No, you weren't.'

'I was. I should never have kissed you. It just happened.'

'I know.'

'I totally misread the situation.'

Anna put her hand on his knee. 'Jonah, I *know*. I misread it, too. And that's what I wanted to say. You were so kind to me, taking me with you at short notice, listening to me talk about my mother and Ben and . . .' She let out a long sigh. 'And I didn't know you had feelings for me.'

'When I saw the bracelet from the bits I'd sent you, I assumed you'd guessed it was from me and were trying to let me know.'

'I can see how you thought that. I'm sorry.'

'I'm sorry, too. I never meant to scare you, Anna, or put you on the spot.'

They fell into silence, watching Bennett chasing around with his newfound friends. Anna knew what was left to say, but also that it wouldn't be what Jonah was hoping for. A mother with a bright-red pushchair passed by, the curly copper-haired baby girl inside it giving them a quizzical look.

Jonah laughed. 'Much easier to be that age, eh? All you

443

have to worry about is playing, eating and sleeping. I don't think she was a fan of us, though.'

'Everyone's a critic,' Anna replied, knowing that the time had come for what she needed to say. 'You know I don't . . . feel the same way about you, don't you?'

His smile faded. 'Aye. I pretty much got that idea.'

'It's not for want of trying, honestly. You're a good man and you mean a lot to me. I don't want to lose that. But I just can't see you as more than a friend.'

'You don't need to explain. I've been doing a lot of thinking and reached the same conclusion. I like you, Anna, always have. But the thought of losing you as a friend has scared the crap out of me these past few days.' He gently placed his hand on hers. 'Start again?'

The outcome was better than Anna could ever have hoped. 'Let's do that.'

When they parted ways by the entrance to Walton Tower – Jonah giving in to his dog's demands for a longer walk to compensate for three days without, Anna went into Spill the Beans, bought coffee and pastries for two and headed up to Tish's apartment. Her conversation with Tish when the book had arrived had helped her make sense of where she was, and now Anna wanted to talk more.

When she reached Tish's floor it became apparent that their friendship wasn't the only one undergoing changes for the better. Seamus Flatley was leaving her friend's apartment, rebuttoning his shirt and looking like the child who had received all the Christmas presents. He flushed a little when he saw Anna, muttering an excuse about 'those troublesome water pipes again' and hurrying down the stairs. Anna knocked on the still-open door.

'Tish?'

'In here . . .' Her friend's voice floated through the apartment, followed a few moments later by its owner. She was smoothing down her hair and sported the same self-satisfied expression as the caretaker. 'Hey. You caught me – uh . . .'

Anna folded her arms. 'Seamus? Really?'

'You know, it's the darnedest thing, my boiler bit the dust – *again* – and Seamus happened to be passing . . .' She stopped, amused by her own preposterous excuse. 'Who am I kidding? The man's gorgeous and I'd be crazy not to take advantage. And it's been a *really* long time since I enjoyed a body like that.'

Anna recoiled a little. Their friendship might be entering more personal territory, but she wasn't sure she was ready yet to hear every detail of Tish's latest liaison. 'Just as long as you're happy.'

'Oh, I am. My mother would probably disown me. Not so much for entertaining a hot guy in my home, but more because he's Irish. So, I finally found my rebellious side, at forty-five years old. Who knew that would happen?' She straightened a cushion on the sofa. 'But I guess you didn't come here to bust me. What's up?'

'When I went away, it was with Jonah. We got our wires massively crossed and he made a pass at me. Since we came back I've avoided him, but I thought about what I'd told you in Spill the Beans last week and decided to sort it out. Which I just have.'

Tish motioned for Anna to sit. 'You did good, honey. Misunderstandings can blow friendships apart. Believe me, I've been trapped in explosions like that before, and they aren't pretty.'

'I feel good about it. I don't like being at odds with anyone.'

'Apart from your mother.' Tish winked. 'But, hey, you're preaching to the choir with me on that one.'

'And my job looks safe for the foreseeable future, too, which is great.'

'So why does your face tell me things aren't so rosy?'

Anna stared back. 'Does it?'

'You suck at lying, Anna Browne. The FBI is unlikely to call on your services any time soon. What happened to the journalist?'

Was it obvious that Ben was still playing on her mind? 'I think he might be leaving the paper. I don't know what to think about him, Tish – that's the truth. I'm angry that he used me; and in the light of what he did, I don't know if any of our friendship was real. But when I considered what you said, I couldn't help feeling I should have listened to his explanation when he tried to give it. Instead I shot him down in flames because I couldn't see past the injustice.'

'The guy used you. You have every right to be upset.'

'I do. But why don't I feel satisfied with how things are?'

'So, the book – if it's from him – changed things?'

'I don't know. I saw him at work yesterday, briefly. But he left before I had a chance to speak to him. I'd just like

446

answers, I suppose. Without them, I'm left hanging and I want to draw a line under this.'

'Keep looking for opportunities,' Tish said. 'But if they don't arrive, let it go. You can't control what someone else wants to do. If he isn't prepared to fight for your respect, he never deserved it from the start.'

Over dinner that night, Anna pieced together her response to Ben, if she was ever able to speak to him. She would hold him to account for his actions, of course, but would make herself listen to his reply. Had he been more interested in her story all along? If so, how much further had he been prepared to go, if she hadn't given him the story he wanted? His answers might hurt her, but if she was ever going to move on, she needed to know.

'Good or bad, Anna, we need truth,' Grandma Morwenna often said. Anna had discovered truths about her beloved grandmother that didn't sit well with her soul, but learning them had been a key component of the person she was becoming. The truth she'd given Jonah today wasn't what he'd wanted to hear, but was necessary if their friendship was to survive. Ben might confirm her worst suspicions, but at least she would know. That knowledge would help her heal, even if it stung.

She would find an opportunity to speak to him tomorrow, she decided. And if that didn't happen, the next day or the one after that, until a resolution came. It was too important to her own peace of mind and forward movement to shrink back now.

Fifty

The invitation for the *Messenger* party was as impressive as Juliet Evans had promised the actual event would be. Made of thick card, it featured a beautifully intricate, three-dimensional hand-cut tree design, complete with tiny birds and swinging apples amid the filigree branches, every edge lined with gold foil. Just holding the work of art took Anna's breath away. The *Messenger* building was humming with excitement, following the discovery of the invitations in thick, purple vellum envelopes on every employee's desk. Rumours of a stellar guest list began to emerge, along with an intriguing report that Juliet had invited the editors of every national newspaper to witness the *Daily Messenger*'s comeback.

Juliet had certainly done her job: online gossip columns and news agencies were already talking about the event, while certain broadsheets discussed the challenge facing every newspaper in the digital age, painting the *Messenger* as a test case for survival. Before the party had even taken place, it was the talk of the town.

The invitations confirmed that the party would be held in the elegant Kensington Palace Orangery, a venue well known for hosting high-profile events on the London party circuit. Sheniece wasted no time informing everyone who would listen of its delights, having seen parties there featured in the celebrity magazines she read religiously. Even Babs, who remained to be convinced that she'd be allowed to work till retirement, promised she'd buy a new outfit for the occasion, 'just in case a handsome actor asks me to dance'.

Anna shared her colleagues' excitement, the party becoming a symbol of better times ahead. Like her, the *Daily Messenger* was evolving, leaving behind the uncertainty of recent months and daring to begin a new chapter.

Whether Ben would be part of that, however, was still unclear. Anna didn't see him for two days after the company meeting; when she asked Rea from the newsroom, she said Ben was working away, although she didn't know where his assignment had taken him. Nobody said it aloud, but the accepted wisdom was that a new position had called him away – the news not being official, in case it affected morale. Anna wondered if she had missed her chance.

A ray of hope emerged, the day before the *Messenger* party, when an intern working for Juliet's PA let slip to Ted that a certain Ben McAra was on the guest list – and had confirmed his attendance.

'You see, girl? Any information you want getting, Uncle Ted's your man.'

That settled it: the party would be the perfect place to talk to Ben. Anna knew it could well be her last opportunity and she was determined not to let it pass.

That afternoon a hesitant-looking man approached the reception desk, looking a little lost.

'Can I help you?' Anna asked.

'This is the address I have, but – ' he checked the folded piece of paper he carried, ' – I think there must be a mistake. This is Messenger House, isn't it?'

'Yes, it is.'

'We don't usually have appointments in the City. Not in places like this, at least . . . I'm sorry – Grant Ogilvy,' he offered his hand, much to Anna's amusement. It wasn't often that a visitor to the building proffered a handshake to her.

'I'm Anna. Nice to meet you. Who are you here to see?'

'Anna? Anna Browne?' Seeing her name badge, Grant beamed broadly. 'Then it would appear, my dear girl, that I am in the right place after all. Stay right where you are . . .' He turned tail and hurried back out of the building.

'What was *that* about?' Sheniece asked.

Anna watched the visitor leaving. 'I'm not sure.' A stranger asking for her by name was unsettling. She had been assured her time as a headliner was over, but what if it wasn't?

Five minutes later the man reappeared, carrying a large flat object under one arm. Placing it on the reception desk, he grinned. 'Sorry for the delay, just been arguing the toss

450

with a most unpleasant traffic warden. Tried to suggest I was parked illegally, would you believe? I digress. This is for *you.*'

The brown-paper-wrapped object bore her name, but no address. Glancing at the corners confirmed that it fit the pattern of Anna's previous parcels.

'Who sent it?' she asked quickly. Grant obviously wasn't a courier – and if the parcel he had brought had been ordered in person, he might have more details about the sender. Anna held her breath, willing him to answer.

'Can't say, sorry. It was stipulated in the terms of the order. Have to say, they were startlingly specific about it. Took my staff the best part of an hour to fold the corners of the wrapping paper correctly.'

'Oh.' She knew she'd been grasping at straws, but Anna felt disappointed to find another dead-end for her search. 'Well, thank you.'

Grant hesitated and brought a hand to his heart. 'Would you mind terribly opening it before I go? Only I don't often get to see the reaction, when people receive my designs.'

'You're a designer? Oh my life, you *have* to open it!' Sheniece and Ashraf flanked Anna like a pair of shaken Prosecco bottles ready to pop.

Given the avid attentions of her audience, how could Anna refuse? 'Okay.' Suppressing an urge to laugh out loud, she removed the wrapping paper to reveal a glossy copper-gold box. It bore the initials 'G.O.' in looping black script.

451

'That's me,' Grant beamed, tapping the box. 'Now, look inside.'

Laid between sheets of bronze-coloured tissue Anna caught a glimpse of scarlet red. She lifted it, the folds falling out as the fullness of the red fabric shivered across the reception desk.

'It's a dress,' she breathed.

'One of our most popular,' Grant said. 'I designed it with the Golden Age of Hollywood in mind. Simple, flowing, cut to emphasise a real woman.'

'Oh, wow, it's beautiful . . . I don't know what to say.'

The designer nodded. 'You've said all I wanted to hear. Have a lovely time at your party.' Taking a last look at his latest customer, he left.

Anna revelled in the feel of the fabric against her fingers. She had never been given a dress before, and certainly would never have chosen one designed to stand out. In the back of her mind Grant's words replayed, gaining in volume until –

'Wait! How do you know about the party?' But Grant Ogilvy had gone. Anna looked down at the empty box and caught sight of a small card tucked into the folds of tissue:

> For the most beautiful woman at the party.
> I will see you there.

Her colleagues were oblivious to this, their attention still caught by the stunning dress. Heart thumping, Anna quickly hid the card in her suit pocket.

'How perfect is this?' Ashraf was saying. 'You *have* to wear it tomorrow night, Anna! It's like Cinderella, only better!'

'Was there a note?' Sheniece looked up from her inspection of the dress. 'There sometimes is with your stuff, right?'

'I'll check.' Anna made a theatrical search of the tissue layers in the box. 'Doesn't seem to be one here.'

'Who cares when you get a gift like this? I am phoning Rea *right now . . .*'

Anna left Sheniece and Ashraf to send the latest news along the *Messenger* grapevine, retreating to the relative calm of the work kitchen. As the kettle boiled, she considered the new parcel's meaning. Was the sender preparing to reveal their identity at the party? Or would they be watching from a distance? She could rule neither out – the message gave little away. What she now knew for certain was that the sender would be there.

What happens when I'm there is my *choice*, she told herself.

Given the evidence at hand, the sender must be Ben. He was conveniently absent from work, but the gift had arrived soon after his attendance at the party had been confirmed. If she didn't already know he would be there, the message with the dress left her in no doubt. He had hurried away from the meeting in the newsroom, but was this because he'd planned to speak to Anna at the party and not before? He had hinted when they last spoke that he could make things right between them: was this what he'd had in mind?

453

If the beautiful Dodie Smith book was an apology, what did he plan to say at the party? And would it be what she wanted to hear? The dress was designed to be noticed by everyone; would whatever he said be heard by them all, too?

And so Anna knew what she would do.

Tomorrow night Anna Browne would stand out from the crowd in a stunning red dress – and would meet the person she'd longed to thank for so long. She would thank them for their gifts and explain that no more were required: she had discovered the woman they had seen in her from the beginning – and so much more.

Because, for the last few days, she had been aware of something she could no longer deny, no matter what had happened before. She knew it on the beach when Jonah tried to kiss her and she knew it now. Despite every reason she shouldn't feel as she did, Anna knew she could no longer deny her heart.

And if what she was almost certain of now were proved to be right, she would forgive Ben McAra and tell him she was falling in love with him . . .

Fifty-One

'*Wow!*'

Anna locked her front door and smiled at Jonah, who was walking up the corridor towards her, a large kit bag slung over one shoulder and a tripod in his hand. He looked tired, but his eyes were bright from doing what he loved most. She had seen it at Godrevy – being in the great outdoors seemed to bring out the best in him.

'Good day's filming?'

'Cold, but good. You look incredible.'

Pleased by his reaction, Anna gave a little twirl. 'It's gorgeous, isn't it?'

'I wasn't talking about the dress . . .'

'*Jonah.*'

'Don't worry, I think we've established the boundaries on that one. But I can say what I see, can't I?'

'Well, you look very nice, too. Rugged.'

'Aye? Is that what you call being dragged through a hedge backwards, when you're being polite?'

'Apparently so.'

The new understanding between them still felt a little out of place, but Anna was glad it existed. She loved Jonah as a friend and was relieved to know he was content to feel the same about her.

'So, what's with the glad rags? You off out somewhere nice?'

'It's the *Messenger* party tonight.'

'Ah, I see. And will *he* be there?' Jonah's smile was warm. 'It's okay, lass, I guessed. I just hope he's worthy of you.'

'I think he might have sent the parcels,' Anna admitted. 'Well, almost all of them.'

'Except mine was the best, of course. If he did send them, he's a better man than I thought. Just don't take any of his messing, you hear? You're worth more than that.'

Arriving at the gates of Kensington Gardens, Anna saw her colleagues waiting for her.

'Here she is!' Babs called. 'And doesn't she look the belle of the ball?'

Ashraf's jaw made a bid for the pavement. 'Bloody hell, Anna, look at you!'

Sheniece rolled her eyes heavenwards. 'Stop dribbling and let's get into this party. We have celebs to rub shoulders with.'

'If Sheniece has her way, it won't just be her shoulders she's rubbing . . .' Ted offered Anna his arm.

The evening was warmer than expected, although a stiff

breeze had sprung up, shivering through hanging purple and silver banners that marked the way through the gardens and catching the hems of dresses and suit jackets, billowing skirts out as the crowd entered. Large hurricane lanterns illuminated the path, throwing horizontal stripes of light and shade across the gravel. A gaggle of strategically placed paparazzi jostled for position on either side, held back from the arriving party guests by flimsy-looking rope barriers, as grim-faced security guards in bright-yellow jackets prevented any opportunistic journalists from ducking underneath. They were here for the celebrities, of course; rumours of A-list guests had been circulating in the press for several days and speculation was rife. The *Daily Messenger* employees passed by without drawing the flashbulbs of the cameras, but even the act of walking through a bank of photographers made each one feel privileged to be there.

Anna, Sheniece, Ashraf and Babs giggled as they passed the press section, Anna glad that none of the cameras were trained on her. Being old news had its benefits. Wearing the dress from the parcel, she felt like a star – and the prospect of what awaited her at the party put a spring in her step. Sheniece caused passing *Messenger* staff to laugh as she threw dramatic poses for the disinterested journalists. 'I don't care if they're not taking my photo. I'll never get a chance like this again!'

Ashraf stood alongside her. 'I'm her manager,' he called. 'She's the next big thing.'

'Dream on, love,' a photographer shouted back.

'Move along, please.' An unsmiling security man took

a step towards Anna's colleagues, who quickly fell back in line with the arriving guests.

Babs linked arms with Sheniece. 'Better do as he says, flower. He's scary.'

'He's *hot*,' Sheniece grinned, waving over her shoulder as they walked on.

Tall, square hedges hid the Orangery from view as they passed through the security cordon. The sounds of piano and strings drifted on the night air, drawing them onwards.

To Anna, it was like stepping into a movie scene, moving in a soft scarlet blur as the full skirt of her dress danced around her. The music, the beautiful gardens and the happy company of her colleagues played out all around and she was aware of heads turning as she passed. Where before she would have lowered her gaze and tried to hide, she now accepted their approval, her head held high. Tonight she had chosen to stand out, to be noticed. It was an extraordinarily freeing experience and Anna felt her skin tingle as she passed through the crowd.

They rounded the corner of the hedges and the Orangery came into view. The elegant eighteenth-century red-brick building looked like a miniature palace. Its tall windows glowed warmly against the night sky, throwing light across a cream canopy draped out along its length. Huge crystal chandeliers glittered from the canopy roof, while under-neath black-and-white-suited waiters milled between guests, carrying flutes of expensive champagne on silver trays. A string quartet and a grand piano played on the lawn beneath a draped silver-silk gazebo lined with sparkling white lights, watched by an appreciative group of partygoers who applauded politely after each piece.

Everything about the party was designed to impress. Anna wondered how much money had been spent tonight – but the message was clear: the *Daily Messenger* was very much in business and wanted the world to know it. Juliet Evans stood on the Orangery's stone steps in the middle of her creation, draped magnificently in a shimmering purple evening dress, expensive diamonds glittering at her neck and wrist. She received the congratulations of her guests with the poise of Grace Kelly, throwing her head back to laugh at their jokes like a woman without a care in the world. She was the queen of all she surveyed, and every guest at the party knew it.

'Have you seen the Dragon?' Ted asked, joining them. It was strange to see the usually uniformed security chief in black-tie attire. 'Scrubs up well, for an older bird.'

'You fancy your chances then, Ted?' Sheniece playfully dug him in the ribs.

'She might fancy a real man for a change,' he sniffed, straightening his tie. 'Not like those media moguls she insists on dating. That woman wants a bit of Ted Blaskiewicz in her life.'

Anna scanned the party guests, but couldn't see Ben. She had planned everything she would say to him and had made a promise to herself that she wouldn't leave the party until she'd said it all. Last night she had added the dress to the parcel gifts, laid out across her bed. Before her she could see the past six months of her life, each object representing a step on her journey. This time she had included Jonah's rogue gift, because it had played its own part, in a way its sender could never have intended. The dress seemed to be a final chapter in her incredible adventure.

Ted waited until their colleagues were walking towards the Orangery, before tapping Anna's elbow. 'I . . . um . . . wanted to say something, girl. Without them lot hearing.' He rubbed the back of his neck nervously, the exchange of personal comments something he was unaccustomed to. 'Thing is, I was wrong. About those parcels of yours. And I don't often admit I'm wrong. I mean, that dress looks like it was made for you. Whoever sent it knew what he was doing – he wanted to treat you like a princess and, well, I admire him for that. I'm sorry I suggested he was a serial killer.'

Touched by his words, Anna smiled. 'That's lovely of you, Ted, thank you.' She held out her arm and nodded in the direction of the Orangery. 'Shall we?'

The security chief flushed and linked his arm through hers. 'My pleasure, girl.'

The interior of the Orangery had been transformed into an autumnal forest, planters with real red-leaved maple trees lining both sides, each branch picked out with tiny white lights. Fallen leaves, hand-cut from copies of the *Daily Messenger*, were piled beneath and strewn across the white marble floor, while newsprint birds balanced between the tree branches and on every windowsill. The air was filled with the scent of apple Martinis being served at a frosted glass bar in the centre of the Orangery. At the far end of the room a table groaned under the weight

460

of a sumptuous buffet, styled as if it were the centrepiece of a luxury magazine shoot. Every angle of the room and each fine detail was a carefully stage-managed photo opportunity, attested to by the constant burst of flashbulbs from a select group of invited photographers from rival publications. Tomorrow morning, news columns, blogs and society pages would be filled with exquisite images – and the *Daily Messenger* would assume centre-stage.

The delights of the buffet called Ted away as Anna accepted compliments on her dress from a group of journalists.

'You walked in here like a movie star,' Joe Adams remarked, clearly surprised.

'I feel like one,' Anna replied.

'If you don't pull tonight, there's no justice in the world,' Murray Henderson-Vitt leered, paying far too much attention to the swooping neckline of Anna's dress.

She laughed off his attention. 'I *think* that was a compliment, so thank you.' She lifted her head as she took a sip of apple Martini – and saw Ben. He was standing by the bar, a half-empty champagne flute in one hand, looking out across the crowd. The change in him was remarkable from the removed, silent figure Anna had seen at the company meeting. Gone were the dark circles from his eyes, his clean-shaven skin no longer pale. He looked a little uncomfortable in his dinner jacket, his black tie already hanging loosely from the collar of his shirt, but he possessed an energy Anna hadn't witnessed since their mornings together in Freya & Georgie's. Butterflies beset her stomach as she downed the remainder of Martini in

461

her glass and began to weave through the party guests towards him.

'Anna – you look *incredible*,' Rea said, stepping back to block her path. 'That colour is amazing.'

'Thank you.'

'So, what's the latest gossip? And have you seen Sheniece?'

Anna could see Ben moving away from the bar. 'I think I saw her outside near the steps. Sorry, Rea, there's someone I need to speak to . . .'

'Ah. McAra's looking good tonight, eh?' Rea grinned and tapped a finger against the side of her nose. 'Don't worry, I won't tell a soul.'

Blushing, Anna moved past her colleague, raising her head above the shoulders of the crowd to find Ben. She was determined not to lose this opportunity, as she had on the day of the company meeting. Finally she spotted him by one of the planted red maple trees and pushed her way over.

Emerging from the huddle of partygoers, she took a breath as he saw her, raising her hand, both in greeting and in reassurance that he could approach. He gave a half-smile and moved towards her. Anna could feel herself smiling as he neared her – the words she'd planned to say temporarily leaving her mind. Ben McAra was wonderful. Yes, there were issues to deal with, injustices to right; but beneath it all, regardless of whether he deserved it or not, were feelings deeper than Anna could fathom. Tonight – not long from this moment – she would throw caution to the wind and tell him.

He was standing in front of her now, his eyes seeking permission to move closer . . .

'Ladies and gentlemen, our esteemed editor is about to address us, so please make your way to the stage to welcome her.' Piers' sudden announcement made them both turn towards a small white stage beside the bar. Ben said nothing, but his hand momentarily touched the small of Anna's back as the crowd pressed forward. The tiny gesture had the power of a thunderbolt and Anna snatched a fresh champagne glass from a passing waiter's tray to steady her nerves.

Piers announced Juliet and the gathered guests in the Orangery broke into warm applause as she took to the stage. The ovation lasted for almost a minute, the assembled *Messenger* employees keen to show their appreciation for the woman who had saved their jobs and secured the future of the newspaper. Juliet received their praise with trademark coolness, eventually raising her hand to silence the room.

'You're all too kind.' She let her gaze sweep theatrically across the crowd, as if acknowledging every face. 'Well, here we are. Brighter and stronger, bolder and not going away any time soon. Tonight we join together as the *Daily Messenger* family, to celebrate what we've achieved so far and to express to the world our intentions for the future. I won't pretend I always knew this day would come, but I believed sufficiently in our resilience and resourcefulness to hope that it would. We are moving into the future, confident that the *Daily Messenger* has not only earned its place as a leading national daily, but that we can better it. In a year's time we aim to have increased our readership significantly to become the market leader . . .'

A murmur of surprised approval passed through the crowd.

Juliet nodded in appreciation. 'There will, of course, be those who say it can't be done. *Some* of them are even in this room tonight,' she raised her glass as laughter rang round the Orangery's white interior, 'and I welcome each and every one of you. To our detractors – both great and insignificant – I say this: do not underestimate what this newspaper can do. With our renewed sense of purpose, and an exciting team whom I believe represent the most passionate advocates of news media in the country, anything is possible . . .'

Anna was acutely aware of how close Ben was standing, the warmth from his body registering on the skin of her bare arm. She maintained her focus on the stage, but knew he was looking at her.

'I believe in this publication. I built it up from its humble beginnings and created the magnificent paper you see today. Nobody in the industry has worked harder than me to raise the profile of a national tabloid. I am happy to take credit, naturally, not only for my own sake, but also on your behalf – because every *Messenger* employee standing in this room tonight has contributed to the vision I have led. We have a wealth of talent, much of which has yet to reach its full potential. With constant belief and top-down encouragement, I believe the *Daily Messenger* will go from strength to strength . . .'

'Juliet Evans: never knowingly under-promoted,' Murray Henderson-Vitt chuckled next to Anna and Ben. They laughed and their eyes met – Anna's breath catching with the intensity of his stare.

'. . . but it will do so without me.'

Juliet paused, surveying the room from her elevated position as the shockwave of her statement filtered through the party guests. Anna and Ben turned, too, the surprise breaking the moment between them.

'What?'

'Did she just . . . ?'

'She can't be serious!'

Pockets of disbelief broke out across the elegant space. Had they heard correctly? Could their editor, who had forged her fame in the crucible of the *Daily Messenger*, be deserting it? Juliet presided over the bubbling commotion, her head high for the eager flashes from invited photographers. Raising her hand, she brought the room to order.

'I have put my heart and soul into this newspaper. I have seen it soaring the heights and nursed it back from the brink. I have done my time and served it well. It is time for a new breed to assume the mantle and take it on. At the end of this year I will step down as editor, bringing a brand-new chapter of *Messenger* history into being. No doubt this will come as a surprise, not least because I am announcing my intention to leave at the moment of our greatest triumph. But I am more than happy with my decision.' She granted her rapt audience a beatific smile. 'Together, we are magnificent! And now is the time to celebrate. I would like to thank you all, for your hard work, your dedication and your faith in me.

Tomorrow, we face the future knowing what that will look like. Tonight, we celebrate. Raise your glasses with me: to the *Daily Messenger* – the best in the business!'

The guests repeated the toast, shock still rumbling through their ranks. The applause lasted longer than the first, as the employees saluted their outgoing editor – and wondered who could possibly replace her . . .

'Bit of a curveball.' Ben smiled.

'You didn't know?'

'Not a clue. Nobody did. As far as we were aware in the newsroom, Juliet had masterminded a coup and was going to milk it for all it was worth. She must have had a better offer.'

Anna was tempted to ask about Ben's rumoured career change, but held back. This was not the place for it. 'Can we talk, somewhere a little less public?'

Ben raised an eyebrow. 'You're not going to shout at me again, are you?'

'I haven't decided yet. Are you ready to take the risk?'

The strong wind outside had calmed to an autumnal breeze as Anna and Ben left the Orangery, the last of the light gone from the sky. They walked away from the noise of the party, following the gravel path to a small section of formal gardens behind the tall hedges. Finding an ornate carved stone bench, they sat down and Anna knew her moment had arrived.

'I wanted to thank you—' she began, but Ben raised his hand, halting her before she could say more.

'First, let me say sorry. A real sorry, not a journalist's apology. I hurt you, Anna. I hate that I did that. I never

466

set out to write a story on you – okay, that's a lie, I admit the parcels might have been my initial focus. I might have decided to get to know you first because of them. I liked working with you when you were shadowing me, and I thought that gave me a way in. But you have to believe me, when we started hanging out at Freya & Georgie's that changed. I like you, Anna. I care what you think of me. But my boss was pressuring me for a new story. It sounds incredibly lame when I say that, but it's the truth. I needed something to get her off my back for a while. You were the only trump card I had. I'm not proud of that.'

'There was no need to engineer a friendship with me. You could have just asked . . .'

He rubbed his eyes. 'I know. Of course I could. But I was involved before I could back out, and then – well, then it was too late to tell you. My editor sent the story to print, and you know the rest. But I am sorry.'

'I think I know why you did what you did, Ben. And it came from a good place. That's what I wanted to say. The parcels have made such a difference to my life. I didn't understand it in the beginning, but I think I do now. You wanted me to feel special, to be noticed by other people. I've never had that before, so when it happened I didn't know what to do at first. But then I liked people noticing me. What I never explained to you before is that for most of my life I wanted to be invisible. My mother was the kind of person who preferred to be the centre of attention and, as you can guess from the story she sold, her nearest and dearest were often collateral damage. When I came

467

to London it was a relief to be one face in a crowd of thousands. But I never realised I could be noticed in a good way. Your parcels unlocked that discovery.'

Ben was staring at her, a growing frown across his brow. Anna chided herself for not sharing this before; if she had, maybe Ben's article wouldn't have existed.

'Anna, I think you—'

'Please, let me say this. If I don't tell you now, I might lose my nerve. I don't know why you chose to send the parcels to me – whether it was to manufacture a story or because you saw in me something I've only just recognised – but thank you. Thank you for giving me a reason to want more in life; for daring to find my own confidence and make my own choices. Without your gifts, I might never have given myself permission to explore those things. But you don't need to send any more. I know who I am now and—'

'Wait, Anna . . . Stop! You think *I* sent the parcels?'

'Ben, you really don't have to pretend. I'm pleased you did.'

He shook his head. 'I'm sorry, but I didn't. I wish I did, seeing the way you've blossomed since I got to know you. Without the parcels, I might never have had an excuse to speak to you . . .'

It was a cute notion, but he deserved the truth. 'I thought I'd changed because of the parcels, but I was wrong. They gave me the excuse I needed to become who I wanted to be. I have you to thank for it – don't deny it now. It's okay.'

'Why do you think I sent them?'

468

Was he playing with her? 'It was obvious. You noticed the necklace I was wearing, before anybody else. We talked about music and an old record arrived. I told you books were special to me and, after we rowed, I received a copy of my favourite childhood book . . .' Clutching at straws, she added, 'And Ted overheard you warning anyone else in the newsroom off my story.'

Ben lowered his voice. 'What?'

'He said you were saying that if anyone was going to tell my story, it would be you.'

'You think I organised all of that – for the story?'

Anna stared back. 'What else should I think?'

He groaned. 'I don't believe this.'

'Then why did you ask about my parcels?'

'My back was against the wall, okay? I admit that's what it became, but it wasn't my first motivation. To begin with, I asked because I wanted to know more about them. Not because you were a scoop, but because I wanted to know what was responsible for the change I saw in you.'

'Then why warn everyone off my story? Weeks before we started talking?'

'I didn't . . .' His gaze drifted across the darkened formal garden.

'Liar! I know Ted has some pretty wild theories at times, but he wouldn't make up something like that. There must be some truth in it.'

'If I did, it was because I didn't want anyone haranguing you, cheapening what was happening in your life by reducing it to a story.'

'Like *you* did . . .'

469

'It was a mistake! I'd pitched it to Juliet before I had a chance to think. And then it was out of my hands. I know I hurt you, okay? I know I betrayed your trust – and I'm trying my best to apologise for that. But I didn't send the parcels to get a story. Did you really think I was capable of that?'

Anna stared back. Was Ben so pig-headed that he would protect his methods to the end? 'But the dress?'

He followed the movement of her hands to the red fabric. 'It's beautiful. *You're* beautiful.'

'Then – I don't understand . . .'

'Anna, if you're asking me to be some mystery bene-factor, then I'm not the person you're looking for.'

But you are! she protested silently. *At least, I* thought *you were . . .*

'I want to be with you – there, I've said it. I've been miserable without you and I want to see where we could go. But if you're in love with whoever sent the parcels, we have no hope.'

'No, Ben, that's what I wanted to tell you. I think I'm—'

'It's okay, really. I get it. The guy who sent your parcels changed your life. What hope do I have of comparing with someone whose gifts can do that?'

'You said you'd be here tonight . . .' Her thoughts became audible as she tried to make sense of everything. 'When?'

'In the message – with this dress. You said, "I will see you there."'

'So the sender is at this party? Well, you'd better go

and find him then.' Ben made to stand up, but Anna caught his arm.

'No, please – wait . . . I need a minute to work this out.'

This was fast descending into a jumbled mess, and Anna couldn't catch hold of her thoughts before they knotted together. Was Ben right: was she in love with the parcel-sender because she believed it was Ben, or could she have fallen for someone she'd never met?

'I like you, Anna. More than I realised when you refused to speak to me. I've tried to put you out of my head, but I can't.' Even as he said it, Ben's eyes registered defeat. 'But if the only way you want me is to be someone I'm not, there's no point.'

Hurt and confused, Anna rounded on him. 'Don't you dare turn this around on me! What gives you the right to take the moral high ground? You admitted you only started meeting up with me because of the parcels – doesn't exactly qualify you for Man of the Year, does it?'

He ran a hand through his hair. 'I never said it did. I *said* I was sorry, Anna . . .'

'I thought you'd sent the parcels. And I wanted to thank you, because I've wanted to thank the person responsible for a long time. Obviously I was mistaken thinking it was you. Maybe I wanted it to be you – but you haven't even considered that, have you?' She was on her feet now, blood as scarlet as her beautiful dress pumping through her body. 'Instead you accuse me of being some kind of gift-junkie who is only looking for someone to feed her addiction . . . Well, thanks for nothing, Ben. Have a nice life.'

He said nothing, just stood and headed back towards the light and music of the party. Turning on her heels, Anna stormed in the opposite direction, into the darkness of the gardens.

It was all wrong. The way she had pictured this evening didn't fit with its unfolding reality. Ben was meant to make a confession; she was meant to forgive him for the story and thank him for his kindness and then . . . What did she expect to happen next?

With Ben ruled out as the sender, who else could it be? Had she already seen them this evening? She thought back to the people she had spoken to: at least twenty *Messenger* journalists, Ted, Sheniece, Ashraf, Babs . . . Any of them could have sent the parcels.

The beautiful notes of Chopin's Nocturne No. 2 began dancing on the night air. Laughter and the hubbub of voices floated across the gardens towards her. It should have been serene, Anna basking in the glow of the end of her journey. Instead she felt numb, bombarded by questions she hadn't anticipated as another road stretched out before her. The challenge was far from over.

I have to find the sender, she vowed, the orange-blackness of the city night her witness. *I won't leave here until I know who they are.* Separated from the lavish party by more than the hedge behind her, she felt utterly alone.

But where do I begin?

Fifty-Two

'Anna? What are you doing here all by yourself?'

Anna looked up to see Rea's concerned smile. 'Oh, I just – I needed a breath of fresh air. It's a bit crowded in there.'

'Isn't it just?' Rea bent down, slipping off her party shoes and rubbing her feet. 'Although there are a fair few blokes in there I'd happily be squashed up against.'

Anna welcomed the chance to talk about something other than the mess she found herself in with Ben. 'Anyone I know?'

'Hugo Benedict. He's new. We just poached him from the *Post*. You have to see the guy – looks of Henry Cavill, voice as smooth as Tom Hiddleston – and, most importantly, single *and* straight.' She chuckled. 'He's been snapping at McAra's heels since he arrived, so I reckon he'll make himself at home, once Ben's gone.'

The mention of Ben leaving held greater significance

than before. Emotion constricted Anna's throat, but she fought to constrain it. 'That's definite, is it?'

'As good as. Course, nobody's said anything official, but we all know how these things work. I don't think it'll be long.' She patted Anna's knee. 'Not that you care, huh? Sooner that toerag is out of the building, the better for you. So – anyone on the cards for Miss Flippin' Stunning Anna Browne?'

Not now, Anna thought. 'I don't think so. I'm having too much fun on my own.'

'Looks like it. Come back to the party with me. We can get hammered on apple Martinis and leer at handsome men?'

'I think I might just stay here for a while.'

'Shame. In that dress you've caused quite a stir. Everyone's talking about you.'

'Are they?'

'You bet. You look incredible, lady! Like a different woman. You really should take advantage of the situation. There are tons of potential dates here tonight.'

'I'll come and find you a little later, okay?'

Rea shrugged. 'Fine by me. Whatever makes you happy.'

When she was alone again, Anna stood and wandered further away from the party. She followed the path that wound through the formal lawns and beds, feeling the cooling air prickle against her skin. Tonight had promised to be special, but now she was uncertain of what lay ahead.

Turning a corner, the path widened into a small court-yard with a beautiful stone fountain at its centre. The gentle flow of water created music of its own, drops glistening in the light from the moon that had broken through the night clouds. As she neared it, Anna could see silver and copper flashes within the shimmering water. She smiled. There was something irrepressibly hopeful about coins tossed into a fountain – hopes and dreams captured in a moment. She remembered the wishing well in the centre of Polperro and the thrill, as a small child, of hearing the tinkle of the bell suspended over the water within, as she threw in coins given to her by Uncle Jabez.

'If you hear the bell, your wish'll be granted,' he would grin, handing over more coins if her first attempt missed its mark.

Feeling nostalgic, she found a coin in her purse and tossed it into the fountain. One more wish couldn't hurt . . .

'They don't work, you know.'

Juliet Evans gave a cough, the rising cigarette smoke revealing her location, obscured behind the fountain. Anna walked around it to see the *Daily Messenger* editor sitting on a stone bench.

'I'm sorry, I didn't see you.'

'Wishes. Overrated, in my opinion. I never got anything in life by wishing. You make your own luck.' Two empty champagne glasses were propped in the gravel at her feet, a full whisky tumbler sloshing in her hand as she spoke.

'Call it insurance,' Anna smiled. 'Just in case.'

'Whatever floats your boat. Never had much time for superstition myself. Although, given recent events, perhaps I should have.' There was a certain elongation in the way she pronounced her S's, her head movements exaggerated by liquid fortification.

Anna sat a little way from the editor. 'I thought your speech was wonderful this evening.'

Genuinely surprised, Juliet stared back. 'Did you? Funny how one can make falling on one's sword appear a triumph . . .' She rubbed at her eyes with the back of her hand, her heavy eyeliner smudging across her skin. 'I'm tired.'

'Organising the party must have been exhausting,' Anna offered, unsure why she was trying to make conversation with a woman famed for being an ivory tower.

'Not *that*,' Juliet scoffed. 'I have *people* to do that. I just give the orders and sign the cheques. Although I don't even do that any more . . . Everything exhausts me these days. I've seen it all and done it all – and none of it satisfies me like it used to. I should've seen what was coming months before it arrived. Ten years ago I'd have nipped it in the bud before it amounted to anything. Bloody Damien Kendal and his overfed, shiny-arsed cronies.'

'It wasn't your decision to leave? But I thought you said—'

'I *said* a lot of things . . . Sure, it was my decision to resign, but they made it impossible to do anything else. It was the condition of the buyout. You think I want to retire?'

The editor's candour threw Anna and she was unsure of how to answer. 'I thought it was a brave decision, if you don't mind me saying.'

Juliet snorted into her whisky.

'I do. You've shown everyone that the newspaper is

surviving and has a future – so much so that you feel safe leaving it. I think that's a brave thing to do. You leave on a high.'

Juliet said nothing, her eyes trained on Anna. Distant music from the party warmed the air around them. Anna didn't know if she had offended the editor – her expression was impossible to read. The woman clearly wanted to be alone.

'You're sweet.'

The compliment was a bolt from the blue and seemed wrong coming from Juliet's lips.

'Um, thank you . . .'

'Not many people are sweet to me. They say what they think I want to hear. I like that you didn't.' She downed the remainder of her drink and gazed up at the sky. 'Thank you.'

'You're welcome.' Sensing her chance to end the conversation, Anna made to leave. 'I should probably get back.'

'Beautiful dress,' Juliet said, suddenly.

'Thank you. I love it.'

'I thought you would.'

Anna looked at the editor, who still wore the same, vague expression. 'Sorry?'

'What were you wishing for, just then?'

Thrown by the sudden turn in the conversation, Anna took a while to reply. 'I . . . um – I can't tell you. Otherwise it won't come true.'

'By the look of you, it already has. People lay far too much store by wishes. As if unfounded hopes are enough.

They are not. You have to make things happen. Like I did.'

She was speaking in riddles now. Feeling uncomfortable, Anna pressed her luck. 'Why did you think I would love the dress?'

'Seemed the right decision. All of the gifts did.'

And then the full force of the revelation hit Anna. 'You? You sent the parcels?'

Juliet chuckled and spread her hands wide. 'Ta-daa!'

'But why? I hardly know you.'

'That was the point. You weren't supposed to know. It was my clever, clever plan.'

Anna remembered what Ben had said about being backed into a corner by his editor. By Juliet Evans – who was sending parcels to the woman he was trying to get to know . . . It was all horribly clear now: the newspaper was in financial trouble and needed a story that would go viral, trumping the competition and re-establishing its name. Anna had been the unwitting victim of it all. So Ben *had* exploited her, but Juliet had drawn him into it as much as she had Anna – two *Daily Messenger* puppets made to dance to the editor's whim. Of course, now it made perfect sense: Juliet didn't care about the subject of her masterstroke story, only that she needed someone unremarkable and trusting enough to make the story authentic. Anna's response and transformation were of no importance.

'How *dare* you play with my life?' Anna didn't care that she was shouting, her voice splitting the peace of the garden. 'I am worth more than your need to save the newspaper!'

478

Shocked, Juliet stared blurrily up at her.

'Why did you choose me? Because I was gullible, or insignificant enough to fall for it? You had the headline written long before you asked Ben . . .'

'Excuse me? What does Ben McAra have to do with this?'

Anna rounded on her. 'He has *everything* to do with this! Did he know your plan from the beginning? Or did you use him like you've used me?'

'Hold on for one minute and listen. It was never about the story. I'll admit it was useful that McAra became involved, and the publicity went a long way to convincing Kendal and his cronies that the *Messenger* was worth a punt, but that wasn't my motivation.'

'I don't believe you.'

'Which you are quite at liberty to do, Ms Browne. The fact remains, however, that the story was immaterial.'

'Then why?'

'Because, on the only day that I needed permission to be heartbroken in my life, you were the one who gave it. That impressed me.'

Anna could see the pronounced rise and fall of Juliet's chest, the only indication of her true feelings in a body trained to give nothing away.

'I don't understand. I've never given you permission for anything . . .'

'Sit down, Anna.'

'I don't have to do anything you say.'

'Of course you don't. But you want an explanation and I'm offering one – if you're willing to hear it.'

Anna folded her arms, still standing. 'Fine.'

'The day I returned to work after losing my mother, I found, to my great surprise, that I had actually loved her all along. I had fought with her for years, never once feeling her love or approval. But I'm not ashamed to admit that I was assaulted by grief. On that day you and I shared a lift together. You said something I'll never forget: *But still, your mum's your mum.* In all I'd endured with my mother, I'd lost sight of that. What you said made me realise that my grief for her wasn't an admission that she'd been right about me. It was *permissible* for a daughter to grieve the passing of her mother. It was about me, not her.'

'I don't even remember saying that,' Anna returned, her voice wavering as her anger subsided.

'I'm not surprised. For you, it was a kind compliment that came from a good heart. For me, it was gift. I left that conversation and walked straight into a call with Damien Kendal that sealed my fate with the paper. That's when I decided to send the gifts.'

'So you made me your little project?'

'You were hardly a project, Anna.'

'Then what was I, Juliet? Forgive me, but I'm struggling to understand. You say you've always been willing to step over anyone who gets in your way – what's the difference between that and what you did to me? You used me . . .'

'I did. But not in the way you imagine. I couldn't have predicted the story, but when McAra mentioned it, the timing was fortuitous, I'll admit. I certainly couldn't have predicted the interest it would attract around the world.

Besides, I couldn't have prevented its publication without revealing my identity.'

'What right do you have to meddle with other people's lives? You made sure the parcels arrived at work so that other people saw. Did it give you a thrill watching me being manipulated?'

'You weren't manipulated. The gifts made you believe you were worth more than you thought you were. That decision came from yourself. Look at you tonight – unafraid to stand out from the crowd, welcoming the compliments of strangers. The dress isn't responsible for that, it's merely a pretty set-dressing for the choices you have made. I'm not trying to make you into the daughter I never had, or absolve my guilty conscience for my selfishness. I stand by everything I've done in my life because they were *my* choices. But I realised that, during my entire adult life, I'd never done anything for anyone other than me.' She paused, rubbing her hands across her bare arms as if the chill of the air had only just permeated her skin. 'I've had it easy for many years. I've never wanted for anything. I simply wanted to pass that on. And I don't expect anything in return, either. I don't want to be your best friend or surrogate mother. I'm not looking for a companion in my dotage. I just wanted to do something for someone who wasn't me.'

The sender had said they would see Anna at the party. And here Juliet was: the last person in the world Anna would have expected.

'Oh.'

Anna thought about all she had planned to say to the

revealed sender of her parcels tonight. She had pictured this moment in her head so many times – but now what? She took a long look at Juliet, the revelation of her generosity completely at odds with the powerful, detached personality she had become infamous for. Now that her chance to thank her in person was here, words deserted Anna's lips.

'*Oh*? That's all I get?' Juliet shook her head. 'So much for philanthropy.'

Pulling her thoughts together, Anna sat next to the editor. 'No – no, I'm sorry. It's a lot to take in, you know? I'm still not sure I'm happy being anyone's "project", but thank you. The gifts were beautiful and I loved receiving them. It's been amazing, actually. I never thought anyone would do something so generous for me. It's changed how I see myself and, well, it's meant the world to me. But you don't need to send any more – not that I'm suggesting you were going to, of course . . .' She let her gaze follow the progress of the moonlit water as it danced into the fountain's basin. 'This is not how I expected this evening to pan out.'

'You and me both.' Juliet grabbed a packet from her purse. 'Smoke?'

'No, thanks.'

'Good. More for me.' The tip of her cigarette glowed as she inhaled. 'So, Anna Browne, where do you go from here? After your work on McAra's exclusive I think you should consider a career change to the newsroom.'

'It's not what I want to do. I think . . . I think I just want to keep discovering what makes me happy. I like my job, my friends, my life. But I feel like I want to find out what else is out there.' She turned to Juliet. 'How about you?'

'Not a clue. Other than I know that my days of anonymous benevolence are probably over.' Her cigarette smoke snaked up into the night. 'I can't see myself taking up golf or moving to the south of France. I expect I'll find something to sink my teeth into. I'm not like you, Anna. Work is all I have. And I like it that way.'

'You could move to another newspaper. When the news breaks of your announcement they'll be lining up for you.'

'You'd think. No, I'm done with the newspaper business. I've made my mark. The only way would be down for me, and I'm not giving my rivals the satisfaction. I'll figure it out.'

The sound of a muffled announcement from the Orangery caused them both to lift their heads.

'Sounds like Piers is getting microphone-happy. I do hope he doesn't try to start a karaoke competition. He's a terribly maudlin loser.' She ground the remains of the cigarette beneath her expensive heel. 'I should get back.'

'Thank you, Juliet – for the parcels. I'm sorry I shouted at you.'

'You had every right to. I'd have been incandescent with fury. Whatever you decide to do next will be the right decision, but I think a certain journalist needs to be put out of his misery.' She gestured towards the party, where Anna could just make out a figure slowly pacing the pathway.

Her work done, the editor stood and began to walk

483

back to the party. At the corner of the path leading into the courtyard she paused, without looking back. 'The parcels – did they really make a difference?'

'They helped me to change my life.' It was the truth and yet, even as Anna confessed it, she felt sad that her adventure was at an end.

'Good.' Juliet nodded, walking slowly out of view.

Seeing Ben, Anna realised she had the answer that had eluded her. There was one thing left to do, to draw a line under the parcels. Rising, she took a breath and began to walk towards him . . .

Fifty-Three

The moon emerged fully over the garden, its light casting long shadows between the high hedges and ornamental features. It painted the garden with a blue-white eeriness, as if time had frozen and those moving through its expanse were pale memories of people who had once walked here. In the distance, the orange-yellow glow of the party burned like a setting sun on a dark horizon.

Anna was aware of every step, the gravel path crunching beneath her shoes, her heart keeping time. But her mind blazed brighter than the lights from within the Orangery, a thousand and one new thoughts sparkling. The last piece of the puzzle had been placed – and now the way ahead was open for her to enter. She felt transported by an unseen energy. Now she knew who she was and where she wanted to be.

Ben's despondent figure edged closer into view. His back was turned, his eyes trained downwards as he kicked at the gravel. Gone was his bravado, his anger that caused him to walk away before. Instead he looked like a small, lost boy, beset by regrets he wouldn't rescue himself from.

'Ben.'

He didn't reply. Anna moved closer.

'Ben . . .'

He turned. 'Hi.'

'It's getting cold out here, don't you think?'

'I . . . um – I can't say I'd noticed. Are you . . . ?' Looking at the jacket in his hand, he held it out to her.

'No, thank you. Ben . . .'

He closed his eyes. 'Don't say it.'

'But—'

'I mean it, Anna, don't say it. I was stupid and I was angry. But I had no right to be. You were right: I used you. Not in the beginning, but when I had the chance to write your story I didn't hesitate. You didn't deserve that.'

'It's done. No hard feelings. There are more important things in life.'

Bravely she reached for his hand and took it, feeling an initial hesitance as he almost pulled back. But then his fingers began a tentative exploration of hers, moving and turning until they laced tightly together. For some time, neither spoke – the sensation of each other's skin replacing the need for words. When Ben rediscovered his voice, it was soft and small, barely more than a whisper.

'I thought you couldn't trust me again.'

'So did I.'

'What changed?'

'I realised it's my choice. *Life* is my choice. So I choose you to be part of it. If you still want to be?'

'More than you know. Anna, I'm so sorry for what I did.'

'I know.'

Should she kiss him? Their bodies had moved a little closer when their hands met and now Anna could feel the warm waves of Ben's breath caressing her cheek. She had never been the one to make the first move before, but she had never before been the Anna Browne she now felt she was, either. Realising that, nothing prevented her from following her heart. With a boldness that thrilled her, she stepped forward and brought her lips to his. He didn't hesitate this time – his arm wrapped around her body, pulling them closer, as one hand still intertwined with hers. It was beautiful and shocking, raw and strong all at once, Anna finding a home in Ben's embrace.

When they broke apart they observed one another, as if seeing the other for the first time. The power of the moment caused their laughter to reverberate around the garden.

'What was *that*?' he asked.

'That was a kiss,' she teased. 'Any complaints?'

'Mmm, jury's out . . .' He was already pulling her back into his arms. 'Better try again, just to be sure.'

They traded kisses, laughing as they did so, the mood between them dancing between playfulness and passion. The tension that had built between them for so long finally broke as an intense flood of revelation swept them both up.

When Ben managed to break free he asked, 'And the parcel-sender?'

'What about her?' Anna moved to kiss him again, but he held her away from him.

'*Her?*'

She nodded. 'So I can say, with the greatest certainty, that I am *not* in love with her.'

'Who was it?'

'Can't say.'

'Yes, you can. You can tell me anything, now we've kissed.'

'And risk it appearing in your next exclusive report? No, thank you.'

'Aw, come on, Anna! You can't leave me hanging like that.'

'I think you'll find I can,' she giggled, not resisting when he kissed her again. Perhaps she would tell him one day – maybe when the *Daily Messenger*'s esteemed outgoing editor had finally retired. But, for now, it was a secret she was happy to keep.

And so, under an ink-black London sky illuminated by a dazzling moon, Anna Browne received her final gift. It was not wrapped in brown paper with perfectly symmetrical corners. No courier delivered it and none of her colleagues were present to witness its arrival. This time, the sender's details were full and complete – and the gift was worth more than she could ever have hoped or dreamed.

It was a gift of her own choosing.

And it was perfect.

Fifty-Four

'Today's the day the Dragon flies Smoke Mountain, eh? It's a day for celebration, I reckon,' Ted Blaskiewicz grinned, patting Ashraf's shoulder as he headed towards his security office.

Ashraf turned to Anna, swallowing hard. 'I hope that doesn't mean he expects me to match him drink for drink in the pub tonight. Last time I was hungover for a *week*.'

Anna smiled as she finished entering the last of Monday's appointments into the reception system. 'Never drink with Ted. It's really the first lesson any new employee should learn.'

Sheniece folded her arms. 'There shouldn't *be* any new employees on the reception team. The newspaper's secure, for now at least, and we all still have our jobs. Nobody should be *giving* theirs away.'

Gathering her colleague into a hug, Anna whispered, 'I'll miss you too, Shen.'

'I don't know what you're moaning for, Sheniece. Anna

going means you get to be Senior Team Leader – which means you can legitimately make my life hell from the end of the month.'

'You'll love it, Ashraf Guram, and don't you try to deny it. I wonder how the old bag's doing on the sixth floor? Probably still barking orders at poor Piers. When does she go?'

'Ben said her office is pretty much cleared out now, so I don't think it'll be long before she leaves for good,' Anna said, rolling her eyes when Sheniece mimed a silent movie-style swoon.

'*Ben* says . . . You two are enough to make anyone throw up. How is the man himself?'

'Settling into a TV newsroom. He seems happy, though.'

'And now he's dragging you away, too.'

'No, he isn't. This was my decision.'

With each task being one less that she would ever have to do at the *Daily Messenger*, Anna felt strangely wistful. So much had happened since she'd first set foot in the glass-and-steel atrium – and she would miss it. But the spark of an idea that had begun a few months ago had blossomed into something new and exciting. It was time for a new start.

Her interview with the not-for-profit business-support agency had passed like a dream, her soon-to-be employers drinking in every word of her carefully prepared presenta-tion. She was offered a job before the end of the interview and now a brand-new position awaited her. It would be a challenge – bringing her firmly into the spotlight when meeting new clients and potential investors – but for the first time in her working life Anna didn't fear what that might bring. Ben said her new employers didn't know what they were letting themselves in for. But the pride in his smile told her all she needed to know.

She thought about Juliet Evans now, facing a new challenge of her own. Her career had been her life for so many years – how was she going to fare, now that it no longer defined her? Anna hadn't told Sheniece, Ted, Ashraf or her other workmates that Juliet was her secret parcel-sender. Instead she had told them that whoever it was must have bottled out at the last minute. Ted had said it was probably for the best, while Sheniece had been far more interested in the details of how Anna and Ben had got together to push for any more.

The parcels had returned to being Anna's secret. And she liked it that way.

'Anna, you coming? Beer is calling our names, girl.'

Ted, Sheniece and Ashraf were standing on the other side of the reception desk, coats and bags at the ready. Signing off and switching the reception phones to night service, Anna picked up her things and joined her colleagues.

'Everyone's going to be there,' Sheniece babbled as they headed for the front door. 'Rea, Ali, Pervy-Henderson-Vitt. Oh, and the new chap from the newsroom everyone's lusting after . . .'

In the doorway of the *Daily Messenger* building, Anna met a familiar figure walking in.

'Hey, Anna. I've got a parcel,' Narinder grinned, winking at her.

Anna nodded, knowing full well that it wasn't meant for her this time. 'Take it straight up. Top floor.'

Fifty-Five

Juliet Evans handed the last box of belongings to Piers and closed the door behind him. Turning back, she surveyed the oddly empty space that had signified her life for so long. Pale patches of carpet were the only reminders of where expensive furniture once stood, designer-made cabinets and couches given as gifts by grateful Board members in recognition of her work. Within these walls she had masterminded the *Daily Messenger's* risc from almost-forgotten title to leading national daily, back in the heady Eighties gold rush. Gazing from the floor-to-ceiling windows across thc city, she had planned scheme after scheme to rise above the competition, set the *Messenger* apart and – crucially – ensure her name was set in the very stone of Fleet Street grcats. In hcr office, given back to her by a smarmy Damien Kendal following her triumphant party speech, she had witnessed her last hurrah: confirmation yesterday of *Messenger* sales and circulation beating the top national tabloid title by 7 per cent. It was her parting shot to the industry that had made her name, and it sealed her notoriety forever. She might be leaving today, but she was leaving in a blaze of glory. It was exactly how she had wanted it to be.

She took more than a little satisfaction in the fact that she had been given leave to hand-pick her successor, Joanne Malin, a flame-haired star of broadcast media. The *Daily Messenger* would be safe in her capable hands and Fleet Street would learn to give her due honour, as they had Juliet. She was already being hailed as the helmswoman of a new era for the paper. And rightly so, thought Juliet, kicking away the burn of irritation at how quickly she was being forgotten. Success would surround this newspaper for many years to come, she was certain, built upon the solid foundations she had toiled to establish. That, in the end, was what she wanted.

And yet her decision to vacate the top office carried with it a sadness that surprised her. Many times over her career she had longed for days not governed by the steaming juggernaut of her ambition. Tomorrow morning, it would finally be a reality. The thought terrified her.

A knock on her door called her attention away from what lay ahead. 'Enter.'

Piers' expression was all apology. 'I'm sorry, Juliet, I just wanted to check . . .'

'Check *what*?' She stopped herself. Her loyal assistant deserved better than to be a punchbag for her angst. 'Forgive me. Come in.'

He seemed as surprised as her by the emptiness of her

494

former seat of power. 'It looks wrong,' he said, his smile conveying more than his words.

'Does it?' The drag of melancholy returned to Juliet's stomach. Annoyed by its arrival when her employee was there to witness it, she pushed it away. 'What can I do for you?'

'Actually, I wanted to check that you were okay.'

Taken aback, she stared at him. 'Oh?'

'Because I imagine this,' he indicated the space with a sweep of his hand, 'is a little strange to deal with.'

In fifteen years of Piers and Juliet working together, they had never so much as shared a passing anecdote about their personal lives. She didn't know his partner's name, or whether he had children. She seemed to recall him mentioning once that he lived in Bloomsbury. Beyond that, for all Juliet knew, Piers Langley might well have stopped existing the moment he left the building.

'It is.' The admission felt momentous.

'The place won't be the same without you,' her PA ventured. 'You *are* the *Daily Messenger*. I don't know how anyone will fill your shoes.'

'She doesn't have to,' Juliet replied. 'My successor is eminently capable. She's still at the stage in her career where success matters. I have grown tired of it.'

'Forgive me if I don't believe you. You have success coursing through your veins.' Reddening, he grinned. 'I can be forward, now I know you can't sack me.'

'I still have an hour before I officially retire,' Juliet returned, grateful of the light relief. 'You should be warned.'

'Message received and understood, Ms Evans. Is there anything you need?'

A Plan B, Juliet thought. But who was she kidding? She had never needed a Plan B in her life. 'I'm fine, thanks. You may as well finish now, Piers. I doubt I'll have more orders for you.'

To her surprise, her PA's eyes glistened as he extended his hand. 'I won't say goodbye, then, only *adieu*. If you should need assistance for your next venture, you have my number. I come highly recommended by the best in the business, you know.'

Juliet took his hand and didn't protest when Piers moved closer to plant two kisses on her cheeks. 'Thank you. Sincerely. I wish you every success.'

Watching her former assistant hurry from her office, it occurred to Juliet that he might well be the only person here who would truly miss her. This business mourned nobody for long, the course of continuous global news forever moving forward. Those who furthered its advance were, in the end, as disposable as the subjects of the stories that fuelled it.

She kicked at a scrap of cardboard that had fallen from one of the many boxes now making their way to the storage unit she knew she would never visit. On top of the one remaining carton of her former belongings, she saw the small frame that contained a photograph of her mother. Picking it up, she surveyed the unsmiling elderly lady – an expression she had faced for much of her life. Disappointment. Irritation. Judgement.

Your father wanted a son.

How was any child supposed to answer that? Her father had only lived long enough to see her first job and had been singularly unimpressed by his daughter's chosen career. *You're no better than a rag merchant, Juliet. Airing others' private business for all and sundry to see – you call* that *a decent way to make a living?* Perhaps that was why she had never wanted children. No child deserved to be the disappointment of its parents – and she suspected she had inherited more of their lack of compassion than she liked to think. She couldn't offer a child what it needed.

'Well, I did it, Mother,' she said to the old woman's too-blue eyes. 'Like it or not, I'm a success.'

There had been one time – one blissful moment in the muted beige surroundings of the hospice – when she'd had a glimpse of a different Vivienne Taylor-Evans, as her mother slipped into a rare moment of lucidity in the middle of her confusion. As had become usual, Juliet had been listening to her mother's pitifully bewildered questions, from the eight-year-old Vivienne assumed she still was: *Where's my mummy? When's she coming to take me home? I don't like it here. I'm scared. Are you my mummy?*

As she had done countless times before, Juliet had answered patiently, reassuring Vivienne that all was well. Then Vivienne blinked – and a glimpse of her mother returned.

'You've done well, haven't you, Ju-Ju?'

Juliet had gawped at her mother, torn between wanting to cry and wanting to leave. 'I have,' she managed.

'The nurse said you're famous. That would have annoyed your father.'

'And you?' Juliet had pushed her luck, not knowing how long this shadow would remain. 'What do you think?'

'Oh, I'm quite happy.' And then the elderly woman retreated to the terrified child, intense blue fear reclaiming her eyes. 'Can I go home now?'

In forty-nine years of motherhood, these were the only words of comfort Vivienne had given her daughter.

Bracing against the old, familiar pain, Juliet placed the photo frame underneath a pile of journals in the box and glared out at the city, as if denying the hurt it might have seen in the top-floor office of the *Daily Messenger* building. She had grieved for her mother, but now it was time to move on. She had to leave as she had arrived, thirty years before: head held high and ambition powering her steps. That she was leaving to a wide, empty void was a truth only she needed to know . . .

'I'm *still* fine, Piers,' she barked irritably when another knock came at the door. When her assistant didn't enter, she marched over and swung it open, preparing to unleash one final tirade on her almost-ex-colleague. 'Oh.'

The courier gave a sheepish smile. 'Parcel for the editor?'

'This should have been signed for in reception.'

'They said to bring it up.' He offered the package to Juliet. 'I need a signature.'

Juliet was about to tell the courier – Narinder, according to his name badge – exactly what he could do with the parcel that was clearly intended for her successor, not wanting so physical a reminder of the end of her reign. But then a thought occurred to her: this could be the last delivery she would open as editor of the *Daily Messenger*.

It was a sorry excuse for a sentimental symbol, but in the face of an already emptied office, it would have to suffice.

'Fine.' She snatched the parcel from the courier's hands and quickly scribbled her surname on the delivery sheet.

'Cheers.' He paused, his smile steady.

'Was there something else?'

'Just – all the best for the future, yeah? Have a good one, you know. Be happy and that.'

Juliet stared after him as he strolled back down the corridor. Perhaps it was good she was leaving today, if random sentimentality was breaking out across the building. She closed the door and wandered back into her office, inspecting the parcel. It was about the size of a shoebox, the name and address written in a neat hand. Turning it over, she noticed that both ends of the brown-paper covering had been folded to identical length – something her mother had insisted upon whenever they wrapped presents for Hanukkah and birthdays.

'Tidy wrapping equals a calm mind,' Vivienne would intone, watching over Juliet as she folded and refolded the wrapping paper to perfect her skills. It was one thing Juliet had retained from her childhood to which she still adhered today. Achieving the perfect folds was strangely comforting; as if by doing so she would earn the approval from her mother that she had sought all her life.

A single chair remained by the window – her beloved white Italian leather seat, which would be making its way to her Berkshire home as soon as her driver arrived. Sitting down, the view of the city stretching away from her feet, she carefully lifted one corner, then the other, taking care to open each tape-fastening as if unpacking a priceless object. She had driven her parents half to distraction with her fastidiousness as a child, but Juliet secretly liked to make the moment last. Surprises were something she generally loathed, but a little magic still remained around the opening of gifts – even if she suspected this one was not intended for her.

Inside the innocuous brown wrapping she discovered a sea-green box, and beneath its lid a covering of sunshine-yellow tissue paper. It reminded her of the few happy holidays she had spent on the Kent coast with her grandparents, before their deaths the year she started boarding school. The tissue whispered apart to reveal a reproduction Victorian cut-out paper doll. An accompanying card featured a series of outfits printed in gaudy colours: an explorer's outfit with tight bodice, long skirt, heeled boots and a pith helmet; a beautiful turquoise evening dress with elegant fan and pearls at the neck; a pirate queen's garb with striped bodice and a black shawl tied across the hips of the wide purple skirt; and a bride's lace-layered gown. Each outfit's outline included square tabs that, when prised from the card, could be folded over the doll to 'dress' it. Beneath the doll was a small, leather-bound travel journal, embossed with a faded gold design of ancient seafaring maps. Opening the journal, Juliet found a sea-green envelope, with her name written in identical hand to the parcel's address label. Inside, on a single sheet of cream paper, was a letter:

Dear Juliet

From today you can be whatever you want to be. It's your choice, your decision, and won't be swayed one bit by this parcel. But I've sent this to help you decide.

Who do you want to be today?

And where do you want to go?

Thank you for showing me that life is a choice and a journey. Whatever you choose to do and wherever you decide to go, it will be the right decision. Because life is too exciting to sit still for long.

Brightest wishes

Anna Browne x

THE END

*Read on for exclusive material from
Miranda Dickinson, including how to wrap
the perfect gift . . .*

Book locations used in
A Parcel for Anna Browne.

Polperro – the setting for Anna's childhood home. I need to stress that Polperro is a gorgeous village in Cornwall, and Anna doesn't hate it! But I wanted an idyllic, isolated location that contrasted with the difficulty Anna has growing up with her mother, in a community where nothing is hidden. I hope the community spirit and care for the young Anna and her brother Ruari come across in the story.

Talland Bay (mentioned in Anna's recollections) – this is just around the cliff path from Polperro, a very special place that I remember from childhood holidays. There's a gorgeous café there now, which is well worth a visit.

Godrevy – the place Anna and Jonah escape to. Godrevy is incredibly special to me and I've wanted to write about it for a long time. I was first taken there by my husband

Bob and his family and it's one of the most wildly romantic, ruggedly gorgeous places I've ever been to. While I was writing *A Parcel for Anna Browne* I visited Godrevy on holiday with Bob, Flo and Bob's family, and I just knew Anna had to go there to rediscover her love for her home county. It's a haven for surfers, has a gorgeous sandy beach perfect for families, and mile upon mile of cliff walks where skylarks wheel overhead in the summer and seals play in the coves around the feet of the cliffs. You have to go there!

London – Anna's home, and the setting for most of the book. Until I became a published author I'd always been nervous of my capital city. The constant busyness and detached attitude of people there can be a shock to the system when, like me, you come from a place where random strangers regularly strike up conversations with you! But, for Anna, I knew London would be the perfect place to live, precisely because she can be anonymous there, interacting with people she chooses to, whereas in her childhood home privacy was impossible. She also suspects that her absent father lives in the city, which keeps alive in her mind the tantalising possibility that she might one day bump into him. What I've learned to love about London now is the sheer diversity of characters and locations for a story. I loved creating venues like Tish's favourite home-accessories shop in Marylebone High Street, Freya & Georgie's coffee shop near the *Daily Messenger* building on Fleet Street and the vintage shop in Notting Hill. While these aren't based on real shops, there are plenty of businesses like these in the city.

My favourite gift companies

Not On the High Street: www.notonthehighstreet.com – I've lost count of the number of amazing gifts I've found on this website. I love that it supports small craft businesses, and the attention to detail that many of the sellers give to wrapping their deliveries makes them extra-special.

Bluebasil Brownies: www.bluebasilbrownies.co.uk – Not only are these quite possibly the most amazing brownies you've ever tasted, but the way they are lovingly packaged makes a delivery from them feel like the biggest treat.

Aspire Style: www.aspirestyle.co.uk – This company has lovely shops (my favourite one is in Stratford-upon-Avon) filled with gorgeous, unusual gifts. Every purchase is wrapped in blush-pink tissue paper, which I particularly love!

Wrapping the perfect gift
by Lucy Ledger

Gift-wrapping is usually an after-thought as we pass down supermarket aisles or run into a shop and grab whatever will make do. Very little time is spent on it, but as we learned from Anna's experience, a beautifully wrapped gift is as memorable as the gift itself. It heightens the excitement and anticipation of what is inside and if we have spent money on a beautiful gift surely it deserves to be presented in a way that makes it extra special? Gift-wrapping doesn't have to be complicated or expensive; it just requires a little thought and preparation. I have compiled my top five tips below to help give you ideas for creating a memorable wrap.

1. Think ribbons, buttons and luggage tags! A trip to a local haberdashery or looking at online boutiques (eBay is also brilliant) can unearth a treasure trove of lovely inexpensive extras to add to your parcels and really make them stand out.

2. If you don't have the time to shop every time a special occasion comes around and you'd like to stock up, then try to stick to plain paper – Kraft brown parcel paper is a great idea because it's very inexpensive and neutral. You can dress it up in all sorts of ways with any colour combination from your lovely new collection of ribbons, tags and buttons!

3. To get a good idea of your recipient's taste, take a look at their home. How do they decorate it? Do they love monochrome? Then a lovely parcel wrapped in black paper with luxurious white ribbon will really wow them. Do they love florals and vintage style? Think brown paper, floral tissue paper, twine and a craft brown luggage tag.

4. A really fun and thoughtful idea for wrapping a birthday gift is the 'Pass the Parcel' idea. Lots of beautiful layers and a little note in every layer, each saying a thing the recipient did that year that made them so special to you.

5. Another great and inexpensive idea is to keep hold of old boxes so you can cover them with beautiful paper. That way you can make your own mini gift sets and hampers, which are so much more thoughtful than pre-packed versions.

Have fun and remember – the details are not just details. They all make up the special experience of receiving a very memorable gift!

By award-winning greetings and gifts designer Lucy Ledger
(www.lucyledger.com)

A Parcel for
Anna Browne playlist

I put together this playlist to inspire me and create the right mood while I was writing *A Parcel for Anna Browne*. I hope you enjoy it!

1. 'All My Days', Alexi Murdoch (*Time Without Consequence*)
2. 'Tiny Parcels', Rue Royale (*Remedies Ahead*)
3. 'Falling Off the Face of the Earth', Matt Wertz (*Twenty Three Places*)
4. 'Frozen', Madonna (*Ray of Light*)
5. 'I Followed Fires', Matthew and the Atlas (*Kingdom of Your Own* EP)
6. 'Allegory', Kris Drever (*Mark the Hard Earth*)
7. 'Try', Jillian Edwards (*Galaxies & Such*)
8. 'Take It from Me', The Weepies (*Say I Am You*)

9. 'You've Found Love', I Am Arrows (*Sun Comes Up Again*)
10. 'Mo Ghruagach Dhonn', Julie Fowlis (*Cuilidh*)
11. 'Pipe Dreams', Travis (*The Invisible Band*)
12. 'Shine', Sam Palladio (The Music of *Nashville*, Season 1, Vol. 2)
13. 'Time', Sarah McLachlan (*Afterglow*)
14. 'Lon-dubh / Blackbird', Julie Fowlis (*Cuilidh*)
15. 'I Choose You', Sara Bareilles (*The Blessed Unrest*)

Author Q&A

1. Have you always wanted to be a writer?
Yes, for as long as I can remember. I grew up in a family who loved books and my favourite place as a little girl was my local library. I decided when I was about five that I wanted to write a book that could be on the shelves in Kingswinford Library (a tiny place in reality but a palace of dreams to me) – and that started a lifelong passion.

2. How long did it take you to write *A Parcel for Anna Browne*?
I've actually wanted to write Anna's story for about three years, so I would say it took two and a half years to daydream the story and just under six months to write and edit it!

3. Is there a particular place you like to write?
At the moment I have an office tucked away in the spare bedroom of our house, but very soon this will become my

daughter Flo's bedroom, so I'll have to find somewhere else!

I'm quite partial to writing on the sofa – a throwback to when it was the only place I could write in the one-bedroom flat I was renting (and where my first four novels were written). If I have enough cushions and a blanket over my knees, I'm happy there! Coffee shops are another favourite place to write – I like the bustle and chat going on around me as I'm writing.

For *A Parcel for Anna Browne*, I wrote the Godrevy and Polperro scenes during a family holiday, sitting at a kitchen table in an apartment overlooking Carbis Bay. Hearing the crash of waves and call of gulls really added to the story – perhaps one day I'll be lucky enough to do all my writing there . . .

4. Do you have a routine as a writer?
Not really! I would love to be able to say I have a set routine, but I never have. For many years I juggled writing with a day job, so I fitted it in whenever and wherever I could. I naturally write better at night, so now we have Flo I'm writing after she goes to bed. Having a baby has meant I've had to become far more disciplined about my writing, so I keep notebooks everywhere (including the loo!) and grab moments to write and plan during the day. That way, when I write at night I know exactly what I'm doing and don't waste time.

5. How are you going to celebrate publication day?
I'm famously rubbish at celebrating, so I plan to do

something special with Bob and Flo to celebrate this novel. We'll probably go to Birmingham to see the book in my favourite Waterstones in New Street (which is housed in an old Victorian bank) and have a celebratory lunch.

6. Which books have inspired you?

For *A Parcel for Anna Browne*, I was particularly inspired by the books of Sarah Addison Allen. I've been a fan of hers since I read *The Sugar Queen* and I adore the sense of magic she infuses into her stories. I wanted Anna's parcels to have that feeling of magic about them – and for the story to feel like a fable.

7. How did you come up with the title of the book?

This one was really easy to come up with! It's the arrival of the parcels in Anna's life that begins a change in how she sees herself. I liked the sense of expectation in the title, too – I feel excited if I receive a parcel, so I wanted to convey that thrill.

8. What would you like readers to take away from *A Parcel for Anna Browne*?

Firstly, I hope they love the story! I think the main thing I'd love readers to take away from Anna's story is that the parcels, while magical and lovely, aren't responsible for the changes in her life. They merely give her permission to be the person she wants to be. I hope readers finish *A Parcel for Anna Browne* believing that anything is possible.

9. Are you writing a new novel at the moment?
Yes, I've already started writing the next book and I'm very excited about it! I don't have a deadline yet, so I'm at the lovely stage of researching, dreaming and having fun creating characters.

10. What advice would you give to aspiring authors?
Firstly, write. Don't put it off, hide in 'How To' books and writing conferences (which can be fab but can also be a legitimate excuse to delay starting to write), or tell yourself you can't do it. Writing is a constant apprenticeship: you learn how to do it by doing it!

Secondly, when you start writing, chuck away the 'aspiring' tag. You're only an aspiring writer if you want to write but aren't doing it yet. Once you're writing, you're a writer.

And lastly, always, ALWAYS write for you first. The lovely, much-missed Terry Pratchett said, 'The first draft is just you telling yourself the story.' So write it for you. Don't worry about the market, trends, genre or anything else: tell the story you want to tell. And have fun doing it! Fun isn't frivolous – it's a vital writing tool. If you love what you do, you'll keep doing it, and nothing will deter you.

It's time to relax with your next good book

THEWINDOWSEAT.CO.UK

If you've enjoyed this book, but don't know what
to read next, then we can help. The Window Seat is
a site that's all about making it easier to discover your
next good book. We feature recommendations,
behind-the-scenes tales from the world of publishing,
creative writing tips, competitions, and, if we're honest,
quite a lot of lists based on our favourite reads.

You'll find stories and features
by authors including Lucinda Riley, Karen Swan,
Diane Chamberlain, Jane Green, Lucy Diamond
and many more. We showcase brand-new talent
as well as classic favourites, so you'll never be
stuck for what to read again.

We'd love to know what you think of the site, our books,
and what you'd like us to feature, so do let us know.

 @panmacmillan

 facebook.com/TheWindowSeat

WWW.THEWINDOWSEAT.CO.UK